WITHDRAWN
UTSA Libraries

WITHDRAWN
UTSA Libraries

A SELECTED EDITION OF W. D. HOWELLS

Volume 18

The Quality of Mercy

HOWELLS EDITION

David J. Nordloh, *General Editor*
Don L. Cook, *Textual Editor*
Christoph K. Lohmann, *Associate Editor*

HOWELLS EDITION EDITORIAL BOARD

George Arms, *Executive Committee*
Louis J. Budd
Edwin H. Cady, *Executive Committee*
Everett Carter
Don L. Cook, *Executive Committee*
William M. Gibson, *Executive Committee*
Ronald Gottesman, *Executive Committee*
Christoph K. Lohmann
David J. Nordloh, *Executive Committee*
James Woodress

CONSULTING EDITORS

Edwin H. Cady
Bernard Perry, *for the Indiana University Press*
John K. Reeves

W. D. HOWELLS

The Quality of Mercy

Introduction and Notes to the Text
by James P. Elliott

Text Established by
James P. Elliott, with David J. Nordloh

INDIANA UNIVERSITY PRESS

Bloomington and London

1979

Editorial expenses for this volume have been met in part by grants from the National Endowment for the Humanities administered through the Center for Editions of American Authors of the Modern Language Association.

Copyright © 1979 by Indiana University Press and the Howells Edition Editorial Board

All rights reserved

No part of this book may be reproduced or utilized in any form or by any means, electronic or mechanical, including photocopying and recording, or by any information storage and retrieval system, without permission in writing from the publisher. The Association of American University Presses' Resolution on Permissions constitutes the only exception to this prohibition.

Manufactured in the United States of America

Library of Congress Cataloging in Publication Data

Howells, William Dean, 1837–1920.
  The quality of mercy.

  (His A selected edition of W. D. Howells ; v. 18)
  Includes bibliographical references.
  I. Elliott, James Paul, 1945– II. Title.
PS2020.F68 vol. 18 [PZ3] [PS2025] 813'.4 78–20655
  ISBN 0–253–35789–6

LIBRARY
The University of Texas
At San Antonio

Acknowledgments

The editors of this volume and of the Howells Edition Center are grateful for the support given their research by the administrative officers of Indiana University, particularly Herman B Wells, University Chancellor, and Harrison Shull, former Dean of the Office of Research and Development. We are especially happy to thank the Ball Brothers Foundation of Muncie, Indiana, for direct financial assistance which made possible the completion and publication of this book. And we continue to appreciate the kind cooperation of William White Howells and the other heirs of W. D. Howells.

The editors are indebted to the hard work and endless patience of the following former and present staff members of the Howells Edition Center: Pam Bennett, Velma Carmichael, Jerry Herron, Trish Johnston, David Kleinman, Melissa Kuramoto, Cindy Nagy, Connie Perry, Daniel Rubey, Robert Schildgen, Ann Webster, and Robin Wheeler. Finally, we want to thank the staff of the Houghton Library, Harvard University, for its assistance and cooperation.

The primary editor wishes to acknowledge with thanks the efforts of his dissertation committee—Don L. Cook, Edwin H. Cady, Philip B. Daghlian, and David J. Nordloh—who have provided invaluable aid at every stage of this edition. Thanks go also to Edmund Berkeley, Jr., of the University of Virginia Library, and Robert O. Dougan of the Huntington Library, for permission to quote from letters in their respective collections; and to Carolyn Jakeman of the Houghton Library.

Contents

Introduction

WITH the writing of *The Quality of Mercy*, W. D. Howells once again attempted the kind of broad novelistic canvas he had painted in *A Hazard of New Fortunes* (1889). Certainly it is more ambitious in character and incident than his intervening works, the autobiographical *A Boy's Town* (1890) and the novellas *The Shadow of a Dream* (1890) and *An Imperative Duty* (1891). Its topicality, too, recalls the earlier novel; as he had used the New York streetcar strike of 1889 for the ending of *A Hazard of New Fortunes*, so he turned to another dislocation of contemporary society—the crime of defalcation —as material for his new novel. He made his protagonist a defaulter, a type of criminal regularly in the news in the 1890's and certain to generate the popular attention he probably wanted for the only novel he was to serialize in the newspapers. And consistent with the ideal suggested by the Shakespearean title of the new novel, Howells stressed the complexity of responses to the criminal—from the haughty disbelief in J. M. Northwick's guilt on the part of his daughters to the gradual involvement of the Hilary family and the anger, condescension, pity, and vengefulness of numerous inhabitants of East Hatboro' and Boston.[1] Unlike *A Hazard of New Fortunes*, Howells worked at *The Quality of Mercy* without the distraction of family problems that plagued him in 1889. What difficulty he had with the new novel was caused by problems of conceptualization, especially during the early stages of his composition. Despite these problems, however, Howells grew

---

1. *The Merchant of Venice*, IV, i, 184. The well-known line—"The quality of mercy is not strained"—seems to be finally an ironic comment on these people, for mercy is the least frequent of all responses to Northwick and his family.

to have a personal confidence in the novel which was bolstered by its public reception.

That *The Quality of Mercy* appeared as a newspaper serial probably resulted from tension between Howells and his regular American publishers, Harper and Brothers. When he was writing *A Boy's Town* in the winter of 1890, he proposed *The World of Chance* as the novel he owed the firm for 1891; but soon he was apparently preparing to do more creative work than was necessary to fulfill his contractual obligations. On 26 February 1890 he acknowledged H. M. Alden's acceptance of *The World of Chance*, adding, "it is not probable that I can write more than one novel in a year, but there are no conditions in my agreement with H. & B [sic] limiting my work for 1891."[2] Alden replied that the Harpers did not mean to tell Howells what he could publish. Rather, "whatever serials you might write in 1891, there should be none whose publication should precede that of your proposed novel, 'The World of Chance,' in our magazine" (1 March 1890).

Perhaps S. S. McClure, the energetic young entrepreneur of a burgeoning newspaper syndicate, heard rumors that Howells was restless. In any case, to lure the well-known author into his growing stable of contributors, McClure asked if Howells would write a serial novel for the New York *Sun* which McClure could then distribute through his syndicate.[3] Howells was cautious but intrigued.[4] He wrote a guarded letter to Harper and Brothers on 9 April, asking if the firm had "any wish or intention in regard to my work beyond the year 1891."

2. The manuscripts of this and all other letters cited are in the Houghton Library, Harvard University, unless otherwise noted. Permission to quote from the unpublished letters owned by Harvard has been granted by the Harvard College Library. Permission to quote from unpublished material by Howells has been granted by William White Howells for the heirs of the Howells estate. Republication of these materials requires the same permissions. Unless otherwise indicated, Howells' reports on progress on his novel all come from his letters to his father, William Cooper Howells.

3. No record of McClure's request survives, but Howells appears to be referring to such a suggestion from McClure in a letter to him of 6 April 1890.

4. In the letter of 6 April, Howells advised McClure to "let the matter of the story rest till we see other [sic] again . . . ."

"We beg leave to say," the Harpers replied, "that we are not prepared at present to make any engagement beyond the year 1891, as kindly proposed by you, further than we have already made" (14 April 1890). Howells exploded: "If you will kindly refer to my letter of last week you will see that I did not, as you seem from your reply to think, 'propose' any prolongation of our relations beyond 1891. In view of some matters offering for the future, I wished to consider any possible plans of yours; for I thought this your due. Your letter of yesterday leaves me free to act . . ." (15 April 1890). On 18 April the Harpers apologized, but Howells had already acted, for McClure inquired about the name of the pending newspaper story that same day. Mr. Dana of the *Sun* "would really like to know right off. He was very much gratified when I informed him that you would write the serial for him." Howells answered McClure with the synopsis of *The Quality of Mercy.* "I have thought of calling the story 'The Mercy of God,' or 'The Grace of God'," Howells wrote. It would be the "story of a man of great force, great apparent wealth and high social standing . . . . At the opening of the story . . . he has embezzled and muddled away the company's money to an amount that makes him a hopeless defaulter."[5]

The news of Howells' arrangement with McClure and the *Sun* provided Harper and Brothers with a fortuitous exit from an "embarrassing situation."[6] Why not, they appear to have asked the author, publish the *Sun* serial in 1891 and serialize *The World of Chance* in the 1892 *Harper's Monthly?* But they insisted that they retain the rights to book publication for the *Sun* serial and that its run be completed before 1 January 1892.[7] Howells agreed. Finishing *An Imperative Duty* by 25

---

5. The complete text of the synopsis may be found in the Appendix to this Introduction, pp. xxiii–xxv.

6. The Harpers had accepted a novel by Mary Noilles Murfree for serialization in 1891 and did not want to run two serial novels simultaneously. "I wish your proposed novel [*The World of Chance*] had been offered for 1892," Alden had mused to Howells on 20 February 1890.

7. See H. M. Alden to WDH, 12 May 1890.

September 1890, he began *The Quality of Mercy* with the new year.

Besides newspaper accounts reporting a new defaulter almost every day, Howells looked to many other sources for his material. He based the train wreck which disguises the defaulter on reports of the catastrophe of 5 February 1887, "when a passenger train of the Vermont Central Railroad ran off Woodstock Bridge."[8] He pressed his sister Aurelia for details about Quebec; as he explained to his father, he hoped she would "jot me down some of the more characteristic aspects of life at Quebec in the winter—the look of the streets, sleighs, etc.; things that would most strike and concern a stranger" (11 January 1891). He had Sylvester Baxter tell him how reporters " 'get onto' things" like impending defalcations.[9] He discussed questions of plausibility with O. M. Hanscom of the Boston Pinkerton Detective Agency.[10] And he sent his friend John C. Ropes a questionnaire concerning the legal steps involved in a defalcation proceeding.[11]

With facts and suggestions gathered from many quarters, Howells built the "constant play of incident" which he had projected in his synopsis of the novel. But he also suggested in the synopsis that McClure look beneath the incidents for the "deeper, interior way" the story was realistic—the moral and psychological currents which would elicit his "strongest dramatic effects." When play of incident generates valid psychological development, Howells implied, the novel's thematic statements would reflect the "modern, immediate" society he constantly examined in his fiction. But that goal was not easily reached. On one hand, he had superb control over his conception of Northwick, the protagonist; the manuscript leaves

---

8. Everett Carter, *Howells and the Age of Realism* (Philadelphia, 1954), p. 109.

9. WDH to Sylvester Baxter, 25 February 1891. MS at Huntington Library.

10. In gratitude Howells had Houghton, Mifflin send the detective copies of his works which the firm had published in paper; see WDH to [Houghton, Mifflin], 2 March 1891.

11. WDH to John C. Ropes, 25 March 1891. MS at University of Virginia.

comprising the opening chapters of Part II, which describe Northwick's lonely flight into Canada, for example, are virtually unrevised except for occasional adjustments of words and phrases. On the other hand, his efforts to dramatize the responses of Northwick's family—especially his daughter Suzette —and the society of Hatboro' and Boston to the crime necessitated a new start after more than a month of writing. Though not quite so drastic as starting over, the revision involved much of the content of the social sections of the manuscript, including the conclusion, for which Howells wrote three increasingly complex versions.[12]

The energy which Howells devoted to this process of self-editing also finds expression in his correspondence during the composition of *The Quality of Mercy*. "I knew that long palaver I read you was ringing false at the time," he wrote to Hamlin Garland on 27 February 1891. "Thanks for your criticism. I've just been knocking the stuffing out of it."[13] He explained himself to his father at greater length: "Three days ago I was in despair about my story; I had gone off on a false tack, and I shall have to throw away two hundred pages, but now I'm all straight again, and shall start fair tomorrow" (1 March). On 22 March he told his father he had six hundred pages of his new start written, and was about one-third done.

With Northwick's escape to Canada, a breakthrough occurred. The largely unrevised nature of the manuscript at this point supports Howells' assertion to his father on 9 April that he had been "booming on my story this week, and seem really to have got my grip on it after a long season of despair." The work continued to flow, with some foreboding occasionally coloring his thoughts: "If I have such favoring gales as in the last week, I shall soon be in port. But what squalls may beat me about! It's an awful trade . . ." (12 April). By 3 May he was

---

12. See A Note on the Manuscript, pp. 379–384, for a description of the manuscript of *The Quality of Mercy*.

13. WDH to Hamlin Garland, 27 February 1891. MS at University of Southern California.

able to report, "My story gets on; but it is long, and seems to grow longer as I write. I have so many more things to say now than I used." Inevitably, he ran into other rough places, but he persevered. Though he announced to his father on 17 May that the story "has given me no end of trouble, either because the subject is difficult, or because I'm less facile than I was," he had "a clear light on it at last" on 30 May. On 6 July he finished the first of the three versions of the concluding chapters. Two weeks later, he had his conclusion, and removed himself and his family from Boston to Intervale, New Hampshire, for the summer.

Howells continued revising as he began "pushing through the proof" he received from S. J. Parkhill and Co. of Boston, the typesetters.[14] All of these revisions are recorded in the Emendations list of this edition. One group of them, dealing with Brice Maxwell, the struggling young reporter, and his relationship to Louise Hilary, Suzette Northwick's best friend, provides a good example of the changes the novel was undergoing at this stage.

One of Howells' motives in this particular case may have been to preserve Maxwell and Louise for future use (in *The Story of a Play* in 1898). The manuscript which he sent to Parkhill portrayed a bitter, worldly reporter, unequivocally Louise's social and moral inferior; through deletions in proof Howells significantly adjusted his portrayal of the young man and left Louise's attraction to him dimmed but undestroyed. Such revisions keep the characterization of Maxwell from undercutting the reporter's perceptive philosophical article on the defalcation. This passage, for instance, is cancelled: "[Matt Hilary] was asking himself whether the artistic use of life, which Maxwell evidently prided himself on was so much higher, or so very different from those businesses, which he scorned" (see the Emendations list at 260.14). Louise's en-

---

14. WDH to Aurelia Howells, 17 July 1891. On 5 August Howells was still proofreading and had begun *The World of Chance*; see WDH to Sylvester Baxter, 5 August 1891 (MS in Huntington Library).

counter with Maxwell's brittle manner crushes her budding sympathy for him: " 'he is hard and ambitious and selfish!' " she says to her mother in yet another cancelled passage; " 'It's over, quite over! . . . I found him a mere egotist at heart!' " (299.36). Through cancellation of such passages, Maxwell's worldliness is toned down; his appreciation of Matt is more sincere and supports the sincerity of his article. When Matt and his mother speak of his deficiencies they call attention to his low position and his unlearned manners rather than to his lack of compassion. Louise is discouraged by his attitude but not alienated from him.

Howells' work on proofs continued through August. "I am stereotyping the *Sun* story in book-form before beginning to print it in the paper," he wrote to his father on 26 July, "so as to not to [sic] have to do proof-reading for the serial. When the book is all cast, I hope to come out to you, some time between the middle of August and the beginning of September; but I can't be exact about the date yet." Stereotyping must have been completed on schedule, for Howells spent a late August fortnight in Ohio with his father, and returned to Intervale via New York City in order to "cash up" the novel at the *Sun* office on 31 August and collect his ten thousand dollars.[15] This proofreading was evidently the last time he touched the text. Howells seemed satisfied that the text of *The Quality of Mercy* needed no further adjustments.

Obviously unaware of the internal complexity that lay behind the proof sheets he received, S. S. McClure trumpeted in a syndicate announcement of 11 September, designed to be sent to thirty newspapers across the country, that "I have secured complete copy of probably the most important novel I have ever offered to the newspaper press." On 9 October came another announcement to ten more newspapers.[16] *The Quality*

15. See WDH to William Cooper Howells, 2 September 1891, and WDH to Aurelia Howells, 6 September 1891.

16. A typescript with manuscript revisions of the September circular and a manuscript of the October circular are located in the McClure Papers, Lilly Library, Indiana University.

of Mercy began its run of fourteen installments in the New York *Sun* on Sunday, 4 October 1891. Eventually McClure sold the serial to seven other newspapers: the Boston *Herald*, the Buffalo *Express*, the Chicago *Inter-Ocean*, the Cincinnati *Commercial-Gazette*, the Cleveland *Leader*, the Philadelphia *Inquirer*, and the Toronto *Globe*. The novel also appeared serially under the title *John Northwick, Defaulter*, in the weekly London journal *Wit and Wisdom*, but, though Mc-Clure had a London syndicate office, whether or not he was responsible for publication there is unknown.

Of course Howells' switch from Harper and Brothers to McClure made news. On 11 October Howells wrote to his father, "I don't know what statements you have seen about my story, but it was sold to the N. Y. Sun, which is publishing it simultaneously with several other papers, to which it had the right to sub-let it. You may generally rely upon any statement in the press being at least half wrong." "My story, The Quality of Mercy, seems to be taking well, here," Howells reported from Boston a week later, "and in Chicago the Inter-Ocean had to print a second edition of the first number."[17] Howells must have been pleased with the attention his serial was getting. McClure said it was "one of the most satisfactory and successful novels I ever published."[18]

In addition to being the only novel Howells serialized in newspapers, *The Quality of Mercy* initiated a new procedure in the publication of his books. The principal stipulation of the new International Copyright Agreement, which went into effect in July 1891, was that, in order to secure American copyright, a book had to be "printed from type set within the limits

---

17. Howells apparently got the information about the *Inter-Ocean* from McClure, who quotes Mr. Nixon, the editor of the newspaper, in a letter to Howells on 9 October 1891. In addition to this extra printing of the Sunday, 4 October, newspaper, the *Inter-Ocean* brought out a special supplement on Monday, 26 October, which reprinted the first four installments of the novel, chapters I–XVI.

18. See the McClure Syndicate Circular dated 4 December 1891. MS in the McClure Papers, Lilly Library, Indiana University.

of the United States, or from plates made therefrom."[19] Howells could no longer have David Douglas of Edinburgh, his
British publisher, prepare plates for him at lower cost, print
the British edition, and ship the plates to America for use by
Howells' American publisher. Since by supplying the plates
for printing Howells could establish a better bargaining position for royalties, he had Parkhill and Co. prepare plates of
The Quality of Mercy. The Parkhill typesetting was the basis
of all the early forms of publication—from the type itself were
pulled the sheets Howells turned over to the New York *Sun*,
the sheets which he sent to David Douglas for the British edition of the novel, probably the sheets which McClure obtained
as copy for the other seven newspapers, and possibly the sheets
used by the London journal *Wit and Wisdom*. Then, with
proofreading completed, Parkhill sent the plates made from
this type to Harper and Brothers, who used them to print the
first American edition.[20]

The Douglas edition of the novel, entitled *Mercy*, was deposited on 31 December, but evidently because of confusion
entailed by the new publishing procedures, it was not announced until 5 February 1892.[21] Howells and Harper and
Brothers seem to have agreed to publish the novel immediately after the first of the year. The Harpers did not want to
issue it before the serial was finished, yet they could not postpone publication too long without conflicting with *The
World of Chance*, which would begin its serialization in the
March *Harper's Monthly*. Howells wanted Douglas' publication to coincide with that of Harper and Brothers in order that
Douglas might secure a reciprocal quasi-copyright in England.

---

19. Quoted in G. Thomas Tanselle, "Copyright Records and the Bibliog-
rapher," *Studies in Bibliography*, XXII (1969), 98.

20. See the Textual Commentary, pp. 372–375, for the significance of this
sequence to the establishment of the critical text of *The Quality of Mercy*.

21. "Literary and Trade Notes," *Publishers' Weekly*, XLI (1892), 294, explains that "a [British] contemporary was printing a story under the same title
as *The Quality of Mercy*." This situation probably accounts for Douglas' alternate title, *Mercy*.

Douglas put on all speed to have the novel set from the sheets
Howells had sent him and printed and bound by the first of
the year. But something delayed the transfer of plates from
Parkhill to Harper, and Howells advised Douglas to wait.
Douglas answered on 5 January 1892 that he could delay distribution of the novel a month but not its publication, as it
had already been registered at Stationers' Hall.

The first American edition was officially issued on 26 March
1892. It appears to have generated immediate interest: "The
new book (Q. of M.) seems to start off pretty well," Howells
wrote his father, adding, however, "I don't know how far it
will go" (17 April 1892). A paperbound reimpression as Number 726 in the Harper "Franklin Square Library, New Series,"
was deposited on 1 October 1892. Howells' royalties were
twenty per cent on the cloth edition and twelve and one-half
per cent on the paper. Interest in the novel must have kept up,
for the plates were used four more times by 1900, and shortly
after a new edition was set in the typography of the Harper
"Library Edition" of Howells' works. When that project was
abandoned before *The Quality of Mercy* appeared, the new
plates were used instead in reprinting for the regular trade
edition. The novel has not been reprinted since.

The variety of event and character in *The Quality of Mercy*
became the focus of critical attention.[22] Some reviewers found
the many incidents distracting, but others began to probe the
interior dramatic effects Howells had worked into his story.
On the one hand, the *Athenæum* found the basic story un-
convincing, and noted in *The Quality of Mercy* "the almost
indefinable sense of commonness pervading the whole";
though the situation is a "strong one," "the book drags heavily," suffering from "the absence of imaginative suggestion

22. Reviews of *The Quality of Mercy* appeared in the following journals
and newspapers: *Athenæum*, no. 3359 (12 March 1892), 339; *Westminster Review*, CXXXVII (1892), 464–465; New York *Times*, 10 April 1892, p. 19; H. E.
Scudder, "Recent American and English Fiction," *Atlantic Monthly*, LXIX
(1892), 702–704; *Critic*, XX (1892), 262; George William Curtis, "Editor's Study,"
Harper's Monthly, LXXXV (1892), 316–317; *Nation*, LV (1892), 33–34; William
Morton Payne, *Dial*, XIII (1892), 102; *Saturday Review*, LXXIII (1892), 307.

INTRODUCTION xxi

off[and] of real human humour in the working out of the plot."
On the other hand, the *Westminster Review* called the story
"interesting throughout, and in parts deeply pathetic," and
paid a measured tribute to the realism of Howells' characters:
"None of the actors in the little drama are so perfect as to be
insipid . . . and not one—not even the poor absconding treasurer—is utterly detestable."

American reviews often found the theme of *The Quality of
Mercy* its most noteworthy attribute. In a somewhat incoherent review for the New York *Times,* an anonymous critic re-
iterated the censure of the plot first stated by the *Athenæum,*
taking offense at Howells' "morbidity" and penchant for
"mental dissections." After praising the portrayal of Northwick, the review shifted to a discussion of the contrasting
journalists, Pinney and Maxwell. Through them, the reviewer
grudgingly conceded, Howells is making "us ponder over what
may be that curious production of 1892, which he designates
as 'commercial civilization'." To the reviewer for the *Critic,*
the plot of the novel possessed not "an element of entertain-
ment" and depended completely on "uninteresting" conversation. What is valuable is Howells' treatment of Northwick,
who is not a fictional character at all, but a "study in sociology," or a "masterly bit of psychological analysis." Northwick
provides Howells with a means to disclose the source of America's "financial laxity"—the "substitution of a personal code of
self-justification for that unreflective emotional honesty which
is the race-conscience." Howells' topical treatment, this critic
concludes, eventually leads the reader to consider, "not the
crudely thought-out ethics of a single man or period, but the
accumulated experience of all men from all time."

The fullest examination of the novel's social themes was
H. E. Scudder's review article in the *Atlantic.* According to
Scudder, the book is inferior to *A Hazard of New Fortunes.*
Howells' tame use of his material creates characters who are
not truly outstanding and memorable. But if one considers
that the reader's attention is thus more easily focused on the
motives for Howells' choice and treatment of his subject, such

characterization might be justified, for it points the reader to the theme of complicity: "[Howells] finds himself drawn to consider how this act of moral decadence affected the man himself, his family, his neighbors, the corporation . . . the whole community . . . ." Scudder acknowledges the power of Howells' handling of Northwick, but concludes, "we doubt if a novel has justified itself fully when its persons fade in the mind of the reader, and a few abstract principles remain as his chief possession."

Other reviewers perceived the characters as vivid and lasting. William Morton Payne in the *Dial* praised Howells for his ability to know "how to tell in artistic manner a story of real human interest," and he concluded, "When the work of Mr. Howells shall have been duly threshed by time, this work, at least, will not be left with the chaff." George William Curtis, writing in the "Editor's Study" of *Harper's Monthly*, focused entirely on Northwick's flight to Canada, calling it an episode "which would make the reputation of a new writer." Though the author narrates these events "with singular fidelity to the common aspects of life," they have a deeper effect, Curtis felt: "an apprehension of the unseen and the spiritual that makes this flight a high achievement of the artist." After similarly praising the portrayal of Northwick, the reviewer for the *Nation* took a wider view of the effects of Howells' characterization: "The perusal of 'The Quality of Mercy' must increase the admiration of the author's constant readers for the fidelity with which he has pursued his chosen way, to present a series of pictures of common American life. They must also be impressed by that steady advance in knowledge which is helping him in his later works to represent his people as, after all, more human than American." Such criticism responded to Howells' ability as a realist to portray the "strongest dramatic effects" he projected in his synopsis: *The Quality of Mercy* had touched readers with its sense of life and moral vision.

J.P.E.

APPENDIX

[Howells' synopsis of *The Quality of Mercy* is reproduced here in its entirety. The manuscript, on deposit in the Houghton Library, consists of three leaves of light-weight, wove, unlined white paper measuring 8¼ in. x 10½ in. and watermarked LACROIX FRÈRES. The text is typewritten in blue on the recto in the script-face type which was characteristic of Howells' typing during the 1890's. There are a few revisions in Howells' black ink holograph. The text is reproduced exactly, and errors in the synopsis are recorded without being accompanied by [sic]. Howells' deletions are printed within angle brackets at the points where they occur in the manuscript, and the insertions are printed within vertical arrows at the points where they appear in the manuscript. A clear text of the synopsis is printed in Edwin H. Cady, *The Realist at War* (Syracuse, N. Y., 1958), pp. 164–165.]

Synopsis

I have thought of calling the story "The Mercy of God," or "The Grace of God," but I have not decided about that; perhaps either title would be too grave. But it would be the story of a man of great force, great apparent wealth and high social standing, who ↑has↓ worked himself up from simple New England beginnings, to the head of a great manufacturing interest. At the opening of the story, he is in the secret which cannot be kept any longer <th> that he has embezzled and muddled away the company's money to an amount that makes him a hopeless defaulter. Three courses are then open to him: <t> to kill himself as Grey did; to stand trial and go to prison as Snelling did; to go to Canada as so many others have done. His lawyer, a man of conscience and certain rigid principles, advises him to stand his trial. <The> A young fellow, not a very good young fellow, who has been sufficiently foolish in his way, and has not been very constant in his thoughts <of> ↑to↓ the defaulter's daughter, finds himself made a man of by the crisis, and agrees with the lawyer; the daughter, rather a hard, fashionable girl, agrees with him, too. She and the young ↑fellow↓ confirm their engagement in view of the calamity, the disgrace; and are ready to meet the worst together. But the defaulter himself has not the heart for it. He goes to Canada, and the story follows him to Quebec, on ground that I know very well. I should make a close study of his life and circumstance there, and try to show how without resources in himself, life must begin to pall upon him, there or anywhere<.> ↑away from his old interests.↓ He goes back and forth to Europe, keeping out of the reach of extradition, but he is always an exile, always cut off from his old occupations, associations, and above all from his country place, where he used to find the highest pleasures,—common ones, of course: <—> horses, fine cattle, &c.—he was capable of. He is homesick, bored and lonesome. A detective appears, <a> and shadows him; and he knows it, with a curious longing to make the man's acquaintance. He finds him, as I shall try to show him, not the conventional detective of fiction, but a human being ↑with a family he is very fond of.↓. They rather like one <O> another, <a> and I shall try to make the reader like the detective, without romancing him in the least, or blinking any of his professional characteristics. The defaulter begins to toy with the notion of going home and taking his chances; he and the detective talk it over, and the detective is enthusiastic about it; he tries to make interest with the defaulter to let him t take him back and get the reward. The notion ↑at first↓ amuses the defaulter, but when he has fully made up his mind to return, he telegraphs for the detective and puts himself in his power inside the American border. The detective is puzzled; in view of the past kindness between them, he wishes to be magnanimous, and he gives him a last chance to escape (supposing the equivalent of the reward to be secured) if he has changed his mind. But the defaulter has not changed his mind. The idea of expiation has fully taken possession of it. He refuses the chance offered him and goes home. He is kept out of prison on bail, and while waiting his trial, he suddenly dies.

I can give only a meagre outline of my scheme, without suggesting any but the principal figures. I should try to have a strong love interest in the story, and I should try to give it humorous grace in the character of the detective ↑and the Quebec people, and others.↓. The whole design shows fantastic in some points, but I believe it to be thoroughly realistic, in the deeper, interior way, where I I should ↑seek↓ my strongest dramatic <inciden> effects, while on the surface I should try to keep a constant play of incident for those who could not <beh> look below it. The subject is modern, immediate, such as I like to treat, and I feel the motive to be strong. But of course, everything depends with me upon the working out, or rather the working in.

I should like thia synopsis back again, for I expect to make no other memoranda for the story.

W. D. Howells in 1893

The Quality of Mercy

I

———

NORTHWICK'S man met him at the station with the cutter. The train was a little late, and Elbridge was a little early; after a few moments of formal waiting, he began to walk the clipped horses up and down the street. As they walked they sent those quivers and thrills over their thin coats which horses can give at will; they moved their heads up and down, slowly and easily, and made their bells jangle noisily together; the bursts of sound evoked by their firm and nervous pace died back in showers and falling drops of music. All the time, Elbridge swore at them affectionately, with the unconscious profanity of the rustic Yankee whose lot has been much cast with horses. In the halts he made at each return to the station, he let his blasphemies bubble sociably from him in response to the friendly imprecations of the three or four other drivers who were waiting for the train; they had apparently no other parlance. The drivers of the hotel 'bus, and of the local express wagon were particular friends; they gave each other to perdition at every other word; a growing boy who had come to meet Mr. Gerrish, the merchant, with the family sleigh, made himself a fountain of meaningless maledictions; the public hackman, who admired Elbridge almost as much as he respected Elbridge's horses (they were really Northwick's; but the professional convention was that they were Elbridge's), clothed them with fond curses as with a garment. He was himself, more literally speaking, clothed in an old ulster, much frayed about the wrists and skirts and polished across the middle of the back by rubbing against counters and window sills. He was bearded like a patriarch and he wore a rusty fur cap pulled down over his ears, though it was not very cold; its peak rested on the point of his nose, so that he had to throw his head far back to get Elbridge in the field of his vision. Elbridge had on a high hat, and was smoothly buttoned to his throat in a plain coachman's coat of black; Northwick had never cared to have him make a closer approach to a livery; and it is doubtful if Elbridge would have done it if he had asked or ordered it of him. He deferred to Northwick in a measure as the owner of his horses, but he did not defer to him in any other quality.

"Say, Elbridge, when you goin' to gi' me that old hat o' your'n?" asked the hackman in a shout that would have reached Elbridge if he had been half a mile off instead of half a rod.

"What do you want of another second-hand hat, you —— —— old fool, you?" asked Elbridge in his turn.

The hackman doubled himself down for joy, and slapped his leg; at the sound of a whistle to the eastward he pulled himself erect again, and said, as if the fact were one point gained, "Well, there she blows, any way." Then he went round the corner of the station to be in full readiness for any chance passenger the train might improbably bring him.

No one alighted but Mr. Gerrish and Northwick. Mr. Gerrish found it most remarkable that he should have come all the way from Boston on the same train with Northwick and not known it; but Northwick was less disposed to wonder at it. He passed rapidly beyond the following of Mr. Gerrish, and mounted to the place Elbridge made for him in the cutter. While Elbridge was still tucking the robes about their legs, Northwick drove away from the station, and through the village up to the rim of the high land that lies between Hatboro' and South Hatboro'. The bare line cut along the horizon where the sunset lingered in a light of liquid crimson, paling and passing into weaker violet tints with every mo-

ment, but still tenderly flushing the walls of the sky, and holding longer the accent of its color where a keen star had here
and there already pierced it and shone quivering through.
The shortest days were past, but in the first week of February
they had not lengthened sensibly, though to a finer perception
there was the promise of release from the winter dark if not
from the winter cold. It was not far from six o'clock when
Northwick mounted the southward rise of the street; it was
still almost light enough to read; and the little slender black
figure of a man that started up in the middle of the road as if
it had risen out of the ground, had an even vivid distinctness.
He must have been lying in the snow; the horses crouched
back with a sudden recoil, as if he had struck them back with
his arm, and plunged the runners of the cutter into the deeper
snow beside the beaten track. He made a slight pause, long
enough to give Northwick a contemptuous glance, and then
continued along the road at a leisurely pace to the deep cut
through the snow from the next house. Here he stood regard-
ing such difficulty as Northwick had in quieting his horses,
and getting underway again. He said nothing, and Northwick
did not speak; Elbridge growled, "He's on one of his tears
again," and the horses dashed forward with a shriek of all
their bells. Northwick did not open his lips till he entered the
avenue of firs that led from the highway to his house; they
were still clogged with the snowfall, and their lowermost
branches were buried in the drifts.

"What's the matter with the colt?" he asked.

"I don't know as that fellow understands the colt's feet very
well. I guess one of the shoes is set wrong," said Elbridge.

"Better look after it."

Northwick left Elbridge the reins, and got out of the cutter
at the flight of granite steps which rose to the ground-floor of
his wooden palace. Broad levels of piazza stretched away from
the entrance under a portico of that carpentry which so often
passes with us for architecture. In spite of the effect of organic
flimsiness in every wooden structure but a log cabin, or a fish-

erman's cottage shingled to the ground, the house suggested a perfect functional comfort. There were double windows on all round the piazzas; a mellow glow from the incandescent electrics penetrated to the outer dusk from them; when the door was opened to Northwick, a pleasant heat gushed out, together with the perfume of flowers, and the odors of dinner.

"Dinner is just served, sir," said the inside man, disposing of Northwick's overcoat and hat on the hall table with respectful scruple.

Northwick hesitated. He stood over the register, and vaguely held his hands in the pleasant warmth indirectly radiated from the steam-pipes below.

"The young ladies were just thinking you wouldn't be home till the next train," the man suggested, at the sound of voices from the dining-room.

"They have some one with them?" Northwick asked.

"Yes, sir. The rector, sir; Mr. Wade, sir."

"I'll come down by and by," Northwick said, turning to the stairs. "Say I had a late lunch before I left town."

"Yes, sir," said the man.

Northwick went on up stairs with footfalls hushed by the thickly padded thick carpet, and turned into the sort of study that opened out of his bedroom. It had been his wife's parlor during the few years of her life in the house which he had built for her, and which they had planned to spend their old age in together. It faced southward, and looked out over the greenhouses and the gardens, that stretched behind the house to the bulk of woods shutting out the stage-picturesqueness of the summer settlement of South Hatboro'. She had herself put the rocking chair in the sunny bay window, and Northwick had not allowed it to be disturbed there since her death. In an alcove at one side he had made a place for the safe where he kept his papers; his wife had intended to keep their silver in it, but she had been scared by the notion of luring burglars so close to them in the night, and had always left the silver in the safe in the dining room.

She was all her life a timorous creature, and after her marriage had seldom felt safe out of Northwick's presence. Her portrait, by Hunt, hanging over the mantelpiece, suggested something of this, though the painter had made the most of her thin, middle-aged blond good looks, and had given her a substance of general character which was more expressive of his own free and bold style than of the facts in the case. She was really one of those hen-minded women, who are so common in all walks of life, and are made up of only one aim at a time, and of manifold anxieties at all times. Her instinct for saving long survived the days of struggle in which she had joined it to Northwick's instinct for getting; she lived and died in the hope, if not the belief, that she had contributed to his prosperity by looking strictly after all manner of valueless odds and ends. But he had been passively happy with her; since her death, he had allowed her to return much into his thoughts, from which her troublesome solicitudes and her entire uselessness in important matters, had obliged him to push her while she lived. He often had times when it seemed to him that he was thinking of nothing, and then he found he had been thinking of her. At such times, with a pang, he realized that he missed her; but perhaps the wound was to habit rather than affection. He now sat down in his swivel chair and turned it from the writing-desk which stood on the rug before the fireplace, and looked up into the eyes of her effigy with a sense of her intangible presence in it, and with a dumb longing to rest his soul against hers. She was the only one who could have seen him in his wish to have not been what he was. She would have denied it to his face, if he had told her he was a thief; and as he meant to make himself more and more a thief, her love would have eased the way by full acceptance of the theories that ran along with his intentions and covered them with pretences of necessity. He thought how even his own mother could not have been so much comfort to him; she would have had the mercy, but she would not have had the folly. At the bottom of his heart, and under all his pretenses, Northwick knew that it was not mercy which would help him; but he wanted it, as we all want what is comfortable and bad for us at times. With the performance and purpose of a thief in his heart, he turned to the pictured face of his dead wife as his refuge from the face of all living. It could not look at him as if he were a thief.

The word so filled his mind that it seemed always about to slip from his tongue. It was what the president of the board had called him when the fact of his fraudulent manipulation of the company's books was laid so distinctly before him that even the insane refusal which the criminal instinctively makes of his crime in its presence, was impossible. The other directors sat blankly round and said nothing; not because they hated a scene, but because the ordinary course of life among us had not supplied them with the emotional materials for making one. The president, however, had jumped from his seat and advanced upon Northwick. "What does all this mean, sir? I'll tell you what it means. It means that you're a thief, sir: the same as if you had picked my pocket, or stolen my horse, or taken my overcoat out of my hall."

He shook his clenched fist in Northwick's face, and seemed about to take him by the throat. Afterwards he inclined more to mercy than the others; it was he who carried the vote which allowed Northwick three days' grace, to look into his affairs, and lay before the directors the proofs that he had ample means, as he maintained, to meet the shortage in the accounts. "I wish you well out of it, for your family's sake," he said at parting; "but all the same, sir, you are a thief."

He put his hands ostentatiously in his pockets, when some others meaninglessly shook hands with Northwick, at parting, as Northwick himself might have shaken hands with another in his place; and he brushed by him out of the door without looking at him. He came suddenly back to say, "If it were a question of you alone, I would cheerfully lose something more than you've robbed me of for the pleasure of seeing you handcuffed in this room and led to jail through the street by a constable. No honest man, no man who was not always a rogue at heart, could have done what you've done: juggled with the books for years, and bewitched the record so by your infernal craft, that it was never suspected till now. You've given *mind* to your scoundrelly work, sir; all the mind you had; for if you hadn't been so anxious to steal successfully, you'd have given more mind to the use of your stealings. You *may* have some of them left, but it looks as if you'd made ducks and drakes of them, like any petty rascal in the hands of the Employees' Insurance Company. Yes, sir, I believe you're of about the intellectual caliber of that sort of thief. I can't respect you even on your own ground. But I'm willing to give you the chance you ask, for your daughter's sake. She's been in and out of my house with my girl like one of my own children, and I wont send her father to jail if I can help it. Understand! I haven't any sentiment for *you*, Northwick. You're the kind of rogue I'd like to see in a convict's jacket, learning to make shoe-brushes. But you shall have your chance to go home and see if you can pay up, somehow, and you sha'n't be shadowed while you're at it. You shall keep your outside to the world three days longer, you whited sepulchre; but if you want to know, I think the best thing that could happen to you on your way home would be a good railroad accident.''

The man's words and looks were burnt into Northwick's memory, which now seemed to have the faculty of simultaneously reproducing them all. Northwick remembered his purple face, with its prominent eyes, and the swing of his large stomach, and just how it struck against the jamb as he whirled a second time out of the door. The other directors, some of them, stood round buttoned up in their overcoats with their hats on, and a sort of stunned aspect; some held their hats in their hands, and looked down into them with a decorous absence of expression, as people do at a funeral. Then they left him alone in the Treasurer's private room, with its official luxury of thick Turkey rugs, leathern armchairs, and nickel-plated cuspidors standing one on each side of the hearth where a fire of soft coal in a low down grate burned with a subdued and respectful flicker.

II

IF IT had not been for the boisterous indignation of the president Northwick might have come away from the meeting, after the exposure of his defalcations with an unimpaired personal dignity. But as it was he felt curiously shrunken and shattered, till the prevailing habit of his mind enabled him to piece himself together again and resume his former size and shape. This happened very quickly. He had conceived of himself so long as a man employing funds in his charge in speculations sometimes successful and sometimes not, but at all times secured by his personal probity and reliability. He had in fact more than once restored all that he had taken, and he had come to trust himself in the course of these transactions as fully as he was trusted by the men who were ignorant of his irregularities. He was somehow flattered by the complete confidence they reposed in him; though he really felt it to be no more than his due: he had always merited and received the confidence of men associated with him in business, and he had come to regard the funds of the corporation as practically his own. In the early days of his connection with the company it largely owed its prosperity to his wise and careful management; one might say that it was not until the last when he got so badly caught by that drop in railroads that he had felt anything wrong in his convertible use of its money. It was an informality; he would not have denied that, but it was merely an informality. Then his losses suddenly leaped beyond his ability to make them good; then for the first time he began to practice that system in keeping the books which the furious president called juggling with them. Even this measure he considered a justifiable means of self-defence pending the difficulties which beset him, and until he could make his losses good by other operations. From time to time he was more fortunate; and whenever he dramatized himself in an explanation to the directors, as he often did, especially of late, he easily satisfied them as to the nature of his motives and the propriety of his behavior, by calling their attention to these successful deals, and to the probability, the entire probability, that he could be at any moment in a position to repay all he had borrowed of the company. He called it borrowing, and in his long habit of making himself these loans and returning them, he had come to have a sort of vague feeling that the company was privy to them; that it was almost an understood thing. The president's violence was the first intimation to reach him in the heart of his artificial consciousness that his action was at all in the line of those foolish peculators whose discovery and flight to Canada was the commonplace of every morning's paper: such a commonplace that he had been sensible of an effort in the papers to vary the tiresome repetition of the same old fact by some novel grace of wit, or some fresh picturesqueness in putting it. In the presence of the directors, he had refused to admit it to himself; but after they adjourned, and he was left alone, he realized the truth. He was like those fools, exactly like them, in what they had done, and in the way of doing it; he was like them in motive and principle. All of them had used others' money in speculation, expecting to replace it, and then had not been able to replace it, and then had skipped, as the newspapers said.

Whether he should complete the parallel, and skip, too, was a point which he had not yet acknowledged to himself that he had decided. He never had believed that it need come to that; but for an instant, when the president said he could wish him nothing better on his way home than a good railroad accident, it flashed upon him that one of the three alternatives before him was to skip. He had the choice to kill himself, which was supposed to be the gentlemanly way out of his difficulties, and would leave his family unstained by his crime: that matter had sometimes been discussed in his presence, and every one had agreed that it was the only thing for a gentleman to do after he had pilfered people of money he could not pay back. There was something else that a man of other instincts and weaker fibre might do, and that was to stand his trial for embezzlement, and take his punishment. Or a man, if he was that kind of a man, could skip. The question with Northwick was whether he was that kind of man, or whether if he skipped, he would be that kind of man; whether the skipping would make him that kind of man.

The question was a cruel one for the self-respect which he had so curiously kept intact. He had been respectable ever since he was born; if he was born with any instinct it was the instinct of respectability, the wish to be honored for what he seemed. It was all the stronger in him, because his father had never had it; perhaps an hereditary trait found expression in him after passing over one generation; perhaps an antenatal influence formed him to that type. His mother was always striving to keep the man she had married worthy of her choice in the eyes of her neighbors; but he had never seconded her efforts. He had been educated a doctor but never practiced medicine; in carrying on the drug and book business of the village he cared much more for the literary than the pharmaceutical side of it; he liked to have a circle of cronies about the wood-stove in his store till midnight, and discuss morals and religion with them; and one night, when denying the plenary inspiration of the scriptures, he went to the wrong jar for an ingredient of the prescription he was making up; the patient died of his mistake. The disgrace and the disaster broke his wife's heart; but he lived on to a vague and colorless old age, supported by his son in a total disoccupation. The elder Northwick used sometimes to speak of his son and his success in the world: not boastfully, but with a certain sarcasm for the source of his bounty, as a boy who had always disappointed him by a narrowness of ambition. He called him Milt, and he said he supposed, now, Milt was the most self-satisfied man in Massachusetts; he implied that there were better things than material success. He did not say what they were, and he could have found very few people in that village to agree with him; or to admit that the Treasurer of the Ponkwasset Mills had come in anywise short of the destiny of a man whose father had started him in life with the name of John Milton. They called him Milt, too, among themselves, and perhaps here and there a bolder spirit might have called him so to his face if he had ever come back to the village. But he had not. He had, as they had all heard, that splendid summer place at Hatboro', where he spent his time when he was not at his house in Boston; and when they verified the fact of his immense prosperity by inquiry of some of the summer-folks who knew him or knew about him, they were obscurely flattered by the fact; just as many of us are proud of belonging to a nation in which we are enriched by the fellow-citizenship of many manifold millionaires. They did not blame Northwick for never coming to see his father, or for never having him home on a visit; they daily saw what old Northwick was, and how little he was fitted for the society of a man whose respectability, even as it was reflected upon them, was so dazzling. Old Northwick had never done anything for Milt; he had never even got along with him; the fellow had left him, and made his own way; and the old man had no right to talk; if Milt was ever of a mind to cut off his rations, the old man would soon see.

III

THE LOCAL opinion scarcely did justice to old Northwick's imperfect discharge of a father's duties; his critics could not have realized how much some capacities, if not tastes, which Northwick had inherited, contributed to that very effect of respectability which they revered. The early range of books, the familiarity with the mere exterior of literature, restricted as it was, helped Northwick later to pass for a man of education, if not of reading with men who were themselves less read than educated. The people whom his ability threw him with in Boston were all Harvard men, and they could not well conceive of an acquaintance, so gentlemanly and quiet as Northwick, who was not college bred, too. By unmistakable signs, which we carry through life, they knew he was from the country, and they attributed him to a freshwater college. They said, "You're a Dartmouth man, Northwick, I believe," or, "I think you're from Williams," and when Northwick said no, they forgot it, and thought that he was a Bowdoin man; the impression gradually fixed itself that he was from one or other of those colleges. It was determined in like manner—partly on account of his name—that he was from one of those old ministerial families that you find up in the hills, where the whole brood study Greek while they are sugaring off in the spring; and that his own mother had fitted him for college. There was in fact something clerical in Northwick's bearing; and it was felt by some that he had studied for the ministry, but had gone into business to help his family. The literary

14

phase of the superstition concerning him was humored by the library which formed such a striking feature of his house in Boston as well as his house in Hatboro'; at Hatboro' it was really vast, and was so charming and so luxurious that it gave the idea of a cultivated family; they preferred to live in it, and rarely used the drawing room, which was much smaller, and was a gold and white sanctuary on the north side of the house only opened when there was a large party of guests, for dancing. Most people came and went without seeing it, and it remained shut up, as much a conjecture, as the memory of Northwick's wife. She was supposed to have been taken from him early, to save him and his children from the mortifying consequences of one of those romantic love-affairs in which a conscientious man had sacrificed himself to a girl he was certain to outgrow. None of his world knew that his fortunes had been founded upon the dowry she brought him, and upon the stay her belief in him had always been. She was a churchmember, as such women usually are, but Northwick was really her religion; and as there is nothing that does so much to sanctify a deity as the blind devotion of its worshippers, Northwick was rendered at times worthy of her faith by the intensity of it. In his sort he returned her love; he was not the kind of man whose affections are apt to wander, perhaps because they were few and easily kept together; perhaps because he was really principled against letting them go astray. He was not merely true in a passive way, but he was constant in the more positive fashion. When they began to get on in the world, and his business talent brought him into relations with people much above them socially, he yielded to her shrinking from the opportunities of social advancement that opened to them, and held aloof with her. This kept him a country person in his experiences much longer than he need have remained; and tended to that sort of defensive secretiveness which grew more and more upon him, and qualified his conduct in matters where there was no question of his knowledge of the polite world. It was not until after his wife's death, and until his daughters began to grow up into the circles where his money and his business associations authorized them to move, that he began to see a little of that world. Even then he left it chiefly to his children; for himself he continued quite simply loyal to his wife's memory, and apparently never imagined such a thing as marrying again.

He rose from the chair where he had sat looking up into her pictured face, and went to open the safe near the window. But he stopped, in stooping over to work the combination, and glanced out across his shoulder into the night. The familiar beauty of the scene tempted him to the window for what, all at once, he felt might be his last look, though the next instant he was able to argue the feeling down, and make his meditated act work into his scheme of early retrieval and honorable return. He must have been thinking there before the fire a long time, for now the moon had risen, and shone upon the black bulk of firs to the southward, and on the group of outbuildings. These were in a sort the mechanism that transacted the life of his house, ministering to all its necessities and pleasures. Under the conservatories, with their long stretches of glass, catching the moon's rays like levels of water, was the steam furnace that imparted their summer climate, through heavy mains carried below the basement, to every chamber of the mansion; a ragged plume of vapor escaped from the tall chimney above them, and dishevelled itself in diaphanous silver on the night breeze. Beyond the hot-houses lay the cold graperies; and off to the left were the stables; in a cosy nook of their low mass Northwick saw the lights of the coachman's family rooms; beyond the stables were the cow-barn and the dairy, with the farmer's cottage; it was a sort of joke with Northwick's business friends that you could buy butter of him sometimes at less than half it cost him, and the joke flattered Northwick's sense of baronial consequence with regard to his place. It was really a farm, in extent, and it was mostly a grazing farm; his cattle were in the herd-books, and he raised horses, which he would sell now and then to a friend; they were so distinctly varied from the original stock as to form almost a breed of themselves; they numbered scores in his stalls and pastures. The whole group of the buildings was so great that it was like a sort of communal village. In the silent moonlight Northwick looked at it as if it were an expansion or extension of himself, so personally did it seem to represent his tastes, and so historical was it of the ambitions of his whole life; he realized that it would be like literally tearing himself from it, when he should leave it. That would be the real pang; his children could come to him, but not his home. But he reminded himself that he was going only for a time, until he could rehabilitate himself and come back upon the terms he could easily make when once he was on his feet again. He thought how fortunate it was that in the meanwhile this property could not be alienated; how fortunate it was that he had originally deeded it to his wife in the days when he had the full right to do so, and she had willed it to their children by a perfect entail. The horses and the cattle might go, and probably must go; and he winced to think of it; but the land, and the house,—all but the furniture and pictures,—were the children's and could not be touched. The pictures were his, and would have to go with the horses and cattle; but ten or twelve thousand dollars would replace them, and he must add that sum to his other losses, and bear it as well as he could.

After all, when everything was said and done, he was the chief loser. If he was a thief, as that man said, he could show that he had robbed himself of two dollars for every dollar that he had robbed anybody else of; if now he was going to add to his theft by carrying off the forty-three thousand dollars of the company's which he found himself possessed of, it was certainly not solely in his own interest. It was to be the means of recovering all that had gone before it, and that the very men whom it would enable him to repay finally in full, supposed it to have gone with.

Northwick felt almost a glow of pride in clarifying this

point to his reason. The additional theft presented itself almost in the light of a duty: it really was his duty to make reparation to those he had injured, if he had injured any one, and it was his first duty to secure the means of doing it. If that money, which it might almost be said was left providentially in his hands, were simply restored now to the company, it would do comparatively no good at all, and would strip him of every hope of restoring the whole sum he had borrowed. He arrived at that word again, and reinforced by it he stooped again to work the combination of his safe, and make sure of the money, which he now felt an insane necessity of laying his hands on; but he turned suddenly sick, with a sickness at the heart or at the stomach, and he lifted himself, and took a turn about the room.

He perceived that in spite of the outward calm which it had surprised him to find in himself, he was laboring under some strong inward stress; and he must have relief from it if he was to carry this business through. He threw up the window, and stood with his hand on the sash, quivering in the strong in-rush of the freezing air. But it strengthened him, and when he put down the window after a few moments, his faintness passed altogether. Still he thought he would not go through that business at once; there was time enough; he would see his girls and tell them that he was obliged to leave by an early train in the morning.

He took off his shoes and put on his slippers, and his house-coat, and went to the stairs-landing outside, and listened to the voices in the library below. He could hear only women's voices, and he inferred that the young man who had been dining with his daughters was gone. He went back into his bed-room, and looked at the face of an unmasked thief in his glass. It was not to get that aspect of himself, though, that he looked; it was to see if he was pale or would seem ill to his children.

IV

Northwick was fond of both his daughters; if he was more demonstrative in meeting the younger, it was because she had the more modern and more urban habit of caressing her father; the elder, who was very much the elder, followed an earlier country fashion of self-repression, and remained seated and silent when he came into the room, though she watched with a pleased interest the exchange of endearments between him and her sister. Her name was Adeline, which was her mother's name, too; and she had the effect of being the aunt of the young girl. She was thin and tall, and she had a New England indigestion which kept her looking frailer than she really was. She conformed to the change of circumstances which she had grown into almost as consciously as her parents, and dressed richly in sufficiently fashionable gowns, which she preferred to have of silk, cinnamon or brown in color; on her slight, bony fingers she wore a good many rings.

Suzette was the name of the other daughter; her mother had fancied that name; but the simple monosyllable it had been shortened into somehow suited the proud-looking girl better than the whole name, with its suggestion of coquettishness.

She asked, "Why didn't you come down, papa? Mr. Wade was calling, and he staid to dinner." She smiled, and it gave him a pang to see that she seemed unusually happy; he could have borne better, he perceived, to leave her miserable; at least, then, he would not have wholly made her so.

19

"I had some matters to look after," he said. "I thought I might get down before he went." A deep leathern arm chair stood before the hearth where the young rector had been sitting, with the ladies at either corner of the mantel; Northwick let himself sink into it, and with a glance at the face of the faintly ticking clock on the black marble shelf before him, he added casually, "I must get an early train for Ponkwasset in the morning, and I still have some things to put in shape."

"Is there any trouble there?" the girl asked from the place she had resumed. She held by one hand from the corner of the mantel and let her head droop over on her arm. Her father had a sense of her extraordinary beauty, as a stranger might have had.

"Trouble?" he echoed.

"With the hands."

"Oh, no; nothing of that sort. What made you think so?" asked Northwick, rapidly exploring the perspective opened up in his mind by her question, to see if it contained any suggestion of advantage to him. He found an instant's relief in figuring himself called to the mills by a labor trouble.

"That tiresome little wretch of a Putney is going about circulating all sorts of reports."

"There is no reason as yet, to suppose the strike will affect us," said Northwick. "But I think I had better be on the ground."

"I should think you could leave it to the Superintendent," said the girl, "without wearing your own life out about it."

"I suppose I might," said Northwick, with an effect of refusing to acquire merit by his behavior, "but the older hands all know me so well, that"—

He stopped as if it were unnecessary to go on, and the elder daughter said, "He is on one of his sprees, again. I should think something ought to be done about him, for his family's sake, if nothing else. Elbridge told James that you almost drove over him, coming up."

"Yes," said Northwick. "I didn't see him until he started up under the horses' feet."

"He will get killed, some of these days," said Adeline, with the sort of awful satisfaction in realizing a catastrophe which delicate women often feel.

"It would be the best thing for him," said her sister, "and for his family too. When a man is nothing but a burden and a disgrace to himself and everybody belonging to him, he had better die as soon as possible."

Northwick sat looking into his daughter's beautiful face, but he saw the inflamed and heated visage of the president of the board, and he heard him saying, "The best thing that could happen to you on your way home would be a good railroad accident."

He sighed faintly, and said, "We can't always tell. I presume it isn't for us to say." He went on, with that leniency for the shortcomings of others which we feel when we long for mercy to our own: "Putney is a very able man; one of the ablest lawyers in the State, and very—honest. He could be almost anything if he would let liquor alone. I don't wish to judge him. He may have"—Northwick sighed again, and ended vaguely—"his reasons"—

Suzette laughed. "How moderate you always are, papa! And how tolerant!"

"I guess Mr. Putney knows pretty well whom he's got to deal with, and that he's safe in abusing you all he likes," said Adeline. "But I don't see how such respectable people as Doctor Morrell and Mrs. Morrell can tolerate him. I've no patience with Doctor Morrell, or his wife, either. To be sure, they tolerate Mrs. Wilmington, too."

Suzette went over to her father to kiss him. "Well, I'm going to bed, papa. If you'd wanted more of my society you ought to have come down sooner. I suppose I sha'n't see you in the morning; so it's good-bye as well as good-night. When will you be home?"

"Not for some days, perhaps," said the unhappy man.

"How doleful! Are you always so homesick when you go away?"

"Not always; no."

"Well, try to cheer up, this time, then. And if you have to be gone a great while, send for me, wont you?"

"Yes, yes; I will," said Northwick. The girl gave his head a hug, and then glided out of the room. She stopped to throw him a kiss from the door.

"There!" said Adeline. "I didn't mean to let Mrs. Wilmington slip out; she can't bear the name, and I *know* it drove her away. But you mustn't let it worry you, father. I guess it's all going well, now."

"What's going well?" Northwick asked, vaguely.

"The Jack Wilmington business. I know she's really given him up, at last; and we can't be too thankful for that much, if it's no more. I don't believe he's bad, for all the talk about him, but he's been weak, and that's a thing she couldn't forgive in a man; she's so strong herself."

Northwick did not think of Wilmington; he thought of himself, and in the depths of his guilty soul, in those secret places underneath all his pretences, where he really knew himself a thief, he wondered if his child's strength would be against her forgiving his weakness. What we greatly dread we most unquestioningly believe; and it did not occur to him to ask whether impatience with weakness was a necessary inference from strength. He only knew himself to be miserably weak.

He rose and stood a moment by the mantel, with his impassive, handsome face turned toward his daughter as if he were going to speak to her. He was a tall man, rather thin; he was clean shaven, except for the grayish whiskers just forward of his ears and on a line with them; he had a regular profile, which was more attractive than the expression of his direct regard. He took up a crystal ball that lay on the marble, and looked into it as if he were reading his future in its lucid depths, and then put it down again, with an effect of helplessness. When he spoke it was not in connection with what his daughter had been talking about. He said, almost dryly, "I think I will go up and look over some papers I have to take with me, and then try to get a little sleep before I start."

"And when shall we expect you back?" asked his daughter, submissively accepting his silence concerning her sister's love affairs. She knew that it meant acquiescence in anything that Sue and she thought best.

"I don't know, exactly; I can't say, now. Good-night."

To her surprise he came up and kissed her; his caresses were for Sue, and she expected them no more than she invited them. "Why, father!" she said in a pleased voice.

"Let James pack the small bag for me, and send Elbridge to me in about an hour," he said, as he went out into the hall.

V

NORTHWICK was now fifty-nine years old, but long before he
reached this age he had seen many things to make him doubt
the moral government of the universe. His earliest instruction had been such as we all receive. He had been taught to
believe that there was an overruling power which would punish him if he did wrong, and reward him if he did right; or
would at least be displeased in one case, and pleased in the
other. The precept took primarily the monitory form, and
first enforced the fact of the punishment or the displeasure;
there were times when the reward or the pleasure might not
sensibly follow upon good behavior, but evil behavior never
escaped the just consequences. This was the doctrine which
framed the man's intention if not his conduct of life and continued to shape it years after experience of the world, and
especially of the business world, had gainsaid it. He had seen
a great many cases in which not only good behavior had apparently failed of its reward, but bad behavior had failed of
its punishment. In the case of bad behavior his observation
had been that no unhappiness, not even any discomfort came
from it unless it was found out; for the most part it was not
found out. This did not shake Northwick's principles; he still
intended to do right, so as to be on the safe side, even in a remote and improbable contingency; but it enabled him to
compromise with his principles and to do wrong provisionally
and then repair the wrong before he was found out, or before
the overruling power noticed him.

But now there were things that made him think, in the surprising misery of being found out, that this power might have had its eye upon him all the time, and was not sleeping, or gone upon a journey, as he had tacitly flattered himself. It seemed to him that there was even a dramatic contrivance in the circumstances to render his anguish exquisite. He had not read many books; but sometimes his daughters made him go to the theatre, and once he had seen the play of Macbeth. The people round him were talking about the actor who played the part of Macbeth, but Northwick kept his mind critically upon the play, and it seemed to him false to what he had seen of life in having all those things happen just so, to fret the conscience and torment the soul of the guilty man; he thought that in reality they would not have been quite so pat; it gave him rather a low opinion of Shakespeare, lower than he would have dared to have if he had been a more cultivated man. Now that play came back into his mind, and he owned with a pang that it was all true. He was being quite as aptly visited for his transgression; his heart was being wrung, too, by the very things that could hurt it most. He had not been very well, of late, and was not feeling physically strong; his anxieties had preyed upon him, and he had never felt the need of the comfort and quiet of his home so much as now when he was forced to leave it. Never had it all been so precious; never had the beauty and luxury of it seemed so great. All that was nothing, though, to the thought of his children, especially of that youngest child, whom his heart was so wrapt up in, and whom he was going to leave to shame and ruin. The words she had spoken from her pride in him, her ignorant censure of that drunkard, as a man who had better die since he had become nothing but a burden and disgrace to his family, stung on as if by incessant repetition. He had crazy thoughts, impulses, fantasies, in which he swiftly dreamed renunciation of escape. Then he knew that it would not avail anything to remain; it would not avail anything even to die; nothing could avail anything at once, but in the end, his going would avail most.

He must go; it would break the child's heart, to face his shame, and she must face it. He did not think of his eldest daughter, except to think that the impending disaster could not affect her so ruinously.

"My God, my God!" he groaned, as he went up stairs. Adeline called from the room he had left, "Did you speak, father?"

He had a conscience, that mechanical conscience which becomes so active in times of great moral obliquity, against telling a little lie, and saying he had not spoken. He went on up stairs without answering anything. He indulged the self pity, a little longer, of feeling himself an old man forced from his home, and he had a blind reasonless resentment of the behavior of the men who were driving him away, and whose interests, even at that moment he was mindful of. But he threw off this mood when he entered his room, and settled himself to business. There was a good deal to be done in the arrangement of papers for his indefinite absence, and he used the same care in providing for some minor contingencies in the company's affairs as in leaving instructions to his children for their action until they should hear from him again. Afterwards this curious scrupulosity became a matter of comment among those privy to it; some held it another proof of the ingrained rascality of the man, a trick to suggest lenient construction of his general conduct in the management of the company's finances, others saw in it an interesting example of the involuntary operation of business instincts which persisted at a juncture when the man might be supposed to have been actuated only by the most intensely selfish motives.

The question was not settled even in the final retrospect, when it appeared that at the very moment that Northwick showed himself mindful of the company's interests on those minor points, he was defrauding it further in the line of his defalcations, and keeping back a large sum of money that belonged to it. But at that moment Northwick did not consider that this money necessarily belonged to the company, any more than his daughters' house and farm belonged to it. To

be sure it was the fruit of money he had borrowed or taken
from the company and had used in an enormously successful
deal; but the company had not earned it, and in driving him
into a corner, in forcing him to make instant restitution of all
its involuntary loans, it was justifying him in withholding this
part of them. Northwick was a man of too much sense to reason explicitly to this effect, but there was a sophistry, tacitly
at work in him to this effect, which made it possible for him
to go on and steal more where he had already stolen so much.
In fact it presented the further theft as a sort of duty. This
sum, large as it was, really amounted to nothing in comparison
with the sum he owed the company; but it formed his only
means of restitution, and if he did not take it and use it to that
end, he might be held recreant to his moral obligations. He
contended, from that vestibule of his soul where he was not a
thief, with that self of his inmost where he was a thief, that it
was all most fortunate, if not providential, as it had fallen
out. Not only had his broker sent him that large check for his
winnings in stocks the day before, but Northwick had, contrary to his custom, cashed the check, and put the money in
his safe instead of banking it. Now he could perceive a leading in the whole matter, though at the time it seemed a fla-
grant defiance of chance, and a sort of invitation to burglars.
He seemed to himself like a burglar, when he had locked the
doors and pulled down the curtains, and stood before the safe
working the combination. He trembled, and when at last the
mechanism announced its effect with a slight click of the
withdrawing bolt, he gave a violent start. At the same time
there came a rough knock at the door, and Northwick called
out in the choking, incoherent voice of one suddenly roused
from sleep: "Hello! Who's there? What is it?"

"It's me," said Elbridge.

"Oh, yes! Well! All right! Hold on, a minute! Ah—you can
come back in ten or fifteen minutes. I'm not quite ready for
you, yet." Northwick spoke the first broken sentences from
the safe where he stood in a frenzy of dismay; the more col-

lected words were uttered from his desk where he ran to get his pistol. He did not know why he thought Elbridge might try to force his way in; perhaps it was because any presence on the outside of the door would have terrified him. He had time to recognize that he was not afraid for the money, but that he was afraid for himself in the act of taking it.

Elbridge gave a cough on the other side of the door, and said with a little hesitation, "All right," and Northwick heard him tramp away, and go down stairs.

He went back to the safe and pulled open the heavy door, whose resistance helped him shake off his nervousness. Then he took the money from the drawer where he had laid it, counted it, slipped it into the inner pocket of his waistcoat, and buttoned it in there. He shut the safe and locked it. The succession of these habitual acts calmed him more and more, and after he had struck a match and kindled the fire on his hearth, which he had hitherto forgotten, he was able to settle again to his preparations in writing.

VI

————

WHEN Elbridge came back, Northwick called out, "Come in!" and then went and unlocked the door for him. "I forgot it was locked," he said carelessly. "Do you think the colt's going to be lame?"

"Well, I don't like the way she behaves, very well. Them shoes have got to come off." Elbridge stood at the corner of the desk, and diffused a strong smell of stable through the hot room.

"You'll see to it, of course," said Northwick. "I'm going away in the morning, and I don't know just how long I shall be gone." Northwick satisfied his mechanical scruple against telling a lie by this formula; and in its shelter he went on to give Elbridge instructions about the management of the place in his absence. He took some money from his pocket book and handed it to him for certain expenses, and then he said, "I want to take the five o'clock train, that reaches Ponkwasset at nine. You can drive me up with the black mare."

"All right," said Elbridge; but his tone expressed a shadow of reluctance that did not escape Northwick.

"Anything the matter?" he asked.

"I dunno. Our little boy don't seem to be very well."

"What ails him?" asked Northwick, with the sympathy it was a relief for him to feel.

"Well, Doctor Morrell's just been there, and he's afraid it's the membranous crou"— The last letter stuck in Elbridge's throat; he gulped it down.

29

"Oh, I *hope* not," said Northwick.

"He's comin' back again—he had to go off to another place —but I could see 'twa'n't no use," said Elbridge with patient despair; he had got himself in hand again, and spoke clearly.

Northwick shrank back from the shadow sweeping so near him: a shadow thrown from the skies, no doubt, but terrible in its blackness on the earth. "Why, of course, you mustn't think of leaving your wife. You must telephone Simpson to come for me."

"All right." Elbridge took himself away.

Northwick watched him across the icy stable-yard, going to the coachman's quarters in that cosy corner of the spreading barn; the windows were still as cheerily bright with lamplight as when they struck a pang of dumb envy to Northwick's heart. The child's sickness must have been very sudden, for his daughters not to have known of it. He thought he ought to call Adeline and send her in there to those poor people; but he reflected that she could do no good, and he spared her the useless pain; she would soon need all her strength for herself. His thought returned to his own cares, from which the trouble of another had lured it for a moment. But when he heard the doctor's sleighbells clash into the stable yard, he decided to go himself and show the interest his family ought to feel in the matter.

No one answered his knock at Elbridge's door, and he opened it and found his way into the room, where Elbridge and his wife were with the doctor. The little boy had started up in his crib, and was struggling, with his arms thrown wildly about.

"There! There, he's got another of them chokin' spells!" screamed the mother. "Elbridge Newton, ain't you goin' to do anything? Oh help him, save him, Dr. Morrell! Oh, I should think you'd be ashamed, to let him suffer so!" She sprang upon the child, and caught him from the doctor's hands, and turned him this way and that trying to ease him; he was suddenly quiet, and she said, "There, I just knew I

could do it! What are you big strong men good for, any"—
She looked down at the child's face in her arms, and then up
at the doctor's, and she gave a wild screech, like the cry of one
in piercing torment.

It turned Northwick heartsick. He felt himself worse than
helpless there; but he went to the farmer's house, and told the
farmer's wife to go over to the Newtons'; their little boy had
just died. He heard her coming before he reached his own
door, and when he reached his room, he heard the bells of the
doctor's sleigh clashing out of the avenue.

The voice and the look of that childless mother haunted
him. She had been one of the hatshop hands, a flighty nervous
thing, madly in love with Elbridge, whom she ruled with a
sort of frantic devotion since their marriage, compensating his
cool quiet with a perpetual flutter of exaggerated sensibilities
in every direction. But somehow she had put Northwick in
mind of his own mother, and he thought of the Chance or the
Will that had bereaved one and spared the other, and he en-
vied the little boy who had just died.

He considered the case of the parents who would want to
make full outward show of their grief, and he wrote Elbridge
a note, to be given him in the morning, and enclosed one of
the bills he was taking from the company; he hoped Elbridge
would accept it from him towards the expenses he must meet
at such a time.

Then he wheeled his chair about to the fire and stretched
his legs out to get what rest he could before the hour of starting. He would have liked to go to bed, but he was afraid of
oversleeping himself in case Elbridge had neglected to telephone Simpson. But he did not believe this possible and he
had smoothly confided himself to his experience of Elbridge's
infallibility, when he started awake at the sound of bells before the front door, and then the titter of the electric bell
over his bed in the next room. He thought it was an officer
come to arrest him, but he remembered that only his household was acquainted with the use of that bell, and then he

wondered that Simpson should have found it out. He put on his overcoat and arctics and caught up his bag, and hurried down stairs and out of doors. It was Elbridge who was waiting for him on the threshold, and took his bag from him.

"Why! Where's Simpson?" he asked. "Couldn't you get him?"

"It's all right," said Elbridge opening the door of the booby, and gently bundling Northwick into it. "I could come just's easy as not. I thought you'd ride better in the booby; it's a little mite chilly for the cutter." The stars seemed points of ice in the freezing sky; the broken snow clinked like charcoal around Elbridge's feet. He shut the booby door and then came back and opened it slightly. "I wa'n't agoin' to let no Simpson carry you to no train, noway."

The tears came into Northwick's eyes, and he tried to say, "Why, thank you, Elbridge," but the door shut upon his failure, and Elbridge mounted to his place and drove away. Northwick had been able to get out of his house only upon condition that he should behave as if he were going to be gone on an ordinary journey. He had to keep the same terms with himself on the way to the station. When he got out there he said to Elbridge, "I've left a note for you on my desk. I'm sorry to be leaving home—at such a time—when you're"—

"You'll telegraph when to meet you?" Elbridge suggested.

"Yes," said Northwick. He went inside the station, which was deliciously warm from the large register in the centre of the room, and brilliantly lighted in readiness for the train now almost due. The closing of the door behind Northwick roused a little black figure drooping forward on the benching in one corner. It was the drunken lawyer. There had been some displeasures, general and personal, between the two men, and they did not speak; but now, at sight of Northwick, Putney came forward, and fixed him severely with his eye.

"Northwick! Do you know who you tried to drive over, last evening?"

Northwick returned his regard with the half-ironical half-patronizing look a dull man puts on with a person of less fortune but more brain. "I didn't see you, Mr. Putney, until I was quite upon you. The horses"—

"It was the *Law* you tried to drive over!" thundered the little man with a voice out of keeping with his slender body. "Don't try it too often! You can't drive over the Law, *yet*— you haven't quite millions enough for that. Heigh? That so?" he queried, sensible of the anti-climax of asking such a question in that way, but tipsily helpless in it.

Northwick did not answer; he walked to the other end of the station, set off for ladies, and Putney did not follow him. The train came in, and Northwick went out and got aboard.

VII

THE PRESIDENT of the board, who had called Northwick a thief, and yet had got him a chance to make himself an honest man, was awake at the hour the defaulter absconded, after passing quite as sleepless a night. He had kept a dinner engagement, hoping to forget Northwick, but he seemed to be eating and drinking him at every course. When he came home toward eleven o'clock, he went to his library and sat down before the fire. His wife had gone to bed, and his son and daughter were at a ball; and he sat there alone, smoking impatiently.

He told the man who looked in to see if he wanted anything that he might go to bed; he need not sit up for the young people. Hilary had that kind of consideration for servants, and he liked to practice it; he liked to realize that he was practicing it now, in a moment when every habit of his life might very well yield to the great and varying anxieties which beset him.

He had an ideal of conduct, of what was due from him to himself, as a gentleman and a citizen, and he could not conceal from himself that he had been mainly instrumental in the escape of a rogue from justice, when he got the Board to give Northwick a chance. His ideals had not hitherto stood in the way of his comfort, his entire repose of mind, any more than they had impaired his prosperity, though they were of a kind far above those which commercial honor permits a man to be content with. He held himself bound, as a man of a certain origin and social tradition, to have public spirit, and he had a great deal of it. He believed that he owed it to the community to do nothing to lower its standards of personal integrity and responsibility; and he distinguished himself by a gratified consciousness from those people of chromo-morality, who held all sorts of loose notions on such points. His name stood not merely for so much money; many names stood for far more; but it meant reliability, it meant honesty, it meant good faith. He really loved these things, though no doubt he loved them less for their own sake than because they were spiritual properties of Eben Hilary. He did not expect everybody else to have them, but his theory of life exacted that they should be held the chief virtues. He was so conscious of their value that he ignored all those minor qualities in himself which rendered him not only bearable, but even lovable; he was not aware of having any sort of foibles, so that any error of conduct in himself surprised him even more than it pained him. It was not easy to recognize it; but when he once saw it, he was not only willing but eager to repair it.

The error that he had committed in Northwick's case, if it was an error, was one that presented peculiar difficulties, as every error in life does: the errors love an infinite complexity of disguise, and masquerade as all sorts of things. There were moments when Hilary saw his mistake so clearly that it seemed to him nothing less than the repayment of Northwick's thefts from his own pocket would satisfy the claims of justice to his fellow-losers if Northwick ran away; and then again, it looked like the act of wise mercy, which it had appeared to him when he was urging the Board to give the man a chance as the only thing which they could hopefully do in the circumstances, as common sense, as business. But it was now so obvious that a man like Northwick could and would do nothing but run away if he were given the chance, that he seemed to have been his accomplice when he used the force of his personal character with them in Northwick's behalf. He was in a ridiculous position, there was no doubt of that, and he was not going to get out of it without much painful wear and tear of pride, of self-respect.

After a long time he looked at the clock, and found it still early for the return of his young people. He was impatient to see his son, and to get the situation in the light of his mind, and see how it looked there. He had already told him of the defalcation, and of what the Board had decided to do, with Northwick; but this was while he was still in the glow of action, and he had spoken very hurriedly with Matt who came in just as he was going out to dinner; it was before his cold fit came on. He had reached that time of life when a man likes to lay his troubles before his son; and in the view his son usually took of his troubles, Hilary seemed to find another mood of his own. It was a fresher, different self dealing with them; for the fellow was not only younger and more vigorous; he was another temperament with the same interests, and often the same principles. He had disappointed Hilary in some ways, but he had gratified his pride in the very ways he had disappointed him. The father had expected the son to go into business, and Matt did go into the mills at Ponkwasset, where he was to be superintendent in the natural course. But one day he came home and told his father that he had begun to have his doubts of the existing relations of labor and capital; and until he could see his way clearer he would rather give up his chance with the company. It was a keen disappointment to Hilary; he made no concealment of that; but he did not quarrel with his son about it. He robustly tolerated Matt's queer notions, not only because he was a father who blindly doted on his children and behaved as if everything they did was right, no matter if it put him in the wrong, but because he chose to respect the fellow's principles, if those were his principles. He had his own principles, and Matt should have his if he liked. He bore entirely well the purpose of going abroad that Matt expressed, and he wished to give him much more money than the fellow would take to carry on those researches which he made in his travels. When he came back and published his monograph on work and wages in Europe, Hilary paid the expense, and took as unselfish an interest in the slow and meager sale of the little book as if it had cost him nothing.

Eben Hilary had been a crank, too, in his day, so far as to have gone counter to the most respectable feeling of business in Boston when he came out an abolitionist. His individual impulse to radicalism exhausted itself in that direction; we are each of us good for only a certain degree of advance in opinion; few men are indefinitely progressive; and Hilary had not caught on to the movement that was carrying his son with it. But he understood how his son should be what he was, and he loved him so much that he almost honored him for what he called his balderdash about industrial slavery. His heart lifted when at last he heard the scratching of the night-latch at the door below, and he made lumbering haste down stairs to open and let the young people in. He reached the door as they opened it, and in the momentary lightness of his soul at sight of his children he gave them a gay welcome, and took his daughter, all a fluff of soft silken and furry wraps into his arms.

"Oh, don't kiss my nose!" she called out. "It'll freeze you to death, papa! What in the world are you up, for? Anything the matter with mamma?"

"No. She was in bed when I came home; I thought I would sit up and ask what sort of time you'd had."

"Did you ever know me to have a bad one? I had the best time in the world. I danced every dance, and I enjoyed it just as much as if I had 'shut and been a Bud again.' But don't you know it's very bad for old gentlemen to be up so late?"

They were mounting the stairs, and when they reached the library, she went in and poked her long-gloved hands well in over the fire on the hearth while she lifted her eyes to the clock. "Oh, it isn't so very late. Only five."

"No, it's early," said her father with the security in a feeble joke which none but fathers can feel with none but their grown-up daughters. "It's full an hour yet before Matt would be getting up to feed his cattle, if he were in Vardley." Hilary had given Matt the old family place there; and he always liked to make a joke of his getting an honest living by farming it.

"Don't *speak* of that agricultural angel!" said the girl, pulling her draperies back with one hand and confining them with her elbow, so as to give her other hand greater comfort of the fire. To do better yet she dropped on both knees before it.

"Was he nice?" asked the father, with confidence.

"Nice! Ask all the plain girls he danced with, all the dull girls he talked with! When I think what a good time I should have with him as a plain girl, if I were not his sister, I lose all patience." She glanced up in her father's face, with all the strange charm of features that had no regular beauty; and then, as she had to do whenever she remembered them, she asserted the grace which governed every movement and gesture in her, and got as lightly to her feet as if she were a wind-bowed flower tilting back to its perpendicular. Her father looked at her with as fond a delight as a lover could have felt in her fascination. She was, in fact, a youthful, feminine version of himself in her plainness; though the grace was all her own. Her complexion was not the leathery red of her father's, but a smooth and even white from cheek to throat. She let her loose cloak fall to the chair behind her, and showed herself tall and slim, with that odd visage of hers drooping from a perfect neck. "Why," she said, "if we had all been horned cattle, he couldn't have treated us better."

"Do you hear that, Matt?" asked the father, as his son came in, after a methodical and deliberate bestowal of his outer garments below; his method and his deliberation were part of the joke of him in the family.

"Complaining of me for making her walk home?" he asked in turn, with the quiet which was another part of the joke. "I didn't suppose you'd give me away, Louise."

"I didn't; I knew I only had to wait and you would give yourself away," said the girl.

"Did he make you walk home?" said the father. "That's the reason your hands are so cold."

"They're not very cold—now; and if they were, I shouldn't mind it in such a cause."

"What cause?"

"Oh the general shamefulness of disusing the feet God had given me. But it was only three blocks, and I had my arctics." She moved a little away toward the fire again and showed the arctics on the floor where she must have been scuffling them off under her skirts. "Ugh! But it's cold!" She now stretched a satin slipper in toward the fire.

"Yes, it's a cold night; but you seem to have got home alive, and I don't think you'll be the worse for it, now if you go to bed at once," said her father.

"Is that a hint?" she asked, with a dreamy appreciation of the warmth through the toe of her slipper.

"Not at all; we should be glad to have you sit up the whole night with us."

"Ah, now I know you're hinting. Is it business?"

"Yes, it's business."

"Well, I'm just in the humor for business; I've had enough pleasure."

"I don't see why Louise shouldn't stay and talk business with us, if she likes. I think it's a pity to keep women out of it, as if it didn't concern them," said the son. "Nine tenths of the time it concerns them more than it does men." He had a bright, friendly, philosophical smile in saying this, and he stood waiting for his sister to be gone, with a patience which their father did not share. He stood something over six feet in his low shoes and his powerful frame seemed starting out of the dress suit, which it appeared so little related to. His whole face was handsome and regular, and his full beard did not wholly hide a mouth of singular sweetness.

"Yes; I think so too, in the abstract," said the father. "If the business were mine, or were business in the ordinary sense of the term"—

"Why, why did you say it was business at all, then?" The girl put her arms round her father's neck and let her head-scarf fall on the rug a little way from her cloak and her arctics. "If you hadn't said it was business, I should have been in bed long ago." Then, as if feeling her father's eagerness to have her gone, she said, "Good night!" and gave him a kiss, and a hug or two more, and said "Good night, Matt," and got herself away, letting a long glove trail somewhere out of her dress, and stretch its weak length upon the floor after her, as if it were trying to follow her.

VIII

Louise's father, in turning to look from her toward his son, felt himself slightly pricked in the cheek by the pin that had transferred itself from her neck-gear to his coat collar, and Matt went about picking up the cloak, the arctics, the scarf and the glove. He laid the cloak smoothly on the leathern lounge, and arranged the scarf and glove on it, and set the arctics on the floor in a sort of normal relation to it, and then came forward in time to relieve his father of the pin that was pricking him, and that he was rolling his eyes out of his head to get sight of.

"What in the devil is that?" he roared.

"Louise's pin," said Matt, as placidly as if that were quite the place for it, and its function were to prick her father in the cheek. He went and pinned it into her scarf, and then he said, "It's about Northwick, I suppose."

"Yes," said his father, still furious from the pin prick. "I'm afraid the miserable scoundrel is going to run away."

"Did you expect there was a chance of that?" asked Matt, quietly.

"Expect!" his father blustered. "I don't know what I expected. I might have expected any thing of him but common honesty. The position I took at the meeting was that our only hope was to give him a chance. He made all sorts of professions of ability to meet the loss. I didn't believe him, but I thought that he might partially meet it, and that nothing was to be gained by proceeding against him. You can't get blood out of a turnip, even by crushing the turnip."

41

"That seems sound," said the son with his reasonable smile.

"I didn't spare him, but I got the others to spare him. I told him he was a thief"—

"Oh!" said Matt.

"Why, wasn't he?" returned his father angrily.

"Yes, yes. I suppose he might be called so." Matt admitted it with an air of having his reservations, which vexed his father still more.

"Very well, sir!" he roared. "Then I called him so; and I think that it will do him good, to know it." Hilary did not repeat all of the violent things he had said to Northwick; though he had meant to do so, being rather proud of them; the tone of his son's voice somehow stopped him for the moment. "I brought them round to my position, and we gave him the chance he asked for."

"It was really the only thing you could do."

"Of course it was! It was the only business-like thing, though it wont seem so when it comes out that he's gone to Canada. I told him I thought the best thing for him would be a good thorough railroad accident on his way home; and that if it were not for his family, for his daughter who's been in and out here so much with Louise, I would like to see him hand-cuffed, and going down the street with a couple of constables."

Matt made no comment upon this, perhaps because he saw no use in criticising his father, and perhaps because his mind was more upon the point he mentioned. "It will be hard for that pretty creature."

"It will be hard for a number of creatures, pretty and plain," said his father. "It wont break any of us; but it will shake some of us up abominably. I don't know but it may send one or two people to the wall, for the time being."

"Ah, but that isn't the same thing at all. That's suffering; it isn't shame. It isn't the misery that the sin of your father has brought on you."

"Well, of course not!" said Hilary impatiently granting it. "But Miss Northwick always seemed to me a tolerably tough kind of young person. I never quite saw what Louise found to like in her."

"They were at school together," said the son. "She's a sufficiently offensive person, I fancy; or might be. But she sometimes struck me as a person that one might be easily unjust to, for that very reason. I suppose she has the fascination that a proud girl has for a girl like Louise."

Hilary asked, with a divergence more apparent than real, "How is that affair of hers with Jack Wilmington?"

"I don't know. It seems to have that quality of mystery that belongs to all affairs of the kind when they hang fire. We expect people to get married, and be done with it, though that may not really be the way to be done with it."

"Wasn't there some scandal about him, of some kind?"

"Yes; but I never believed in it."

"He always struck me as something of a cub, but somehow he doesn't seem the sort of a fellow to give the girl up because"—

"Because her father is a fraud?" Matt suggested. "No, I don't think he is, quite. But there are always a great many things that enter into the matter besides a man's feelings, or his principles, even. I can't say what I think Wilmington would do. What steps do you propose to take next in the matter?"

"I promised him he shouldn't be followed up, while he was trying to right himself. If we find he's gone, we must give the case into the hands of the detectives, I suppose." The disgust showed itself in Hilary's face, which was an index to all his emotions, and his son said, with a smile of sympathy:

"The apparatus of justice isn't exactly attractive, even when one isn't a criminal. But I don't know that it's any more repulsive than the apparatus of commerce, or business, as we call it. Some dirt seems to get on everybody's bread by the time he's earned it, or on his money even when he's made it in large sums as our class do."

The last words gave the father a chance to vent his vexation with himself upon his son. "I wish you wouldn't talk that walking-delegate's rant with me, Matt. If I let you alone in your nonsense, I think you may fitly take it as a sign that I wish to be let alone myself."

"I beg your pardon," said the young man. "I didn't wish to annoy you."

"Don't do it, then." After a moment, Hilary added with a return to his own sense of deficiency, "The whole thing's as thoroughly distasteful to me as it can be. But I can't see how I could have acted otherwise than I've done. I know I've made myself responsible, in a way, for Northwick's getting off; but there was really nothing to do but to give him the chance he asked for. His having abused it, wont change that fact at all; but I can't conceal from myself that I half-expected him to abuse it."

He put this tentatively, and his son responded, "I suppose that naturally inclines you to suppose he'll run away."

"Yes."

"But your supposition doesn't establish the fact."

"No. But the question is whether it doesn't oblige me to act as if it had; whether I oughtn't, if I've got this suspicion, to take some steps at once to find out whether Northwick's really gone or not, and to mix myself actively up in the catchpole business of his pursuit, after I promised him he shouldn't be shadowed in any way till his three days were over."

"It's a nice question," said Matt. "Or rather, it's a nasty one. Still, you've only got your fears for evidence, and you must all have had your fears before. I don't think that even a bad conscience ought to hurry one into the catchpole business." Matt laughed again with that fondness he had for his father. "Though as for any peculiar disgrace in catchpoles as catchpoles, I don't see it. They're a necessary part of the administration of justice, as we understand it and have it; and I don't see how a detective who arrests, say, a murderer, is not as respectably employed as the judge who sentences him, or the hangman who puts the rope round his neck. The distinction we make between them is one of those tricks for shirking responsibility which are practiced in every part of the system. Not that I want you to turn catchpole. It's all so sorrowful and sickening that I wish you hadn't any duty at all in the matter. I suppose you feel at least that you ought to let the Board know that you have your misgivings?"

"Yes," said Hilary ruefully, with his double chin on his breast. "I felt like doing it at once; but there was my word to *him!* And I wanted to talk with you."

"It was just as well to let them have their night's rest. There isn't really anything to be done." Matt rose from the low chair where he had been sprawling, and stretched his stalwart arms abroad. "If the man was going he's gone past recall by this time; and if he isn't gone, there's no immediate cause for anxiety."

"Then you wouldn't do anything at present?"

"I certainly shouldn't. What could you do?"

"Yes, it might as well all go till morning, I suppose."

"Good night," the son said, suggestively. "I suppose there isn't really anything more?"

"No; what could there be? You had better go to bed."

"And you too, I hope, father."

"Oh, I shall go to bed—as a matter of form."

The son laughed. "I wish you could carry your formality so far as to go to sleep, too. I shall."

"I sha'n't sleep," said the father, bitterly. "When things like this happen, some one has to lie awake and think about them."

"Well, I dare say Northwick's doing that."

"I doubt it," said Hilary. "I suspect Northwick is enjoying a refreshing slumber on the Montreal express somewhere near St. Albans about this time."

"I doubt if his dreams are pleasant. After all, he's only going to a larger prison if he's going into exile. He may be on the Montreal express, but I guess he isn't sleeping," said Matt.

"Yes," his father admitted. "Poor devil! He'd much better be dead."

IX

THE GROOM who drove Miss Sue Northwick down to the station at noon that day, came back without her an hour later. He brought word to her sister that she had not found the friend she expected to meet at the station, but had got a telegram from her there and had gone into town to lunch with her. The man was to return and fetch her from the six o'clock train.

She briefly explained at dinner that her friend had been up at four balls during the week, and wished to beg off from the visit she had promised until after the fifth, which was to be that night.

"I don't see how she lives through it," said Adeline. "And at her age, it seems very odd to be just as fond of dancing as if she were a bud."

"Louise is only twenty-three," said Suzette. "If she were married, she would be just in the heart of her gayeties at that age, or even older."

"But she isn't married, and that makes all the difference."

"Her brother is spending the month at home, and she makes the most of his being with them."

"Has he given up his farming? It's about time."

"No; not at all, I believe. She says he's in Boston merely as a matter of duty, to chaperone her at parties, and save her mother from having to go with her."

"Well," said Adeline, "I should think he would want to be of *some* use in the world; and if he wont help his father in business, he had better help his mother in society."

46

Suzette sat fallen back in her chair for the moment, and she said as if she had not heeded, "I think I will give a little dance here, next week. Louise can come up for a couple of days, and we can have it Thursday. We made out the list—just a few people. She went out with me after lunch, and we saw most of the girls, and I ordered the supper. Mrs. Lambert will matronize them; it'll be an old dance, rather, as far as the girls are concerned, but I've asked two or three buds; and some of the young married people. It will be very pleasant, don't you think?"

"Very. Do you think Mr. Wade would like to come?"

Suzette smiled. "I dare say he would. I wasn't thinking of him in making it, but I don't see why he shouldn't look in."

"He might come to the supper," Adeline mused aloud. "If it isn't one of his church days. I never can keep the run of them."

"We were talking about that and we decided that Thursday would be perfectly safe. Louise and I looked it up together; but we knew we could make everything sure by asking Mrs. Lambert first of all: she would have been certain to object if we had made any mistake."

"I'm very glad," said Adeline. "I know father will be glad to have Mr. Wade here. He's taken a great fancy to him."

"Mr. Wade's very nice," said Suzette, coolly. "I shouldn't have liked to have it without him."

They left the table and went into the library, to talk the dance over at larger leisure. Suzette was somewhat sleepy from the fatigues of her escapade to Boston, and an afternoon spent mostly in the cold air, and from time to time she yawned, and said she must really go to bed, and then went on talking.

"Shall you have any of the South Hatboro' people?" her sister asked.

"Mrs. Munger and her tribe?" said Suzette with a contemptuous little smile. "I don't think she would contribute much. Why not the Morrells; or the Putneys, at once?" She added abruptly, "I think I shall ask Jack Wilmington." Adeline gave a start, and looked keenly at her; but she went on quite imperviously. "The Hilarys know him. Matt Hilary and he were quite friends at one time. Besides," she said, as if choosing now to recognize the quality of Adeline's gaze, "I don't care to have Louise suppose there's the shadow of anything between us any more, not even a quarrel."

Adeline gave a little sigh of relief. "I'm glad that's it. I'm always afraid you'll get"—

"To thinking about him again? You needn't be. All that's as thoroughly dead and gone as anything can be in this world. No," she continued, in the tone that is more than half for one's self in such dealings, "whatever there was of that, or might have been, Mr. Wilmington has put an end to, long ago. It never was anything but a fancy, and I don't believe it could have been anything else if it had ever come to the point."

"I'm glad it seems so to you now, Sue," said her sister, "but you needn't tell *me* that you weren't very much taken with him at one time; and if it's going to begin again I'd much rather you wouldn't have him here."

Suzette laughed at the old-maidish anxiety. "Do you think you shall see me at his feet before the evening is over? But I should like to see him at mine, for a moment and to have the chance of hearing his explanations."

"I don't believe he's ever been bad!" cried Adeline. "He's just weak."

"Very well. I should like to hear what a man has to say for his weakness, and then tell him that I had a little weakness of my own, and didn't think I had strength to endure a husband that had to be explained."

"Ah, you're in love with him, yet! You shall never have him here in the world, after the way he's treated you!"

"Don't be silly, Adeline! Don't be romantic! If you had ever been in love yourself, you would know that people outlive that as well as other things. Let's see how the drawing-room will do for the dance."

She jumped from her chair and touched the electric button

at the chimney. "You think that nothing but death can kill a fancy, and yet nobody marries their first love, and lots of women have second husbands." The man showed himself at the door, and she said to him in a rapid aside, "Turn up the lights in the drawingroom, James," and resumed to her sister. "No, Adeline! The only really enduring and undying thing is a—slight. That lasts—with *me!*"

Adeline was moved to say, in the perverse honesty of her soul, and from the inborn New England love of justice, "I don't believe he ever meant it, Sue. I don't believe but what he was influenced"—

Suzette laughed, not at all bitterly. "Oh, *you're* in love with him! Well, you may have him if ever he offers himself to me. Let's look at the drawing room!"

She caught Adeline round her bony waist, where each rib defined itself to her hand, and danced her out of the library across the hall into the white and gold saloon beyond. "Yes," she said, with a critical look at the room, "it will do splendidly. We shall have to put down linen, of course; but then the dancing will be superb—as good as a bare floor. Yes, it will be a grand success. Ugh! Come out, come out, come out! How deathly cold it is!"

She ran back into the warm library, and her sister followed more slowly.

"You shouldn't think," she said, as if something in Sue's words had reminded her of it, "that coming so soon after Mrs. Newton's little boy"—

"Well, that's *like* you Adeline! To bring *that* up! *No*, indeed! It'll be a whole week, nearly; and besides he *isn't* quite one of the family. What an idea!"

"Of course," her sister assented, abashed by Sue's scornful surprise.

"It's too bad it should have happened—just at this time," said the girl, with some relenting. "When is it to be?"

"Tomorrow, at eleven," said Adeline. She perceived that Sue's selfishness was more a selfishness of words, perhaps, than of thoughts or feelings. "You needn't have anything to do with it. I can tell them you were not very well, and didn't feel exactly like coming. They will understand." She was used to making excuses for Suzette, and a motherly fib like this seemed no harm to her.

X

IN THE morning before her sister was astir, Adeline went out to the coachman's quarters in the stabling, and met the mother of the dead child at the door. "Come right in!" she said fiercely, as she set it wide. "I presume you want to know if there's anything you can do for me: that's what they all ask. Well, there ain't, unless you can bring him back to life. I've been up and doin', as usual, this mornin'," she said, and a sound of frying came from the kitchen where she had left her work to let her visitor in. "We got to eat; we got to live."

The farmer's wife came in from the next chamber, where the little one lay; she had her bonnet and shawl on as if going home after a night's watching. She said, "I tell her he's better off where he's gone; but she can't seem to sense the comfort of it."

"How do you know he's better off?" demanded the mother, turning upon her. "It makes me tired to hear such stuff. Who's goin' to take more care of the child where he's gone, than what his mother could? Don't you talk nonsense, Mrs. Saunders! You don't know anything about it, and nobody does. I can bear it; yes, I've got the stren'th to stand up against death, but I don't want any *comfort*. You want to see Elbridge, Miss Northwick? He's in the harness-room, I guess. He's got to keep about, too, if he don't want to go clear crazy. One thing, he don't have to stand any comfortin'. I guess men don't say such things to each other as women do, big fools as they be!"

Mrs. Saunders gave Miss Northwick a wink of pity for Mrs.

Newton, and expressed that she was hardly accountable for what she was saying.

"He used to complain of me for lettin' Arty get out into the stable among the horses; but I guess he wont be troubled that way *much* more," said the mother; and then something in Miss Northwick's face seemed to stay her in her wild talk; and she asked, "Want I should call him for you?"

"No, no," said Adeline, "I'll go right through to him, myself." She knew the way from the coachman's dwelling into the stable, and she found Elbridge oiling one of the harnesses, with a sort of dogged attention to the work, which he hardly turned from to look at her. "Elbridge," she asked, "did you drive father to the depot yesterday morning?"

"Yes, ma'am, I did."

"When did he say he would be back?"

"Well, he said he couldn't say, exactly. But I understood in a day or two."

"Did he expect to be anywhere but Ponkwasset?"

"No, ma'am, I didn't hear him say as he did."

"Then it's a mistake; and of course I knew it was a mistake. There's more than one Northwick in the world, I presume." She laughed a little hysterically; she had a newspaper in her hand, and it shook with the nervous tremor that passed over her.

"Why, what is it, Miss Northwick?" said Elbridge with a perception of the trouble in her voice through the trouble in his own heart. He stopped pulling the greasy sponge over the trace in his hand, and turned towards her.

"Oh, nothing. There's been an accident on the Union and Dominion Railroad; and of course it's a mistake."

She handed him the paper, folded to the column which she wished to show, and he took it between two finger-tips, so as to soil it as little as possible and stood, reading it. She went on saying, "He wouldn't be on the train if he was at Ponkwasset. I got the paper when I first came down stairs, but I didn't happen to read the account till just now; and then I thought

I'd run out and see what father said to you about where he was going. He told us he was going to the Mills, too, and"— Her voice growing more and more wistful, died away in the fascination of watching the fascination of Elbridge as he first took in the half-column of scare-heads, and then followed down to the meagre details of the dispatch eked out with double-leading to cover space.

It appeared that the Northern express had reached Wellwater Junction on the Union and Dominion line, several hours behind time, and after the usual stop there for supper had joined the Boston train on the United States and Canada for Montreal and had run off the track just after leaving the Junction. "The deadly car stove got in its work" on the wreck, and many lives had been lost by the fire, especially in the parlor car. It was impossible to give a complete list of the killed and wounded, but several bodies were identified, and among the names of passengers in the Pullman that of T. W. Northwick was reported, from a telegram received by the conductor at Wellwater asking to have a seat reserved from that point to Montreal.

"It aint him, I know it aint, Miss Northwick," said Elbridge. He offered to give her the paper, but took another look at it before he finally yielded it. "There's lots of folks of the same name, I don't care what it is, and the initials aint the ones."

"No," she said, doubtfully, "but I didn't like the last name being the same."

"Well, you can't help that; and as long as it aint the initials, and you know your father is safe and sound at the mills, you don't want to worry."

"No," said Adeline. "You're sure he told you he was going to the mills?"

"Why, didn't he tell *you* he was? I don't recollect just what he said. But he told me about that note he left for me, and that had the money in it for the fun'al"— Elbridge stopped for a moment before he added, "He said he'd telegraph just which

train he wanted me to meet him when he was comin' back—
Why, dumn it! I guess I *must* be crazy. We can settle it in half
an hour's time—or an hour or two at the outside—and no need
to worry about it. Telegraph to the mills and find out whether
he's there or not."

He dropped his harness, and went to the telephone and
called up the Western Union operator at the station. He had
the usual telephonic contention with her as to who he was, and
what he wanted, but he got her at last to take his dispatch to
Ponkwasset Falls, asking whether Northwick was at the mills.

"There!" he said. "I don't believe but what that'll fix it all
right. And I'll bring you in the answer myself, when it comes,
Miss Northwick."

"I do hate to trouble you with my foolishness, when"—

"I guess you needn't mind about that," said Elbridge. "I
guess it wouldn't make much difference to me, if the whole
world was burnt up. Be a kind of a relief." He did not mean
just the sense the words conveyed, and she, in her preoccupa-
tion with her own anxiety, and her pity for him, interpreted
them aright.

She stayed to add, "I don't know what he could have been
on that train for, any way, do you?"

"No, and he wa'n't on it; you'll find that out."

"It'll be very provoking," she said, forecasting the minor
trouble of the greater trouble's failure. "Everybody will wonder if it isn't father, and we shall have to tell them it isn't."

"Well, that wont be so bad as havin' to tell 'em it is," said
Elbridge, getting back for the moment to his native dryness.

"That's true," Adeline admitted. "Don't speak to anybody
about it till you hear." She knew from his making no answer
that he would obey her, and she hid the paper in her pocket,
as if she would hide the intelligence it bore from all the rest
of the world.

She let Suzette sleep late after the fatigues of her day in
Boston, and the excitement of their talk at night, which she
suspected had prevented the girl from sleeping early. El-

bridge's sympathetic incredulity had comforted her, if it had not convinced her, and she possessed herself in such patience as she could till the answer should come from the mills. If her father were there, then it would be all right; and in the mean-time she found some excuses for not believing the worst she feared. There was no reason in the world why he should be on that train; there was no reason why she should identify him with that T. W. Northwick, in the burnt up car; that was not his name, and that was not the place where he could have been.

———

THERE was trouble with the telegraph and telephone connections between Hatboro' and Ponkwasset, and Adeline had to go to the funeral without an answer to Elbridge's message. Below her surface interest in the ceremony and the behavior of the mourners and the friends, which nothing could have alienated but the actual presence of calamity, she had a nether misery of alternating hope and fear, of anxieties continually reasoned down, and of security lost the instant it was found. The double strain told so upon her nerves that when the rites at the grave were ended, she sent word to the clergyman and piteously begged him to drive home with her.

"Why, aren't you well, Miss Northwick?" he asked with a glance at her troubled face, as he got into the covered sleigh with her.

"Oh, yes," she said, and she flung herself back against the cushioning and began to cry.

"Poor Mrs. Newton's grief has been very trying," he said gently, and with a certain serenity of smile he had, and he added, as if he thought it well to lure Miss Northwick from the minor affliction that we feel for others' sorrows to the sorrow itself, "It has been a terrible blow to her—so sudden, and her only child."

"Oh, it isn't that," said Adeline frankly. "Have—have you seen the—paper this morning?"

"It came," said the clergyman. "But in view of the duty before me, I thought I wouldn't read it. Is there anything particular in it?"

"No, nothing. Only—only"— Adeline had not been able to separate herself from the dreadful thing, and she took it out of the carriage pocket. "There has been an accident on the railroad," she began firmly; but she broke down in the effort to go on: "And I wanted to have you see—see"— She stopped, and handed him the paper.

He took it and ran over the account of the accident, and came at her trouble with an instant intelligence that was in itself a sort of reassurance: "But had you any reason to suppose your father was on the train?"

"No," she said from the strength he gave her. "That is the strange part about it. He went up to the mills, yesterday morning, and he couldn't have been on the train at all. Only the name"—

"It isn't quite the name," said Wade with a gentle moderation, as if he would not willingly make too much of the difference, and felt truth to be too sacred to be tampered with even while it had merely the form of possibility.

"No," said Adeline, eager to be comforted, "and I'm sure he's at the mills. Elbridge has sent a dispatch to find out if he's there, but there must be something the matter with the telegraph. We hadn't heard before the funeral; or at least he didn't bring me word; and I hated to keep round after him when"—

"He probably hadn't heard," said the clergyman, soothingly, "and no news is good news, you know. But hadn't we better drive round by the station, and find out whether any answer has been"—

"O, no! I couldn't do that!" said Adeline, nervously. "They will telephone the answer up to Elbridge. But come home with me, if you haven't something to do and stay with us till we"—

"Oh, very willingly." On the way the young clergyman talked of the accident, guessing that her hysterical conjectures had heightened the horror, and that he should make it less dreadful by exploring its facts with her. He did not declare it impossible her father should have been on the train, but he urged the extreme improbability.

Elbridge and his wife passed them, driving rapidly in Simpson's booby, which Adeline had ordered for their use at the funeral; and when she got into the house Elbridge was waiting there for her. He began at once, "Miss Northwick, I don't believe but what your father's staid over at Springfield for something. He was talkin' to me last week about some hosses there"—

"Isn't he at the mills?" she demanded sharply.

Elbridge gave his hat a turn on his hand, before he looked up. "Well, no, he hain't been, yet"—

Adeline made no sound, but she sank down as a column of water sinks.

At the confusion of movements and voices that followed, Suzette came to the door of the library, and looked wonderingly into the hall, where this had happened, with a book clasped over her finger. "What in the world is the matter?" she asked with a sort of sarcastic amaze, at sight of Elbridge lifting something from the floor.

"Don't be alarmed, Miss Suzette," said Mr. Wade. "Your sister seems a little faint, and"—

"It's this sickening heat!" cried the girl, running to the door, and setting it wide. "It suffocates me when I come in from the outside. I'll get some water." She vanished and was back again instantly, stooping over Adeline, to wet her forehead and temples. The rush of the cold air began to revive her. She opened her eyes, and Suzette said, severely, "What has come over you, Adeline? Aren't you well?" and as Adeline answered nothing, she went on: "I don't believe she knows where she is. Let us get her into the library on the lounge."

She put her strength with that of the young clergyman and they carried Adeline to the lounge; Suzette dispatched Elbridge, hanging helplessly about, for some of the women. He sent the parlor maid, and did not come back.

Adeline kept looking at her sister as if she were afraid of

her. When she was sufficiently recovered to speak, she turned her eyes on the clergyman, and said huskily, "Tell her."

"Your sister has had a little fright," he began; and with his gentle eyes on the girl's he went on to deal the pain that priests and physicians must give. "There's the report of a railroad accident in the morning paper, and among the passengers—the missing—was one of the name of Northwick"—

"But father is at the mills!"

"Your sister had telegraphed before the funeral, to make sure—and word has come that he—isn't there."

"Where is the paper?" demanded Suzette, with a kind of haughty incredulity.

Wade found it in his pocket, where he must have put it instead of giving it back to Adeline in the sleigh. Suzette took it and went with it to one of the windows. She stood reading the account of the accident, while her sister watched her with tremulous eagerness for the help that came from her contemptuous rejection of the calamity.

"How absurd! It isn't father's name, and he couldn't have been on the train. What in the world would he have been going to Montreal for, at this time of year? It's ridiculous!" Suzette flung the paper down, and came back to the other two.

"I felt," said Wade, "that it was extremely improbable"—

"But where," Adeline put in faintly, "could he have been if he wasn't at the mills?"

"Anywhere in the world except Wellwater Junction," returned Suzette, scornfully. "He may have stopped over at Springfield, or"—

"Yes," Adeline admitted, "that's what Elbridge thought."

"Or he may have gone on to Willoughby Junction. He often goes there."

"That is true," said the other, suffering herself to take heart a little. "And he's been talking of selling his interest in the quarries there; and"—

"He's there, of course," said Suzette with finality. "If he'd been going farther, he'd have telegraphed us. He's always very careful. I'm not in the least alarmed, and I advise you not to be, Adeline. When did you see the paper first?"

"When I came down to breakfast," said Adeline guiltily.

"And I suppose you didn't eat any breakfast?"

Adeline's silence made confession.

"What I think is, we'd better all have *lunch*," said Suzette, and she went and touched the bell at the chimney. "You'll stay with us, wont you, Mr. Wade? We want lunch at once, James," she said to the man who answered her ring. "Of course you must stay, Mr. Wade, and help see Adeline back to her right mind." She touched the bell again, and when the man reappeared, "My sleigh at once, James," she commanded. "I will drive you home, Mr. Wade, on my way to the station. Of course I shall not leave anything in doubt about this silly scare. I fancy it will be no great difficulty to find out where father is. Where is that railroad guide? Probably my father took it up to his room." She ran up stairs and came down with the book in her hand. "Now we will see. I don't believe he could get any train at Springfield, where he would have to change for the mills, that would take him beyond the Junction at that hour last night. The express has to come up from Boston"— She stopped, and ran over the time table of the route. "Well, he *could* get a connecting train at the Junction; but that doesn't prove at all that he did."

She talked on, mocking the mere suggestion of such a notion, and then suddenly rang the bell, once more, to ask sharply, "Isn't lunch ready yet? Then bring us tea, here. I shall telegraph to the mills again, and I shall telegraph to Mr. Hilary in Boston: he will know whether father was going anywhere else. They had a meeting of the board day before yesterday, and father went to the mills unexpectedly. I shall telegraph to Ponkwasset Junction, too; and you may be sure I shall not come home, Adeline, till I know something definite."

The tea came, and Suzette served the cups herself with nerves that betrayed no tremor in the clash of silver or china. But she made haste, and at the sound of sleighbells without, she put down her own cup untasted.

"Oh, must you take Mr. Wade away?" Adeline feebly pleaded. "Stay till she comes back!" she entreated.

Suzette faltered a moment, and then with a look at Mr. Wade she gave a harsh laugh. "Very well!" she said.

She ran into the hall and up the stairs, and in another moment they heard her coming down again; the outer door shut after her, and then came the flutter of the sleighbells as she drove away.

Over the lunch the elder sister recovered herself a little, and ate as one can in the suspense of a strong emotion.

"Your sister is a person of great courage," said the clergyman, as if he were a little abashed by it.

"She would never show that she's troubled. But I know well enough that she's troubled, by the way she kept talking and doing something every minute; and now, if she hadn't gone to telegraph, she'd—I mustn't keep you here any longer, Mr. Wade," she broke off, in the sense of physical strength the food had given her. "Indeed I mustn't. You needn't be anxious. I shall do very well, now. Yes! I shall!"

She begged him to leave her, but he perceived that she did not really wish him to go, and it was nearly an hour after Suzette drove away before he got out of the house. He would not let her send him home; and he walked toward the village in the still sunny cold of the early winter afternoon, thinking of the sort of contempt with which that girl had spurned the notion of calamity, as if it were something to be resented, and even snubbed, in its approach to her. It was as if she had now gone to trace it to its source and defy it there; to stamp upon the presumptuous rumor and destroy it.

Just before he reached the crest of the upland that shut out the village from him, he heard the clash of sleighbells; a pair of horses leaped into sight, and came bearing down upon him with that fine throw of their feet which you get only in such a direct encounter. He stepped into the side track, and then he heard Miss Sue Northwick call to her horses, and saw her pulling them up. She had her father's fondness for horses, and the pair of little grays were a gift from him with the picturesque sledge they drew. The dasher swelled forward like a swan's breast, and then curved deeply backward; from either corner of the band of iron filagree at the top, dangled a red horsetail. The man who had driven her to the station sat in a rumble behind; on the seat with Suzette was another young lady who put out her hand to Wade, with a look of uncommon liking across the shining bearskin robe and laughed at his astonishment in seeing her. While they talked the clipped grays nervously lifted and set down their forefeet in the snow, as if fingering it; they inhaled the cold air with squared nostrils, and blew it out in blasts of white steam.

Suzette said, in explanation of her friend's presence, "Louise had seen the account, and she made her brother bring her up. They think just as I do, that there's nothing of it; one of the papers had the name Nordeck; but we've left Mr. Hilary at the station, fighting the telephone and telegraph in all directions, and he isn't to stop till he gets something positive. He's trying Wellwater now." She said all this very haughtily, but she added, "The only thing is, I can't understand why my father hasn't been heard of at the mills. Some one was asking for him there yesterday."

"Probably he went on to Willoughby Junction, as you suggested."

"Of course he did," said Louise. "We haven't heard from there yet."

"Oh, I'm not in the least troubled," said Sue. "But it's certainly very provoking." She lifted her reins. "I'm hurrying home to let Adeline know."

"She'll be very glad," Wade returned, as if it were the certainty of good news she was carrying. "I think I'll join Matt at the station," he suggested to Louise.

"Do!" she answered. "You can certainly manage something between you. Matt will be almost as glad of your coming as my going. I thought we were coming up here to reassure Sue, but I seem strangely superfluous."

"You can reassure Adeline," said Sue. She added to Wade,

"I keep thinking what an annoyance it will be to my father, to have all this fuss made over him. I sometimes feel vexed with Adeline. Good-bye!" she called back to him as she drove away, and she stopped again to add, "Won't you come up with Mr. Hilary, when you've heard something definite?"

Wade promised, and they repeated their good-byes all round, with a resolute cheerfulness.

XII

THE AFFAIR had been mixed up with tea and lunch, and there was now the suggestion of a gay return to the Northwick place and an hour or two more in that pleasant company of pretty and lively women which Wade loved almost as well as he loved righteousness. He knew that there was such a thing as death in the world; he had often already seen its strange, peaceful face; he had just stood by an open grave; but at the moment, his youth denied it all, and he swung along over the hardpacked roadway thinking of the superb beauty of Suzette Northwick, and the witchery of Louise Hilary's face. It was like her, to come at once to her friend in this anxiety; and he believed a strength in her to help bear the worst, the worst that now seemed so remote and impossible.

He did not find Matt Hilary in the station; but he pushed through to the platform outside and saw him at a little distance standing between two of the tracks, and watching a group of men there who were replacing some wornout rails with new ones.

"Matt!" he called to him, and Matt turned about and said, "Hello, Caryl!" and yielded him a sort of absent minded hand, while he kept his face turned smilingly upon the men. Some were holding the rails in position, and another was driving in the spike that was to rivet the plate to the sleeper. He struck it with exquisite accuracy from a wide, rhythmical, free handed swing of his hammer.

"Beautiful! Isn't it?" said Matt. "I never see any sort of manual labor, even the kinds that are brutified and demoral-

64

ized by their association with machinery, without thinking how far the arts still come short of the trades. If any sculptor could feel it, what a magnificent bas-relief just that thing would make!" He turned round to look at the men again: in their different poses of self-forgetfulness and interest in their work, they had a beauty and grace, in spite of their clumsy dress, which ennobled the scene.

When Matt once more faced round he smiled serenely on his friend. Wade, who knew his temperament and his philosophy, was deceived for the moment. "Then you don't share Miss Northwick's anxiety about her father," he began, as if Matt had been dealing directly with that matter, and had been giving his reasons for not being troubled about it. "Have you heard anything yet? But of course you haven't, or"—

Matt halted him, and looked down into his face from his greater height with a sort of sobered cheerfulness. "How much do you know about Miss Northwick's father?"

"Very little—nothing in fact but what she and her sister showed me in the morning paper. I know they're in great distress about him; I just met Miss Suzette and your sister, and they told me I should find you at the station."

Matt began to walk on again. "I didn't know but you had heard some talk from the outside. I came off to escape the pressure of inquiry at the station; people had found out somehow that I had been put in charge of the telegraphing when the young ladies left. I imagined they wouldn't follow me if I went for a walk." He put his hand through Wade's arm, and directed their course across the tracks toward the street winding away from the station, where Elbridge had walked his horses up and down the evening he met Northwick. "I told them to look out for me, if they got anything; I should keep in sight somewhere. Isn't it a curious commentary on our state of things," he went on, "that when any man in a position of trust can't be accounted for twenty-four hours after he leaves home, the business like supposition is that he has run away with money that doesn't belong to him?"

"What do you mean, Matt?"

"I mean that the popular belief in Hatboro' seems to be that Northwick was on his way to Canada on the train that was wrecked."

"Shocking, shocking!" said Wade. "What makes you think they believe that?"

"The conjecture and speculation began in the station the moment Miss Northwick left it, and before it could be generally understood that I was there to represent her. I suppose there wasn't a man among them that wouldn't have trusted Northwick with all he had, or wouldn't have felt that his fortune was made if Northwick had taken charge of his money. In fact I heard some of them saying so before their deference for me shut their mouths. Yet I haven't a doubt they all think he's an absconding defaulter."

"It's shocking," said Wade, sadly, "but I'm afraid you're right. These things are so common that people are subjected to suspicion on no kind of"— But just at this juncture Matt lifted his head from the moment's revery in which he seemed to have been far absent.

"Have you seen much of the family this winter?"

"Yes; a good deal," said Wade. "They're not communicants, but they've been regular attendants at the services, and I've been a good deal at their house. They seem rather lonely; they have very little to do with the South Hatboro' people, and nothing at all with the villagers. I don't know why they've spent the winter here. Of course one hears all kinds of gossip. The gossips at South Hatboro' say that Miss Suzette was willing to be on with young Wilmington again, and that *she* kept the family here. But I place no faith in such a conjecture."

"It has a rustic crudity," said Matt. "But if Jack Wilmington ever cared anything for the girl, now's his chance to be a man and stand by her."

Something in Matt's tone made Wade stop and ask, "What do you mean Matt? Is there anything besides"—

"Yes." Matt took a fresh grip of his friend's arm, and walked him steadily forward, and kept him walking in spite of his involuntary tendency to come to a halt, every few steps, and try to urge something that he never quite got from his tongue, against the probability of what Matt was saying. "I mean that these people are right in their suspicions."

"Right?"

"My dear Caryl, there is no doubt whatever that Northwick is a defaulter to the company in a very large amount. It came out at a meeting of the directors on Monday. He confessed it, for he could not deny it in the face of the proof against him, and he was given a number of days to make up his shortage. He was released on parole; it was really the best thing, the wisest as well as the mercifullest, and of course he broke his word, and seized the first chance to run away. I knew all about the defalcation from my father just after the meeting. There is simply no question about it."

"Gracious powers!" said Wade, finally helpless to dispute the facts which he still did not realize. "And you think it possible—do you suppose—imagine—that it was really he who was in that burning car? What an awful fate!"

"An awful fate?" asked Matt. "Do you think so? Yes, yours is the safe ground in regard to a thing of that kind—the only ground."

"The only ground?"

"I was thinking of my poor father," said Matt. "He said some sharp things to that wretched creature at the meeting of the Board—called him a thief, and I dare say other hard names—and told him that the best thing that could happen to him was a railroad accident on his way home"—

"Ah!"

"You see? When he read the account of that accident in the paper this morning, and found a name so much like Northwick's among the victims, he was fearfully broken up, of course. He felt somehow as if he had caused his death—I could see that, though of course he wouldn't admit anything of the kind."

"Of course," said Wade, compassionately.

"I suppose it isn't well to invoke death in any way. He is like the devil, and only too apt to come, if you ask for him. I don't mean anything superstitious, and I don't suppose my father really has any superstitious feeling about the matter. But he's been rather a friend—or a victim—of that damnable theory that the gentlemanly way out of a difficulty like Northwick's is suicide, and I suppose he spoke from association with it, or by an impulse from it. He has been telegraphing right and left, to try to verify the reports, as it was his business and duty to do, anyway; and he caught at the notion of my coming up here with Louise to see if we could be of any use to those two poor women."

"Poor women!" Wade echoed. "The worst must fall upon them, as the worst always seems to do."

"Yes, wherever a cruel blow falls there seems to be a woman for it to fall on. And you see what a refinement of cruelty this is going to be when it reaches them? They have got to know that their father met that awful death, and that he met it because he was a defaulter and was running away. I suppose the papers will be full of it."

"That seems intolerable. Couldn't anything be done to stop them?"

"Why the thing has to come out. You can keep happiness a secret, but sorrow and shame have to come out—I don't know why; but they do. Then when they come out we feel as if the means of their publicity were the cause of them. It's very unphilosophical." They walked slowly along in silence for a few moments, and then Matt's revery broke out again in words. "Well, it's to be seen now whether she has the strength that bears, or the strength that breaks. The way she held her head, as she took the reins and drove off, with poor Louise beside her palpitating with sympathy for her trouble and anxiety about her horses, was—yes, it was superb; there's no other word for it. Ah, poor girl!"

"Your sister's presence will be a great help to her," said Wade. "It was very good of her to come."

"Oh, there wasn't anything else for it," said Matt flinging

his head up. "Louise has my father's loyalty. I don't know much about her friendship with Miss Northwick—she's so much younger than I, and they came together when I was abroad—but I've fancied she wasn't much liked among the girls, and Louise was her champion, in a way. When Louise read that report, nothing would do but she must come."

"Of course."

"But our being here must have its embarrassments for my father. It was a sacrifice for him to let us come."

"I don't understand."

"It was he who carried through the respite the directors gave Northwick; and now he will have the appearance before some people of helping to cover up the miserable facts, of putting a good face on things while a rogue was getting away from justice. He might even be supposed to have some interest in getting him out of the way."

"Oh, I don't think any such suspicion can attach itself to such a man as Mr. Hilary," said Wade with a certain resentment of the suggestion even from the man's son.

"In a commercial civilization like ours any sort of suspicion can attach to any sort of man in a case like this," said Matt.

Wade took off his hat and wiped his forehead. "I can't realize that the case is what you say. I can't realize it at all. It seems like some poor sort of play, of make-believe. I can't forgive myself for being so little moved by it. We are in the presence of a horror that ought to make us uncover our heads and fall to our knees and confess our own sins to God!"

"Ah, I'm with you *there!*" said Matt, and he pushed his hand further through his friend's arm.

They were both still well under thirty, and they both had that zest for mere experience, any experience, that hunger for the knowledge of life, which youth feels. In their several ways they were already men who had thought for themselves, or conjectured, rather; and they were eager to verify their speculations through their emotions. They thought a good deal alike on many things, though they started from such opposite points in their thinking; and they both had finally the same ideal of life. Their intimacy was of as old a date as their school days; at Harvard they were in the same clubs as well as the same class. Wade's father was not a Boston man, but his mother was a Bellingham, and he was nurtured in the traditions of Hilary's social life. Both had broken with them: Wade not so much when he became a ritualist as Hilary when he turned his back on manufacturing.

They were now not without a kind of pride in standing so close to the calamity they were the fated witnesses of, and in the midst of their sympathy they had a curiosity which concerned itself with one of the victims because she was a young and beautiful girl. Their pity not so much ignored as forgot Northwick's elder daughter, who was a plain, sick old maid, and followed the younger with a kind of shrinking and dread of her doom, which Matt tried to put into words.

"I assure you, if I couldn't manage to pull away from it at moments, I don't see how I could stand it. I had a sense of personal disgrace, when I met that poor girl with what I had in my mind. I felt as if I were taking some base advantage of her in knowing that about her father, and I was so glad when she went off with Louise and left me to struggle with my infamous information alone. I hurried Louise away with her in the most cowardly haste. We don't any of us realize it as you say. Why, just imagine! It means sorrow, it means shame, it means poverty. They will have to leave their house, their home; she will have to give up everything to the company. It isn't merely friends and her place in the world; it's money, it's something to eat and wear, it's a roof over her head!"

Wade refused the extreme view portrayed by his friend's figures. "Of course she wont be allowed to come to want."

"Of course. But there's really no measuring the sinuous reach of a disaster like this. It strikes from a coil that seems to involve everything."

"What are you going to do if you get bad news?" asked Wade.

"Ah, I don't know! I must tell her, somehow; unless you think that you"— Wade gave a start which Matt interpreted aright; he laughed nervously. "No, no! It's for me to do it. I know that; unless I can get Louise . . . Ah! I wonder what that is."

They were walking back toward the station again, and Matt had seen a head and arm projected from the office window, and a hand waving a sheet of yellow paper. It seemed meant for them. They both began to run, and then they checked themselves; and walked as fast as they could.

"We must refer the matter to your sister," said Wade, "and if she thinks best, remember that I shall be quite ready to speak to Miss Northwick. Or, if *you* think best, I will speak to her without troubling your sister."

"Oh, *you*'re all right, Wade. You needn't have any doubt of that. We'll see. I wonder what there is in that dispatch."

The old station master had come out of the station and was hurrying to meet them with the message, now duly enclosed in an envelope. He gave it to Matt and promptly turned his back on him.

Matt tore it open, and read: "Impossible to identify parlor car passengers." The telegram was signed "Operator," and was dated at Wellwater. It fell blankly on their tense feeling.

"Well," said Wade, after a long breath. "It isn't the worst."

Matt read it frowningly over several times; then he smiled. "Oh, no. This isn't at all bad. It's nothing. But so far, it's rather comforting. And it's something, even if it is nothing. Well, I suppose I'd better go up to Miss Northwick with it. Wait a moment: I must tell them where to send, if anything else comes."

"I'll walk with you as far as St. Michael's," said Wade, when they left the station. "I'm going to my study, there."

They set off together, up the middle of the street, which gave them more elbow-room than the side walk narrowly blocked out of the snow.

From a large store as they were passing, a small, dry-looking, pompous little man advanced to the middle of the street, and stopped them. "I beg your pardon, Mr. Wade! I beg your pardon, sir!" he said, nimbly transferring himself, after the quasi self-introduction, from Wade to Matt. "May I ask whether you have received any further information?"

"No," said Matt, amiably, "the only answer we have got is that it is impossible to identify the passengers in the parlor car."

"Ah, thank you! Thank you very much, sir! I felt sure it couldn't be *our* Mr. Northwick. Er—good-morning, sir."

He bowed himself away, and went into his store again, and Matt asked Wade, "Who in the world is that?"

"He's a Mr. Gerrish—keeps the large store, there. Rather an unpleasant type."

Matt smiled. "He had the effect of refusing to believe that anything so low as an accident could happen to a man of Northwick's business standing."

"Something of that," Wade assented. "He worships Northwick on the altar of material success."

Matt lifted his head and looked about. "I suppose the whole place is simply seething with curiosity."

Just after they reached the side-street where Wade left him to go down to his church, he met Sue Northwick driving in her sleigh. She was alone, except for the groom impassive in the rumble.

"Have you heard anything?" she asked sharply.

Matt repeated the dispatch from the operator at Wellwater.

"I knew it was a mistake," she said with a kind of resolute scorn. "It's perfectly ridiculous! *Why* should he have been there? I think there ought to be some way of punishing the newspapers for circulating false reports. I've been talking with the man who drove my father to the train yesterday morning, and he says he spoke lately of buying some horses at Springfield. He got several from a farm near there once. I'm going down to telegraph the farmer; I found his name among father's bills. Of course he's there. I've got the dispatch all written out."

"Let me take it back to the station for you, Miss Northwick," said Matt.

"No; get in with me, here, and we'll drive down, and then

I'll carry you back home. Or! Here, Dennis!" she said to the man in the rumble, and she handed him the telegram. "Take this to the telegraph-office, and tell them to send it up by Simpson the instant the answer comes."

The Irishman said "Yes, ma'am," and dropped from his perch with the paper in his hand.

"Get in, Mr. Hilary," she said, and after he had mounted she skillfully backed the sleigh and turned the horses homeward. "If I hear nothing from my dispatch, or if I hear wrong, I am going up to Wellwater Junction myself, by the first train. I can't wait any longer. If it's the worst, I want to know the worst."

Matt did not know what to say to her courage. So he said, "Alone?" to gain time.

"Of course! At such a time, I would *rather* be alone."

At the house Matt found Louise had gone to her room for a moment, and he said he would like to speak with her there.

She was lying on the lounge, when he announced himself, and she said "Come in," and explained, "I just came off a moment, to give my sympathies a little rest. And then, being up late so many nights this week. What have you heard?"

"Nothing, practically. Louise, how long did you expect to stay?"

"I don't know. I hadn't thought. As long as I'm needed, I suppose. Why? Must you go back?"

"No—not exactly."

"Not exactly? What are you driving at?"

"Why, there's nothing to be found out by telegraphing. Some one must go up to the place where the accident happened. She sees that, and she wants to go. She can't realize at all what it means to go there. Suppose she could manage the journey, going alone, and all that; what could she do after she got there? How could she go and look up the place of the accident, and satisfy herself whether her father was"—

"Matt!" shrieked his sister. "If you go on, you will drive me wild. She mustn't go; that's all there is of it. You mustn't think of letting her go." She sat up on the lounge in expression of her resolution on this point. "She must send somebody —some of their men. She mustn't go. It's too hideous!"

"No," said Matt, thoughtfully. "I shall go."

"You!"

"Why not? I can be at the place by four or five in the morning and I can ascertain all the facts, and be able to relieve this terrible suspense for her."

"For both of them," suggested Louise. "It must be quite as bad for that poor, sick old maid."

"Why, of course," said Matt, and he felt so much ashamed of having left her out of the account that he added, "I dare say it's even worse for her. She's seen enough of life to realize it more."

"Sue was his favorite, though," Louise returned. "Of course you must go, Matt. *You* couldn't do *less!* It's magnificent of you. Have you told her, yet, that you would go?"

"Not yet. I thought I would talk it over with you, first."

"Oh, *I* approve of it. It's the only thing to do. And I had better stay here till you come back"—

"Why, no; I'm not sure." He came a little nearer and dropped his voice. "You'd better know the whole trouble, Louise. There's great trouble for them whether he's dead or alive. There's something wrong in his accounts with the company, and if he was on that train he was running away to Canada to escape arrest."

He could see that only partial intelligence of the case had reached her.

"Then if he's killed, it will all be hushed up. I see! It makes you hope he's killed."

Matt gave a despairing groan. "If he's killed it makes it just so much the worse. The defalcation has to come out, anyway."

"When must it come out?"

"A good many people know of it; and such things are hard to keep. It may come out—some rumor of it—in the morning papers. The question is whether you want to stay till they know it here—whether it would be wise, or useful"—

"Certainly not! I should want to kill anybody that was by when such a thing as that came out, and I should despise Sue Northwick if she let me get away alive. I must go at once!"

She slid herself from the lounge, and ran to the glass where she put up a coil of hair in the knot it had escaped from.

"I had my doubts," Matt said, "about letting you come here, without telling you just what the matter was; but mother thought you would insist upon coming, anyway, and that you would be embarrassed"—

"Oh, *that* was quite right," said Louise. "The great thing now is to get away."

"I hope you wont let her suspect"—

"Well, I *think* you can trust me for that, Matt," said Louise, turning round upon him with a hairpin in her mouth, long enough to give him as sarcastic a glance as she could. If her present self possession was a warrant of future performance, Matt thought he could trust her; but he was afraid Louise had not taken in the whole enormity of the fact; and he was right in this. As a crime, she did not then, or ever afterwards fully imagine it. It may be doubted whether she conceived of it as other than a great trouble, and as something that ought always to be kept from her friend.

Matt went down stairs and found Sue Northwick in the library.

"I feel perfectly sure," she said, "that we shall hear of my father at Springfield. One of the horses he got there has gone lame, and it would be quite like him to stop and look up another in the place of it on the same farm."

The logic of this theory did not strike Matt, but the girl held her head in such a strong way, she drew her short breaths with such a smoothness, she so visibly concealed her anxiety in the resolution to believe herself what she said that he could not refuse it the tribute of an apparent credence. "Yes, that certainly makes it seem probable."

"At any rate," she said, "if I hear nothing from him there, or we get no news from Wellwater, I shall go there at once. I've made up my mind to that."

"I shouldn't wish you to go alone, Sue," Adeline quavered. Her eyes were red, and her lips swollen as if she had been crying; and now the tears came with her words. "You could never get there alone in the world. Don't you remember, it took us all day to get to Wellwater the last time we went to Quebec?"

Sue gave her sister a severe look, as if to quell her open fears at least, and Matt asked aimlessly, "Is it on the way to Quebec?"

Sue picked up the railroad guide from the desk where she had left it. "Yes; it is and it isn't." She opened the book and showed him the map of the road. "The train divides at Wellwater, and part goes to Montreal and part to Quebec. There are all sorts of stops and starts on the Quebec branch, so that you don't arrive till next morning, but you get to Montreal in five or six hours. But the whole thing seems perfectly frantic. I don't see why we pay the slightest attention to it! Of *course* papa has stayed over in Springfield, for something; only, he's usually so careful about telegraphing us if he changes his plans"—

She faltered, and let the book drop. Matt picked it up for her, and began to look at the time-table, at first to hide the pain he felt at the self-discouragement in which she ended, and then to see if he might not somehow be useful to her. "I see that a train from Boston meets the Springfield train at Wellwater."

"Does there?" She bent to look over the book with him, and he felt the ungovernable thrill at being near the beauty of a woman's face which a man never knows whether to be ashamed of or glad of, but which he cannot help feeling. "Then perhaps I had better go by way of Boston. What time does it start? Oh, I see! Seven thirty. I could get that train—if I don't hear from him at Springfield. But I know I shall hear."

A stir of drapery made them aware of Louise at the library door. Suzette went toward her. "Are you going?" she asked, without apparently sharing the surprise Matt felt at seeing his sister with her hat and gloves on, and her jacket over her arm.

"Yes, I'm going, Sue. I just ran up to see you—I had to do that—but we both know I'm of no use here; and so we wont make any pretences." Louise spoke very steadily, almost coldly; her brother did not quite know what to make of her; she was pale, and she looked down, while she spoke. But when she finished buttoning the glove she was engaged with, she went up and put both her hands in Suzette's. "I don't need to tell you that I'm going, just to get myself out of your way. It isn't a time for ornamental friendshipping, and you've got all the good you could out of seeing me, and knowing that I'm anxious with you. That's about all there is of it, and I guess we'd better not spin it out. But remember, Sue, whenever you need me, when you really want me, you can send for me, and if I don't come again till you do, you'll know that I'm simply waiting. Will you remember that—*whatever* happens?"

Matt gave a long tacit sigh of relief.

"Yes, I will, Louise," said Suzette. They kissed each other as if in formal ratification of their compact, which meant so much more to one of them than it could to the other.

"Come, Matt!" said Louise.

She added hastily, to prevent insistence against her plan, that they would have time to walk to the station, and she wished to walk. Then Matt said, "I will see you aboard the train, and then I'll come back and wait till you hear from Springfield, Miss Suzette."

"That is a good idea," said Louise.

"But," Adeline urged tremulously, "sha'n't you be afraid to go to Boston alone? It'll be dark by the time you get there!"

"The journey can't be very dangerous," said Louise, "and when I arrive, I shall put myself in charge of a faithful Boston hackman, and tell him I'm very valuable, and am to be taken the best of care of. Then I shall be set down at our door in perfect safety."

They all had the relief of a little laugh; even Adeline joined reluctantly in it.

When they were once free of the house, Matt said, "I wonder, whether she will remember after the worst comes, what you said, and whether she will trust you enough to turn to us?"

"I don't know. Probably she will be too proud at first. But I shall come, whether she asks me or not. If they had relations or connections, as everybody else has, it would be different. But as it is"—

"Yes, of course," said Matt.

"I wish I could realize that Sue was fond of him, as we are of papa. But I can't. He always made me feel creepy; didn't he you?"

"He was a secret person. But as far as I had anything to do with him at the mills, when I was there, I found him square enough. He was a country person."

"I suppose Sue's pride is countrified," said Louise.

Matt went on: "His secrecy may have been only a sort of shyness. Heaven knows I don't want to judge him. I suppose that that slow deliberation of his was an effort to maintain himself with dignity. Of course we see him now in the light of his rascality, poor man, and most of his traits seem ugly."

They had a little time after they reached the station, and they walked up and down the platform, talking, and Matt explained how his father might be glad to have him go to Wellwater and settle the question whether Northwick was in the accident or not. It would be a great relief for him to know. He tried to make out that he was going from a divided motive.

"Oh, you needn't be at the trouble to say all that to me, Matt," said Louise. "I don't blame you for wanting to go, even out of kindness."

"No, I suppose there's no guilt attaching to a thing of that kind," Matt answered.

There were a good many loungers about the sation, young men and girls, released from the shops for the day; in such towns they find the station an agreeable resort, and enjoy a never-failing excitement in the coming and going of the trains. They watched the Hilarys, as they walked, with envy of that something distinguished which both of them had. They were both tall and handsomely made, and they had the ease before their fellow beings which perhaps comes as much from the life-long habit of good clothes as from anything else. Matt had a conscience against whatever would separate him from his kind, but he could not help carrying himself like a swell, for all that; and Louise did not try to help it, for her part. She was an avowed worldling, and in this quality she now wore a drab cloth costume, bordered with black fur down the front of her jacket and around it at the hips; the skirt, which fell plain to her feet, had a border of fur there, and it swirled and swayed with her long dashing stride in a way that filled all those poor girls who saw it with despair. It seemed to interest almost as painfully a young man with a thin, delicate face whom she noticed looking at her; she took him at first for one of those educated or half-educated operatives who are complicating the labor problem more and more. He was no better dressed than others in the crowd, and there was no reason why he could not be a hat-shop or a shoe-shop hand, and yet, at a second glance, she decided that he was not. He stood staring at her with a studious frown, and with the faint suggestion of a sneer on his clean shaven, fine lips; but she knew that he was admiring her however he might be hating her, and she spoke to Matt about him as they turned from him in their walk and promised to point him out. But when they came up again to where he had been standing, he was gone.

The train came in, and Louise got aboard, and Matt made his way into the station, and went to ask the operator in the telegraph office if she had got anything for Miss Northwick. She said, "Something just come. I was waitin' for the hack to send it up."

"Oh, I will take it, if you please. I am going back to Mr. Northwick's," said Matt.

"All right."

Matt took the dispatch, and hurried out to find some means

of getting quickly to Miss Northwick with it. There was no conveyance about the station, and he started up the street at a gait which was little short of a run, and which exposed him to the ridicule of such small boys as observed his haste in their intervals of punging. One, who dropped from the runner of a sleigh which came up behind him, jeered him for the awkwardness with which he floundered out of its way in the deep snow of the roadside. The sleigh was abruptly halted, and Sue Northwick called from it, "Mr. Hilary! I couldn't wait at home; and I've just been at the depot—by the lower road. You have a dispatch."

"Yes, I have a telegram."

"Oh, give it to me!"

He withheld it a moment. "I don't know what it is, Miss Northwick. But if it isn't what you expected, will you let—will you allow me"—

As if she did not know what she was doing, she caught the dispatch from his hand, and tore it open. "Well," she said, "I knew it! He hasn't been there; now I shall go to Wellwater." She crumpled the telegram nervously in her hand, and made a motion to lift the reins.

Matt put his hand on her wrist. "You couldn't. You—you must let me go."

"You?"

"Me. I can get into Boston in time for that half past seven train, and I can do all the things when I get to Wellwater that you couldn't do. Come; be reasonable! You must see that what I propose is best. I solemnly promise you that nothing shall be left undone, or omitted or forgotten, that could set your mind at rest. Whatever you would wish done, I will do. Go home; your sister needs you; you need yourself; if you have a trial to meet greater than this suspense which you've borne with such courage, you want all your strength for it. I beg you to trust me to do this for you. I know that it seems recreant to let another go in your place on such an errand, but it really isn't so. You ought to know that I wouldn't offer to go if I were not sure that I could do all that you could do, and more. Come! Let me go for you!"

He poured out his reasons vehemently, and she sat like one without strength to answer. When he stopped, she still waited before she answered simply, almost dryly, "Well," and she gave no other sign of assent in words. But she turned over the hand, on which he was keeping his, and clutched his hand hard; the tears, the first she had shed that day, gushed into her eyes. She lifted the reins and drove away, and he stood in the road gazing after her till her sleigh vanished over the rise of ground to the southward.

XIII

THE PALE light in which Matt Hilary watched the sleigh out of sight thickened into the early winter dusk before his train came, and he got off to Boston. In the meantime the electrics came out like sudden moons, and shed a lunar ray over the region round about the station, where a young man who was in the habit of describing himself in print as one of *The Boston Events* young men found his way into an eating-house not far from the track. It had a simple, domestic effect inside, and the young man gave a sigh of comfort in the pleasant warmth and light. There was a woman there who had a very conversable air, a sort of eventual sociability, as the young man realized when she looked up from twitching the white, clean cloths perfectly straight on the little tables set in rows on either side of the room.

She finally reached the table where the young man had taken a chair for his overcoat and hat, and was about taking another for himself.

"Well," he said, "let's see. No use asking if you've got coffee?" He inhaled the odor of it coming from the open door of another room, with a deep breath. "Baked beans?"

"Yes."

"Well, I don't think there's anything much better than baked beans. Do you?"

"Well, not when you git 'em *good*," the woman admitted. "*Ril* good."

"And what's the matter with a piece of mince pie?"

"I don't see's there's any great deal. Hot?"

"Every time."

"I *thought* so," said the woman. "We have it both ways, but I'd as soon eat a piece of I don't know what as a piece o' *cold* mince pie."

"We have mince pie right along at our house," said the young man. "But I guess if I was to eat a piece of it cold my wife would have the doctor round inside of five minutes."

The woman laughed as if for joy in the hot mince-pie fellowship established between herself and the young man. "Well, I guess she need to. Nothin' else you want?"

She brought the beans and coffee, with a hot plate, and a Japanese paper napkin, and she said as she arranged them on the table before the young man, "Your pie's warmin' for you; I got you some rolls; they're just right out the oven; and here's some the best butter I ever put a knife to, if I *do* say so. It's just as good and sweet as butter can be, if it *didn't* come from the Northwick place at a dollar a pound."

"Well, now, I should have thought you'd have used the Northwick butter," said the young man with friendly irony.

"You know the Northwick butter?" said the woman charmed at the discovery of another tie.

"Well, my wife likes it for cooking," said the young man. "We have a fancy brand for the table."

The woman laughed out her delight in his pleasantry. "Land! I'll bet you grumble at it, too!" she said, with a precipitate advance in intimacy which he did not disallow.

"Well, I'm pretty particular," said the young man. "But I *have* to be, to find anything to find fault with in the way *my* wife manages. I don't suppose I shall be able to get much more Northwick butter, now."

"Why not?"

"Why, if he was killed in that accident"—

"Oh, I guess there ain't anything to that," said the woman. "I guess it was some other Northwick. Their coachman—Elbridge Newton—was tellin' my husband that Mr. Northwick had stopped over at Springfield to look at some hosses there. He's always buyin' more hosses. I guess he must have as much as eighty or ninety hosses now. I don't place any dependence on that report."

"That so?" said the young man. "Why, what did that fellow mean, over at the drugstore, just now, by his getting out for Canada?"

"What fellow?"

"Little slim chap, with a big black moustache, and blue eyes, blue and blazing, as you may say."

"Oh,—Mr. Putney! That's just one of his jokes. He's always down on Mr. Northwick."

"Then I suppose he's just gone up to Ponkwasset about the trouble there."

"Labor trouble?"

"I guess so."

The woman called toward an open door at the end of the room. "William!" and a man in his shirt sleeves showed himself. "You heard of any labor trouble to Mr. Northwick's mills?"

"No, I don't believe there is any," said the man. He came forward inquiringly to the table where his wife was standing by the *Events* young man.

"Well, I'm sorry," said the young man, "but it shows that I haven't lost so much in missing Mr. Northwick after all. I came up here from Boston to interview him for our paper about the labor troubles."

"I want to know!" said the hostess. "You an editor?"

"Well, I'm a reporter—same thing," the young man answered. "Perhaps you've got some troubles of your own here in your shops?"

"No," said the host, "I guess everybody's pretty well satisfied here in Hatboro'." He was tempted to talk by the air of confidence which the *Events* young man somehow diffused about him, but his native Yankee caution prevailed, and he did not take the lead offered him.

"Well," said the young man, "I noticed one of your citizens over at the drugstore that seemed to be pretty happy."

"Oh, yes: Mr. Putney. I heard you tellin' my wife."

"Who *is* Mr. Putney, anyway?" asked the *Events* man.

"Mr. Putney?" the host repeated, with a glance at his wife, as if for instruction or correction in case he should go wrong. "He's one of the old Hatboro' Putneys, here."

"All of 'em preserved in liquor, the same way?"

"Well, no, I can't say as they are." The host laughed, but not with much liking, apparently. His wife did not laugh at all, and the young man perceived that he had struck a false note.

"Pity," he said, "to see a man like that, goin' that way. He said more bright things in five minutes, drunk as he was, than I could say in a month on a strict prohibition basis."

The good understanding was restored by this ready self-abasement. "Well, I d' know as you can say that, exactly," said the hostess, "but he *is* bright, there ain't any two ways about it. And he ain't always that way you see him. It's just one of his times, now. He has 'em about once in every four or five months, and the rest part he's just as straight as anybody. It's like a disease, as I tell my husband."

"I guess if he was a mind to steady up, there ain't any lawyer could go ahead of him, well, not in *this* town," said the husband.

"Seems to be pretty popular, as it is," said the young man. "What makes him so down on Mr. Northwick?"

"Well, I dunno," said the host, "*what* it is. He's always been so. I presume it's more the kind of a man Mr. Northwick is, than what it is anything else."

"Why, what kind of a man *is* Mr. Northwick, anyway?" the young man asked, beginning to give his attention to the pie which the woman had now brought. "He don't seem to be so popular. What's the reason."

"Well, I don't know as I could say, exactly. I presume, one thing, he's only been here summers till this year, since his wife died, and he never did have much to do with the place, before."

"What's he living here, for, this winter? Economizing?"

"No; I guess he no need to do that," the host answered.

His wife looked knowing, and said with a laugh, "I guess Miss Sue Northwick could tell you if she was a mind to."

"Oh, I see," said the reporter with an irreverence that seemed to be merely provisional and held subject to instant exchange for any more available attitude. "Young man in the case. Friendless minister whose slippers require constant attention?"

"I guess he ain't very friendless," said the hostess, "as far forth as that goes. He's about the *most* popular minister, especially with the workin' folks, since Mr. Peck."

"Who was Mr. Peck?"

"Well, he was the one that was run over by the cars at the depot here two or three years back. Why, this house was started on his idea. Sort of co-operation at first; we run it for the Social Union."

"And the co-operation petered out," said the reporter making a note. "Always does; and then you took it, and began to make money. Standard history of co-operation."

"I guess we ain't gettin' rich any too fast," said the hostess dryly.

"Well, you will if you use the Northwick butter. What's the reason he isn't popular here when he *is* here? Must spend a good deal of money on that big place of his; and give work."

"Mr. Putney says it's corruptin' to have such a rich man in the neighborhood; and he does more harm than good with his money." The hostess threw out the notion as if it were something she had never been quite able to accept herself, and would like to see its effect upon a man of the reporter's wide observation. "*He* thinks Hatboro' was better off before there was a single hat shop or shoe shop in the place."

"And the law offices had it all to themselves," said the young man; and he laughed. "Well, it *was* a halcyon period. What sort of a man is Mr. Northwick, personally?"

The woman referred the question to her husband, who pondered it a moment. "Well, he's a kind of a close-mouthed man. He's never had anything to do with the Hatboro' folks much. But I never heard anything against him. I guess he's a pretty good man."

"Wouldn't be likely to mention it round a great deal if he *was* going to Canada. Heigh? Well, I'm sorry I can't see Mr. Northwick, after all. With these strikes in the mills everywhere, he must have some light to throw on the labor question generally. Poor boy, himself, I believe?"

"I don't believe his daughters could remember when," said the hostess, sarcastically.

"That so? Well, we *are* apt to lose our memory for dates as we get on in the world, especially the ladies. Ponkwasset isn't on the direct line of this road, is it?" He asked this of the host, as if it followed.

"No, you got to change at Springfield, and take the Union and Dominion road there. Then it's on a branch."

"Well; I guess I shall have to run up and see Mr. Northwick, there. *What* did you say the young man's name was that's keeping the Northwick family here this winter?" He turned suddenly to the hostess, putting up his note book, and throwing a silver dollar on the table to be changed. "Married man myself, you know."

"I guess I hain't mentioned any names," said the woman, in high glee. Her husband went back to the kitchen, and she took the dollar away to a desk in the corner of the room, and brought back the change.

"Who'd be a good person to talk with about the labor situation here?" the young man asked, in pocketing his money.

"I d' know as I could hardly tell," said the hostess thoughtfully. "There's Colonel Marvin, he's got the largest shoe shop; and some the hat shop folks, most any of 'em would do. And then there's Mr. Wilmington that owns the stocking mills; him or Mr. Jack Wilmington, either one'd be good. Mr. Jack'd be the best, I guess. Or I don't suppose there's anybuddy in the place'd know more, if they's a mind to talk, than Mrs. Wilmington; unless it *was* Mis' Doctor Morrell."

"Is Mr. Jack their son?" asked the reporter.

"Land! Why she ain't a day older, if she's that. He's their nephew."

"Oh, I see: second wife. Then *he's* the young man, heigh?"

The hostess looked at the reporter with admiration. "Well, you do beat the witch. If he hain't, I guess he might 'a' b'en."

The reporter said he guessed he would take another piece of that pie, and some more coffee if she had it, and before he had finished them he had been allowed to understand that if it was not for his being Mrs. Wilmington's nephew Mr. Jack would have been Miss Northwick's husband long ago; and that the love lost between the two ladies was not worth crying for.

The reporter, who had fallen into his present calling by a series of accidents not necessarily of final result in it, did not use arts so much as instincts in its exercise. He liked to talk of himself and his own surroundings, and he found that few men, and no women could resist the lure thrown out by his sincere expansiveness. He now commended himself to the hostess by the philosophical view he took of the popular belief that Mrs. Wilmington was keeping her nephew from marrying any one else so as to marry him herself when her husband died. He said that if you were an old man and you married a young woman he guessed that was what you had got to expect. This gave him occasion to enlarge upon the happiness to be found only in the married state if you were fitly mated, and on his own exceptional good fortune in it. He was in the full flow of an animated confidence relating to the flat he had just taken and furnished in Boston, when the door opened, and the pale young man whom Louise Hilary had noticed at the station, came in.

The reporter broke off with a laugh of greeting. "Hello, Maxwell! You onto it, too?"

"Onto what?" said the other, with none of the reporter's effusion.

"This labor trouble business," said the reporter, with a wink for him alone.

"Pshaw, Pinney! You'd grow a bush for the pleasure of beating about it." Maxwell hung his hat on a hook above the table, but sat down fronting Pinney with his overcoat on; it was a well worn overcoat, irredeemably shabby at the buttonholes. "I'd like some tea," he said to the hostess, "some English breakfast tea, if you have it; and a little toast." He rested his elbows on the table, and took his head between his hands, and pressed his fingers against his temples.

"Headache?" asked Pinney with the jocose sympathy men show one another's sufferings, as if they could be joked away. "Better take something substantial. Nothing like ham and eggs for a headache."

The other unfolded his paper napkin. "Have you got anything worth while?"

"Lots of public opinion and local color," said Pinney. "Have you?"

"I've been half crazy with this headache. I suppose we brought most of the news with us," he suggested.

"Well, I don't know about that," said Pinney.

"I do. You got your tip straight from headquarters. I know all about it, Pinney; so you might as well save time, on that point, if time's an object with you. They don't seem to know anything here; but the consensus in Hatboro' is that he was running away."

"The what is?" asked Pinney.

"The consensus."

"Anything like the United States Census?"

"It isn't spelt like it."

Pinney made a note of it. "I'll get a headline out of that. I take my own wherever I find it, as George Washington said."

"Your own, you thief!" said Maxwell, with sardonic amusement. "You don't know what the word means."

"I can make a pretty good guess, thank you," said Pinney, putting up his book.

"Do you want to trade?" Maxwell asked, after his tea came, and he had revived himself with a sip or two.

"Any scoops?" asked Pinney, warily. "Anything exclusive?"

"Oh, come!" said Maxwell. "No, I haven't; and neither have you. What do you make mysteries for? I've been over the whole ground, and so have you. There are no scoops in it."

"I think there's a scoop if you want to work it," said Pinney darkly.

Maxwell received the vaunt with a sneer. "You ought to be a detective—in a novel." He buttered his toast and ate a little of it, like a man of small appetite and invalid digestion.

"I suppose you've interviewed the family?" suggested Pinney.

"No," said Maxwell gloomily, "there are some things that even a space-man can't do."

"You ought to go back on a salary," said Pinney with compassion and superiority. "You'll ruin yourself trying to fill space, if you stick at trifles."

"Such as going and asking a man's family whether they think he was burnt up in a railroad accident and trying to make copy out of their emotions? Thank you, I prefer ruin. If that's your scoop, you're welcome to it."

"They're not obliged to see you," urged Pinney. "You send in your name, and"—

"They shut the door in your face, if they have the presence of mind."

"Well! What do you care if they do? It's all in the way of business, anyhow. It's not a personal thing."

"A snub's a pretty personal thing, Pinney. The reporter doesn't mind it, but it makes the man's face burn."

"Oh, very well! If you're going to let uncleanly scruples like that stand in your way, you'd better retire to the poet's corner, and stay there. You can fill that much space anyway; but you're not built for a reporter. When are you going to Boston?"

"Six fifteen. I've got a scoop of my own."

"What is it?" asked Pinney incredulously.

"Come round in the morning, and I'll tell you."

"Perhaps I'll go in with you, after all. I'll just step out into the cold air and see if I can harden my cheek for that interview. Your diffidence is infectious, Maxwell."

—————

PINNEY was really somewhat dashed by Maxwell's attitude, both because it appealed to the more delicate and generous self which he was obliged to pocket so often in the course of business, and because it made him suspect that Maxwell had already interviewed Northwick's family. They would be forewarned, in that case and would of course refuse to see him. But he felt that as a space-man, with the privilege of filling all the space he chose with this defalcation, his duty to his family required him to use every means for making copy.

He encouraged himself by thinking of his wife, and what she was probably doing at that moment in their flat at Boston, and he was feeling fairly well when he asked for Miss Northwick at the door of the great wooden palace. He had time to take in its characteristics, before James, the inside man, opened the door, and scanned him for a moment with a sort of baffled intelligence. To the experience of the inside man his appearance gave no proof that he was or was not an agent, a peddler in disguise, or a genteel mendicant of the sort he was used to detecting and deterring.

"I don't know, sir. I'll go and see." He let rather than invited Pinney in, and in his absence, the representative of the *Events* made note of the interior both of the hall which he had been allowed to enter, and of the library where he found himself upon his own responsibility. The inside man discovered him there with his back to the fire when he returned with his card still in his hand.

"Miss Northwick thinks it's her father you wish to see. He's not at home."

"Yes, I know that. I did wish to see Mr. Northwick, and I asked to see Miss Northwick because I knew he wasn't at home."

"Oh!" The man disappeared, and after another interval Adeline came in. She showed the trepidation she felt at finding herself in the presence of an interviewer.

"Will you sit down?" she said timidly, and she glanced at the card which she had brought back this time. It bore the name of Lorenzo A. Pinney, and in the left hand corner the words *Representing the Boston Events*. Mr. Pinney made haste to re-assure her by a very respectful and business-like straightforwardness of manner; he did not forbid it a certain shade of authority.

"I am sorry to disturb you, Miss Northwick. I hoped to have some conversation with you in regard to this—this rumor —accident. Can you tell me just when Mr. Northwick left home?"

"He went up to the Mills, yesterday morning, quite early," said Adeline. She was in the rise of hope which she and Suzette both felt from the mere fact that Matt Hilary was on the way to hunt the horrible rumor to its source; it seemed to her that he must extinguish it there. She wanted to tell this friendly-looking reporter so; but she would not do this without Suzette's authority. Suzette had been scolding her for not telling her what was in the paper as soon as she read it in the morning; and they were both so far respited for the moment from their fear as to have had some words back and forth about the propriety of seeing this reporter at all. Adeline was on her most prudent behavior.

"Did you expect him back soon when he left?" Pinney asked respectfully.

"Oh, no; he said he wouldn't be back for some days."

"It's several hours to Ponkwasset, I believe?" suggested Pinney.

"Yes, three or four. There *is* one train—at half past twelve, I think," said Miss Northwick, with a glance at the clock, "that takes you there in three hours."

"The early train doesn't connect right through, then?"

"No; my father would have to wait over at Springfield. He doesn't often take the early train; and so we thought, when we found he wasn't at the Mills, that he had stopped over a day at Springfield to buy some horses from a farmer there. But we've just heard that he didn't. He may have run down to New York; he often has business there. We don't place any reliance on that story"—she gasped the rest out—"about—that accident."

"Of course not," said Pinney with real sympathy. "It's just one of those flying rumors—they get the names all mixed up, those country operators."

"They spelt the name two ways in different papers," said Adeline. "Father had no earthly business up that way; and he always telegraphs."

"I believe the Mills are on the line of the Union and Dominion Road, are they not?" Pinney fell into the formal style of his printed questionings.

"Yes, they are. Father could get the Northern Express at Springfield, and drive over from Ponkwasset Junction; the express doesn't stop at the Falls."

"I see. Well, I wont trouble you any farther, Miss Northwick. I hope you'll find out it's all a mistake about"—

"Oh, I know it is!" said Adeline. "A gentleman—a friend of ours—has just gone up to Wellwater to see about it."

"Oh, well, that's good," said Pinney. "Then you'll soon have good news. I suppose you've telegraphed?"

"We couldn't get *anything* by telegraph. That is the reason he went."

It seemed to Pinney that she wished to tell him who went; but she did not tell him; and after waiting for a moment in vain, he rose and said, "Well I must be getting back to Boston. I should have been up here to see your father about these labor troubles night before last, if I'd taken my wife's advice. I always miss it when I don't," he said smiling.

There is no reason why a man should acquire merit with other women by seeming subject to his wife or dependant upon her; but he does. They take it as a sort of tribute to themselves, or to the abstract woman; their respect for that man rises; they begin to honor him; their hearts warm to him. Pinney's devotion to his wife had already been of great use to him, on several occasions, in creating an atmosphere of trust about him. He really could not keep her out of his talk for more than five minutes at a time; all topics led up to her sooner or later.

When he now rose to go Miss Northwick said, "I'm sorry my father isn't at home, and I'm sorry I can't give you any information about the troubles."

"Oh, I shall go to the Mills, tomorrow," he interrupted cheerily. Her relenting emboldened him to say, "You must have a beautiful place, here, in summer, Miss Northwick."

"*I* like it all times of the year," she answered. "We've all been enjoying the winter so much; it's the first we've spent here for a long time." She felt a strange pleasure in saying this; her reference to their family life seemed to reassure her of its unbroken continuity, and to warrant her father's safety.

"Yes," said Pinney, "I knew you had let your house in town. I think my wife would feel about it just as you do; she's a great person for the country and if it wasn't for my work on the paper, I guess I should have to live there."

Miss Northwick took a mass of heavy-headed jacqueminot roses from the vase where they drooped above the mantel and wrapping them in a paper from the desk, stiffly offered them to Pinney. "Wont you carry these to your wife?" she said. This was not only a recognition of Pinney's worth in being so fond of his wife, but a vague attempt at propitiation. She thought it might somehow soften the heart of the interviewer in him and keep him from putting anything in the paper about her. She was afraid to ask him not to do so.

"Oh, thank you," said Pinney. "I didn't mean to—it's very kind of you—I assure you"— He felt very queer to be remanded to the purely human basis in relation to these people, and he made haste to get away from that interview. He had nothing to blame himself for, and yet he now suddenly somehow felt to blame. In the light of the defaulter's home-life Northwick appeared his victim. Pinney was not going to punish him, he was merely going to publish him; but all the same, for that moment, it seemed to him that he was Northwick's persecutor and was hunting him down, running him to earth. He wished that poor old girl had not given him those flowers; he did not feel that he could take them to his wife; on the way back to the station he stepped aside from the road and dropped them into the deep snow.

His wife met him at the door of their flat, eager to know what success he had; and at sight of her his spirits rose again, and he gave her an enthusiastic synopsis of what he had done.

She flung herself on his knees, where he sat, and embraced him. "Ren, you've done splendidly! And I know you'll beat the *Abstract* clear out of sight. Oh Ren, Ren!" She threw her arms round his neck again, and the happy tears started to her eyes. "This will give you any place on the paper you choose to ask for! Oh, I'm the happiest girl in the world!"

Pinney gave her a joyful hug. "Yes, it's all right. There are ninety-nine chances to one that he was going to Canada. There's a big default running up into the hundred thousands and they gave him a chance to make up his shortage— it's the old story. I've got just the setting I wanted for my facts, and now as soon as Manton gives us the word to go ahead"—

"Wait till Manton gives the word!" cried Mrs. Pinney. "Well you shall do no such thing, Ren. We wont wait a minute!"

Pinney broke out into a laugh, and gave her another hug for her enthusiasm, and explained between laughing at her and kissing her, why he had to wait: that if he used the matter before the detective authorized him, it would be the last tip he would ever get from Manton.

"We sha'n't lose anything. I'm going to commence writing it out, now. I'm going to make it a work of art. Now, you go and get me some coffee, Hat. There isn't going to be any let up on this till it's all blocked out, any way; and I'm going to leave mighty few places to fill in, I can tell you."

He pulled off his coat, and sat down at his desk.

His wife stopped him. "You'd better come out into the kitchen, and work on the table there. It's bigger than this desk."

"Don't know but I had," said Pinney. He gathered up his work and followed her out into the cosy little kitchen where she cooked their simple meals, and they ate them. "Been living on tea since I been gone?" He pulled open the refrigerator built into the wall, and glanced into it. "Last night's dinner all there yet."

"You know I don't care to eat when you're away, Ren," she said, with a pathetic little mouth.

Pinney kissed her and then he sat down to his work again; and when he was tired with writing, his wife took the pen, and wrote from his dictation. As they wrought on they lost the sense, if they ever had it, of a fellow creature inside of the figure of a spectacular defaulter which grew from their hands; and they enjoyed the impersonality which enables us to judge and sentence one another in this world, and to do justice, as we say. It is true that Pinney having seen Northwick's home, and faced his elderly, invalid daughter, was moved to use him with a leniency which he would not otherwise have felt. He recognized a merit in this forbearance of his, and once, towards the end of his work, when he was taking a little rest, he said: "Reporters get as much abuse as plumbers; but if people only knew what we kept back, perhaps they would sing a different tune. Of course, it's a temptation to describe his daughter, poor old thing, and give the interview in full, but I don't quite like to. I've got to cut it down to the fact that she evidently hadn't the least idea of the defalcation, or why he was on the way to Canada. Might work a little pathos in with that, but I guess I mustn't!"

His wife pushed the manuscript away from her, and flung down the pen. "Well, Ren, if you go on talking in that way, you'll take the pleasure out of it for *me*; I can tell you that much. If I get to thinking of his family, I can't help you any more."

"Pshaw!" said Pinney. "The facts have got to come out, any way, and I guess they wont be handled half as mercifully anywhere else as I shall handle 'em." He put his arms round her, and pulled her tight up to him. "Your tender heartedness is going to be the ruin of me, yet, Hat. If it hadn't been for thinking how you'd have felt, I should gone right up to Wellwater, and looked up that accident, myself, on the ground. But I knew you'd go all to pieces if I wasn't back at the time I said, and so I didn't go."

"Oh, what a story!" said the young wife fondly, with her adoring eyes upon him. "I shouldn't have cared, I guess, if you'd never come back."

"Shouldn't you? How many per cent of that am I going to believe?" he asked, and he drew her to him again in a rapture with her pretty looks, and the love he saw in them.

Pinney was a handsome little fellow himself, with a gay, give-and-take air that had always served him well with women, and that, as his wife often told him, had made her determine to have him the first time she saw him.

This was at the opening of the Promontory House, two summers before, when Pinney was assigned to write the affair up for the *Events*. She had got her first place as operator in the new hotel; and he brought in a despatch for her to send to Boston just as she was going to shut up the office for the night, and go in to see the dancing in the main dining-room, and perhaps be asked to dance herself by some of the clerks. At the sound of a pencil tapping on the ledge of the little window in the castiron filagree wall of her den, she turned quickly round ready to cry with disappointment; but at sight of Pinney with his blue eyes, and his brown fringe of moustache curling closely in over his lip, under his short, straight nose, and a funny cleft in his chin, she felt more like laughing, somehow, as she had since told him a hundred times. He wrote back to her from Boston, on some pretended business; and they began to correspond, as they called it; and they were engaged before the summer was over. They had never yet tired of talking about that first meeting, or of talking about themselves and each other in any aspect. They found out, as soon as they were engaged, and that sort of social splendor which young people wear to each other's eyes had passed, that they were both rather simple and harmless folks, and they began to value each other as being good. This tendency only grew upon them with the greater intimacy of marriage. The chief reason for thinking that they were good was that they loved each other so much: she knew that he was good because he loved her; and he believed that he must have a great deal of good in him, if such a girl loved him so much. They thought it a virtue to exist solely for one another as they did; their mutual devotion seemed to them a form of unselfishness. They felt it a great merit to be frugal and industrious that they might prosper; they prospered solely to their own advantage, but the advantage of persons so deserving through their frugality and industry seemed a kind of altruism; it kept them in constant good humor with themselves and content with each other. They had risked a great deal in getting married on Pinney's small salary, but apparently their courage had been rewarded, and they were not finally without the sense that their happiness had been achieved somehow in the public interest.

XV

_____

MAXWELL's headache went off after his cup of tea, but when he reached the house in Clover street where he had a room in the boarding house his mother kept, he was so tired that he wanted to go to bed. He told her he was not tired; only disappointed with his afternoon's work.

"I didn't get very much. Why of course, there was a lot of stuff lying round in the gutters that I can work up, if I have the stomach for it. You'll see it in Pinney's report, whether I do it or not. Pinney thinks it's all valuable material. I left him there interviewing the defaulter's family and making material out of their misery. I couldn't _do_ that."

"I shouldn't want you to, Brice," said his mother. "I couldn't bear to have you."

"Well, we're wrong, both of us, from one point of view," said the young fellow. "As Pinney says, it's business to do these things, and a business motive ought to purify and ennoble any performance. Pinney is getting to be a first-class reporter; he'll be a managing editor and an owner, and be refusing my work in less than ten years."

"I hope you'll be out of such work long before that," said the mother.

"I'm likely to be out of all kinds of work before that, if I keep on at this gait. Pinney hasn't got the slightest literary instinct: he's a wood-chopper, a stable-boy by nature; but he knows how to make copy and he's sure to get on."

"Well, you don't want to get on in his way," the mother urged soothingly.

"Yes; but I've got to get on in his way while I'm trying to get on in my own. I've got to work eight hours at reporting for the privilege of working two at literature. That's how the world is built. The first thing is to earn your bread."

"Well, you *do* earn yours, my son—and no one works harder to earn it."

"Ah, but it's so damned dirty when I've earned it."

"Oh, my son!"

"Well, I wont swear at it. That's stupid, too; as stupid as all the rest." He rose from the chair he had dropped into, and went toward the door of the next room. "I must beautify my person with a clean collar and cuffs. I'm going down to make a call on the Back Bay, and I wish to leave a good impression with the fellow that shows me the door when he finds out who I am and what I want. I'm going to interview Mr. Hilary on the company's feelings towards their absconding treasurer. What a dose! He'll never know I hate it ten times as bad as he does. But it's my only chance for a scoop."

"I'm sure he'll receive you well, Brice. He must see that you're a gentleman"—

"No, I'm not a gentleman, mother," the son interrupted harshly from the room where he was modifying his linen. "I'm not in that line of business. But I'm like most people in most other lines of business: I intend to be a gentleman as soon as I can afford it. I shall have to pocket myself as usual, when I interview Mr. Hilary. Perhaps *he* isn't a gentleman either. There's some consolation in that. I should like to write an article some day on business methods and their compatibility with self-respect. But Mr. Ricker wouldn't print it."

"He's very kind to you, Brice."

"Yes, he's as kind as he dares to be. He's the oasis in the desert of my life; but the counting-room simoom comes along and dries him up, every now and then. Suppose I began my article by a study of the counting-room in independent journalism?"

Mrs. Maxwell had nothing to say to this suggestion, but much concerning the necessity of wearing the neck muffler, which she found her son had not had on all day. She put it on for him now, and made him promise to put it on for himself when he left the house where he was going to call.

The man who came to the door told him Mr. Hilary was not at home, but was expected shortly, and consented to let him come in and wait. He tried to classify Maxwell in deciding where to let him wait: his coat and hat looked like a chair in the hall; his pale, refined, rather haughty face like the drawing-room. The man compromised on the library, and led him in there.

Louise rose upright on the lounge where she had thrown herself after dinner, to rest in the dim light, and think over the day's strange experience, and stared at them helplessly. For her greater ease and comfort, she had pushed off her shoes, and they had gone over the foot of the lounge. She found herself confronted with the contumacious looking workman she had noticed at the station in Hatboro', with those thin, mocking lips, and the large dreamy eyes that she remembered.

The serving-man said, "Oh, I didn't know you were here, miss," and stood irresolute. "The gentleman wishes to see your father."

"Will you sit down?" she said to Maxwell. "My father will be in very soon, I think." She began to wonder, whether she could edge along unobserved to where her shoes lay, and slip her feet into them. But for the present she remained where she was, and not merely because her shoes were off, and she could not well get away, but because it was not in her nature not to wish every one to be happy and comfortable. She was as far as any woman can be from coquetry, but she could not see any manner of man without trying to please him. "I'm sorry he isn't here," she said, and then as there seemed nothing for him to answer, she ventured, "It's very cold, out, isn't it?"

"It's grown colder since nightfall," said Maxwell.

He remembered her, and she saw that he did, and this somehow promoted an illogical sense of acquaintance with him.

"It seems," she ventured farther, "very unusual weather for the beginning of February."

"Why, I don't know," said Maxwell, with rather more self-possession than she wished him to have so soon. "I think we're apt to have very cold weather after the January thaw."

"That's true," said Louise, with inward wonder that she had not thought of it. His self-possession did not comport with his threadbare clothes any more than his neat accent and quiet tone comported with the proletarian character she had assigned him. She decided that he must be a walking delegate, and that he had probably come on mischief from some of the workpeople in her father's employ; she had never seen a walking-delegate before, but she had heard much dispute between her father and brother as to his usefulness in society; and her decision gave Maxwell fresh interest in her mind. Before he knew who Louise was, he had made her represent the millionaire's purse-pride, because he found her in Hilary's house, and because he had hated her for a swell, as much as a young man can hate a pretty woman, when he saw her walking up and down the platform at Hatboro'. He looked about the rich man's library with a scornful recognition of its luxury. His disdain, which was purely dramatic, and had no personal direction, began to scare Louise; she wanted to go away, but even if she could get to her shoes, without his noticing, she could not get them on without making a scraping noise on the hard wood floor. She did not know what to say next, and her heart warmed with gratitude to Maxwell when he said, with no great relevancy to what they had been saying, but with much to what he had in mind, "I don't think one realizes the winter, except in the country."

"Yes," she said, "one forgets how lovely it is, out of town."

"And how dreary," he added.

"Oh, do you feel that?" she asked, and she said to herself, "We shall be debating whether summer is pleasanter than winter, if we keep on at this rate."

"Yes, I think so," said Maxwell. He looked at a picture over the mantel, to put himself at greater ease, and began to speak of it, of the color and drawing. She saw that he knew nothing of art, and felt only the literary quality of the picture, and she was trying compassionately to get the talk away from it, when she heard her father's step in the hall below.

Hilary gave a start of question, when he looked into the library, that brought Maxwell to his feet. "Mr. Hilary, I'm connected with the *Daily Abstract*, and I've come to see if you are willing to talk with me about this rumored accident to Mr. Northwick."

"No, sir! No, sir!" Hilary stormed back. "I don't know any more about the accident than you do! I haven't a word to say about it. Not a word! Not a syllable! I hope that's enough?"

"Quite," said Maxwell, and with a slight bow to Louise he went out.

"Oh, papa!" Louise moaned out, "how *could* you treat him so?"

"Treat him so? Why shouldn't I treat him so? Confound his impudence! What does he mean by thrusting himself in here and taking possession of my library? Why didn't he wait in the hall?"

"Patrick showed him in here. He saw that he was a gentleman!"

"Saw that he was a gentleman?"

"Yes, certainly. He is very cultivated. He's not—not a common reporter, at *all!*" Louise's voice trembled with mortification for her father, and pity for Maxwell, as she adventured this assertion from no previous experience of reporters. It was shocking to feel that it was her father who had not been the gentleman. "You—you might have been a little kinder, papa; he wasn't at all obtrusive; and he only asked you whether you would say anything. He didn't persist."

"I didn't intend he should persist," said Hilary. His fire of straw always burnt itself out in the first blaze; it was uncomfortable to find himself at variance with his daughter who was usually his fond and admiring ally; but he could not give up at once. "If you didn't like the way I treated him why did you stay?" he demanded. "Was it necessary for you to entertain him till I came in? Did he ask for the family? What does it all mean?"

The tears came into her eyes, and she said with indignant resentment: "Patrick didn't know I was here when he brought him in; I'm sure I should have been glad to go, when you began raging at him, papa, if I *could*. It wasn't very pleasant to hear you. I wont come any more, if you don't want me to. I thought you liked me to be here. You said you did."

Her father blustered back, "Don't talk nonsense. You'll come, just as you always have. I suppose," he added, after a moment in which Louise gathered up her shoes, and stood with them in one hand behind her, a tall figure of hurt affection and wounded pride, "I suppose I might have been a little smoother with the fellow, but I've had twenty reporters after me, to-day, and between them, and you and Matt, in all this bother, I hardly know what I'm about. Didn't Matt see that his going to Wellwater on behalf of Northwick's family must involve me more and more?"

"I don't see how he could help offering to go when he found Suzette was going alone. He couldn't do less."

"Oh, do less!" said Hilary, with imperfectly sustained passion. He turned to avoid looking at Louise, and his eyes fell on a strange-looking note book on the table where Maxwell had sat. "What's this?"

He took it up, and Louise said, "He must have left it," and she thought, "Of course he will come back for it!"

"Well, I must send it to him. And I'll—I'll write him a note," Hilary groaned.

Louise smiled eager forgiveness. "He seemed very intelligent, poor fellow, in some ways. Didn't you notice what a cultivated tone he had? It's shocking to think of his having to go about and interview people, and meet all kinds of rebuffs."

"I guess you'd better not waste too much sympathy on him," said Hilary with some return to his grudge.

"Oh, I didn't mean *you*, papa," said Louise sweetly.

The doorbell rang, and after some parley at the threshold, Patrick came up to say, "The gentleman that was just here thinks he left his note-book; he"—

Hilary did not let him get the words out: "Oh, yes; show him up! Here it is!" He ran half down the stairs himself to meet Maxwell.

XVI

LOUISE stole a glance at herself across the room in the little triptych mirror against one of the shelves. Her hair was not tumbled, and she completed her toilet to the eye by dropping her shoes and extending the edge of her skirt over them where she stood.

Her father brought Maxwell in by the arm, and she smiled a fresh greeting to him. "We—I had just picked your note-book up. I—I'm glad you came back. I—was a little short with you a moment ago. I—I— Mayn't I offer you a cigar?"

"No, thanks. I don't smoke," said Maxwell.

"Then a glass of— It's pretty cold out?"

"Thank you; I never drink."

"Well, that's good! That's—sit down; sit down!—that's a very good thing. I assure you, I don't think it's the least use, though I do both. My boy doesn't, he's a pattern to his father."

In spite of Hilary's invitation Maxwell remained on foot, with the effect of merely hearing him out as he went on. "I— I'm sorry I haven't anything to tell about that accident. I've been telegraphing all day, without finding out anything beyond the fact as first reported; and now my son's gone up to Wellwater, to look it up on the ground. It may have been our Mr. Northwick, or it may not. May I ask how much you know?"

"I don't know that I'm quite free to say," answered Maxwell.

"Oh!"

"And I didn't expect you to say anything unless you wished to make something known. It's a matter of business."

"Exactly," said Hilary. "But I think I might been a little civiller in saying what I did. The rumor's been a great annoyance to me; and I like to share my annoyances with other people. I suppose your business often brings you in contact with men of that friendly disposition? Heigh?" Hilary rolled the cigar he was about to light between his lips.

"We see the average man," said Maxwell not at all flattered from his poise by Hilary's apologies. "It's a bore to be interviewed; I know that from the bore it is to interview."

"I dare say that's often the worst part of it," said Hilary, lighting his cigar, and puffing out the first great clouds. "Well, then, I may congratulate myself on sparing you an unpleasant duty. I didn't know I should come off so handsomely."

There seemed nothing more to say, and Maxwell did not attempt to make conversation. Hilary offered him his hand, and he said, as if to relieve the parting of abruptness, "If you care to look in on me again, later on, perhaps"—

"Thank you," said Maxwell, and he turned to go. Then he turned back, and after a moment's hesitation, bowed to Louise, and said very stiffly "Good evening!" and went out.

Louise fetched a deep breath. "Why didn't you keep him longer, papa, and find out all about him?"

"I think we know all that's necessary," said her father dryly. "At least he isn't on my conscience any longer; and now I hope you're satisfied."

"Yes—yes," she hesitated. "You don't think you were too patronizing in your reparation, papa?"

"Patronizing?" Hilary's crest began to rise.

"Oh, I don't mean that; but I wish you hadn't let him see that you expected him to leap for joy when you stooped to excuse yourself."

Hilary delayed, for want of adequate terms, the violence he was about to permit himself. "The next time, if you don't like my manner with people, don't stay, Louise."

"I knew you wanted me to stay, papa, to see how beautifully

you would do it; and you *did* do it beautifully. It was magnificent—perhaps *too* magnificent." She began to laugh and to kiss away the vexation from her father's face, keeping her hands behind her with her shoes she had picked up again, in them, as she came and leaned over him, where he sat.

"And did I want you to stay and entertain him here till I came in?" he demanded, to keep from being mollified too soon.

"No," she faltered. "*That* was a work of necessity. He looked so sick and sad, that he appealed to my sympathy, and besides— Do you think I could trust you with a secret, papa?"

"What are you talking about?"

"Why you see I thought he was a walking delegate at first."

"And was that the reason you stayed."

"No. That was what frightened me, and then interested me. I wanted to find out what they were like. But that isn't the secret."

"It's probably quite as important," Hilary growled.

"Well, you see it's such a good lesson to me! I had slipped off my shoes when I was lying down, and I couldn't get away, he came in so suddenly."

"And do you mean to tell me, Louise, that you were talking to that reporter all the time in"—

"How should he know it? You didn't know it yourself, papa. I couldn't get my shoes on after he came, of course!" She brought them round before her in evidence.

"Well, it's scandalous, Louise, simply scandalous! I never come in after you've been here without finding some part of your gear lying round—hair pins, or gloves, or ribbons, or belts, or handkerchiefs, or something—and I wont have it. I want you to understand that I think it's disgraceful. I'm ashamed of you."

"Oh, no! Not *ashamed*, papa!"

"Yes, I am!" said her father; but he had to relent under her look of mock-imploring, and say, "Or I ought to be. I don't see how you could hold up your head."

"I held it very *high* up. When you haven't got your shoes

on—in company—it gives you a sort of—internal majesty; and I behaved very loftily. But it's been a fearful lesson to me, papa!" She made her father laugh, and then she flung herself upon him, and kissed him for his amiability. She said, at the end of this rite, "He didn't seem much impressed even after you had apologized, do you think papa?"

"No, he didn't," Hilary grumped. "He's as stiff-necked as need be."

"Yes," said Louise thoughtfully. "He must be proud. How funny proud people are, papa! I can't understand them. That was what always fascinated me with Suzette."

Hilary's face saddened as it softened. "Ah, poor thing! She'll have need of all her pride, now."

"You mean about her father," said Louise, sobered too. "Don't you hope he's got away?"

"What do you mean, child? That would be a very rascally wish in me."

"Well, you'd rather he had got away than been killed?"

"Why, of course, of course," Hilary ruefully assented. "But if Matt finds he wasn't—in the accident, it's my business to do all I can to bring him to justice. The man's a thief."

"Well, then, *I* hope he's got away."

"You mustn't say such things, Louise."

"Oh, *no*, papa! Only *think* them."

XVII

HILARY had to yield to the pressure on him and send detectives to look into the question of Northwick's fate at the scene of the accident. It was a formal violation of his promise to Northwick that he should have three days unmolested; but perhaps the circumstances would have justified Hilary to any business man, and it could really matter nothing to the defaulter, dead or alive. In either case he was out of harm's way. Matt, all the same, felt the ghastliness of being there on the same errand with these agents of his father, and reaching the same facts with them. At moments it seemed to him as if he were tacitly working in agreement with them, for the same purpose as well as to the same end; but he would not let this illusion fasten upon him; and he kept faith with Suzette in the last degree. He left nothing undone which she could have asked if he had done; he invented some quite useless things to do, and did them, to give his conscience no cause against him afterwards. The fire had left nothing but a few charred fragments of the wreck. There had been no means of stopping it, and it had almost completely swept away the cars in which it had broken out. Certain of the cars to the windward were not burnt; these lay capsized beside the track, bent and twisted, and burst athwart, fantastically like the pictures of derailed cars as Matt had seen them in the illustrated papers; the locomotive, pitched into a heavy drift, was like some dead monster that had struggled hard for its life. Where the fire had raged, there was a wide black patch in the whiteness glistening everywhere else; there were ashes, and writhen iron work; and bits of charred wood work; but nothing to tell who or how many had died there. It was certain that the porter and the parlor car conductor were among the lost; and his list of passengers had perished with the conductor; there was only left with the operator the original of that telegram, asking to have a chair reserved in the Pullman from Wellwater, and signed with Northwick's name, but those different initials, which had given rise to the report of his death.

This was the definite fact which Matt could carry back with him to Northwick's family, and this they knew already. It settled nothing; it left the question of his death just where it was before. But Matt struggled with it as if it were some quite new thing, and spent himself in trying to determine how he should present it to them. In his own mind he had very great doubt whether Northwick was in the accident, and whether that dispatch were not a trick, a ruse to cover up the real course of his flight. But then there was no sense in his trying to hide his track, for he must have known that as yet there was no pursuit. If the telegram were a ruse, it was a ruse to conceal the fact that Northwick was still in the country, and had not gone to Canada at all. But Matt could not imagine any reason for such a ruse; the motive must be one of those illogical impulses which sometimes govern criminals. In any case, Matt could not impart his conjectures to the poor women who must be awaiting his return with such cruel anxiety. If the man were really dead, it would simplify the matter beyond the power of any other fact; Matt perceived how it would mitigate the situation for his family; he could understand how people should hold that suicide was the only thing left for a man in Northwick's strait. He blamed himself, for coming a moment to that ground, and owned the shame of his interested motive; but it was nevertheless a relief which he did not know how to refuse when Suzette Northwick took what he had to tell as final proof that her father was dead.

She said that she had been talking it all over with her sister, and they were sure of it; they were prepared for it; they expected him to tell them so.

Matt tried to have her realize that he had not told her so; and he urged, as far as he could, the grounds for hoping that her father was not in the accident.

She put them all aside. The difference in the initials was really no difference; and besides, and above all, there was the fact that if her father were anywhere alive, he must have seen the report of his death by this time, and sent some word, made some sign for their relief. She was doubly sure of this because he was so anxiously thoughtful of them when they were separated. He expected them to notify him of every slight change in their plans when they were away, and always telegraphed as to his own. The only mystery was his going to Canada without letting them know his plans before or afterwards. It must have been upon some very suddenly urgent business that took his mind off of everything else.

Matt silently hung his head, dreading lest she should ask him what he thought, and wondering how he must answer if she did. He perceived that he had no choice but to lie, if she asked him; but when he volunteered nothing she did not ask him.

It was the second morning after he had left her; but he could see that she had lived long since their parting. He thought, "That is the way she will look as she grows old." The delicate outline of her cheeks showed a slight straightening of its curve; her lips were pinched; the aquiline jut of her nose was sharpened. There was no sign of tears in her eyes; but Adeline wept, and constantly dried her tears with her handkerchief. She accepted her affliction meekly, as Suzette accepted it proudly, and she seemed to leave all the conjectures and conclusions to her sister.

Suzette was in the exaltation which death first brings to the bereaved, when people say that they do not realize it yet, and that they will feel it later. Then they go about, especially if they are women, in a sort of hysterical strength; they speak calmly of what has happened; they help those beyond the immediate circle of their loss to bear up against it; these look to see them break suddenly under the stress of their bereavement, and wonder at their impassioned fortitude.

Matt knew neither how to stay nor to get away; it seemed intrusive to linger and inhuman to go when he had told the little he had to tell. Suzette had been so still, so cold, in receiving him, that he was astonished at her intensity when he rose to leave her at last.

"I shall never forget what you have done for us, Mr. Hilary. Never! Don't belittle it, or try to make it seem nothing! It was everything! I wonder you could do it!"

"Yes!" Adeline put in, as if they had been talking his kindness over as well as their loss, and were of one mind about it.

"Oh, indeed!" he began. "Any one would have done it"—

"Don't say so!" cried Suzette. "You think that because *you* would have done it for *any* one! But you have done it for *us*; and as long as I live I shall remember that! Oh"— She broke off; and dropped her face with a pathetic, childlike helplessness on her lifted arm; and now he was less than ever able to leave her. They all sat down again after they had risen to part; Matt felt the imperative necessity of encouraging them; of rescuing her from the conjecture which she had accepted as certainty. He was one of those men in whom passion can be born only of some form of unselfish kindness; and who alone can make women happy. If it was love that was now stirring so strangely at his heart he did not know it was love; he thought it was still the pity that he had felt for the girl's immense calamity. He knew that from every phase of it he could not save her, but he tried to save her from that which now confronted them, and from which he saw her suffering. He went over all the facts again with the hapless creatures, and reasoned from them the probability that their father was still alive. It was respite from sorrow which misery must follow; it was insane, it was foolish, it was even guilty, but he could not help trying to win it for them; and when he left them at last, they were bright with the hope he had given them, and that the event, whether it was death or whether it was disgrace, must quench in a blacker despair.

The truth of this rushed upon him when he found himself staggering away from the doomed house which cast its light gayly out upon the snow, and followed him with a perverse sense of its warmth and luxury into the night. But a strange joy mixed with the trouble in his soul; and for all that sleepless night, the conflict of these emotions seemed to toss him to and fro as if he were something alien and exterior to them. North-wick was now dead, and his death had averted the disgrace which overhung his name; now he was still alive, and his escape from death had righted all the wrong he had done. Then his escape had only deepened the shame he had fled from; his death had fixed a stain as of blood guiltiness on his misdeeds, and was no caprice of fate but a judgment of the eternal justice. Against this savage conclusion Matt rebelled, and made his stand.

XVIII

FOR FORTY-EIGHT hours longer the fact of the defalcation was kept back; but then, in view of the legal action urged by those who did not accept the theory of Northwick's death, it had to come out, and it broke all bounds in overwhelming floods of publicity.

Day after day the papers were full of the facts, and it was weeks before the editorial homilies ceased. From time to time, fresh details and unexpected revelations, wise guesses and shameless fakes, renewed the interest of the original fact. There were days when there was nothing about it in the papers, and then days when it broke out in vivid paragraphs and whole lurid columns again. It was not that the fraud was singular in its features; these were common to most of the defalcations, great and small, which were of daily fame in the newspapers. But the doubt as to the man's fate and the enduring mystery of his whereabouts, if he were still alive, were qualities that gave peculiar poignancy to Northwick's case. Its results in the failure of people not directly involved were greater than could have been expected; and the sum of his peculations mounted under investigation. It was all much worse than had been imagined, and in most of the editorial sermons upon it the moral gravity of the offence was measured by the amounts stolen and indirectly lost by it. There was a great deal of mere astonishment, as usual, that the crime should have been that of a man whom no one would have dreamed of suspecting, and there was some sufficiently ridiculous consternation at the presence of such moral decay in the very heart of the commercial life of Boston.

In the *Events*, Pinney made his report of the affair the work of art which he boasted should come from his hand. It was really a space-man's masterpiece; and it appealed to every nerve in the reader's body with its sensations repeated through many columns, and continued from page to page with a recurrent efflorescence of scare-heads and catch lines. In the ardor of production all scruples and reluctances became fused in a devotion to the interests of the *Events* and its readers. With every hour, the painful impressions of his interview with Miss Northwick grew fainter, and the desire to use it stronger, and he ended by sparing no color of it. But he compromised with his sympathy for her by deepening the shadows in the behavior of the man who could bring all this sorrow upon those dearest to him. He dwelt upon the unconsciousness of the family, the ignorance of the whole household, in which life ran smoothly on while the head of both was a fugitive from justice, if not the victim of a swift retribution. He worked in all the pathos which the facts were capable of holding, and at certain points he enlarged the capacity of the facts. He described with a good deal of graphic force the Northwick interior. Under his touch the hall expanded, the staircase widened and curved, the carpets thickened, the servants multiplied, the library into which "the *Events* representative was politely ushered," was furnished with "all the appliances of a cultured taste." The works of the standard authors in costly bindings graced its shelves; magnificent paintings and groups of statuary adorned its walls and alcoves. The dress of the lady who courteously received the *Events* reporter was suitably enriched; her years were discounted, and her beauty approached to the patrician cast. There was nothing mean about Pinney, and while he was at it he lavished a manorial grandeur upon the Northwick place outside as well as inside. He imparted a romantic consequence to Hatboro' itself: "a thriving New England town, proud of its historic past, and rejoicing in its modern prosperity, with a population of some five or six thousand souls, among whose working men and women modern ideas of the most advanced character had been realized in the well-known Peck Social Union, with its cooperative kitchen, and its clientèle of intelligent members and patrons." People of all occupations became leading residents in virtue of taking Pinney into their confidence, and A Prominent Proletarian achieved the distinction of a catch-line by freely imparting the impressions of J. M. Northwick's character among the working-classes. The Consensus of Public Feeling, in portraying which Pinney did not fail to exploit the proprietary word he had seized formed the subject of some dramatic paragraphs; and the whole formed a rich and fit setting for the main facts of Northwick's undoubted fraud and flight, and for the conjectures which Pinney indulged concerning his fate.

Pinney's masterpiece was, in fine, such as he could write only at that moment of his evolution as a man, and such as the *Events* could publish only at that period of its development as a newspaper. The report was flashy and vulgar and unscrupulous; but it was not brutal, except by accident, and not unkind except through the necessities of the case. But it was helplessly and thoroughly personal, and it was no more philosophized than a monkish chronicle of the middle ages.

The *Abstract* addressed a different class of readers and aimed at a different effect in its treatment of public affairs. We look upon newspapers as having a sort of composite temperament, formed from the temperaments of all the different men employed on them; but as a matter of fact they each express the disposition and reflect the temperament of one controlling spirit, which all the other dispositions and temperaments yield to. This is so much the case that it is hard to efface the influence of a strong mind from the journal it has shaped even when it is no longer actively present in it. A good many years before the time of the Northwick defalcation, the *Events* had been in the management of a journalist once well-known in Boston, a certain Bartley Hubbard, who had risen from the ranks of the reporters, and who had thoroughly reporterized it in the worst sense. After he left it, the owner tried several devices for elevating and reforming it, but failed, partly because he was himself a man of no ideals but those of the counting room, and largely because the paper could not recover from the strong slant given it without self-destruction. So the *Events* continued what Bartley Hubbard had made it, and what the readers he had called about it liked it to be: a journal without principles and without convictions, but with interests only; a map of busy life, indeed, but glaringly colored, with crude endeavors at picturesqueness, and with no more truth to life than those railroad maps where the important centres converge upon the broad black level of the line advertised, and leave rival roads wriggling faintly about in uninhabited solitudes. In Hubbard's time the *Abstract*, then the *Chronicle-Abstract*, was in charge of the editor who had been his first friend on the Boston press, and whom he finally quarreled with on a point which this friend considered dishonorable to Hubbard. Ricker had not since left the paper, and though he was called a crank by some of the more progressive and reckless of the young men, he clung to his ideal of a conscience in journalism; he gave the *Abstract* a fixed character and it could no more have changed than the *Events*, without self destruction. The men under him were not so many as Cæsar's soldiers, and that perhaps was the reason why he knew not only their names but their qualities. When Maxwell came with the fact of the defalcation which the detectives had entrusted to him for provisional use, and asked to be assigned to the business of working it up, Ricker consented, but he consented reluctantly. He thought Maxwell was better for better things; he knew he was a ravenous reader of philosophy and sociology, and he had been early in the secret of his being a poet; it had since become an open secret among his fellow reporters, for which he suffered both honor and dishonor.

"I shouldn't think you'd like to do it, Maxwell," said Ricker kindly. "It isn't in your line is it? Better give it to some of the other fellows."

"It's more in my line than you suppose, Mr. Ricker," said

the young fellow. "It's a subject I've looked up a great deal lately. I once thought"—he looked down bashfully—"of trying to write a play about a defaulter, and I got together a good many facts about defalcation. You've no idea how common it is; it's almost the commonest fact of our Civilization."

"Ah! Is that so?" asked Ricker with ironical deference to the bold generalizer. "Who else is 'onto' this thing?"

"Pinney, of the *Events.*"

"Well, he's a dangerous rival, in some ways," said Ricker. "When it comes to slush and a whitewash brush, I don't think you're a match for him. But perhaps you don't intend to choose the same weapons." Ricker pulled down the green-lined paste board peak that he wore over his forehead by gaslight, and hitched his chair round to his desk again, and Maxwell knew that he was authorized to do the work.

He got no word from the detective who had given him a hint of the affair, to go ahead the night after his return from Hatboro' as he had expected but he knew that the fact could not be kept back, and he worked as hard at his report as Pinney and Pinney's wife had worked at theirs. He waited till the next morning to begin, however, for he was too fagged after he came home from the Hilarys'; he rose early and got himself a cup of tea over the gas-burner; before the house was awake he was well on in his report. By nightfall he had finished it, and then he carried it to Ricker. The editor had not gone to dinner, yet, and he gave Maxwell's work the critical censure of a hungry man. It was in two separate parts: one a careful and lucid statement of all the facts which had come to Maxwell's knowledge, in his quality of reporter, set down without sensation, and in that self-respectful decency of tone which the *Abstract* affected; the other an editorial comment upon the facts. Ricker read the first through without saying anything; when he saw what the second was, he pushed up his green-lined peak and said, "Hello, young man! Who invited you to take the floor?"

"Nobody. I found I couldn't embody my general knowledge

of defalcation in the report without impertinence, and as I had to get my wisdom off my mind somehow, I put it in editorial shape. I don't expect you to take it. Perhaps I can sell it somewhere."

Ricker seemed to pay no attention to his explanation. He went on reading the manuscript, and when he ended, he took up the report again, and compared it with the editorial in length. "If we printed these things as they stand it would look like a case of the tail wagging the dog."

Maxwell began again, "Oh, I didn't expect"—

"Oh, yes, you did," said Ricker. "Of course, you felt that the report was at least physically inadequate."

"I made as much as I honestly could of it. I knew you didn't like padding or faking, and I don't myself."

Ricker was still holding the two manuscripts up before him. He now handed them over his shoulder to Maxwell, where he stood beside him. "Do you think you could weld these two things together?"

"I don't know."

"Suppose you try."

"As editorial, or"—

"Either. I'll decide after you've done. Do it here."

He pushed some papers off the long table beside him, and Maxwell sat down to his task. It was not difficult. The material was really of kindred character throughout. He had merely to write a few prefatory sentences in the editorial attitude to his report, and then append the editorial, with certain changes again. It did not take him long; in half an hour he handed the result to Ricker.

"Yes," said Ricker, and he began to read it anew with his blue pencil in his hand.

Maxwell had come with nerves steeled to bear the rejection of his article entire, but he was not prepared to suffer the erasure of all his pet phrases and favorite sentences, sometimes running to entire paragraphs.

When Ricker handed it back to him at last with "What do

you think of it now?" Maxwell had the boldness to answer, "Well, Mr. Ricker, if I *must* say, I think you've taken all the bones and blood out of it."

Ricker laughed. "Oh, no! Merely the fangs and poison sacks. Look here, young man! Did you believe all those cynical things when you were saying them?"

"I don't know"—

"*I* know. I know you *didn't*. Every one of them rang false. They were there for literary effect, and for the pleasure of the groundlings. But by and by, if you keep on saying those things, you'll get to thinking them, and what a man thinks a man is. There are things there that you ought to be ashamed of, if you really thought them, but I knew you didn't; so I made free to strike them all out." Maxwell looked foolish; he wished to assert himself, but he did not know how. Ricker went on: "Those charming little sarcasms and innuendoes of yours would have killed your article for really intelligent readers. They would have suspected a young fellow having his fling, or an old fool speaking out of the emptiness of his heart. As it is, we have got something unique, and I don't mind telling you I'm very glad to have it. I've never made any secret of my belief that you have talent."

"You've been very good," said Maxwell, a little rueful still. The surgeon's knife hurts though it cures.

When Maxwell went home, he met his mother. "Why, mother," said the young fellow, "Old Ricker is going to print my report as editorial; and we're not going to have any report."

"I *told* you it was good!"

Maxwell felt it was due to himself to keep some grudge, and he said, "Yes; but he's taken all the life out of it with his confounded blue pencil. It's perfectly dead."

It did not seem so when he saw it in proof at the office later, and it did not seem so when he got it in the paper. He had not slept well; he was excited by several things, by the use Ricker had made of his work, and by the hopes of advancement which this use quickened in him. He was not ashamed of it; he was very proud of it; and he wondered at its symmetry and force, as he read and read it again. He had taken very high philosophical ground in his view of the matter, and had accused the structure of society. There must be something rotten, he said, at the core of our civilization, when every morning brought the story of a defalcation, great or small, in some part of our country: not the peculations of such poor clerks and messengers as their employers could be insured against, but of officials, public and corporate, for whom we had no guaranty but the average morality of our commercial life. How low this was might be inferred from the fact that while such a defalcation as that of J. M. Northwick created dismay in business and social circles, it could not fairly be said to create surprise. It was, most unhappily, a thing to be expected, in proof of which no stronger evidence need be alleged than that patent to the *Abstract* reporter in the community where the defaulter had his home, and where in spite of his reputation for the strictest probity it was universally believed that he had run away with other people's money merely because he had been absent twenty-four hours without accounting for his whereabouts.

At this point Maxwell wove in the material he had gathered in his visit to Hatboro', and without using names or persons contrived to give a vivid impression of the situation and the local feeling. He aimed at the historical attitude, and with some imitation of Taine's method and manner, he achieved it. His whole account of the defalcation had a closeness of texture which involved every significant detail, from the first chance suspicion of the defaulter's honesty, to the final opinions and conjectures of his fate. At the same time the right relation and proportion of the main facts were kept, and the statement was throughout so dignified and dispassionate that it had the grace of something remote in time and place. It was when the narrative ended and the critical comment began that the artistic values made themselves felt. Ricker had been free in his recognition of the excellence of Maxwell's work, and quick to appreciate its importance to the paper. He made the young fellow disjointed compliments and recurrent predictions concerning it when they were together, but there were qualities in it that he felt afterwards he had not been just to. Of course it owed much to the mere accident of Maxwell's accumulation of material about defalcations for his play; but he had known men break down under the mass of their material, and it surprised and delighted him to see how easily and strongly Maxwell handled his. That sick little youngster carried it all off with an air of robust maturity that amused as well as surprised Ricker. He saw where the fellow had helped himself out, consciously or unconsciously, with the style and method of his favorite authors; and he admired the philosophic poise he had studied from them; but no one except Maxwell himself was in the secret of the forbearance, the humane temperance, with which Northwick was treated. This was a color from the play which had gone to pieces in his hands; he simply adapted the conception of a typical defaulter, as he had evolved it from a hundred instances, to the case of the defaulter in hand, and it fitted perfectly. He had meant his imaginary defaulter to appeal rather to the compassion than the justice of the theatre, and he presented to the reader the almost fatal aspect of the offence. He dwelt upon the fact that the case, so far from being isolated or exceptional, was without peculiarities, was quite normal. He drew upon his accumulated facts for the proof of this, and with a rapid array of defaulting treasurers, cashiers, superintendents and presidents, he imparted a sense of the uniformity in their malfeasance which is so evident to the student. They were all comfortably placed and in the way to prosperity if not fortune; they were all tempted by the possession of means to immediate wealth; they all yielded so far as to speculate with the money that did not belong to them; they were all easily able to replace the first loans they made themselves; they all borrowed again and then could not replace the loans; they were all found out, and all were given a certain time to make up their shortage. After that a certain diversity appeared: some shot themselves, and some hanged themselves; others decided to stand their trial; the vastly greater number ran away to Canada.

In this presentation of the subject, Maxwell had hardly to do more than to copy the words of a certain character in his play: one of those cynical personages, well known to the drama, whose function is to observe the course of the action and to make good humored sarcasms upon the conduct and motives of the other characters. It was here that Ricker employed his blue pencil the most freely, and struck out passages of almost diabolical persiflage and touched the colors of the black pessimism with a few rays of hope. The final summing up, again, was adapted from a drama that had been rejected by several purveyors of the leg-burlesque as immoral. In a soliloquy intended to draw tears from the listener, the hero of Maxwell's play, when he parted from his young wife and children before taking poison, made some apposite reflections on his case, in which he regarded himself as the victim of conditions, and in prophetic perspective beheld an interminable line of defaulters to come, who should encounter the same temptations and commit the same crimes under the same circumstances. Maxwell simply recast this soliloquy in editorial terms; and maintained that not only was there nothing exceptional in Northwick's case, but that it might be expected to repeat itself indefinitely. On one hand you had men educated to business methods which permitted this form of dishonesty and condemned that; their moral fibre was strained if not weakened by the struggle for money going on all around us; on the other hand you had opportunity, the fascination of chance, the uncertainty of punishment. The causes would continue the same, and the effects would continue the same. He declared that no good citizen could wish a defaulter to escape the penalty of his offence against society; but it behooved society to consider how far it was itself responsible, which it might well do without ignoring the responsibility of the criminal. He ended with a paragraph in which he forecast a future without such causes and without such effects; but Ricker would not let this pass even in the semi-ironical temper Maxwell had given it. He said it was rank socialism, and he cut it out in the proof, where he gave the closing sentences of the article an interrogative instead of an affirmative shape.

XIX

THE HILARYS always straggled down to breakfast as they chose. When Matt was at home, his mother and he were usually first; then his father came, and Louise last. They took the *Events*, as many other people did, because with all its faults it was a thorough newspaper; and they maintained their self-respect by taking the *Abstract*. The morning that the defalcation came out, Matt sent and got all the other papers, which he had glanced through and talked over with his mother before his father joined them at nine o'clock. Several of them had illustrations: likenesses of Northwick, and views of his house in Boston, and his house in Hatboro'; views of the Company's Mills at Ponkwasset; views of the railroad wreck at Wellwater; but it was Pinney's masterpiece which really made Hilary sick. All the papers were atrocious, but that was loathsome. Yet there was really nothing more to blame in the attitude of the papers than in that of the directors who gave the case to the detectives and set the machinery of publicity at work. Both were acting quite within their rights; both were fulfilling an official duty. Hilary, however, had been forced against his grain into the position, almost, of Northwick's protector; he had suffered keenly from the falsity of this position, for no one despised the sort of man Northwick was more than he; but when you have suffered even for a rogue, you begin to feel some kindness for him. All these blows fell upon his growing sympathy—for the poor devil, as he called him. He got through the various accounts in the various papers, by broken efforts taking them as if in successive shocks from these terrible particulars, which seemed to shower themselves upon him, when he came in range of them, till he felt bruised and beaten all over.

"Well, at least it's out, my dear," said his wife, who noted the final effect of his sufferings across the table, and saw him pause bewildered from the last paper he had dropped. "There's that comfort."

"Is that a comfort?" he asked huskily.

"Why, yes, I think it is. The suspense is over, and now you can begin to pick yourself up."

"I suppose there's something in that." He kept looking at Matt, or rather at the copy of the *Abstract* which Matt was hiding behind, and he said, "What have you got there, Matt?"

"Perhaps I'd better read it out," said Matt. "It seems to me most uncommonly good. I wonder who could have done it!"

"Suppose you do your wondering afterwards," said his father impatiently; and Matt began to read. The positions of the article were not such as Hilary could have taken, probably, if he had been in a different mood; its implications were some of them such as he must have decidedly refused; but the temper of the whole was so humane, so forbearing, so enlightened, that Hilary was in a glow of personal gratitude to the writer for what he called his common decency by the time the reading was over. "That is a very extraordinary article," he said, and he joined Matt in wondering who could have done it, with the usual effect in such cases.

"I wish," said Mrs. Hilary, "that every other newspaper could be kept from those poor things." She meant Northwick's daughters, and she added, "If they must know the facts they couldn't be more mercifully told them."

"Why, that was what I was thinking, mother," said Matt. "But they can't be kept to this version, unhappily. The misery will have to come on them shapelessly as all our miseries do. I don't know that the other papers are so bad"—

"Not bad!" cried his father.

"No. They're not unkind to them, except as they are just

to him. They probably represent fairly enough the average thinking and feeling about the matter: the thing they'll have to meet all their lives and get used to. But I wish I knew who did this *Abstract* article; I should like to thank him."

"The question is now," said Mrs. Hilary, "what we can do for them, there. Are you sure you made it clear to them, Matt, that we were willing to have them come to us, no matter *what* happened?"

"Louise and I both tried to do that," said her son, "when we were there together, and, when I reported to them after Wellwater I told them again and again what our wish was."

"Well," said Mrs. Hilary, "I am glad we have done everything we could. At first I doubted the wisdom of your taking Louise to see them; but now I'm satisfied that it was right. And I'm satisfied that your father did right in getting that wretched creature the chance he abused."

"Oh, yes," said Matt. "That was right. And I'm thoroughly glad he's out of it. If he's still alive I'm glad he's out of it."

Hilary had kept silent, miserably involved in his various remorses and misgivings, but now he broke out. "And I think you're talking abominable nonsense, Matt. I didn't get Northwick given that chance to enable him to escape the consequences of his rascality. Why shouldn't he be punished for it?"

"Because it wouldn't do the least good, to him or to any one else. It wouldn't reform him, it wouldn't reform anything. Northwick isn't the disease; he's merely the symptom. You can suppress him; but that wont cure the disease. It's the whole social body that's sick, as this article in the *Abstract* implies."

"I don't see any such implication in it," his father angrily retorted. "Your theory would form an excuse for the scoundrelism of every scoundrel unhung. Where is the cure of the social body to begin if it doesn't begin at home, with every man in it? I tell you, it would be a very good thing for Northwick, and every rogue like him if he could be made serve his term in State's prison."

The controversy raged a long time without departing from

these lines of argument on either side. Mrs. Hilary listened with the impatience women feel at every absence from the personal ground, the only ground of reality. When Matt had got so far from it as to be saying to his father, "Then I understand you to maintain that if A is properly punished for his sins, B will practice virtue in the same circumstances and under the same temptations that were too much for A," his mother tried to break in upon them. She did not know much about the metaphysical rights and wrongs of the question; she only felt that Matt was getting his father, who loved him so proudly and indulgently, into a corner, and she saw that this was unseemly. Besides, when anything wrong happens, a woman always wants some one punished: some woman, first, or then some other woman's men kindred. Every woman is a conservative in this, and Mrs. Hilary made up her mind to stop the talk between her son and husband because she felt Matt to be doubly wrong.

But when she spoke, her husband roared at her, "Don't interrupt, Sarah!" and then he roared at Matt, "I tell you that the individual is not concerned in the matter! I tell you that it is the interest, the necessity, of the community to punish A for his sins wihout regard to B, and for my part I shall leave no stone unturned till we have found Northwick, dead or alive, and if he is alive, I shall spare no effort to have him brought to trial, conviction and punishment." He shouted these words out, and thumped the breakfast table so that the spoons clattered in the cups, and Mrs. Hilary could hardly hear what Patrick was saying just inside the door.

"To see Mr. Hilary? A lady? Did she send her card?"

"She wouldn't give her name, ma'am; she said she didn't wish to, ma'am. She wished to see Mr. Hilary just a moment in the reception room."

Hilary was leaning forward to give the table another bang, with his fist, but his wife succeeded in stopping him, with a repetition of Patrick's message.

"I wont see her," he answered. "It's probably a woman re-

porter. They're in our very bread trough. I tell you," he went
on to Matt, "there are claims upon you as a citizen, as a social
factor, which annul all your sentimental obligations to B as
a brother. God rest my soul! Isn't C a brother, too, and all
the rest of the alphabet? If A robs the other letters, then let
B take a lesson from the wholesome fact that A's little game
has landed him in jail."

"Oh, I admit that the A's had better suffer for their sins;
but I doubt if the punishment which a man gets against his
will is the right kind of suffering. If this man had come forward voluntarily, and offered to bear the penalty he had risked
by his misdeed, it would have been a good thing for himself
and for everybody else: it would have been a real warning.
But he ran away."

"And so he ought to be allowed to stay away! You are a
pretty Dogberry come to judgment! You would convict a thief
by letting him steal out of your company!"

"It seems to me that's what *you* did, father. And I think
you did right, as I've told you."

"What *I* did?" shouted Hilary. "No, sir, I did nothing of
the kind! I gave him a chance to make himself an honest
man"—

"My dear," said Mrs. Hilary, "you *must* go and get rid of
that woman, at least; or let *me.*"

Hilary flung down his napkin, and red from argument cast
a dazed look about him, and without really quite knowing
what he was about rushed out of the room.

His wife hardly had time to say, "You oughtn't to have got
into a dispute with your father, Matt, when you know he's
been so perplexed," before they heard his voice call out,
"Good heavens, my poor child!" For the present they could
not know that this was a cry of dismay at the apparition of
Suzette Northwick, who met him in the reception-room with
the demand:

"What is this about my father, Mr. Hilary?"

"About your father, my dear?" He took the hands she put

out to him with her words, and tried to think what pitying and helpful thing he could say. She got them away from him, and held one fast with the other.

"Is it true?" she asked.

He permitted himself the pretence of not understanding her; he had to do it. "Why, we hope—we hope it isn't true. Nothing more is known about his being in the accident than we knew at first. Didn't Matt"—

"It isn't *that*. It's worse than that. It's that other thing—that the papers say—that he was a—defaulter—dishonest. Is *that* true?"

"Oh, no, no! Nothing of the kind, my dear!" Hilary had to say this; he felt that it would be inhuman to say anything else; nothing else would have been possible. "Those newspapers—confound them!—you know how they get things all— You needn't mind what the papers say!"

"But why should they say anything about my father, at such a time, when he's— What does it all mean, Mr. Hilary? I don't believe the papers, and so I came to you—as soon as I could, this morning. I knew you would tell me the truth. You have known my father so long; and you know how *good* he is! You know that he never wronged any one—that he *couldn't*!"

"Of course, of course!" said Hilary. "It was quite right to come to me—quite right. How—how is your sister? You must stay now,—Louise isn't down, yet—and have breakfast with her. I've just left Mrs. Hilary at the table— You must join us. She can assure you—Matt is quite confident that there's nothing to be distressed about in regard to the— He"—

Hilary kept bustling aimlessly about as he spoke these vague phrases, and he now tried to have her go out of the room before him; but she dropped into a chair, and he had to stay.

"I want you to tell me, Mr. Hilary, whether there is the slightest foundation for what the papers say this morning?"

"How, foundation? My dear child"—

"Has there been any trouble between my father and the company?"

"Well—well, there are always questions arising"—

"Is there any question of my father's accounts—his honesty?"

"People question everything, nowadays, when there is so much—want of confidence in business.— There have to be investigations, from time to time."

"And has there been any reason to suspect my father? Does any one suspect him?"

Hilary looked round the room with a roving eye, that he could not bring to bear upon the girl's face. "Why I suppose that some of us—some of the directors—have had doubts"—

"Have *you?*"

"My dear girl—my poor child! You couldn't understand. But I can truly say, that when this examination—when the subject came up for discussion at the board meeting, I felt warranted in insisting that your father should have time to make it all right. He said he could; and we agreed that he should have the chance." Hilary said this for the sake of the girl; and he was duly ashamed of the magnanimous face it put upon his part in the affair. He went on: "It is such a very, very common thing for people in positions of trust to use the resources in their charge, and then replace them, that these things happen every day, and no harm is meant and none is done—unless—unless the venture turns out unfortunately. It's not an isolated case!" Hilary felt that he was getting on, now, though he was aware that he was talking very immorally; but he knew that he was not corrupting the poor child before him, and that he was doing his best to console her, to comfort her. "The whole affair was very well put in the *Abstract.* Have you seen it? You must see that and not mind what the other papers say. Come in to Mrs. Hilary; we have the paper"—

Suzette rose. "Then some of the directors believe that my father has been taking the money of the company, as the papers say?"

"Their believing this or that, is nothing to the point"—

"Do *you?*"

"I can't say—I don't think he meant— He expected to restore it, of course. He was given time for that"— Hilary hesitated, and then he thought he had better say, "But he had certainly been employing the company's funds in his private enterprises."

"That is all," said the girl, and she now preceded Hilary out of the room. It was with inexpressible relief that he looked up and saw Louise coming down the stairs.

"Why, Sue!" she cried; and she flew down the steps, and threw her arms round her friend's neck. "Oh, Sue, Sue!" she said in that voice a woman uses to let another woman know that she understands and sympathizes utterly with her.

Suzette coldly undid her clasping arms. "Let me go, Louise"—

"No, no! You sha'n't go. I want you—you must stay with us, now. I know Matt doesn't believe at all in that dreadful report."

"That wouldn't be anything, now, even if it were true. There's another report—don't you know it, in the paper this morning." Louise tried to look unconscious in the slight pause Suzette made before she said: "And your father has been saying my father is a thief."

"Oh, papa!" Louise wailed out.

It was outrageously unfair and ungrateful of them both; and Hilary gave a roar of grief and protest. Suzette escaped from Louise, and before he could hinder it, flashed by Hilary to the street door and was gone.

X X

THE SORROW that turned to shame in other eyes remained sorrow to Northwick's daughters. When their father did not come back or make any sign of being anywhere in life they reverted to their first belief, and accepted the fact of his death. But it was a condition of their grief, that they must refuse any thought of guilt in him. Their love began to work that touching miracle which is possible in women's hearts, and to establish a faith in his honor which no proof of his dishonesty could shake.

Even if they could have believed all the things those newspapers accused him of, they might not have seen the blame that others did in his acts. But as women they could not make the fine distinctions that men make in business morality, and as Northwick's daughters they knew that he would not have done what he did if it was wrong. Their father had borrowed other people's money, intending to pay it back, and then had lost his own, and could not; that was all.

With every difference of temperament they agreed upon this, and they were agreed that it would be a sort of treason to his memory if they encouraged the charges against him by making any change in their life. But it was a relief to them, and especially to Suzette, who held the purse, when the changes began to make themselves, and their costly establishment fell away, through the discontent and anxiety of this servant and that till none were left but Elbridge Newton and his wife. She had nothing to do now but grieve for the child she had lost, and she willingly came in to help about the kitchen and parlor work, while her husband looked after the horses and cattle as well as he could, and tended the furnaces, and saw that the plants in the greenhouses did not freeze. He was up early and late; he had no poetic loyalty to the Northwicks; but as nearly as he could explain his devotion, they had always treated him well, and he could not bear to see things run behind.

Day after day went by, and week after week, and the sisters lived on in the solitude to which the compassion, the diffidence or the contempt of their neighbors left them. Adeline saw Wade, whenever he came to the house, where he felt it his duty and his privilege to bring the consolation that his office empowered him to offer in any house of mourning; but Suzette would not see him; she sent him grateful messages and promises, when he called, and bade Adeline tell him each time that the next time she hoped to see him.

One of the ladies of South Hatboro', a Mrs. Munger, who spent her winters as well as her summers there, penetrated as far as the library, upon her own sense of what was due to herself as a neighbor; but she failed to find either of the sisters. She had to content herself with urging Mrs. Morrell, the wife of the doctor, to join her in a second attempt upon their privacy; but Mrs. Morrell had formed a notion of Suzette's character and temper adverse to the motherly impulse of pity which she would have felt for any one else in the girl's position. Mrs. Gerrish, the wife of the leading merchant of Hatboro', who distinguished himself by coming up from Boston with Northwick, on the very day of the directors' meeting, would have joined Mrs. Munger, but her husband forbade her. He had stood out against the whole community in his belief in Northwick's integrity and solvency; and while every one else accused him of running away as soon as he was reported among the missing in the railroad accident, Gerrish had refused to admit it. The defalcation came upon him like thunder out of a clear sky; he felt himself disgraced before

his fellow citizens; and he resented the deceit which Northwick had tacitly practiced upon him. He was impatient of the
law's delays in seizing the property the defaulter had left
behind him, and which was now clearly the property of his
creditors. Other people in Hatboro', those who had been the
readiest to suspect Northwick, cherished a guilty leniency
toward him in their thoughts. Some believed that he had gone
to his account in other Courts; some that he was still alive in
poverty and exile which were punishment enough, as far as
he was concerned. But Gerrish demanded something exemplary, something dramatic from the law. He blamed the
Ponkwasset directors for a species of incivism, in failing to
have Northwick indicted at once, dead or alive.

"Why don't they turn his family out of that house, and
hand it over to the stockholders he has robbed?" he asked one
morning in the chance conclave of loungers in his store. "I
understand it is this man Hilary, in Boston, who has shielded
and—and protected him from the start, and—and right along.
I don't know *why*; but if I was one of the Ponkwasset stockholders, I think I *should*. I should make a point of inquiring
why Northwick's family went on living in my house after he
had plundered me of everything he could lay his hands on."

The lawyer Putney was present, and he shifted the tobacco
he had in one cheek to the other cheek, and set his little, firm
jaw. "Well, Billy, I'll tell you why. Because the house and
farm and all the real estate belong to Northwick's family and
not to Northwick's creditors." The listeners laughed, and
Putney went on. "That was a point that brother Northwick
looked after a good while ago, I guess. I guess he must have
done it as long ago as when you first wanted his statue put on
top of the soldiers' monument."

"I *never* wanted his statue put on top of the soldiers' monument!" Mr. Gerrish retorted angrily.

Putney's spree was past, and he was in the full enjoyment
of the contempt for Gerrish which was apt to turn to profound respect when he was in his cups. He was himself aware

of the anomalous transition by which he then became a leader of conservative feeling on all subjects and one of the staunchest friends of the status; he said it was the worst thing he knew against the existing condition of things. He went on, now: "Didn't you? Well, I think it would look better than that girl they've got there in circus-clothes." They all laughed; Putney had a different form of derision for the Victory of the soldiers' monument every time he spoke of it. "And it would suggest what those poor fellows really died for: that we could have more and more Northwicks and a whole Northwick system of things. Heigh? You see, Billy, I don't have to be so hard on the Northwicks, personally, because I regard them as a necessary part of the system. What would become of the laws and the courts if there were no rogues? We must *have* Northwicks. It's a pity that the Northwicks should have families; but I don't blame the Northwicks for providing against the evil day that Northwickism is sure to end in. I'm glad the roof can't be taken from over those women's heads; I respect the paternal love and foresight of J. Milton in deeding the property to them."

"It's downright robbery of his creditors for them to keep it!" Gerrish shouted.

"Oh, no, it isn't, Billy. It's law. You must respect the law, and the rights of property. You'll be wanting the strikers to burn down the shoe shops the next time we have trouble here. You're getting awfully incendiary, Billy."

Putney carried the laugh against Gerrish, but there were some of the group, and there were many people in Hatboro', including most of the women, who felt the want of exemplary measures in dealing with Northwick's case. These ladies did not see the sense of letting those girls live on just as if nothing had happened, in a house that their father's crimes had forfeited to his victims, while plenty of honest people did not know where they were going to sleep that night or where the next mouthful of victuals was to come from. It was not really the houseless and the hungry who complained of this injustice; it was not even those who toiled for their daily bread in the Hatboro' shops who said such things. They were too busy, and then too tired, to think much about them, and the noise of Northwick's misdeeds died first amid the din of machinery. It was in the close, stove-heated parlors of the respectable citizens, behind the windows that had so long commanded envious views of the Northwicks going by in their carriages and sledges, and among women of leisure and conscience, that his infamy endured, and that the injuries of his creditors cried out for vengeance on those daughters of his; they had always thought themselves too good to speak to other folks. Such women could not understand what the Ponkwasset Mills Company meant by not turning those girls right out of doors, and perhaps they could not have been taught why the company had no power to do this, or why the president at least had no wish to do it. When they learned that his family still kept up friendly relations with the Northwick girls they were not without their suspicions, which were not long in becoming their express belief that the Hilarys were sharing in the booty. They were not cruel, and would not really have liked to see the Northwick girls suffer, if it had come to that; but they were greedy of the vengeance promised upon the wicked, and they had no fear of judging or of meting with the fullest measure.

In the freer air of the streets and stores and offices, their husbands were not so eager. In fact, it might be said that no man was eager but Gerrish. After the first excitement, and the successive shocks of sensation imparted by the newspapers had passed there came over the men of Hatboro' a sort of resignation which might or might not be regarded as proof of a general demoralization. The defalcation had startled them, but it could not be said to have surprised any one; it was to be expected of a man in Northwick's position; it happened every day, somewhere, and the day had come when it should happen there. They did not say God was good and that Mahomet was His prophet, but they were fatalists, all the same.

They accepted the accomplished fact, and, reflecting that the disaster did not really concern them, many of them regarded it dispassionately, even jocosely. They did not care for a lot of rich people in Boston who had been supplying Northwick with funds to gamble in stocks; it was not as if the Hatboro' bank had been wrecked, and hard working folks had lost their deposits. They could look at the matter with an impartial eye, and in their hearts they obscurely believed that any member of the Ponkwasset Company would have done the same thing as Northwick if he had got the chance. Beyond that they were mostly interested in the question whether Northwick had perished in the railroad accident, or had put up a job on the public, and was possessing his soul in peace somewhere in Rogue's Rest, as Putney called the Dominion of Canada. Putney represented the party in favor of Northwick's survival, and Gates, the provision man, led the opposite faction. When Putney dropped in to order his marketing he usually said something like, "Well, Joel, how's cremation, this morning?"

"Just booming, Squire. That stock's coming up, right along. Bound to be worth a hundred cents on the dollar before hayin', yet." This, or something like it, was what Gates usually answered, but one morning he asked, "Heard how it stands with the Ponkwasset folks, I suppose? They say—paper does—that the reason the president hung off from making a complaint was 't he didn't rightly see how he could have the ashes indicted. *He* believes in it, any way."

"Well," said Putney, "the fathers of New England all died in the blessed hope of infant damnation. But that didn't prove it."

"That's something so, Squire. Guess you got me, there," said Gates.

"I can understand old Hilary's not wanting to push the thing, under the circumstances, and I don't blame him. But the law must have its course. Hilary's got his duty to do. *I* don't want to do it for him."

XXI

HILARY could not help himself, though when he took the legal steps he was obliged to it seemed to him that he was wilfully urging on the persecution of that poor young girl and that poor old maid. It was really ghastly to go through the form of indicting a man who, so far as any one could prove to the contrary, had passed with his sins before the tribunal that searches hearts and judges motives rather than acts. But still the processes had to go on, and Hilary had to prompt them. It was all talked over in Hilary's family, where he was pitied and forgiven in that affection which keeps us simple and sincere in spite of the masks we wear to the world. His wife and his children knew how kind he was, and how much he suffered in this business which, from the first, he had tried to be so lenient in. When he wished to talk of it they all agreed that Matt must not vex him with his theories and his opinions; and when he did not talk of it no one must mention it.

Hilary felt the peculiar hardships of his position all the more keenly because he had a conscience that would not permit him to shirk his duty. He had used his influence, the weight of his character and business repute to control the action of the Board towards Northwick when the defalcation became known, and now he was doubly bound to respond to the wishes of the directors in proceeding against him. Most of them believed that Northwick was still alive; those who were not sure regarded it as a public duty to have him indicted, at any rate, and they all voted that Hilary should make the necessary complaint. Then Hilary had no choice but to obey. Another man in his place might have resigned, but he could not, for he knew that he was finally responsible for Northwick's escape.

He made it no less his duty to find out just how much hardship it would work Northwick's daughters, and he tried to lend them money. But Suzette answered for both that her father had left them some money when he went away; and Hilary could only send Louise to explain how he must formally appear in the legal proceedings; he allowed Louise to put whatever warmth of color she wished into his regrets and into his advice that they should consult a lawyer. It was not business-like; if it were generally known it might be criticised; but in the last resort, with a thing like that, Hilary felt that he could always tell his critics to go to the deuce, and fall back upon a good conscience.

It seemed to Louise at first that Suzette was unwilling to separate her father from his office, or fully to appreciate his forbearance. She treated her own father's course as something above suspicion, as something which he was driven to by enemies whom he would soon have returned to put to confusion if he had lived. It made no difference to her and Adeline what was done; their father was safe, now, and some day his name would be cleared. Adeline added that they were in the home where he had left them; it was their house, and no one could take it from them.

Louise compassionately assented to everything. She thought Suzette might have been a little more cordial in the way she received her father's regrets. But she remembered that Suzette was always undemonstrative, and she did not blame her, after her first disappointment. She could see the sort of neglect that was already falling upon the house; the expression in housekeeping terms of the despair that was in their minds. The sisters did not cry, but Louise cried a good deal in pity of their forlornness, and at last her tears softened them into something like compassion for themselves. They had her stay to lunch rather against her will, but she thought she had better stay. The lunch was so badly cooked and so meager that Louise fancied they were beginning to starve themselves, and wanted to cry into her tea cup. The woman who waited, wore such dismal black, and went about with her eyes staring and her mouth tightly pursed, and smelt faintly of horses. It was Mrs. Newton; she had let Louise in when she came, and she was the only servant whom the girl saw.

Suzette said nothing about their plans for the future, and Louise did not like to ask her. She felt as if she were received under a flag of truce, and that there could be no confidence between them. Both of the sisters seemed to stand on the defensive with her; but when she started to come away, Suzette put on her hat and jacket, and said she would go to the avenue gate with her, and meet Simpson who was coming to take Louise back to the station.

It was a clear day of middle March; the sun rode high in a blue sky, and some jays bragged and jeered in the spruces. The frost was not yet out of the ground, but the shaded road was dry underfoot.

They talked at arms' length of the weather; and then Suzette said abruptly, "Of course, Louise, your father will have to do what they want him to against—papa. I understand that."

"Oh, Sue"—

"Don't! I should wish him to know that I wasn't stupid about it."

"I'm sure," Louise adventured, "he would do anything to help you!"

Suzette put by the futile expression of mere good feeling. "We don't believe papa has done anything wrong, or anything he wouldn't have made right if he had lived. We shall not let them take his property from us if we can help it."

"Of course not! I'm sure papa wouldn't wish you to."

"It would be confessing that they were right, and we will *never* do that. But I don't blame your father, and I want him to know it."

Louise stopped short and kissed Suzette. In her affectionate optimism it seemed to her for the moment that all the trouble was over now. She had never realized anything hopelessly wrong in the affair; it was like a misunderstanding that could be explained away, if the different people would listen to reason.

Sue released herself, and said, looking away from her friend: "It has been hard. He is dead; but we haven't even been allowed to see him laid in the grave"—

"Oh, perhaps," Louise sobbed out," he *isn't* dead! So many people think he isn't"—

Suzette drew away from her in stern offence. "Do you think that if he were alive he would leave us without a word—a sign?"

"No, no! He couldn't be so cruel! I didn't mean that! He is dead, and I shall always say it."

They walked on without speaking, but at the gate Suzette offered to return Louise's embrace. The tears stood in her eyes, as she said, "I would like to send my love to your mother —if she would care for it."

"Care for it!"

"And tell your brother I can never forget what he did for us."

"He can never forget that you let him do it," said Louise with eager gratitude. "He would have liked to come with me, if he hadn't thought it might seem intrusive."

"*Intrusive!* Your *brother!*" Sue spoke the words as if Matt were of some superior order of beings.

The intensity of feeling she put into her voice brought another gush of tears into Louise's eyes. "Matt *is* good. And I will tell him what you say. He will like to hear it." They looked down the road, but they could not see Simpson coming yet. "Don't wait, Sue," she pleaded. "Do go back! You will be all worn out."

"No, I will stay till your carriage comes," said Suzette; and they remained a moment silent together.

Then Louise said, "Matt has got a new fad: a young man that writes on the newspapers"—

"The newspapers!" Suzette repeated with an intonation of abhorrence.

"Oh, but he isn't like the others," Louise hastened to explain. "Very handsome, and interesting, and pale and sick. He is going to be a poet, but he's had to be a reporter. He's awfully clever; but Matt says he's awfully poor, and he has had such a hard time. Now they think he wont have to interview people any more—he came to interview papa, the first time; and poor papa was very blunt with him; and then so sorry. He's got some other kind of newspaper place; I don't know what. Matt liked what he wrote about—about your—troubles, Sue."

"Where was it?" asked Sue. "They were all wickedly false and cruel."

"This wasn't cruel. It was in the *Abstract*."

"Yes, I remember. But he said papa had taken the money," Sue answered unrelentingly.

"Did he? I thought he only said *if* he did. I don't believe he said more. Matt wouldn't have liked it so much if he had. He's in *such* bad health. But he's awfully clever."

The hack came in sight over the rise of ground, with Simpson driving furiously as he always did when he saw people. Louise threw her arms round her friend again. "Let me go back and stay with you, Sue! Or come home with me, you and Miss Northwick. We shall all be so glad to have you, and I hate so to leave you here alone. It seems so dreadful!"

"Yes. But it's easier to bear it here than anywhere else. Some day all this falsehood will be cleared up, and then we shall be glad that we bore it where he left us. We have decided what we shall do, Adeline and I. We shall try to let the house furnished for the summer, and live in the lodge here."

Louise looked round at the cottage by the avenue gate, and said it would be beautiful.

"We've never used it for any one, yet," Suzette continued, "and we can move back into the house in the winter."

This again seemed to Louise an admirable notion, and she parted from her friend in more comfort than she could have imagined when they met. She carried her feeling of elation home with her, and was able to report Sue in a state of almost smiling prosperity, and of perfect resignation if not acquiescence in whatever the company should make Hilary do. She figured her father, in his reluctance, as a sort of ally of the Northwicks, and she was disappointed that he seemed to derive so little pleasure from Sue's approval. But he generally approved of all that she could remember to have said for him to the Northwicks, though he did not show himself so appreciative of the situation as Matt. She told her brother what Sue had said when she heard of his unwillingness to intrude upon her and she added that now he must certainly go to see her.

XXII

A DAY or two later, when Matt Hilary went to Hatboro', he found Wade in his study at the church, and he lost no time in asking him, "Wade, what do you know of the Miss Northwicks? Have you seen them lately?"

Wade told him how little he had seen Miss Northwick, and how he had not seen Suzette at all. Then Matt said, "I don't know why I asked you, because I knew all this from Louise; she was up here the other day, and they told her. What I am really trying to get at is whether you know anything more about how that affair with Jack Wilmington stands. Do you know whether he has tried to see her since the trouble about her father came out?"

Adeline Northwick had dropped from the question, as usual, and it really related so wholly to Suzette in the thoughts of both the young men, that neither of them found it necessary to limit it explicitly.

"I feel quite sure he hasn't," said Wade, "though I can't answer positively."

"Then that settles it!" Matt walked away to one of Wade's gothic windows, and looked out. When he turned and came back to his friend, he said, "If he had ever been in earnest about her, I think he would have tried to see her, at such a time, don't you?"

"I can't imagine his not doing it. I never thought him a cad."

"No, nor I."

"He would have done it unless—unless that woman has some hold that gives her command of him. He's shown great weakness, to say the least. But I don't believe there's anything worse."

"What do the village people believe?"

"All sorts of lurid things, some of them; others believe that the affair is neither more nor less than it appears to be. It's a thing that could be just what it is in no other country in the world. It's the phase that our civilization has contributed to the physiognomy of scandal, just as the exile of the defaulter is the phase we have contributed to the physiognomy of crime. Public opinion here isn't severe upon Mrs. Wilmington or Mr. Northwick."

"I'm not prepared to quarrel with it on that account," said Matt, with the philosophical serenity which might easily be mistaken for irony in him. "The book we got our religion from teaches leniency in the judgment of others."

"It doesn't teach cynical indifference," Wade suggested.

"Perhaps that isn't what people feel," said Matt.

"I don't know. Sometimes I dread to think how deeply our demoralization goes in certain directions."

Matt did not follow the lure to that sort of speculative inquiry he and Wade were fond of. He said, with an abrupt return to the personal ground: "Then you don't think Jack Wilmington need be any further considered in regard to her?"

"In regard to Miss Sue Northwick? I don't know whether I quite understand what you mean."

"I mean, is it anybody's duty—yours or mine—to go to the man and find him out: what he really thinks, what he really feels? I don't mean, make an appeal to him. That would be unworthy of her. But perhaps he's holding back from a mistaken feeling of delicacy, of remorse; when if he could be made to see that it was his right, his privilege to be everything to her now that a man could be to a woman and infinitely more than any man could hope to be to a happy or fortunate woman— What do you think? He could be reparation, protection, safety, everything!"

Wade shook his head. "It would be useless. Wilmington knows very well that such a girl would never let him be anything to her, now, when he had slighted her fancy for him before. Even if he were ever in love with her, which I doubt, he couldn't do it."

"No, I suppose not," said Matt. After a little pause, he added, "Then I must go myself."

"Go, yourself? What do you mean?" Wade asked.

"Some one must try to make them understand just how they are situated. I don't think Louise did; I don't think she knew herself how the legal proceedings would affect them; and I think I'd better go and make it perfectly clear."

"I can imagine it wont be pleasant," said Wade.

"No," said Matt, "I don't expect that. But I inferred from what she said to Louise that she would be willing to see me, and I think I had better go."

He put his conviction interrogatively, and Wade said heartily, "Why, of course. It's the only thing," and Matt went away with a face which was cheerful with good will, if not the hope of pleasure.

He met Suzette in the avenue, dressed for walking, and coming forward with the magnificent, haughty movement she had. As she caught sight of him, she started, and then almost ran toward him. "Oh! *You!*" she said, and she shrank back a little, and then put her hand impetuously out to him.

He took it in his two, and bubbled out, "Are you walking somewhere? Are you well? Is your sister at home? Don't let me keep you! May I walk with you?"

Her smile clouded. "I'm only walking here in the avenue. How is Louise? Did she get home safely? It was good of her to come here. It isn't the place for a gay visit."

"Oh, Miss Northwick! It was good of you to see her! And we were very happy—relieved—to find that you didn't feel aggrieved with any of *us* for what must happen. And I hope you don't feel that I've taken an advantage of your kindness in coming?"

"Oh, no!"

"I've just been to see Wade." Matt reddened consciously. "But it doesn't seem quite fair to have met you where you had no choice but to receive me!"

"I walk here every morning," she returned evasively. "I have no where else. I never go out of the avenue. Adeline goes to the village, sometimes. But I can't meet people."

"I know," said Matt, with caressing sympathy, and his head swam in the sudden desire to take her in his arms, and shelter her from that shame and sorrow preying upon her. Her eyes had a trouble in them that made him ache with pity; he recognized, as he had not before, that they were the translation in feminine terms of her father's eyes. "Poor Wade," he went on, without well knowing what he was saying, "told me that he—he was very sorry he had not been able to see you—to do anything"—

"What would have been the use? No one can do anything. We must bear our burden; but we needn't add to it by seeing people who believe that—that my father did wrong."

Matt's breath almost left him. He perceived that the condition on which she was bearing her sorrow was the refusal of her shame. Perhaps it would not have been possible for one of her nature to accept it, and it required no effort in her to frame the theory of her father's innocence; perhaps no other hypothesis was possible to her, and evidence had nothing to do with the truth as she felt it.

"The greatest comfort we have is that none of *you* believe it; and your father knew my father better than any one else. I was afraid I didn't make Louise understand how much I felt that, and how much Adeline did. It was hard to tell her, without seeming to thank you for something that was no more than my father's due. But we do feel it, both of us; and I would like your father to know it. I don't blame him for what he is going to do. It's necessary to establish my father's innocence to have the trial. I was very unjust to your father that first day, when I thought he believed those things against papa. We appreciate his kindness in every way, but we shall not get any lawyer to defend us."

Matt was helplessly silent before this wild confusion of perfect trust and hopeless error. He would not have known where to begin to set her right; he did not see how he could speak a word without wounding her through her love, her pride.

She hurried on walking swiftly as if to keep up with the rush of her freed emotions. "We are not afraid but that it will come out so that our father's name, who was always so perfectly upright, and so good to every one, will be cleared, and those who have accused him so basely will be punished as they deserve."

She had so wholly misconceived the situation and the character of the impending proceedings that it would not have been possible to explain it all to her; but he could not leave her in her error, and he made at last an effort to enlighten her.

"I think my father was right in advising you to see a lawyer. It wont be a question of the charges against your father's integrity, but of his solvency. The proceedings will be against his estate; and you mustn't allow yourselves to be taken at a disadvantage"—

She stopped. "What do we care for the estate if his good name isn't cleared up?"

"I'm afraid—I'm afraid," Matt entreated, "that you don't exactly understand"—

"If my father never meant to keep the money, then the trial will show," the girl returned.

"But a lawyer—indeed you ought to see a lawyer—could explain how such a trial would leave that question where it was. It wouldn't be the case against your father, but against *you*."

"Against us? What do they say *we* have done?"

Matt could have laughed at her heroic misapprehension of the affair, if it had not been for the pity of it. "Nothing!

Nothing! But they can take everything here that belonged to your father—everything on the place, to satisfy his creditors. The question of his wrong-doing wont enter. I can't tell you how. But you ought to have a lawyer who would defend your rights in the case."

"If they don't pretend we've done anything then they can't do anything to us!"

"They can take everything your father had in the world to pay his debts."

"Then let them take it," said the girl. "If he had lived he would have paid them. We will never admit that he did anything for us to be ashamed of; that he ever wilfully wronged any one."

Matt could see that this profession of her father's innocence was essential to her. He could not know how much of it was voluntary, a pure effect of will, in fulfilment of the demands of her pride, and how much was real belief. He only knew that whatever it was, his wish was not to wound her or to molest her in it, but to leave what should be sacred from human touch to the mystery that we call providence. It might have been this very anxiety that betrayed him, for a glance at his face seemed to stay her.

"Don't you think I am right, Mr. Hilary?"

"Yes, yes!" Matt began; and he was going to say that she was right in every way, but he found that his own truth was sacred to him as well as her fiction, and he said, "I've no right to judge your father. It's the last thing I should be willing to do. I certainly don't believe he ever wished to wrong any one if he could have helped it."

"Thank you!" said the girl. "That was not what I asked you. I *know* what my father meant to do, and I didn't need any reassurance. I'm sorry to have troubled you with all these irrelevant questions; and I thank you very much for the kind advice you have given me."

"Oh, don't take it so!" he entreated simply. "I do wish to be of use to you—all the use that the best friend in the world can be; and I see that I have wounded you. Don't take my words amiss; I'm sure you couldn't take my will so, if you knew it! If the worst that anybody has said about your father were ten times true, it couldn't change my will, or"—

"Thank you! Thank you!" she said perversely. "I don't think we understand each other, Mr. Hilary. It's scarcely worth while to try. I think I must say good bye. My sister will be expecting me"— She nodded, and he stood aside lifting his hat. She dashed by him, and he remained staring after her till she vanished in the curve of the avenue. She suddenly reappeared and came quickly back toward him. "I wanted to say that no matter what you think or say, I shall never forget what you have done, and I shall always be grateful for it." She launched these words fiercely at him, as if they were a form of defiance, and then whirled away, and was quickly lost to sight again.

———

THAT EVENING Adeline said to her sister at the end of the meagre dinner they allowed themselves in these days, "Elbridge says the hay is giving out, and we have got to do something about those horses that are eating their heads off in the barn. And the cows: there's hardly any feed for them."

"We must take some of the money and buy feed," said Suzette passively. Adeline saw by her eyes that she had been crying; she did not ask her why; each knew why the other cried.

"I'm afraid to," said the elder sister. "It's going so fast, as it is, that I don't know what we shall do, pretty soon. I think we ought to sell some of the cattle."

"We can't. We don't know whether they're ours."

"Not ours?"

"They may belong to the creditors. We must wait till the trial is over."

Adeline made no answer. They had disputed enough about that trial, which they understood so little. Adeline had always believed they ought to speak to a lawyer about it; but Suzette had not been willing. Even when a man came that morning with a paper which he said was an attachment and left it with them, they had not agreed to ask advice. For one thing they did not know whom to ask. Northwick had a lawyer in Boston; but they had been left to the ignorance in which most women live concerning such matters, and they did not know his name.

Now Adeline resolved to act upon a plan of her own that

154

she had kept from Suzette because she thought Suzette would not like it. Her sister went to her room after dinner, and then Adeline put on her things and let herself softly out into the night. She took that paper the man had left, and she took the deeds of the property which her father had given her soon after her mother died, while Sue was a little girl. He said that the deeds were recorded, and that she could keep them safely enough, and she had kept them ever since in the box where her old laces were, and her mother's watch, that had never been wound up since her death.

Adeline was not afraid of the dark on the road or in the lonely village-streets; but when she rang at the lawyer Putney's door her heart beat so with fright that it seemed as if it must jump out of her mouth. She came to him because she had always heard that in spite of his sprees he was the smartest lawyer in Hatboro'; and she believed that he could protect their rights if any one could. At the same time she wished justice to be done, though they should suffer, and she came to Putney partly because she knew he had always disliked her father, and she reasoned that such a man would be less likely to advise her against the right in her interest than a friendlier person.

Putney came to the door himself as he was apt to do at night when he was in the house, and she saw him control his surprise at sight of her. "Can I see—see—see you a moment," she stammered out, "about some—some law business?"

"Certainly," said Putney with grave politeness. "Will you come in?" He led the way into the parlor where he was reading, when she rang, and placed a chair for her, and then shut the parlor door, and waited for her to offer him the papers that rattled in her nervous clutch.

"It's this one that I want to show you first," she said, and she gave him the writ of attachment. "A man left it this noon, and we don't know what it means."

"It means," said Putney, "that your father's creditors have brought suit against his estate, and have attached his property so that you cannot sell it or put it out of your hands in any way. If the court declares him insolvent, then everything belonging to him must go to pay his debts."

"But what can we do? We can't buy anything to feed the stock, and they will suffer!" cried Adeline.

"I don't think long," said Putney. "Some one will be put in charge of the place, and then the stock will be taken care of by the creditors."

"And will they turn us out? Can they take our house? It is our house—mine and my sister's; here are the deeds that my father gave me long ago; and he said they were recorded." Her voice grew shrill.

Putney took the deeds, and glanced at the recorder's endorsement, before he read them. He seemed to Adeline a long time; and she had many fears till he handed them back to her. "The land, and the houses and all the buildings are yours and your sister's, Miss Northwick, and your father's creditors can't touch them."

The tears started from Adeline's eyes; she fell weakly back in her chair and let them run silently down her worn face. After a while Putney said, gently, "Was this all you wanted to ask me?"

"That is all," Adeline answered, and she began blindly to put her papers together. He helped her. "How much is there to pay?" she asked, with an anxiety she could not keep out of her voice.

"Nothing. I haven't done you any legal service. Almost any man you showed those papers to could have told you as much as I have." She tried to gasp out some acknowledgments and protests as he opened the doors for her. At the outer threshold he said, "Why, you're alone!"

"Yes. I'm not at all afraid"—

"I will go home with you." Putney caught his hat from the rack, and plunged into a shabby over coat that dangled under it.

Adeline tried to refuse, but she could not. She was trem-

bling so that it seemed as if she could not have set one foot before the other without help. She took his arm, and stumbled
along beside him through the quiet, early spring night.

After a while he said, "Miss Northwick, there's a little piece
of advice I *should* like to give you."

"Well?" she quavered meekly.

"Don't let anybody lead you into the expense of trying to
fight this case with the creditors. It wouldn't be any use. Your
father was deeply involved"—

"He had been unfortunate, but he didn't do anything
wrong!" Adeline hastened to put in, nervously.

"It isn't a question of that," said Putney, with a smile which
he could safely indulge in the dark. "But he owed a great deal
of money, and his creditors will certainly be able to establish
their right to everything but the real estate."

"My sister never wished to have anything to do with the
trial. We intended just to let it go."

"That's the best way," Putney said.

"But I wanted to know whether they could take the house
and the place from us."

"That was right, and I assure you they can't touch either.
If you get anxious, come to me again—as often as you like."

"I will indeed, Mr. Putney," said the old maid submissively. She let him walk home with her, and up the avenue till
they came in sight of the house. Then she plucked her hand
away from his arm, and thanked him, with a pathetic little
titter. "I don't know what Suzette would say if she knew I had
been to consult you," she suggested.

"It's for you to tell her," said Putney, seriously. "But you'd
better act together. You will need all your joint resources in
that way."

"Oh, I shall tell her," said Adeline. "I'm not sorry for it
and I think just as you do, Mr. Putney."

"Well, I'm glad you do," said Putney, as if it were a favor.

When he reached home his wife asked, "Where in the world
have you been, Ralph?"

"Oh, just philandering round in the dark a little with Adeline Northwick."

"Ralph, what *do* you mean?"

He told her, and they were moved and amused together at the strange phase their relation to the Northwicks had taken. "To think of her coming to you, of all people in the world, for advice in her trouble!"

"Yes," said Putney. "But I was always a great friend of her father's, you know, Ellen."

"Ralph!"

"Oh, I may have spent my whole natural life in denouncing him as demoralization incarnate, and a curse to the community, but I always *liked* him, Ellen. Yes, I loved J. Milton, and I was merely waiting for him to prove himself a first class scoundrel, to find out just how *much* I loved him. I've no doubt but if we could have him among us again, in the attractive garb of the state's prison inmates I should be hand and glove with brother Northwick."

XXIV

ADELINE's reasons for going to Putney in their trouble had to avail with Suzette against the prejudice they had always felt towards him. In the tangible and immediate pressure that now came upon them they were glad to be guided by his counsel; they both believed it was dictated by a knowledge of law and a respect for justice, and by no regard for them. They had a comfort in it for this reason, and they freely relied upon it as in some sort the advice of an honest and faithful enemy. They remembered that the last evening he was with them, their father had spoken leniently of Putney's infirmity, and admiringly of his wasted ability. Now each step they took was at his suggestion. They left the great house before the creditors were put in possession of the personal property, and went to live in the porter's lodge at the gate of the avenue, which they furnished with the few things they could claim for their own out of their former belongings, and from the ready money Suzette had remaining in her name at the bank. They abandoned everything of value in the house they had left, even to their richer dresses and their jewels: they preferred to do this, and Putney approved; he saw that it saved them more than it cost them in their helpless pride.

The Newtons continued in their quarters unmolested; the furniture was theirs and the building belonged to the North-wick girls, as the Newtons called them. Mrs. Newton went every day to help them to get going in their new place, and Elbridge and she lived there for a few weeks with them, till they said they should not be afraid to stay alone. He stood guard over their rights as far as he could ascertain them in the spoliation that had to come. He locked the avenue gate against the approach of those who came to the assignee's sale, and made them enter and take away their purchases by the farm road; and in all lawful ways he rendered himself obstructive and inconvenient.

His deference to the law was paid entirely through Putney, whose smartness inspired Elbridge with a respect he felt for no other virtue in man. Putney arranged with him to take the Northwick place and manage it on shares for the Northwick girls; he got for him two of the old horses which Elbridge wanted for his work, and one of the cheaper cows. The rest of the stock was sold to gentlemen farmers round about, who had fancies for costly cattle; the horses, good, bad and indifferent, were sent to a sale stable in Boston. The greenhouses were stripped of all that was valuable in them, and nothing was left upon the place, of its former equipment, except the few farm implements, a cart or two, and an ancient carryall that Putney bid off for Newton's use.

Then, when all was finished he advertised the house to let for a term of years, and failing a permanent tenant before the season opened he rented it to an adventurous landlady who proposed to fill it with summer boarders, and who engaged to pay a rental for it monthly in advance that would enable the Northwick girls to live on in the porter's lodge without fear of want. For the future Putney imagined a scheme for selling off some of the land next the villas of South Hatboro', in lots to suit purchasers. That summer sojourn had languished several years in uncertainty of its own fortunes; but now, by a caprice of the fashion which is sending people more and more to the country for the spring and fall months, it was looking up decidedly. Property had so rapidly appreciated there that Putney thought of asking so much a foot, for the Northwick land, instead of offering it by the acre.

In proposing to become a land operator, on behalf of his clients, he had to reconcile his practice with theories he had held concerning unearned land-values; and he justified himself to his crony Dr. Morrell on the ground that these might be justly taken from such rich and idle people as wanted to spend the spring and fall at South Hatboro'. The more land at a high price you could get into the hands of the class South Hatboro' was now attracting, and make them pay the bulk of the town tax, the better for the land that working men wanted to get a living on. In helping the Northwick girls to keep all they could out of the clutches of their father's creditors, he held that he was only defending their rights; and any fight against a corporation was a kind of holy war. He professed to be getting on very comfortably with his conscience, and he promised that he would not let it worry other people. To Mr. Gerrish he made excuses for taking charge of the affairs of two friendless women when he ought to have joined Gerrish in punishing them for their father's sins, as any respectable man would. He asked Gerrish to consider the sort of fellow he had always been, drinking up his own substance while Gerrish was thriftily devouring other people's houses, and begged him to make allowance for him.

The anomalous relation he held to the Northwicks afforded him so much excitement and enjoyment, that he passed his devil's dividend, as he called his quarterly spree. He kept straight, longer than his fellow citizens had known him to do for many years. But Putney was one of those men who could not be credited by people generally with the highest motives. He too often made a mock of what people generally regarded as the highest motives; he puzzled and affronted them; and as none of his most intimate friends could claim that he was respectable in the ordinary sense of the word, people generally attributed interested motives, or at least cynical motives to him. Adeline Northwick profitted by a call she made upon Doctor Morrell for advice about her dyspepsia to sound him in regard to Putney's management of her affairs; and if the doctor's powders had not so distinctly done her good she might not have been able to rely upon the assurance he gave her that Putney was acting wisely and most disinterestedly toward her and her sister.

"He has such a strange way of talking, sometimes," she said.

But she clung to Putney, and relied upon him in everything, not so much because she implicitly trusted him, as because she knew no one else to trust. The kindness that Mr. Hilary had shown for them in the first of their trouble had of course become impossible to both the sisters. He had in fact necessarily ceased to offer it directly, and Sue had steadily rejected all the overtures Louise made her since they last met. Louise wanted to come again to see her; but Sue evaded her proposals; at last she would not answer her letters; and their friendship outwardly ceased. Louise did not blame her; she accounted for her, and pitied and forgave her; she said it was what she herself would do in Sue's place, but probably if she had continued herself she would not have done what Sue did even in Sue's place. She remembered Sue with a tender constancy when she could no longer openly approach her without hurting more than she helped; and before the day of the assignee's sale came, she thought out a scheme which Wade carried into effect with Putney's help. Those things of their own that the sisters had meant to sacrifice, were bidden off, and restored to them in such a way that it was not possible for them to refuse to take back the dresses, the jewels, the particular pieces of furniture which Louise associated with them.

Each of the sisters dealt with the event in her sort; Adeline simply exalted in getting her things again; Sue gave all hers into Adeline's keeping, and bade her never let her see them.

Part Second

I

Northwick kept up the mental juggle he had used in getting himself away from Hatboro', and as far as Ponkwasset Junction he made believe that he was going to leave the main line, and take the branch road to the mills. He had a thousand mile ticket, and he had no baggage check to define his destination; he could stop off and get on where he pleased. At first he let the conductor take up the mileage on his ticket as far as Ponkwasset Junction; but when he got there he kept on with the train northward, in the pretence that he was going on as far as Willoughby Junction, to look after some business of his quarries. He verified his pretence by speaking of it to the conductor who knew him; he was not a person to take conductors into his confidence, but he felt obliged to account to the man for his apparent change of mind. He was at some trouble to make it seem casual and insignificant, and he wondered if the conductor meant to insinuate anything by saying in return that it was a pretty brisk day to be knocking round much in a stone quarry. Northwick smiled in saying, It was, rather; he watched the conductor to see if he should betray any particular interest in the matter when he left him. But the conductor went on punching the passengers' tickets and seemed to forget Northwick as soon as he left him. At the next station, Northwick followed him out on the platform to find if he sent any telegram off. When he had once given way to this anxiety, which he knew to be perfectly stupid and futile, he had to yield to it at every station. He took his bag with him each time he left the car, and he meant not to go back if he saw the conductor telegraphing. It was intensely cold, and in spite of the fierce heat of the stove at the end of the car, the frost gathered thickly on the windows. The train creaked, when it stopped and started, as if it were crunching along on a bed of dry snow; the noises of the wheels seemed at times to lose their rhythmical cadence, and then Northwick held his breath for fear one of them might be broken. He had a dread of accident such as he had never felt before; his life had never seemed so valuable to him as now; he reflected that it was so because it was to be devoted now to retrieving the past, in a new field under new conditions. His life in this view was not his own; it was a precious trust which he held for others, first for his children, and then for those whom he was finally to save from loss by the miscarriage of his enterprises. He justified himself anew in what he was intending; it presented itself as a piece of self sacrifice, a sacred duty which he was bound to fulfill. All the time he knew that he was a defaulter who had used the money in his charge, and tampered with the record so as to cover up the fact, and that he was now absconding and was carrying off a large sum of money that was not morally his. At one of the stations where he got out to see whether the conductor was telegraphing, he noticed the conductor eyeing his bag curiously; and he knew that he believed there was money in it. Northwick felt a thrill of gratified cunning in realizing how mistaken the conductor was; but he was willing the fellow should think he was carrying up money to pay off his quarry hands.

He was impatient to reach the Junction, where this conductor would leave the train, and it would continue northward in the charge of another man; he seldom went beyond Willoughby on that road, and the new conductor would hardly know him. He meant to go on to Blackbrook Junction and take the New England Central there for Montreal; but he saw the conductor go to the telegraph office at Willoughby Junction, and it suddenly occurred to him that he must not go to

Montreal by a route so direct that any absconding defaulter would be expected to take it. He had not the least proof that the conductor's dispatch had anything to do with him; but he could not help acting as if it had. He said good day to the conductor as he passed him, and he went out of the station with his bag, as if he were going up into the town. He watched till he saw the conductor go off in another direction, and then he came back, and got aboard the train just as it was drawing out of the station. He knew that he was not shadowed in any way, but his consciousness of stealth was such that he felt as if he were followed, and that he must act so as to baffle and mislead pursuit.

At Blackbrook where the train stopped for dinner, he was aware that no one knew him, and he ate hungrily; he felt strengthened and encouraged, and he began to react against the terror that had possessed him. He perceived that it was senseless and ridiculous, that the conductor could not possibly have been telegraphing about him from Willoughby, and there was as yet no suspicion abroad concerning him; he might go freely anywhere by any road.

But he had now let the New England Central train leave without him, and it only remained for him to push on to Wellwater where he hoped to connect with the Boston train for Montreal on the Union and Dominion road. He remembered that this train divided at Wellwater and certain cars ran direct to Quebec, up through Sherbrooke and Lennoxville. He meant to go from Montreal to Quebec, but now he questioned whether he had better not go straight on from Wellwater; when he recalled the long, all-night ride without a sleeper which he had once made on that route many summers before, he said to himself that in his shaken condition he must not run the risk of such a hardship. If he were to get sick from it, or die, it would be as bad as a railroad accident. The word now made him think of what Hilary had said, Hilary who had called him a thief. He would show Hilary whether he was a thief or not, give him time; he would make him eat his words, and he figured Hilary retracting and apologizing in the presence of the whole board; Hilary apologized handsomely and Northwick forgave him, while it was also passing through his mind that he must reduce the risks of railroad accident to a minimum by shortening the time. They reduced the risks of ocean travel in that way, by reducing the time, and logically the fastest ship was the safest. If he could get to Montreal from Wellwater in four or five hours, when it would take him twelve hours to get to Quebec, it was certainly his duty to go to Montreal. First of all he must put himself out of danger of every kind. He must not even fatigue himself too much; and he decided to telegraph on to Wellwater and secure a seat in the Pullman car to Montreal. He had been traveling all day in the ordinary car, and he had found it very rough.

It suddenly occurred to him that he must now assume a false name; and he reflected that he must take one that sounded like his own, or else he would not answer promptly and naturally to it. He chose Warwick, and he kept saying it over to himself while he wrote his dispatch to the station-master at Wellwater asking him to secure a chair in the Pullman. He was pleased with the choice he had made; it seemed like his own name when spoken, and yet very unlike when written. But while he congratulated himself on his quickness and sagacity, he was aware of something detached, almost alien, in the operation of his mind. It did not seem to be working normally; he could govern it but it was like something trying to get away from him, like a headstrong, restive horse. The notion suggested the colt that had fallen lame; he wondered if Elbridge would look carefully after it; and then he thought of all the other horses. A torment of heartbreaking homesickness seized him; his love for his place, his house, his children, seemed to turn against him, and to tear him and leave him bleeding, like the evil spirit in the demoniac among the tombs. He was in such misery, with his longing for his children that he thought it must show in his face, and he made a feint of having to rise and rearrange his overcoat so that he could catch sight of himself in the mirror at the end of the car. His face betrayed nothing; it looked, as it always did, like the face of a kindly, respectable man, a financially reliable face, the face of a leading citizen. He gathered courage and strength from it to put away the remorse that was devouring him. If that was the way he looked, that was the way he must be; and he could only be leaving those so dear to him for some good purpose. He recalled that his purpose was to clear the name they bore from the cloud that must fall upon it; to rehabilitate himself; to secure his creditors from final loss. This was a good purpose, the best purpose that a man in his place could have; he recollected that he was to be careful of his life and health because he had dedicated himself to this purpose.

He determined to keep this purpose steadily in mind, not to lose thought of it for an instant; it was his only refuge. Then a new anguish seized him; a doubt that swiftly became certainty; and he knew that he had signed that despatch Northwick and not Warwick; he saw just how his signature looked on the yellow manilla paper of the telegraph blank. Now he saw what a fool he had been to think of sending any dispatch. He cursed himself under his breath, and in the same breath he humbly prayed to God for some way of escape. His terror made it certain to him that he would be arrested as soon as he reached Wellwater. That would be the next stop, the conductor told him, when he halted him with the question on his way through the cars. The conductor said they were behind time, and Northwick knew by the frantic pull of the train that they were running to make up the loss. It would simply be death to jump from the car; and he must not die, he must run the risk. In his prayer he bargained with God that if He would let him escape, he would give every thought, every breath to making up the loss of his creditors; he half promised to return the money he was carrying away, and trust to his own powers, his business talent in a new field, to retrieve himself. He resolved to hide himself as soon as he reached Wellwater; it would be dark, and he hoped that by this understanding with Providence he could elude the officer in getting out of the car. But if there were two, one at each end of the car?

There was none, and Northwick walked away from the station with the other passengers, who were going to the hotel near the station for supper. In the dim light of the failing day and the village lamps he saw with a kind of surprise the deep snow and felt the strong still cold of the winterland he had been journeying into. The white drifts were everywhere; the vague level of the frozen lake stretched away from the hotel like a sea of snow; on its edge lay the excursion steamer in which Northwick had one summer made the tour of the lake with his family long ago.

He was only a few miles from the Canadian frontier; with a rebound from his anxiety, he now exulted in the safety he had already experienced. He remained tranquilly eating after the departure of the Montreal train was cried; and when he was left almost alone the headwaiter came to him and said, "Your train's just going, sir."

"Thank you," he answered, "I'm going out on the Quebec line." He wanted to laugh, in thinking how he had baffled fate. Now, if any inquiry were made for him it would be at the Montreal train before it started, or at the next station, which was still within the American border, on that line. But on the train for Quebec, which would reach Stanstead in half an hour, he would be safe from conjecture, even, thanks to that dispatch asking for a chair on the Montreal Pullman. The Quebec train was slow in starting; but he did not care; he walked up and down the platform, and waited patiently. He no longer thought with anxiety of the long all-night ride before him. If he did not choose to keep straight on to Quebec, he could stop at Lennoxville or Sherbrooke, and take up his journey again the next day. At Stanstead he ceased altogether to deal with the past in his thoughts. He was now safe from it beyond any possible peradventure, and he began to plan for the future. He had prepared himself for the all-night ride, if he should decide to take it, with a cup of strong coffee at Wellwater, and he was alert in every faculty. His mind worked nimbly and docilely now, with none of that perversity which had troubled him during the day with the fear that he was going wrong in it. His thought was clear and quick, and it obeyed his will like a part of it; that sense of duality in himself no longer agonized him. He took a calm and prudent survey of the work before him; and he saw how essential it was that he should make no false step, but should act at every moment with the sense that he was merely the agent of others in the effort to retrieve his losses.

II

AT STANSTEAD a party of three gentlemen came into the car
and their talk presently found its way through Northwick's
revery, at first as an interruption, an annoyance, and afterwards as a matter of intensifying personal interest to him.
They were in very good spirits, and they made themselves at
home in the car; there were only a few other passengers. They
were going to Montreal, as he easily gathered, and some
friends were to join them at the next junction, and go on
with them. They talked freely of an enterprise which they
wished to promote in Montreal; and they were very confident
of it, if they could get the capital. One of them said, It was a
thing that would have been done long ago, if the Yankees had
been in it. "Well, we may strike a rich defaulter, in Montreal," another said, and they all laughed. Their laughter shocked
Northwick; it seemed immoral; he remembered that though
he might seem a defaulter, he was a man with a sacred trust,
and a high purpose. But he listened eagerly: if their enterprise were one that approved itself to his judgment, the chance
of their discussing it before him might be a leading of Providence which he would be culpable to refuse. Providence had
answered his prayer in permitting him to pass the American
frontier safely, and Northwick must not be derelict in fulfilling his part of the agreement. The Canadians borrowed
the brakeman's lantern, and began to study a map which they
spread out on their knees. The one who seemed first among
them put his finger on a place in the map, and said that was

he spot. It was in the region just back of Chicoutimi. Gold
ad always been found there, but not in paying quantity. It
ost more to mine it than it was worth; but with the applica-
ion of this new process of working up the tailings, there was
io doubt of the result. It was simply wealth beyond the dreams
f avarice.

Northwick had heard that song before; and he fell back in
is seat with a smile that was perhaps too cynical for a partner
f Providence, but which was natural in a man of his experi-
nce. He knew something about processes to utilize the tail-
igs of gold mines which would not otherwise pay for work-
ig; he had paid enough for his knowledge: so much that if
e still had the purchase-money he need not be going into
xile now and beginning life under a false name, in a strange
ind.

By and by he found himself listening again, and he heard
he Canadian saying, "And there's timber enough on the tract
ɔ pay twice over what it will cost, even if the mine wasn't
orth a penny."

"Well, we might go down and see the timber, any way,"
iid one of the party who had not yet spoken much. "And
ien we could take a look at Markham's soap-mine, too. Un-
ɛss," he added, "you had to tunnel under a hundred feet of
iow to get at it. A good deal like diggin' the north pole up
y the roots, wouldn't it be?"

"Oh, no! Oh, no!" said he who seemed to be Markham,
vith the optimism of an enthusiast. "There's no trouble about
:. We've got some shanties that we put up about the mouth
f the hole in the ground we made in the autumn, and you
an see the hole without digging at all. Or at least you could
i the early part of January, when I was down there."

"The hole hadn't run away?"

"No. It was just where we left it."

"Well, that's encouragin'. But I say, Markham, how do
ou get down there in the winter?"

"Oh, very easily. Simplest thing in the world. Lots of fellows in the lumber trade do it all winter long. Do it by sleigh from St. Anne's, about twenty miles below Quebec—from Quebec you have your choice of train or sleigh. But I prefer to make a clean thing of it, and do it all by sleigh. I take it by easy stages, and so I take the long route; there's a short cut but the stops are far between. You make your twenty miles to St. Anne from Quebec one day; eighteen to St. Joachim, the next; thirty nine to Baie St. Paul the next; twenty to Mal baie the next; then forty to Tadoussac; then eighteen to Rivière Marguerite. You can do something every day, at that rate, even in new snow; but on the ice of the Saguenay to Ha ha Bay there's a pull of sixty miles; you're at Chicoutimi eleven miles further, before you know it. Good feed, and good beds all along. You wrap up, and you don't mind. Of course," Markham concluded, "it isn't the climate of Stanstead," as if the climate of Stanstead were something like that of St. Augustine.

"Well, it sounds a mere bagatelle," said the more talkative of the other two, "but it takes a week of steady travel."

"What is a week on the way to Golconda, if Golconda's yours when you get there?" said Markham. "Why, Watkins, the young spruce and poplar alone on that tract are worth twice the price I ask for the whole. A pulp mill, which you could knock together for a few shillings, on one of those magnificent water powers, would make you all millionaires in a single summer."

"And what would it do in the winter when your magnificent water power was restin'?"

"Work harder than ever, my dear boy, and set an example of industry to all the lazy *habitans* in the country. You could get your fuel for the cost of cutting, and you could feed your spruce and poplar in under your furnace, and have it come out paper pulp at the other end of the mill."

Watkins and the other listener laughed with loud haw haws at Markham's drolling, and Watkins said, "I say, Markham, weren't you born on the other side of the line?"

"No. But my father was; and I wish he'd staid there till I came. Then I'd be going round with all the capitalists of Wall street fighting for a chance to put their money into my mine, instead of wearing out the knees of my trousers before you Canucks, begging you not to slap your everlasting fortune in the face."

They now all roared together again, and at Sherbrooke they changed cars.

Northwick had to change, too, but he did not try to get into the same car with them. He wanted to think, to elaborate in his own mind the suggestion for his immediate and remoter future which he had got from their talk; and he dreaded the confusion, and possibly he dreaded the misgiving that might come from hearing more of their talk. He thought he knew, now, just what he wanted to do, and he did not wish to be swerved from it.

He felt eager to get on, but he was not impatient. He bore very well the long waits that he had to make both at Sherbrooke and Richmond; but when the train left the Junction for Quebec at last, he settled himself in his seat with a solider content than he had felt before, and gave himself up to the pleasure of shaping the future that was so obediently plastic in his fancy. The brakeman plied the fierce stove at the end of the car with fuel, and Northwick did not suffer from the cold that strengthened and deepened with the passing night outside, though he was not overcoated and booted for any such temperature as his fellow travellers seemed prepared for. They were all Canadians, and they talked now and then in their broad voweled French, but their voices were low, and they came and went quietly at the country stations. The car was old and worn and badly hung; but in spite of all, Northwick drowsed in the fervor of the glowing stove, and towards morning he fell into a long and dreamless sleep.

He woke from it with a vigor and freshness that surprised him, and found the train pulling into the station at Pointe Levis. The sun burned like a soft lamp through the thick frost on the car-window; when he emerged, he found it a cloudless splendor on a world of snow. The vast landscape, which he had seen in summer all green from the edge of the mighty rivers to the hilltops losing themselves in the blue distance, showed rounded and diminished in the immeasurable drifts that filled it, and that hid the streams in depths almost as great above their ice as those of the currents below. The villages of the habitans sparkled from tinned roof and spire, and the city before him rose from shore and cliff with a thousand plumes of silvery smoke. In and out among the frozen shipping swarmed an active life that turned the rivers into high roads, and speckled the expanses of glistening white with single figures and groups of men and horses.

It was all gay and bizarre, and it gave Northwick a thrill of boyish delight. He wondered for a moment why he had never come to Quebec in winter before, and brought his children. He beckoned to the walnut faced driver of one of the carrioles which waited outside the station to take the passengers across the river, and tossed his bag into the bottom of the little sledge. He gave the name of a hotel in the upper town, and the driver whipped his tough, long-fetlocked pony over the space of ice kept clear of snow by diligent sweeping with fir tree tops, and then up the steep incline of Mountain Hill. The streets were roadways from house-front to house-front, smooth, elastic levels of thickly bedded, triply frozen snow; and the foot passengers, muffled to the eyes against the morning cold, came and went among the vehicles in the middle of the street, or crept along close to the housewalls to keep out of the light avalanches of an overnight snow that slipt here and there from the steep tin roofs.

Northwick's unreasoned gladness grew with each impression of the beauty and novelty. It quickened associations of his earliest days, and of the winter among his native hills. He felt that life could be very pleasant in this latitude; he relinquished the notion he had cherished at times of going to South America with his family in case he should finally fail to arrange with the company for his safe return home; he forecast a future in Quebec where he could build a new home for his children among scenes that need not be all so alien. This did not move him from his fixed intention to retrieve himself, though it gave him the courage of indefinitely expanded possibilities. He was bent upon the scheme he had in mind, and as soon as he finished his breakfast he went out to prepare for it.

III

———

THE INN he had chosen was one which he remembered from former visits to Quebec as having seemed a resort of old world folk of humble fortunes. He got a room, and went to it long enough to count the money he had with him, and find it safe. Then he took one of the notes from the others, and went to a broker's to get it changed.

The amount seemed to give the broker pause; but he concerned himself only with the genuineness of the greenback, and after a keen glance at Northwick's unimpeachable face, he paid over the thousand dollars in Canadian bills. "We used to make your countrymen give us something over," he said with a smile for all recognition of Northwick's nationality.

"Yes; that's all changed, now," returned Northwick. "Do I look so very American?" he asked.

"Oh, I don't know that," said the broker, with an airy English inflection. "I suppose it's your hard hat, as much as anything. We all wear fur caps in such weather."

"Ah, that's a good idea," said Northwick. He spoke easily, but with a nether torment of longing to look at the newspaper lying open on the counter. He could see that it was the morning paper; there might be something about him in it. The thought turned him faint; but he knew that if the paper happened to have anything about him, in it, any rumor of his offence, any conjecture of his flight he could not bear it. He could bear to keep himself deaf and blind to the self he had put behind him; but he could not bear anything less. The

176

papers seemed to thrust themselves upon him; newsboys followed him up in the street with them; he saw them in all the shops, where he went for the fur cap and fur overcoat he bought, for the underclothing and the changes of garments that he had to provide; for the belt he got to put his money in. This great sum, which he dared not bank, must be carried about with him; it must not leave him night or day; it must be buckled into the chamois belt and worn round his waist, sleeping and waking. The belt was really for gold, but the forty-two thousand-dollar notes, which were not a great bulk, would easily go into it.

He returned to his hotel and changed them to it, and put the belt on. Then he felt easier, and he looked up the landlord to ask about the route he wished to take. He found, as he expected, that it was one very commonly travelled by lumber merchants going down into the woods to look after their logging camps. Some took a sleigh from Quebec; but the landlord said it was just as well to go by train to St. Anne, and save that much sleighing; you would get enough of it, then. Northwick thought so, too, and after the early dinner they gave him he took the cars for St. Anne.

He was not tired; he was curiously buoyant and strong. He thought he might get a nap on the way; but he remained vividly awake; and even that night he did not sleep much. He felt again that pulling of his mind, as if it were something separate from him, and were struggling to get beyond the control of his will. The hotel in the little native village was very good in its way; he had an excellent supper and an easy bed; but he slept brokenly and he was awake long before the early breakfast which he had ordered for his start next day. The landlord wished to persuade him that there was no need of such great haste; it was only eighteen miles to St. Joachim, where he was to make his first stop, and the road was so good that he would get there in a few hours. He had better stop and visit the church and see the sick people's offerings which they left there every year in gratitude to the saint for healing them of their maladies. The landlord said it was a pity he could not come some time at the season of the pilgrimage; his countrymen often came then. Northwick perceived that in spite of his fur cap and overcoat, and his great Canadian boots he was easily recognizable for an American to this man though he could not definitely decide whether his landlord was French or Irish, and could not tell whether it was in earnest or in irony that he invited him to try St. Anne for any trouble he happened to be suffering from. But he winced at the suggestion, while his heart leaped at the fantastic thought of hanging that money belt at her altar and so easing himself of all his pains. He grotesquely imagined the American defaulters in Canada making a pilgrimage to St. Anne, and devoting emblems of their moral disease to her: forged notes, bewitched accounts, false statements. At the same time, with that part of him which seemed obedient he asked the landlord if he knew of the gold discoveries on the Chicoutimi river, and tried to account for himself as an American speculator going to look into the matter in his own way and at his own time.

In spite of his uncertainty about the landlord in some ways, Northwick found him a kindly young fellow. He treated Northwick with a young fellow's comfortable deference for an elderly man, and helped him forget the hurts to his respectability which rankled so when he remembered them. He explained the difference between the two routes from Malbaie on, and advised him to take the longer, which lay through a more settled district, where he would be safer in case of any mischance. But if he liked to take the shorter, he told him, there were good *campes*, or log house stations, every ten or fifteen miles, where he would find excellent meals and beds, and be well cared for by people who kept them in the winter for travellers. Ladies sometimes made the journey on that route, which the government had lately opened; and the mails were carried that way; he could take passage with the mail carrier.

This fact determined Northwick. He shrank from trusting

himself in government keeping though he knew he would be safe in it. He said he would go by Tadoussac; and the land-lord found a carriole driver, with a tough little Canadian horse, who agreed to go the whole way to Chicoutimi with him.

After an early lunch the man came, with the low-bodied sledge, set on runners of solid wood, and deeply bedded with bearskins for the lap and back. The day was still and sunny, like the day before, and the air, which drove keenly against his face, with the rush of the carriole, sparkled with particles of frost that sometimes filled it like a light shower of snow. The drive was so short that he reached St. Joachim at noon, and he decided to push on part of the way to Baie St. Paul after din-ner. His host at St. Joachim approved of that. "You goin' have snow tonight, and big drift tomorrow," he said, and he gave his driver the name of an habitant whom they could stop the night with. The driver was silent and he looked sinister; Northwick thought how easily the man might murder him on that lonely road and make off with the money in his belt; how probably he would do it if he dreamed that such wealth was within his grasp. But the man did not notice him after their journey began, except once to turn round and say, "Look out you' nose. You goin' freeze him." For the rest he talked to his horse, which was lazy, and which he kept urging forward with, "Marche donc! Marche donc!" finally shortened to " 'Ch donc! 'Ch donc!" and repeated and repeated at regular inter-vals like the tolling of a bell. It made Northwick think of a bell-buoy off a ledge of rocks, which he had spent a summer near. He wished to ask the man to stop, but he reflected that the waves would not let him stop; he had to keep tolling.

Northwick started. He must be going out of his mind, or else he was drowsing. Perhaps he was freezing, and this was the beginning of the death drowse. But he felt himself warm un-der his furs, where he touched himself, and he knew he had merely been dreaming. He let himself go again, and arrived at his own door in Hatboro'. He saw the electric lights through the long piazza windows, and he was going to warn Elbridge again about that colt's shoes. Then he heard a sharp fox-like barking, and found that his carriole had stopped at the cabin of the habitant who was to keep him over night. The open doorway was filled with children; the wild-looking dogs leaping at his horse's nose were in a frenzy of curiosity and suspicion.

Northwick rose from his nap refreshed physically but with a desolate and sinking heart. The vision of his home had taken all his strength away with it; but from his surface consciousness he returned the greeting of the man with a pipe in his mouth and what looked like a blue stocking on his head, who welcomed him. It was a poor place within, but it had a comfort and kindliness of its own, and it was well warmed from the great oblong stove of castiron set in the partition of the two rooms. The meal that the housewife got him was good and savory, but he had no relish for it, and he went early to bed. He did not understand much French, and he could not talk with the people, but he heard them speak of him as an old man, with a sort of surprise and pity at his being there. He felt this surprise and pity, too; it seemed such a wild and wicked thing that he should be driven away from his home and children at his age. He tried to realize what had done it.

The habitant had given Northwick his best bed, in his large room; he went with his wife into the other and they took two or three of the younger children; the rest all scattered up into the loft; each bade the guest a well mannered good night. Before Northwick slept he heard his host get up and open the outer door. Some Indians came in, and lay down before the fire with the carriole driver.

IV

In the morning Northwick did not want to rise; but he forced himself; and that day he made the rest of the stage to Baie St. Paul. It snowed, but he got through without much interruption. The following day, however, the drifts had blocked the roads so that he did not make the twenty miles to Malbaie till after dark. He found himself bearing the journey better than he expected. He was never so tired again as that first day after St. Anne. He did not eat much or sleep much, but he felt well. The worst was that the breach between his will and his mind seemed to grow continually wider: he had a sense of the rift being like a chasm stretching farther and farther, the one side from the other. At first his mind worked clearly but disobediently; then he began to be aware of a dimness in its record of purposes and motives. At times he could not tell where he was going, or why. He reverted with difficulty to the fact that he had wished to get as far as possible not only beyond pursuit, but beyond the temptation to return voluntarily and give himself up. He knew, in those days before the treaty, that he was safe from extradition; but he feared that if a detective approached he would yield to him, and go back, especially as he could not always keep before himself the reasons for not going back. When from time to time these reasons escaped him, it seemed as if nothing could be done to him in case he went home and restored to the company the money he had brought away. It needed a voluntary operation of logic to prove that this partial restitution would not avail;

that he would be arrested, and convicted. He would not be allowed to go on living with his children in his own house. He would be taken from them, and put in prison.

He made an early start for Tadoussac, after a wakeful night. His driver wished to break the forty mile journey midway, but Northwick would not consent. The road was not so badly drifted as before, and they got through, a little after nightfall. Northwick remembered the place because it was here that the Saguenay steamer lay so long before starting up the river. He recognized in the vague nightlight, the contour of the cove, and the hills above it, with the village scattered over them. It was twenty years since he had made that trip with his wife, who had been nearly as long dead, but he recalled the place distinctly, and its summer effect; it did not seem much lonelier now than it seemed in the summer. The lamps shone from the windows where he had seen them then, when he walked about a little just after supper; the village store had a group of habitans and half breeds about its stove, and there was as much show of life in the streets as there used to be at the same hour and season in the little White Mountain village where his boyhood was passed. It did not seem so bad; if Chicoutimi were no worse he could live there well enough till he could rehabilitate himself. He imagined bringing his family there after his mills had got successfully going; then probably other people from the outside world would be living there.

He ate a hearty supper, but again he did not sleep well, and in the night he was feverish. He thought how horrible it would be if he were to fall sick there; he might die before he could get word to his children and they reach him. He thought of going back to Quebec, and sailing for Europe, and having his children join him there. They could sell the place at Hatboro', and with what it brought, and with what he had they could live comfortably in some cheap country which had no extradition treaty with the United States. He remembered reading of a defaulter who went to a little republic called San Marino somewhere in Italy, and was safe there; he found the President treading his own grape vats; and it cost nothing to live there, though it was dull, and the exile became so homesick that he returned and gave himself up. He wondered that he had not thought of that place before; then he reflected that no ships could make their way from Quebec to the sea before May, at the earliest. He would be arrested if he left any American port, or arrested as soon as he reached England. He remembered the advertisement of a line of steamships between Quebec and Brazil; he must wait for the St. Lawrence to open, and go to Brazil, and in the morning he must go back to Quebec.

But in the morning he felt so much better that he decided to keep on to Chicoutimi. He could not bear the thought of being found out by detectives at Quebec, and by reporters who would fill the press with paragraphs about him. He must die to the world, to his family, before he could hope to revisit either.

The morning was brilliant with sunlight, and the glare of the snow hurt his eyes. He went to the store to get some glasses to protect them, and he bought some laudanum to make him sleep, that night, if he should be wakeful again. It was sixty miles to Ha-ha Bay, but the road on the frozen river was good, and he could do a long stretch of it. From Rivière Marguerite, he should travel on the ice of the Saguenay, and the going would be smooth and easy.

All the landscape seemed dwarfed since he saw it in that far-off summer. The tops of the interminable solitudes that walled the river in on both sides appeared lower, as if the snow upon them weighed them down, but doubtless they had grown beyond their real height in his memory. They had lost the mystery of the summer aspect when they were dimmed with rain, or swathed in mist; all their outlines were in plain sight, and the forests that clothed them from the shore to their summits were not that unbroken gloom which they had seemed. The snow shone through their stems, and the inky river at their feet lay a motionless extent of white. As his carriole slipt lightly over it, Northwick had a fantastic sense of his own minuteness and remoteness. He thought of a photograph of a lunar landscape that he had once seen greatly magnified, and of a fly that happened to traverse the expanse of plaster-like white between the ranges of extinct volcanoes.

At times the cliffs rose from the river too sheer for the snow to lodge on; then their rocky faces shone harsh and stern; and sometimes the springs that gushed from them in summer were frozen in long streams of ice, like the tears bursting from the source of some titanic grief. These monstrous icicles, blearing the visage of the rock, which he figured as nothing but icicles, affected Northwick with an awe that he nowhere felt except when his driver slowed his carriole in front of the great Capes Trinity and Eternity, and silently pointed at them with his whip. He had no need to name them: the fugitive would have known them in another planet. It was growing late; the lonely day was waning to the lonely night. While they halted the scream of a catamount broke from the woods skirting the bay between the Capes, and repeated itself in the echo that wandered from depth to depth of the frozen wilderness, and seemed to die wailing away at the point where it first tore the silence.

Here and there at long intervals they passed a point or a recess where a saw mill stood, with a few log houses about it, and with signs of human life in the smoke that rose weakly on the thin dry air from their chimneys, or in the figures that appeared at the doorways as the carriole passed. At the next of these beyond the Capes the driver proposed to stop and pass the night, and Northwick consented. He felt worn out by his day's journey; his nerves were spent as if by a lateral pressure of the lifeless desert he had been travelling through, and by the stress of his thoughts, the intensity of his reveries. His mind ran back against his will and dwelt with his children. By this time, long before this time, they must be wild with anxiety about him; by this time their shame must have come to poison their grief. He realized it all, and he realized

that he could not, must not help them. He must not go back
to them if ever he was to live for them again. But at last he
asked why he should live, why he should not die. There was
laudanum enough in that bottle to kill him.

As he walked up from the carriole at the river's edge to the
door of the sawmiller's cabin, he drew the cork of the vial, and
poured out the poison; it followed him a few steps, a black
dribble of murder on the snow, that the miller's dog smelt
at and turned from in offence. That night he could not sleep
again; toward morning, when all the house was snoring, he
gave way to the sobs that were bursting his heart. He heard
the sleepers, men and dogs, start a little in their dreams; then
they were still, and he fell into a deep sleep.

They let him sleep late, and he had a dream of himself
which must have been caused by the nascent consciousness of
the going and coming around him. People were talking of
him, and one said how old he was; and another looked at his
long, white beard which flowed down over the blanket as far
as his waist. He told them that he wore it so, that they should
not know him when he got home; and he showed them how
he could take it off and put it on at pleasure. He started awake,
and found his carriole driver standing over him.

"You got you' sleep hout, no?"

"What time is it?" said Northwick stupidly, scanning the
man to make sure that it was he, and waiting for a full sense
of the situation to reach him.

"Nine o'clock," said the man, and he turned away.

Northwick got up, and found the place empty of the men
and dogs. A woman, who looked like a half breed, brought
him his breakfast of fried venison and bean-coffee; her little
one held by her skirt, and stared at him. He thought of Elbridge's baby that he had seen die. It seemed ages ago. He
offered the child a shilling; it shyly turned its face into its
mother's dress. The driver said, " 'E do'n' know what money
is, yet," but the mother seemed to know; she showed her teeth,
and took it for the child. Northwick sat a moment thinking,

what a strange thing it was not to know what money was; it had never occurred to him before; he asked himself a queer question: What was money? The idea of it seemed to go to pieces, as a printed word does, when you look steadily at it, and to have no meaning. It affected him as droll, fantastic, like a piece of childish make-believe, when the woman took some more money from him for his meals and lodging. But that was the way the world was worked. You could get anything done for money; it was the question of demand and supply; nothing more. He tried to think where money came in, when he went out to see Elbridge's sick boy; when Elbridge left the dead child to drive him to the station. It was something else that came in there; but that thing and money were the same, after all: he had proved his love for his children by making money for them; if he had not loved them so much he would not have tried to get so much money, and he would not have been where he was.

His mind fought away from his control, as the sledge slipped along over the frozen river again. It was very cold, but the full sun on his head afflicted him like heat. It was the blaze of light, that beat up from the snow, too. His head felt imponderable; and yet he could not hold it up. It was always sinking forward; and he woke from naps without being sure that he had been asleep.

He intended to push through that day to Chicoutimi; but his start was so late that it seemed to him as if they would never get to Ha-ha Bay. When they arrived, late in the afternoon, all sense of progress thither faded away: it was as if the starting and stopping were one, or contained in the same impulse. It might be so if he kept on eleven miles farther to Chicoutimi, but he would not be able to feel it so at the beginning; the wish could involve its accomplishment only at the end. He said to himself that this was unreasonable: it was a poor rule that would not work both ways.

This ran through his mind in the presence of the old man who bustled out of the door of the cabin where his carriole had stopped. It was larger than most of the other cabins of the place, which Northwick remembered curiously well, some with their logs bare, and some sheathed in birch bark. He remembered this man, too, when his white moustache, which branched into either ear, was a glistening brown; and the droop of his left eyelid was more like a voluntary wink. But the gayety of his face was the same, and his welcome was so cordial, that a fear of recognition went through Northwick. He knew the man for the talkative Canadian who had taken him and his wife a drive over the hills around the bay, in the morning, when their boat arrived, and afterwards stopped with them at this cabin, and had them in to drink a glass of milk. Northwick's wife liked the man, and said she would like to live in such a house in such a place, and should not be afraid of the winter that he told her was so terrible. It was almost as if her spirit were there; but Northwick said to himself that he must not let the man know that he had ever seen him before. The resolution cost him something, for he felt so broken and weak that he would have liked to claim his kindness as an old acquaintance. He would have liked to ask if he still caught wild animals for showmen, and how his trade prospered; if he had always lived at Ha-ha Bay since they met. But he was the more decided to ignore their former meeting because the man addressed him in English at once, and apparently knew him for an American. Perhaps other defaulters had been there before; perhaps the mines had brought Americans there prospecting.

"Good morning, sir!" cried the Canadian. "I am glad to see you! Let me 'elp you hout, sir. Well, it is a pleasure to speak a little English with some one! The English close hup with the river in the autumn, but it open early this year. I 'ope you are a sign of many Americans. They are the life of our country. Without the Americans we could not live. No, sir. Not a day. Come in, come in. You will find you' room ready for you, sir."

Northwick hung back suspiciously. "Were you expecting me?" he asked.

"No one!" cried the man with a shrug and opening of the

hands. "But hall the travellers they stop with Bird, and where there are honly two rooms 'eat with one stove between the walls, their room is always ready. Do me the pleasure!" He set the door open, and bowed Northwick in. "Baptiste!" he called to the driver over his shoulder, "take you' 'orse to the stable." He added a long queue of unintelligible French to his English, and the driver responded, "Hall right."

"I am the only person at Ha-ha Bay who speaks English," he said in the same terms he had used twenty years before when he presented himself to Northwick and his wife on their steamboat, and asked them if they would like to drive before breakfast. "But you must know me? Bird—Oiseau? You have been here before?"

"No," said Northwick, with one lie for all. The man, with his cheer and gayety, was even terribly familiar; and North-wick could have believed that the room and the furniture in it were absolutely unchanged. There was the little window that he knew opened on the poor vegetable garden, with its spindling corn, and its beans for soup and coffee. There was the chair his wife had sat in to look out on the things; but for the frost on the pane he could doubtless see them growing, now.

He sank into the chair, and said to himself that he should die there, and it would be as well, it would be easy. He felt very old and weak; and he did not try to take off the wraps which he had worn in the sledge. He wished that he might fall so into his grave, and be done with it.

V

BIRD walked up and down the room, talking: he seemed over-
joyed with the chance, and as if he could not forego it for a
moment. "Well, sir, I wish that I could say as much! But I
have been here forty years, hoff and on. I am born at Quebec"
—in his tremulous inattention, Northwick was aware that
the man had said the same thing to him all those years before
with the same sidelong glance for the effect of the fact upon
him—"and I came here when I was twenty. Now I am sixty.
Hall the Americans know me. I used to go into the bush with
them for bear. Lots of bear in the bush when I first came;
now they get pretty scarce. I have the best moose-dog— But I
don't care much for the hunting now; I am too hold. That's
a fact. I am sixty; and forty winters I 'ave pass at Ha-ha Bay.
You know why it is call Ha-ha Bay? It is the hecho. Well, I
don't hear much haha nowadays round this bay. But it is
pretty here in the summer; yes very pretty. Prettier than Chicoutimi; and more gold in the 'ills."

He let his bold, gay eye rest confidently on Northwick, as
if to say he knew what had brought him there, and he might
as well own the fact at once; and Northwick tried to get his
mind to grapple with his real motive. But his mind kept pulling away from him, like that unruly horse, and he could not
manage it. He knew, in that self which seemed apart from
his mind, that it would be a very good thing to let the man
suppose he was there to look into the question of the mines;
but there was something else that seemed to go with that intention: something like a wish to get away from the past, so

189

remotely and so completely, that no rumor of it should reach him till he was willing to let it; to be absent from all who had known him so long that no one of them would know him if he saw him. He was there not only to start a pulp mill, but to grow a beard that should effectually disguise him. He recalled how he had looked with that long beard in his dream; he put his hand to his chin and felt the eight days' stubble there, and he wondered how much time it would take to grow such a beard.

Bird went on talking. "I know that Chicoutimi Company. I told Markham about the gold when he was here for bear. He is smart; but he don't know heverything. You think he can make it pay with that invention? I doubt—me. There is one place in those 'ills," and Bird came closer to Northwick and dropped his voice, "where you don't 'ave to begin with the tailings. I know the place. But what's the good? All the same, you want capital."

He went to the shelf in the wall above the stove, and took a pipe which he filled with tobacco, and then he drew some coals out on the stove hearth. But before he dropped one of them on his pipe with his horny thumb and finger, he asked politely, "You hobject to the smoking?"

Northwick said he did not, and Bird said, "It is one of three things you can do here in the winter: smoke the pipe, cut the wood, court the ladies." Northwick remembered his saying that before, too, and how it had made his wife laugh. "I used to do all three. Now I smoke the pipe. Well, while you are young, it is all right, and it is fun in the woods. But I was always 'omesick for Quebec, more or less. You know what it is to be 'omesick."

The word pierced Northwick through the vagary which clothed his consciousness like a sort of fog, and made his heart bleed with self-pity.

"Well, I been 'omesick forty years, and I don't know what for, any more. I been back to Quebec; it is not the same. You know 'ow they pull down those city gate? What they want to do that for? The gate did not keep the stranger hout; it let them in! And there were too many people dead! Now I think I am 'omesick just to get away from here. If I had some capital—ten, fifteen thousand dollars—I would hopen that mine, and take hout my hundred, two hundred thousand dollar and then, Good-bye, Ha-ha Bay! I would make it hecho like it never hecho before. I don't want nothing to work up the tailings of my mine, me! There is gold enough there to pay, and I can hire those habitans cheap like dirt. What is their time worth? The bush is cut away; they got nothing to do. It is the time of a setting 'en, as you Americans say, their time."

Bird smoked away for a little while in silence, and then he seemed aware for the first time that Northwick had not taken off his wraps, and he said, hospitably, "I 'ope you will spend the night with me here?"

Northwick said, "Thank you, I don't know. Is it far to Chicoutimi?" He knew, but he asked, hoping the man would exaggerate the distance, and then he would not have to go.

"It is eleven mile, but the road is bad. Drifted."

"I will wait till to-morrow," said Northwick; and he began to unswathe and unbutton, but so feebly that Bird noticed.

"Allow me!" he said, putting down his pipe, and coming to his aid. He was very gentle, and light-handed, like a woman; but Northwick felt one touch on the pouch of his belt, and refused further help.

He let his host carry his two bags into the next room for him: the bag that he had brought with the few things from home, when he pretended that he was coming away for a day or two, and the bag that he had got in Quebec to hold the things he had to buy there. When Bird set them down beside his bed he could not bear to see the bag from home and he pushed it under out of sight. Then he tumbled himself on the bed, and pulled the bearskin robe that he found on it, up over him and fell into a thin sleep, that was not so different from his dim waking that he was sure it had been sleep when Bird came back with a lamp.

"Been 'aving a little nap?" he asked, looking gayly down on Northwick's bewildered face. "Well, that is all right! We have supper, now, pretty soon. You hungry? Well, in a 'alf-hour."

He went out again, and Northwick, after some efforts, made out to rise. His skull felt sore, and his arms as if they had been beaten with hard blows. But after he had bathed his face and hands in the warm water Bird had brought with the lamp, he found himself better, though he was still wrapped in that cloudy uncertainty of himself and of his sleeping or waking. He saw some pictures about on the coarse, white walls: the Seven Stations of the Cross in colored prints; a lithograph of Indians burning a Jesuit priest. Over the bed's head hung a chromo of Our Lady with seven swords piercing her heart; beside the bed was a parian crucifix, with the figure of Christ writhing on it.

These things made Northwick feel very far and strange. His simple and unimaginative nature could in nowise relate itself to this alien faith, this alien language. He heard soft voices of women in the next room, the first that he had heard since he last heard his daughters'. A girl's voice singing was severed by a door that closed and then opened to let it be heard a few notes more, and again closed.

But he found Bird still alone in the next room when he returned to it. "Well, now, we go to supper as soon as Father Étienne comes. He is our curate—our minister—here. And he eats with me—when he heat anywhere. I tell 'im 'e hought to have my appetite, if he wants to keep up his spiritual strength. The body is the foundation of the soul, no? Well you let that foundation tumble hin, and then where you got you' soul, heigh? But Father Étienne speaks very good English. Heducate at Rome. I am the only other educated man at Ha-ha Bay. You don't 'appen to have some papers in you' bag? French? English? It is the same!"

"Papers? No!" said Northwick, with horror and suspicion. "What is in the papers?"

"That is what I like to find hout," said Bird, spreading his hands with a shrug.

The outer door opened, and a young man in a priest's long robe came in. Bird introduced his guest, and Northwick shook hands with the priest, who had a smooth, regular face, with beautiful, innocent eyes, like a girl's. He might have been twenty eight or twenty-nine; he had the spare figure of a man under thirty who leads an active life; his features were refined by study and the thought of others. When he smiled the innocence of his face was more than girlish, it was child-like. Points of light danced in his large, soft, dark eyes; an effect of trusting, alluring kindness came from his whole radiant visage.

Northwick felt its charm with a kind of fear. He shrank away from the priest, and at table he left the talk to him and his host. They supped in a room opening into a sort of wing; beyond it was a small kitchen from which an elderly woman brought the dishes, and where that girl whom he heard singing kept trilling away as if she were excited, like a canary, by the sound of the frying meat. Bird said, by way of introduction, that the woman was his niece; but he did not waste time on her. He began to talk up his conjecture as to Northwick's business with the priest, as if it were an ascertained fact. Northwick fancied his advantage in leaving him to it. They discussed the question of gold in the hills which the young father treated as an old story of faded interest, and Bird entered into with the fervor of fresh excitement. The priest spoke of the poor return from the mines at Chaudière, but Bird claimed that it was different here. Northwick did not say anything; he listened and watched them, as if they were a pair of confidence men trying to work him. The priest seemed to be anxious to get the question off the personal ground, into the region of the abstract, and Northwick believed this was part of his game, a ruse to throw him from his guard, and commit him to something. He made up his mind to get away as early as he could in the morning; he did not think it was a safe place.

"Very well!" the priest cried, at one point. "Suppose you had the capital you wish. And suppose you had taken out all the gold you say is there, and you were rich. What would you do?"

"What I do!" Bird struck the table with his fist. "Leave Ha-ha Bay tomorrow morning!"

"And where would you go?"

"Go? To Quebec, to London, to Paris, to Rome, to the devil! Keep going!"

The young father laughed a laugh as innocent as his looks, and turned with a sudden appeal to Northwick. "Tell me a little about the rich men in your land of millionaires! How do they find their happiness? In what? What is the secret of joy that they have bought with their money?"

"I don't know what you mean," said Northwick with a recoil deeper into himself after the first flush of alarm at being addressed.

"Where do they live?"

Northwick hesitated, and the priest laid his hand on Bird's shoulder, as if to restrain a burst of information from him.

"I suppose most of them live in New York."

"All the time?"

"No. They generally have a house at the seaside, at Newport or Bar Harbor, for the summer, and one at Lenox or Tuxedo for the fall; and they go to Florida for the winter, or Nice. Then they have their yachts."

"The land is not large enough for their restlessness; they roam the sea. My son," said the young priest to the old hunter, "you can have all the advantage of riches at the expense of a gypsies' van!" He laughed again in friendly delight at Bird's supposed discomfiture; and touched him lightly, delicately, as before. "It is the same in Europe; I have seen it there, too." Bird was going to speak, but the priest stayed him a moment. "But how did your rich people get their millions? Not like those rich people in Europe by inheritance?"

"Very few," said Northwick sensible of a remnant of the

pride he used to feel in the fact, hidden about somewhere in his consciousness. "They made it."

"How? Excuse me!"

"By manufacturing, by speculating in railroad stocks, by mining, by the rise in land values."

"What causes the land to rise in value?"

"The demand for it. The necessity."

"Oh! The need of others! And when a man gains in stocks, some other man loses, no? Do the manufacturers pay the operatives all they earn? Are the miners very well paid and comfortable? I have read that they are miserable. Is it so?"

Northwick was aware that there were good and valid answers to all these questions which the priest seemed to be asking rather for the confusion of Bird than as an expression of his own opinions; but in his dazed intelligence, he could not find the answers.

Bird roared out, "Haw! Do not regard him! He is a man of the other world—an angel—a mere imbecile—about business!" The priest threw himself back in his chair, and laughed tolerantly, showing his beautiful teeth. "All those rich men they give work to the poor. If I had a few thousand dollars to hopen up that place in the 'ill I would furnish work to every man in Ha-ha Bay—to hundreds. Are the miners more miserable than those *habitans*, eh?"

"The good God seems to think so," returned the priest seriously. "At least he has put the gold in the rocks so that you cannot get it out. What would you give the devil to help you?" he asked with a smile.

"When I want to make a bargain with the devil, I don't come to you, Père Étienne; I go to a notary. You ever hear, sir," said Bird, turning to Northwick, "about that notary at Montreal"—

"I think I will go to bed," said Northwick, abruptly. "I am not feeling very well—I am very tired, that is."

He had suddenly lost account of what and where he was. It seemed to him that he was both there and at Hatboro': that

there were really two Northwicks, and that there was a third
self somewhere in space, conscious of them both.

It was this third Northwick whom Bird and the priest would
have helped to bed if he had suffered them, but who repulsed
their offers. He made shift to undress himself, while he heard
them talking in French with lowered voices in the next room.
Their debate seemed at an end. After a little while he heard
the door shut, as if the priest had gone away. Afterwards he
appeared to have come back.

VI

_____

THE TALK went on all night in Northwick's head between those
two Frenchmen, who pretended to be of contrary opinions,
but were really leagued to get the better of him and lure him
on to put his money into that mine. In the morning his fever
was gone; but he was weak, and he could not command his
mind, could not make it stay by him long enough to decide
whether any harm would come from remaining over a day
before he pushed on to Chicoutimi. He tried to put in order
or sequence the reasons he had for coming so deep into the
winter and the wilderness; but when he passed from one to
the next, the former escaped him.

Bird looked in with his blue woollen bonnet on his head,
and his pipe in his mouth, and he removed each to ask how
Northwick was, and whether he would like to have some
breakfast; perhaps he would like a cup of tea, and some toast.

Northwick caught eagerly at the suggestion, and in a few
minutes the tea was brought him by a young girl whom Bird
called Virginie; he said she was his grandniece, and he hoped
that her singing had not disturbed the gentleman: she always sang; one could hardly stop her; but she meant no harm.
He stayed to serve Northwick himself, and Northwick tried
to put away the suspicion Bird's kindness roused in him. He
was in such need of kindness that he did not wish to suspect
it. Nevertheless he watched Bird narrowly as he put the milk
and sugar in his tea, and he listened warily when he began
to talk of the priest and to praise him. It was a pleasure, Bird

said, for one educated man to converse with another; and Father Étienne and he often maintained opposite sides of a question merely for the sake of the discussion; it was like a game of cards where there were no stakes; you exercised your mind.

Northwick understood this too little to believe it; when he talked he talked business; even the jokes among the men he was used to meant business.

"Then you haven't really found any gold in the hills?" he asked slyly.

"My faith, yes!" said Bird. "But," he added sadly, "perhaps it would not pay to mine it. I will show you when you get up. Better not go to Chicoutimi today! It is snowing."

"Snowing?" Northwick repeated. "Then I can't go!"

"Stop in bed till dinner. That is the best," Bird suggested. "Try to get some sleep. Sleep is youth. When we wake we are old again, but some of the youth stick to our fingers. No?" He smiled gayly, and went out, closing the door softly after him, and Northwick drowsed. In a dream Bird came back to him with some specimens from his gold mine. Northwick could see that the yellow metal speckling the quartz was nothing but copper pyrites, but he thought it best to pretend that he believed it gold; for Bird, while he stood over him with a lamp in one hand was feeling with the other for the buckle of Northwick's belt as he sat up in bed. He woke in fright, and the fear did not afterwards leave him in the fever which now began. He had his lucid intervals, when he was aware that he was wisely treated and tenderly cared for, and that his host and all his household were his devoted watchers and nurses; when he knew the doctor, and the young priest, in their visits. But all this he perceived cloudily, and as with a thickness of some sort of stuff between him and the fact, while the illusion of his delirium, always the same, was always poignantly real. Then the morning came when he woke from it, when the delirium was past and he knew where and what he was. The truth did not dawn gradually upon him, but possessed him at

once. His first motion was to feel for his belt; and he found
it gone. He gave a deep groan.

The blue woollen bonnet of the old hunter appeared
through the open doorway, with the pipe under the branching
gray moustache. The eyes of the men met.

"Well," said Bird, "you are in you' senses at last!" Northwick did not speak, but his look conveyed a question which
the other could not misinterpret. He smiled. "You want you'
belt?" He disappeared, and then reappeared, this time full
length, and brought the belt to Northwick. "You think you
are among some Yankee defal*cator?*" he asked, for sole resentment of the suspicion which Northwick's anguished look must
have imparted. "Count it. I think you find it hall right." But
as the sick man lay still, and made no motion to take up the
belt where it lay across his breast, Bird asked, "You want me
to count it for you?"

Northwick faintly nodded, and Bird stood over him, and
told the thousand dollar bills over, one by one, and then put
them back in the pouch of the belt.

"Now, I think you are going to get well. The doctor 'e say
to let you see you' money the first thing. Shall I put it hon
you?"

Northwick looked at the belt; it seemed to him that the
bunch the bills made would hurt him, and he said weakly,
"You keep it for me."

"Hall right," said Bird, and he took it away. He went out
with a proud air, as if he felt honored by the trust Northwick
had explicitly confirmed, and sat down in the next room, so as
to be within call.

Northwick made the slow recovery of an elderly man; and
by the time he could go out of doors without fear of relapse,
there were signs in the air and in the earth of the spring, which
when it comes to that northern land possesses it like a passion.
The grass showed green on the low bare hills as the snow un-
covered them; the leaves seemed to break like an illumination
from the trees; the southwind blew back the birds with its

first breath. The jays screamed in the woods; the Canadian nightingales sang in the evening and the early morning when he woke and thought of his place at Hatboro', where the robins' broods must be half grown by that time. It was then the time of the apple-blossoms there; with his homesick inward vision he saw the billowed tops of his orchard, all pink-white. He thought how the apples smelt, when they first began to drop in August on the clean straw that bedded the orchard aisles. It seemed to him that if he could only be there again for a moment he would be willing to spend the rest of his life in prison. As it was he was in prison; it did not matter how wide the bounds were that kept him from his home. He hated the vastness of the half world where he could come and go unmolested, this bondage that masked itself as such ample freedom. To be shut out was the same as to be shut in.

In the first days of his convalescence, while he was yet too weak to leave his room, he planned and executed many returns to his home. He went back by stealth, and disguised by the beard which had grown in his sickness, and tried to see what change had come upon it; but he could never see it different from what it was that clear winter night when he escaped from it. This baffled and distressed him, and strengthened the longing at the bottom of his heart actually to return. He thought that if he could once look on the misery he had brought upon his children he could bear it better; he complexly flattered himself that it would not be so bad in reality as it was in fancy. Sometimes when this wish harassed him, he said to himself, to still it, that as soon as the first boat came up the river from Quebec, he would go down with it, and arrange to surrender himself to the authorities, and abandon the struggle.

But as he regained his health, he began to feel that this was a rash and foolish promise; he thought he saw a better way out of his unhappiness. It appeared a misfortune once more, and not so much a fault of his. He was restored to this feeling in part by the respect, the distinction which he enjoyed in the little village, and which pleasantly recalled his consequence among the mill-people at Ponkwasset. When he was declared out of danger he began to receive visits of polite sympathy from the heads of families, who smoked round him in the evening, and predicted a renewal of his youth by the fever he had come through safely. Their prophecies were interpreted by Bird and Père Étienne, as with one or other of these he went to repay their visits. Everywhere, the inmates of the simple, clean little houses, had begun early to furbish them up for the use of their summer boarders, while they got ready the shanties behind them for their own occupancy; but everywhere Northwick was received with that pathetic deference which the poor render to those capable of bettering their condition. The secret of the treasure he had brought with him remained safe with the doctor and the priest, and with Bird who had discovered it with them; but Bird was not the man to conceal from his neighbors the fact that his guest was a great American capitalist, who had come to develop the mineral, agricultural and manufacturing interests of Ha-ha Bay on the American scale, and to enrich the whole region, buying land of those who wished to sell and employing all those who desired to work. If he was impatient for the verification of these promises by Northwick, he was too polite to urge it; and did nothing worse than brag to him as he bragged about him. He probably had his own opinion of Northwick's reasons for the silence he maintained concerning himself in all respects; he knew from the tag fastened to the bag Northwick had bought in Quebec that his name was Warwick, and he knew from Northwick himself that he was from Chicago; beyond this, if he conjectured that he was the victim of financial errors, he smoothly kept his guesses to himself and would not mar the chances of good that Northwick might do with his money by hinting any question of its origin. The American defaulter was a sort of hero in Bird's fancy; he had heard much of that character; he would have experienced no shock at realizing him in Northwick; he would have accounted for Northwick, and excused him to himself, if need be. The doctor observed a professional reticence; his affair was with Northwick's body, which he had treated skilfully. He left his soul to Père Étienne, who may have had his diffidence, his delicacy, in dealing with it, as the soul of a Protestant and a foreigner.

VII

———

It took the young priest somewhat longer than it would have
taken a man of Northwick's own language and nation to perceive that his gentlemanly decorum and grave repose of manner masked a complete ignorance of the things that interest
cultivated people, and that he was merely and purely a business man, a figment of commercial civilization, with only the
crudest tastes and ambitions outside of the narrow circle of
money making. He found that he had a pleasure in horses
and cattle, and from hints which Northwick let fall, regard-
ing his life at home, that he was fond of having a farm and a
conservatory with rare plants. But the flowers were possessions, not passions; he did not speak of them as if they afforded
him any artistic or scientific delight. The young priest learned
that he had put a good deal of money in pictures: but then
the pictures seemed to have become investments, and of the
nature of stocks and bonds. He found that this curious American did not care to read the English books which Bird offered
to lend him out of the little store of gifts and accidents accumulated in the course of years from bountiful or forgetful
tourists; the books in French Père Étienne proposed to him,
Northwick said he did not know how to read. He showed no
liking for music, except a little for the singing of Bird's niece
Virginie, but when the priest thought he might care to understand that she sang the ballads which the first voyagers
had brought from France into the wilderness, or which had
sprung out of the joy and sorrow of its hard life, he saw that

the fact said nothing to Northwick, and that it rather embarrassed him. The American could not take part in any of those discussions of abstract questions which the priest and the old woodsman delighted in, and which they sometimes tried to make him share. He apparently did not know what they meant. It was only when Père Étienne gave him up as the creature of a civilization too ugly and arid to be borne, that he began to love him as a brother; when he could make nothing of Northwick's mind, he conceived the hope of saving his soul.

Père Étienne felt sure that Northwick had a soul, and he had his misgivings that it was a troubled one. He, too, had heard of the American defaulter, who has a celebrity of his own in Canada penetrating to different men with different suggestion, and touching here and there a pure and unworldly heart such as Père Étienne bore in his breast, with commiseration. The young priest did not conceive very clearly of the make and manner of the crime he suspected the elusive and mysterious stranger of committing; but he imagined that the great sum of money he knew him possessed of was spoil, of some sort; and he believed that Northwick's hesitation to employ it in any way was proof of an uneasy conscience in its possession. Why had he come to that lonely place in midwinter with a treasure such as that; and why did he keep the money by him, instead of putting it in a bank? Père Étienne talked these questions over with Bird and the doctor, and he could find only one answer to them. He wondered if he ought not to speak to Northwick, and delicately offer him the chance to unburden his mind to such a friend as only a priest could be to such a sinner. But he could not think of any approach sufficiently delicate. Northwick was not a Catholic, and the church had no hold upon him. Besides he had a certain plausibility and reserve of demeanor that forbade suspicion as well as the intimacy necessary to the good which Père Étienne wished to do the lonely and silent man. Northwick was in those days much occupied with a piece of writing, which he always locked carefully into his bag when he left his room, and which he copied in part or in whole again and again, burning the rejected drafts in the hearthfire that had now superseded the stove, and stirring the carbonized paper into ashes so that no word was left distinguishable on it.

One day there came up the river a bateau from Tadoussac bringing the news that the ice was all out of the St. Lawrence. "It will not be long time, now," said Bird, "before we begin to see you' countrymen. The steamboats come to Ha-ha Bay in the last of June."

Northwick responded to the words with no visible sensation. His sphinxlike reticence vexed Bird more and more, and intolerably deepened the mystification of his failure to do any of the things with his capital which Bird had promised himself and his fellow-citizens. He no longer talked of going to Chicoutimi, that was true, and there was not the danger of his putting his money into Markham's enterprise there; but neither did he show any interest or any curiosity concerning Bird's discovery of the precious metal at Ha-ha Bay. Bird had his delicacy as well as Père Étienne, and he could not thrust himself upon his guest even with the intention of making their joint fortune.

A few days later there came to Père Étienne a letter which when he read it superseded the interest in Northwick which Bird felt gnawing him like a perpetual hunger. It was from the curé at Rimouski, where Père Étienne's family lived, and it brought word that his mother, who had been in failing health all winter, could not long survive, and so greatly desired to see him that his correspondent had asked their superiors to allow him to replace Père Étienne at Ha-ha Bay while he came to visit her. Leave had been given, and Père Étienne might expect his friend very soon after his letter reached him.

"Where is Rimouski?" Northwick asked, when he found himself alone with the priest that evening.

"It is on the St. Lawrence. It is the last and first point where the steamers touch in going and coming between Quebec and Liverpool." Père Étienne had been weeping, and his heart was softened and emboldened by the anxiety he felt. "It is my native village—where I lived till I went to make my studies in the Laval University. It is going home for me. Perhaps they will let me remain there." He added by an irresistible impulse of pity and love, "I wish you were going home, too, Mr. Warwick!"

"I wish I were!" said Northwick, with a heavy sigh. "But I can't—yet."

"This is a desert for you," Père Étienne pressed on. "I can see that. I have seen how solitary you are."

"Yes. It's lonesome," Northwick admitted.

"My son," said the young priest to the man who was old enough to be his father, and he put his hand on Northwick's, where it lay on his knee as they sat side by side before the fire, "is there something you could wish to say to me? Something I might do to help you?"

For a moment all was open between them, and they knew each other's meaning. "Yes," said Northwick, and he felt the wish to trust in the priest and to be ruled by him well up like a tide of hot blood from his heart. It sank back again. This pure soul was too innocent, too unversed in the world and its ways to know his offence in its right proportion; to know it as Northwick himself knew it; to be able to account for it and condone it. The affair, if he could understand it at all, would shock him; he must blame it as relentlessly as Northwick's own child would if her love did not save him. With the next word he closed that which was open between them, a rift in his clouds that heaven itself had seemed to look through. "I have a letter—a letter that I wish you would take, and mail for me in Rimouski."

"I will take it with great pleasure," said the priest, but he had the sadness of a deep disappointment in his tone.

Northwick was disappointed, too; almost injured. He had something like a perception that if Père Étienne had been a coarser, commoner soul, he could have told him everything and saved his own soul by the confession.

About a month after the priest's departure the first steam-boat came up the Saguenay from Quebec. By this time, Bird was a desperate man. Northwick was still there in his house, with all that money which he would not employ in any way; at once a temptation and a danger if it should in any manner become known. The wandering poor, who are known to the piety of the habitans as the Brethren of Christ, were a terror to Bird, in their visits; when they came by day to receive the charity which no one denies them, he felt himself bound to keep a watchful eye on this old Yankee, who was either a rascal or a madman, and perhaps both, and to see that no harm came to him; and when he heard the tramps prowling about at night, and feeling for the alms that kind people leave out-doors for them, he could not sleep. The old hunter ne-glected his wild-beast traps, and suffered his affairs to fall into neglect; but it was not his failing appetite, or his broken sleep alone that wore upon him. The disappointment with his guest that was spreading through the community, in-volved Bird, and he thought his neighbors looked askance at him: as if they believed he could have moved Northwick to action, if he would. Northwick could not have moved him-self. He was like one benumbed. He let the days go by, and made no attempt to realize the schemes for the retrieval of his fortunes, that had brought him to that region.

The sound of that steamboat's whistle was a joyful sound to Bird. He rose and went into Northwick's room. North-wick was awake; he had heard the whistle, too.

"Now, Mr. Warwick, or what you' name," said Bird, with trembling eagerness, "that is the boat. I want you to take you' money and go hout my 'ouse. Yes, sir. Now! Pack you' things. Don't wait for breakfast. You get breakfast hon board. Go!"

VIII

THE LETTER which Père Étienne posted for Northwick at Rimouski was addressed to the editor of the Boston *Events*, and was published with every advantage which scare-heading could invent. A young journalist newly promoted to the management was trying to give the counting-room proofs of his efficiency in the line of the *Events'* greatest successes, and he wasted no thrill that the sensation in his hands was capable of imparting to his readers. Yet the effect was disappointing, not only in the figure of the immediate sales, but in the cumulative value of the recognition of the fact that the *Events* had been selected by Northwick as the best avenue for approaching the public. The *Abstract*, in copying and commenting upon the letter, skilfully stabbed its esteemed contemporary with an acknowledgment of its prime importance as the organ of the American defaulters in Canada; other papers, after questioning the document as a fake, made common cause in treating it as a matter of little or no moment. In fact there had been many defalcations since Northwick's; the average of one a day in the despatches of the Associated Press had been fully kept up, and several of these had easily surpassed his in the losses involved, and in the picturesqueness of the circumstances. People generally recalled with an effort the supremely tragic claim of his case through the rumor of his death in the railroad accident; those who distinctly remembered it experienced a certain disgust at the man's willingness to shelter himself so long in the doubt to which it had left not only the public, but his own family, concerning his fate.

The evening after the letter appeared Hilary was dining one of those belated Englishmen who sometimes arrive in Boston after most houses are closed for the summer on the Hill and the Back Bay. Mrs. Hilary and Louise were already with Matt at his farm for a brief season before opening their own house at the shore, and Hilary was living *en garçon*. There were only men at the dinner, and the talk at first ran chiefly to question of a sufficient incentive of Northwick's peculations; its absence was the fact which all concurred in owning. In deference to his guest's ignorance of the matter Hilary went rapidly over it from the beginning, and as he did so, the perfectly typical character of the man and of the situation appeared in clear relief. He ended by saying: "It isn't at all a remarkable instance. There is nothing peculiar about it. Northwick was well off and he wished to be better off. He had plenty of other people's money in his hands which he controlled so entirely that he felt as if it were his own. He used it and he lost it. Then he was found out, and ran away. That's all."

"Then as I understand," said the Englishman, with a strong impression that he was making a joke, "this Mr. Northwick was *not* one of your most remarkable men."

Everybody laughed obligingly, and Hilary said, "He was one of our *least* remarkable men." Then, spurred on by that perverse impulse which we Americans often have to make the worst of ourselves to an Englishman, he added, "The defaulter seems to be taking the place of the self-made man among us. Northwick's a type, a little differentiated from thousands of others by the rumor of his death in the first place, and now by this unconsciously hypocritical and nauseous letter. He's what the commonplace American egoist must come to more and more in finance, now that he is abandoning the career of politics, and wants to be rich instead of great."

"Really?" said the Englishman.

Among Hilary's guests was Charles Bellingham, a bachelor of pronounced baldness, who said he would come to meet Hilary's belated Englishman in quality of bear leader to his cousin-in-law, old Bromfield Corey, a society veteran of that period when even the swell in Boston must be an intellectual man. He was not only old, but an invalid, and he seldom left town in summer, and liked to go out to dinner whenever he was asked. Bellingham came to the rescue of the national repute in his own fashion. "I can't account for your not locking up your spoons, Hilary, when you invited me, unless you knew where you could steal some more."

"Ah, it isn't quite like a gentleman's stealing a few spoons," old Corey began, in the gentle way he had, and with a certain involuntary sibillation through the gaps between his front teeth. "It's a much more heroic thing than an ordinary theft; and I can't let you belittle it as something commonplace because it happens everyday. So does death; so does birth; but they're not commonplace."

"They're not so frequent as defalcation with us, quite—especially birth," suggested Bellingham.

"No," Corey went on, "every fact of this sort is preceded by the slow and long decay of a moral nature, and that is of the most eternal and tragical interest; and"—here Corey broke down in an old man's queer, whimpering laugh as the notion struck him—"if it's very common with us, I don't know but we ought to be proud of it as showing that we excel all the rest of the civilized world in the proportion of decayed moral natures to the whole population. But I wonder," he went on, "that it doesn't produce more moralists of a sanative type than it has. Our bad teeth have given us the best dentists in the world; our habit of defalcation hasn't resulted yet in any ethical compensation. Sewell, here, used to preach about such things, but I'll venture to say we shall have no homily on Northwick from him next Sunday."

The Rev. Mr. Sewell suffered the thrust in patience. "What is the use?" he asked, with a certain sadness. "The preacher's voice is lost in his sounding board, now-a-days, when all the Sunday newspapers are crying aloud from twenty-eight pages illustrated."

"Perhaps *they* are our moralists," Corey suggested.

"Perhaps," Sewell assented.

"By the way, Hilary," said Bellingham, "did you ever know who wrote that article in the *Abstract*, when Northwick's crookedness first appeared?"

"Yes," said Hilary. "It was a young fellow of twenty four or five."

"Come off!" said Bellingham, in a slang phrase then making its way into merited favor. "What's become of him? I haven't seen anything else like it in the *Abstract*."

"No. And I'm afraid you're not likely to. The fellow was a reporter on the paper at the time; but he happened to have looked up the literature of defalcation, and they let him say his say."

"It was a very good say."

"Better than any other he had in him. They let him try again on different things, but he wasn't up to the work. So the managing editor said—and he was a friend of the fellow's. He was too literary, I believe."

"And what's become of him?" asked Corey.

"You might get *him* to read to you," said Bellingham to the old man. He added to the company, "Corey uses up a fresh reader every three months. He takes them into his intimacy and then he finds their society oppressive."

"Why," Hilary answered, with a little hesitation, "he was out of health, and Matt had him up to his farm."

"Is he Matt's only beneficiary?" Corey asked, with a certain tone of tolerant liking for Matt. "I thought he usually had a larger colony at Vardley."

"Well, he has," said Hilary. "But when his mother and sister are visiting him, he has to reduce their numbers. He can't very well turn his family away."

"He might board them out," said Bellingham.

"Do you suppose," asked Sewell, as if he had not noticed the turn the talk had taken, "that Northwick has gone to Europe?"

"I've no doubt he wishes me to suppose so," said Hilary, "and of course we've had to cable the authorities to look out for him at Moville and Liverpool; but I feel perfectly sure he's still in Canada, and expects to make terms for getting home again. He must be horribly homesick."

"Yes?" Sewell suggested.

"Yes. Not because he's a man of any delicacy of feeling, or much real affection for his family. I've no doubt he's fond of them, in a way, but he's fonder of himself. You can see, all through his letter that he's trying to make interest for himself, and that he's quite willing to use his children if it will tell on the public sympathies. He knows very well that they're provided for. They own the place at Hatboro'; he deeded it to them long before his crookedness is known to have begun; and his creditors couldn't touch it if they wished to. If he had really that fatherly affection for them which he appeals to in others, he wouldn't have left them in doubt whether he was alive or dead for four or five months, and then dragged them into an open letter asking forbearance in their name, and promising for their sake to right those he had wronged. The thing is thoroughly indecent."

Since the fact of Northwick's survival had been established beyond question by the publication of his letter, Hilary's mind in regard to him had undergone a great revulsion. It relieved itself with a sharp rebound from the oppressive sense of responsibility for his death which he seemed to have incurred in telling Northwick that the best thing for him would be a railroad accident. Now that the man was not killed Hilary could freely declare, "He made a great mistake in not getting out of the world as many of us believed he had—I confess I had rather got to believe it myself—but he ought at least to have had the grace to remain dead to the poor creatures he had dishonored till he could repay the people he had defrauded."

"Ah! I don't know about that," said Sewell.

"No? Why not?"

"Because it would be a kind of romantic deceit that he'd better not keep up."

"He seems to have kept it up for the last four or five months," said Hilary.

"That's no reason he should continue to keep it up," Sewell persisted. "Perhaps he never knew of the rumor of his death."

"Ah, that isn't imaginable. There isn't a hole or corner left where the newspapers don't penetrate, nowadays."

"Not in Boston. But if he were in hiding in some little French village down the St. Lawrence"—

"Isn't that as romantic as the other notion, parson?" crowed old Corey.

"No, I don't think so," said the minister. "The cases are quite different. He might have a morbid shrinking from his own past, and the wish to hide from it as far as he could; that would be natural; but to leave his children to believe a rumor of his death in order to save their feelings would be against nature; it would be purely histrionic; a motive from the theatre; that is, perfectly false."

"Pretty hard on Hilary, who invented it," Bellingham suggested; and they all laughed.

"I don't know," said Hilary. "The man seems to be posing in other ways. You would think from his letter that he was a sort of martyr to principle, and that he'd been driven off to Canada by the heartless creditors whom he's going to devote his life to saving from loss, if he can't do it in a few months or years. He may not be a conscious humbug, but he's certainly a humbug. Take that pretence of his that he would come back and stand his trial if he believed it would not result in greater harm than good by depriving him of all hope of restitution!"

"Why, there's a sort of crazy morality in that," said Corey.

"Perhaps," said Bellingham, "the solution of the whole matter is that Northwick is cracked."

"I've no doubt that he's cracked, to a certain extent," said Sewell, "as every wrong-doer is. You know the Swedenborgians believe that insanity is the last state of the wicked."

"I suppose," observed old Corey thoughtfully, "you'd be very glad to have him keep out of your reach, Hilary?"

"What a question!" said Hilary. "You're as bad as my daughter. She asked me the same thing."

"I wish I were no worse," said the old man.

"You speak of his children," said the Englishman. "Hasn't he a wife?"

"No. Two daughters. One an old maid, and the other a young girl, whom my daughter knew at school," Hilary answered.

"I saw the young lady at your house once," said Bellingham, in a certain way.

"Yes. She's been here a good deal first and last."

"Rather a high-stepping young person, I thought," said Bellingham.

"She is a proud girl," Hilary admitted. "Rather imperious, in fact."

"Ah, what's the pride of a young girl?" said Corey. "Something that comes from her love and goes to it; no separable quality; nothing that's for herself."

"Well, I'm not sure of that," said Hilary. "In this case it seems to have served her own turn. It's enabled her simply and honestly to deny the fact that her father ever did anything wrong."

"That's rather fine," Corey remarked, as if tasting it.

"And what will it enable her to do, now that he's come out and confessed the frauds himself?" the Englishman asked.

Hilary shrugged, for answer. He said to Bellingham, "Charles, I want you to try some of those crabs. I got them for you."

"Why this is touching, Hilary," said Bellingham, getting his fat head round with difficulty to look at them on the dish the man was bringing to his side. "But I don't know that I should have refused them, even if they had been got for Corey."

IX

THEY did not discuss Northwick's letter at dinner parties in Hatboro', because, socially speaking, they never dined, there; but the stores, the shops, the parlors, buzzed with comment on it; it became a part of the forms of salutation, the color of the day's joke. Gates, the provision man, had to own the error of his belief in Northwick's death. He found his account in being the only man to own that he ever had such a belief; he was a comfort to those who said they had always had their doubts of it; the ladies of South Hatboro', who declared to a woman that they had *never* believed it, respected the simple heart of a man who acknowledged that he had never questioned it. Such a man was not one to cheat his customers in quantity or quality; that stood to reason; his faith restored him to the esteem of many.

Mr. Gerrish was very bitter about the double fraud which he said Northwick had practiced on the community, in having allowed the rumor of his death to gain currency. He denounced him to Mrs. Munger, making an early errand from South Hatboro' to the village to collect public opinion, as a person who had put himself beyond the pale of public confidence, and whose professions of repentance for the past and good intention for the future he tore to shreds. "It is said, and I have no question correctly, that hell is paved with good intentions—if you will excuse me, Mrs. Munger. When Mr. Northwick brings forth fruits meet for repentance—when he makes the first payment to his creditors—I will believe that he is sorry for what he has done, and not *till* then."

"That is true," said Mrs. Munger. "I wonder what Mr. Putney will have to say to all this. Can he feel that *his* skirts are quite clean, acting, that way, as the family counsel of the Northwicks, after all he used to say against him?"

Mr. Gerrish expressed his indifference by putting up a bolt of muslin on the shelf while he rejoined, "I care very little for the opinions of Mr. Putney on any subject."

In some places Mrs. Munger encountered a belief, which she did not discourage, that the Northwick girls had known all along that their father was alive, and had been in communication with him, through Putney, most probably. In the light of this conjecture the lawyer's character had a lurid effect which it did not altogether lose when Jack Wilmington said bluntly, "What of it? He's their counsel. He's not obliged to give the matter away. He's obliged to keep it."

"But isn't it very inconsistent," Mrs. Munger urged, "after all he used to say against Mr. Northwick?"

"I suppose it's a professional, not a personal matter," said Wilmington.

"And then, their putting on mourning! Just think of it!" Mrs. Munger appealed to Mrs. Wilmington, who was listening to her nephew's savagery of tone and phrase with the lazy pleasure she seemed always to feel in it.

"Yes. Do you suppose they meant it for a blind?"

"Why, that's what people think now, don't they?"

"Oh, *I* don't know. What do *you* think, Jack?"

"I think they're a pack of fools!" he blurted out, like a man who avenges on the folly of others the hurt of his own conscience. He cast a look of brutal contempt at Mrs. Munger, who said she thought so, too.

"It is too bad the way people allow themselves to talk," she went on. "To be sure, Sue Northwick has never done anything to make herself loved in Hatboro'—not among the ladies, at least."

Mrs. Wilmington gave a spluttering laugh, and said, "And I suppose it's the ladies who allow themselves to talk as they do. I can't get the men in my family to say a word against her."

Jack scowled his blackest. "It would be a pitiful scoundrel that did. Her misfortunes ought to make her sacred to every one that has the soul of a man."

"Well, so it does. That is just what I was saying. The trouble is that they don't make her sacred to every one that has the soul of a woman," Mrs. Wilmington teased.

"I know it doesn't," Jack returned in helpless scorn, as he left Mrs. Munger alone to his aunt.

"*Do* you suppose he still cares anything for her?" Mrs. Munger asked with cosey confidentiality.

"Who knows?" Mrs. Wilmington rejoined indolently. "It would be very poetical, wouldn't it, if he were to seize the opportunity to go back to her?"

"Beautiful!" sighed Mrs. Munger. "I do *like* a manly man!" She drove home through the village slowly, hoping for the chance of a further interchange of conjectures and impressions; but she saw no one she had not already talked with till she met Doctor Morrell, driving out of the avenue from his house. She promptly set her phaeton across the road so that he could not get by if he were rude enough to wish it.

"Doctor," she called out, "what *do* you think of this extraordinary letter of Mr. Northwick's?"

Dr. Morrell's boyish eyes twinkled. "You mean that letter in the *Events?* Do you think Northwick wrote it?"

"Why, don't *you*, doctor?" she questioned back, with a note of personal grievance in her voice.

"I'm not very well acquainted with his style. Then, you think he *did* write it? Of course, there are always various opinions. But I understood you thought he was burned in that accident last winter."

"Now, *doctor!*" said Mrs. Munger, with the pout which Putney said always made him want to kill her. "You're just trying to tease me; I know you are. I'm going to drive right in and see Mrs. Morrell. *She* will tell me what you think."

"I don't believe you can see her," said the doctor. "She isn't at all well."

"Oh, I'm sorry for that. I don't understand what excuse

she has, though, with a physician for her husband. You must turn homœopathy. Dr. Morrell, do you think it's true that Jack Wilmington will offer himself to Sue Northwick, now that it's come to the worst with her? Wouldn't it be romantic?"

"Very," said the doctor. He craned his head out of the buggy, as if to see whether he could safely drive into the ditch, and pass Mrs. Munger. He said politely, as he started, "Don't disturb yourself! I can get by."

She sent a wail of reproach after him, and then continued toward South Hatboro'. As she passed the lodge at the gate of the Northwick avenue, where the sisters now lived, she noted that the shades were closely drawn. They were always drawn on the side toward the street, but Mrs. Munger thought it interesting that she had never noticed it before, and in the dearth of material she made the most of it, both for her own emotion and for the sensation of others when she reached South Hatboro'.

Behind the drawn shades that Mrs. Munger noted, Adeline Northwick sat crying over the paper Elbridge Newton had pushed under the door that morning. It was limp from the nervous clutch and tremor of her hands, and wet with her tears; but she kept reading her father's letter in it, and trying to puzzle out of it some hope or help. "He must be crazy, he must be crazy," she moaned, more to herself than to Suzette, who sat rigidly and silently by. "He couldn't have been so cruel, if he had been in his right mind; he couldn't! He was always so good to us, and so thoughtful; he must have known that we had given him up for dead, long ago; and he has let us go on grieving for him all this time. It's just as if he had come back from death, and the first he did was to tell us that everything they said against him was true, and that everything we said and believed was all wrong. How could he do it, how could he do it! We bore to think he was dead; yes, we bore that, and we didn't complain; but this is more than any one can ask us to bear. Oh, Suzette, what can we say, now? What can we say after he's confessed himself that he took the

money, and that he has got part of it yet? But I know he
didn't! I know he hasn't! He's crazy! Oh, poor, poor father!
Don't you think he must be crazy? And where is he? Why
don't he write to us, and tell us what he wants us to do? Does
he think we would tell any one where he was? That *shows*
he's out of his mind. I always thought that if he could come
back to life somehow, he'd prove that they had lied about
him; and now! Oh, it isn't as if it were merely the company
that was concerned, or what people said; but it's as if our
own father, that we trusted so much, had broken his word to
us. That is what kills me."

The day passed. They sent Mrs. Newton away when she
came to help them at dinner. They locked their doors, and
shut themselves in from the world, as mourners do with
death. Adeline's monologue went on, with the brief responses
which she extorted from Suzette, and at last it ceased, as if
her heart had worn itself out in the futile repetition of its
griefs.

Then Suzette broke her silence with words that seemed to
break from it of themselves in their abrupt irrelevance to
what Adeline had last said. "We must give it up!"

"Give what up?" Adeline quavered back.

"The house—and the farm—and this hovel. Everything! It
isn't ours."

"Not ours?"

"No. That letter makes it theirs—the people's whose money
he took. We must send for Mr. Putney and tell him to give it
to them. He will know how."

Adeline looked at her sister's face in dismay. She gasped
out, "Why, but Mr. Putney says it's ours, and nobody can
touch it!"

"That was *before*. Now it is theirs; and if we kept it from
them we should be stealing it. How do we know that father
had any right to give it to us when he did?"

"Suzette!"

"I keep thinking such things, and I had better say them

unless I want to go out of my senses. Once I would have died before I gave it up because he left it to us, and now it seems as if I couldn't live till I gave it up because he left it to us. No, I can never forgive him, if he *is* my father. I can never speak to him again, or see him; never! He is dead to me, now!"

The words seemed to appeal to the contrary-mindedness that lurks in such natures as Adeline's. "Why, I don't see what there is so wrong about father's letter," she began. "It just shows what I always said: that his mind was affected by his business troubles, and that he wandered away because he couldn't get them straight. And now it's preyed so upon him that he's beginning to believe the things they say are true, and to blame himself. That's the way I look at it."

"Adeline!" Suzette commanded with a kind of shriek, "Be still! You *know* you don't believe that!"

Adeline hesitated between her awe of her sister, and her wish to persist in a theory which, now that she had formulated it for Suzette's confusion, she found effective for her own comfort. She ventured at last, "It is what I said, the first thing, and I shall always say it, Suzette; and I have a right."

"Say what you please. I shall say nothing. But this property doesn't belong to us till father comes back to prove it."

"Comes back!" Adeline gasped. "Why, they'll send him to state's prison!"

"They wont send him to state's prison if he's innocent, and if he isn't"—

"Suzette! Don't you dare!"

"But that has nothing to do with it. We must give up what doesn't belong to us. Will you go for Mr. Putney, or shall I go? I'm not afraid to be seen, if you don't like to go. I can hold up my head before the whole world, now I know what we ought to do, and we're going to do it; but if we kept this place after that letter, I couldn't even look *you* in the face again." She continued to Adeline's silence. "Why we needn't either of us go! I can get Elbridge to go." She made as if to leave the room.

"Wait! I can't let you—yet. I haven't thought it out," said Adeline.

"Not thought it out!" Suzette went back and stood over her where she sat in her rocking chair.

"No!" said Adeline, shrinking from her fierce look, but with a gathering strength of resistance in her heart. "Because *you've* been thinking of it, you expect me to do what you say in an instant. The place was mother's, and when she died, it came to me, and I hold it in trust for both of us; that's what Mr. Putney says. Even supposing that father did use their money—and I don't believe he did—I don't see why I should give up mother's property to them." She waited a moment before she said, "And I wont."

"Is half of it mine?" asked Suzette.

"I don't know. Yes, I suppose so."

"I'm of age, and I shall give up my half. I'm going to send for Mr. Putney." She went out of the room, and came back with her hat and gloves on, and her jacket over her arm. She had never been so beautiful, or so terrible. "Listen to me Adeline," she said. "I'm going out to send Elbridge for Mr. Putney; and when he comes I am not going to have any squabbling before him. You can do what you please with your half of the property, but I'm going to give up my half to the company. Now, if you don't promise you'll freely consent to what I want to do with my own, I will never come back to this house, or ever see you again, or speak to you. Do you promise?"

"Oh well, I promise," said Adeline, forlornly, with a weak dribble of tears. "You can take your half of the place that mother owned, and give it to the men that are trying to destroy father's character! But I shall never say that I wanted you should do it."

"So that you don't say anything against it, I don't care what else you say." Suzette put on her jacket and stood buttoning it at her soft throat, "*I* do it; and I do it for mother's sake and for father's. I care as much for them as you do."

In the evening Putney came and she told him she wished

him to contrive whatever form was necessary to put her father's creditors in possession of her half of the estate. "My sister doesn't feel as I do about it," she ended. "She thinks they
have no right to it, and that we ought to keep it. But she has
agreed to let me give my half up."

Putney went to the door and threw out the quid of tobacco
which he had been absently chewing upon while she spoke.
"You know," he explained, "that the creditors have no more
claim on this estate in law than they have on my house and
lot?"

"I don't know. I don't care for the law."

"The case isn't altered at all, you know, by the fact that
your father is still living, and your title isn't affected by any
of the admissions made in the letter he has published."

"I understand that," said the girl.

"Well," said Putney. "I merely wanted to make sure you
had all the bearings of the case. The thing can be done, of
course. There's nothing to prevent any one giving any one
else a piece of property."

He remained silent for a moment as if doubtful whether
to say more, and Adeline asked, "And do you believe that if
we were to give up the property, they'd let father come back?"

Putney could not control a smile at her simplicity. "The
creditors have got nothing to do with that, Miss Northwick.
Your father has been indicted, and he's in contempt of court
as long as he stays away. There can't be any question of mercy
till he comes back for his trial."

"But if he came back," she persisted, "our giving up the
property would make them easier with him?"

"A corporation has no bowels of compassion, Miss Northwick. I shouldn't like to trust one. The company has no legal
claim on the estate. Unless you think it has a moral claim,
you'd better hold on to your property."

"And do you think it has a moral claim?"

Putney drew a long breath. "Well, that's a nice question."
He stroked his trousers down over his little thin leg as he sat.

"I have some peculiar notions about corporations. I don't think a manufacturing company is a benevolent institution exactly. It isn't even a sanitarium. It didn't come for its health; it came to make money, and it makes it by a profit on the people who do its work and the people who buy its wares. Practically, it's just like everything else that earns its bread by the sweat of its capital—neither better nor worse." Launched in this direction Putney recalled himself with an effort from the prospect of an irrelevant excursion in the fields of speculative economy. "But as I understand, the question is not so much whether the Ponkwasset Mills have a moral claim, as whether you have a moral obligation. And there I can't advise. You would have to go to a clergyman. I can only say, that if the property were mine I should hold on to it, and let the company be damned, or whatever could happen to a body that hadn't a soul for that purpose."

Putney thrust his hand into his pocket for his tobacco; and then recollected himself, and put it back.

"There, Suzette!" said Adeline.

Suzette had listened in a restive silence, while Putney was talking with her sister. She said in answer to him, "I don't want advice about that. I wished to know whether I could give up my part of the estate to the company, and if you would do it for me at once."

"Oh, certainly," said Putney. "I will go down to Boston tomorrow morning and see their attorney."

"Their attorney? I thought you would have to go to Mr. Hilary."

"He would send me to their lawyer, I suppose. But I can go to him first, if you wish."

"Yes. I do wish it," said the girl. "I don't understand about the company, and I don't care for it; I want to offer the property to Mr. Hilary. Don't say anything but just that I wished to give it up, and my sister consented. Don't say a single word more, no matter what he asks you. Will you?"

"I will do exactly what you say," answered Putney. "But

you understand, I suppose, dont you, that in order to make the division the whole place must be sold?"

Suzette looked at him in surprise. Adeline wailed out, "The whole place sold!"

"Yes; how else could you arrive at the exact value?"

"I will keep the house and the grounds, and Suzette may have the farm"—

Putney shook his head. "I don't believe it could be done— Perhaps"—

"Well, then," said Adeline, "I will never let the place be sold in the world. I"— She caught Suzette's eye and faltered, and then went on piteously, "I didn't know what we should have to do when I promised. But I'll keep my promise; yes, I will. We needn't sign the papers to-night, need we, Mr. Putney? It'll do, in the morning?"

"Oh yes; just as well," said Putney. "It'll take a little time to draw up the writings"—

"But you can send word to Mr. Hilary at once?" Suzette asked.

"Oh, yes; if you wish."

"I do."

"It wont be necessary"—

"I wish it."

Since the affair must so soon be known to everybody, Putney felt justified in telling his wife when he went home. "If that poor old girl freely consented, it must have been at the point of the hairpin. Of course the young one is right to obey her conscience, but as a case of conscience, what do you think of it, Ellen? And do you think one ought to make any one else obey one's conscience?"

"That's a hard question, Ralph. And I'm not sure that she's right. Why should she give up her property, if it was hers, so long ago before the frauds began? Suppose he were not their father, and the case stood just as it does."

"Ah, there's something very strange about the duty of blood."

"Blood? I think Suzette Northwick's case of conscience is a case of pride," said Mrs. Putney. "I don't believe she cares anything about the right and wrong of it. She just wishes to stand well before the world. She would do anything for that. She's as *hard!*"

"That's what the world will say, I've no doubt," Putney admitted.

X

THE NEXT morning Adeline came early to her sister's bed and woke her.

"I haven't slept all night—I don't see how *you* could—and I want you shouldn't let Mr. Putney send that letter to Mr. Hilary, just yet. I want to think it over first."

"You want to break your promise?" asked Suzette, wide awake at the first word.

Adeline began to cry. "I want to think. It seems such a dreadful thing to sell the place. And why need you hurry to send off a letter to Mr. Hilary about it? Wont it be time enough, when Mr. Putney has the writings ready. I think it will look very silly to send word beforehand. I could see that Mr. Putney didn't think it was business-like."

"You want to break your promise?" Suzette repeated.

"*No*, I don't want to break my promise. But I do want to do what's right; and I want to do what *I* think is right. I'm almost sick. I want Elbridge should stop for the doctor on his way to Mr. Putney's." She broke into a convulsive sobbing. "Oh, Suzette! *Do* give me a little more time! Wont you? And as soon as I can see it as you do"—

They heard the rattling of a key in the back door of the cottage, and they knew it was Elbridge coming to make the fire in the kitchen stove, as he always did against the time his wife should come to get breakfast.

Suzette started up from her pillow, and pulled Adeline's face down on her neck, so as to smother the sound of her

obs. "Hush! Don't let him hear! And I wouldn't let any one
now for the world that we didn't agree! You can think it
over all day, if you want; and I'll stop Mr. Putney from writ-
ng till you think as *I* do. But be still, now!"

"Yes, yes! I will," Adeline whispered back. "And I wont
quarrel with you, Sue! I know we shall think alike in the end.
Only, don't hurry me! And let Elbridge get the doctor to
ome. I'm afraid I'm going to be down sick."

She crept sighing back to bed, and after a little while Suz-
tte came dressed to look after her. "I think I'm going to get
little sleep, now," she said. "But don't forget to stop Mr.
Putney."

Suzette went out into the thin, sweet summer morning air,
nd walked up and down the avenue between the lodge and
he empty mansion. She had not slept, either; it was from her
irst drowse that Adeline had wakened her. But she was young,
nd the breath of the cool, southwest wind was a bath of rest
o her fevered senses. She felt herself grow stronger in it, and
he tried to think what she ought to do. If her purpose of the
day before still seemed so wholly and perfectly just, it seemed
ery difficult; and she began to ask herself whether she had
right to compel Adeline's consent to it. She felt the per-
plexities of the world where good and evil are often so mixed
hat when the problem passes from thoughts to deeds the
udgment is darkened and the will palsied. Till now the
wrong had always appeared absolutely apart from the right;
or the first time she perceived that a great right might in-
olve a lesser wrong; and she was daunted. But she meant to
ght out her fight wholly within herself, before she spoke
with Adeline again.

That day Matt Hilary came over from his farm to see
Wade, whom he found as before in his study at the church,
nd disposed to talk over Northwick's letter. "It's a miserable
ffair; humiliating; heart sickening. That poor soul's juggle
with his conscience is a most pathetic spectacle. I can't bring
myself to condemn him very fiercely. But while others may

make allowance for him, it's ruinous for him to excuse him self. That's truly perdition. Don't you feel that?" Wade asked.

"Yes. Yes," Matt assented, with a kind of absence. "But there is something else I wanted to speak with you about and I suppose it's this letter that's made it seem rather urgen now. You know when I asked you once about Jack Wilming ton"—

Wade shook his head. "There isn't the least hope in that direction. I'm sure there isn't. If he had cared anything for the girl, he would have shown it long ago!"

"I quite agree with you," said Matt, "and that isn't what I mean. But if it would have been right and well for him to come forward at such a time, why shouldn't some other man who does love her?" He hurried tremulously on: "Wade, let me ask you one thing more! You have seen her so much more than I; and I didn't know— Is it possible— Perhaps I ought to ask if *you* are at all—if *you* care for her?"

"For Miss Northwick? What an idea? Not the least in the world! *Why* do you ask?"

"Because *I* do!" said Matt. "I care everything for her. So much that when I thought of my love for her, I could no bear that it should be a wrong to any living soul, or that it should be a shadow's strength between her and any possible preference. And I came here with my mind made up, that if you thought Jack Wilmington had still some right to a hear ing from her, I would stand back. If there were any hope for him from himself or from her, I should be a fool not to stand back. And I thought,—I thought that if you, old fellow— But now, it's all right—*all* right"—

Matt wrung the hand which Wade yielded him with a dazed air, at first. A great many things went through Wade's mind, which he silenced on their way to his lips. It would not do to impart to Matt the impressions of a cold and arro gant nature which the girl had sometimes given him, and which Matt could not have received in the times of trouble and sorrow when he had chiefly seen her. Matt's confession

was a shock; Wade was scarcely less dismayed by the complications which it suggested; but he could no more impart his
misgivings than his impressions; he could no more tell Matt
that his father would be embarrassed and compromised by
his passion than he could tell him that he did not think Sue
Northwick was worthy of it. He was in the helpless predicament that confidants often find themselves in but his final
perception of his impossibilities enabled him to return the
fervid pressure of Matt's hand, and even to utter some of
those incoherencies which serve the purpose when another
wishes to do the talking.

"Of course," said Matt, "I'm ridiculous. I know that. I
haven't got anything to found my hopes on but the fact that
there's nothing in my way to the one insuperable obstacle:
to the fact that she doesn't and can't really care a straw for
me. But just now that seems a mere bagatelle." He laughed
with a nervous joy, and he kept talking, as he walked up and
down Wade's study. "I don't know that I have the hope of
anything; and I don't see how I'm to find out whether I have
or not, for the present. You know, Wade," he went on with
a simple-hearted sweetness which Wade found touching,
"I'm twenty-eight years old, and I don't believe I've ever
been in love before. Little fancies, of course; summer flirta-
tions; every one has them; but never anything serious, anything like *this*. And I could see, at home, that they would be
glad to have had me married. I rather think my father believes that a good sensible wife would bring me back to faith
in commercial civilization." He laughed out his relish of the
notion, but went on gravely: "Poor father! This whole business has been a terrible trial to him."

Wade wondered at his ability to separate the thought of
Suzette from the thought of her father; he inferred from his
ability to do so that he must have been thinking of her a
great deal, but he asked, "Isn't it all rather sudden, Matt?"
Wade put on a sympathetic, yet diplomatic smile for the purposes of this question.

"Not for me!" said Matt. He added, not very consequently,

"I suppose it must have happened to me the first moment I saw her here that day Louise and I came up about the accident. I couldn't truly say that she had ever been out of my mind a moment since. No, there's nothing sudden about it. Though I don't suppose these things usually take a great deal of time," Matt ended philosophically.

Wade left the dangerous ground he found himself on. He asked: "And your family, do they know of your—feeling?"

"Not in the least!" Matt answered radiantly. "It will come on them like a thunder-clap! If it ever comes on them at all," he added despondently.

Wade had his own belief that there was no cause for despondency in the aspect of the affair that Matt was looking at. But he could not offer to share his security with Matt, who continued to look serious, and said presently, "I suppose my father might think it complicated his relation to the Northwick trouble, and I have thought that, too. It makes it very difficult. My father is to be considered. You know, Wade, I think there are very few men like my father?"

"There are none, Matt!" said Wade.

"I don't mean he's perfect; and I think his ideas are wrong, most of them. But his conduct is as right as the conduct of any quick-tempered man ever was in the world. I honor him, and I don't believe a son ever loved his father more; and so I want to consider him all I can."

"Ah, I know that my dear fellow!"

"But the question is, how far can I consider him? There are times," said Matt, and he reddened, and laughed consciously, "when it seems as if I couldn't consider him at all: the times when I have some faint hope that she will listen to me, or wont think me quite a brute to speak to her of such a thing at such a moment. Then there are other times when I think he ought to be considered to the extreme of giving her up altogether; but those are the times when I know that I shall never have her to *give* up. Then it's an easy sacrifice."

"I understand," said Wade responding with a smile to Matt's self satire.

Matt went on, and as he talked he sometimes walked to Wade's window and looked out, sometimes he stopped and confronted him across his desk. "It's cowardly, in a way, not to speak at once—to leave her to suffer it out to the end alone; but I think that's what I owe to my father. No real harm can come to her from waiting. I risk the unfair chance I might gain by speaking now when she sorely needs help; but if ever she came to think she had given herself through that need— No, it wouldn't do! My father can do more for her if he isn't hampered by my feeling, and Louise can be her friend— What do you think, Wade? I've tried to puzzle it out, and this is the conclusion I've come to. Is it rather cold-blooded? I know it isn't at all like the lovemaking in the books. I suppose I ought to go and fling myself at her feet, in defiance of all the decencies and amenities and obligations of life, but somehow I can't bring myself to do it. I've thought it all conscientiously over, and I think I ought to wait."

"I think so, too, Matt. I think your decision is a just man's, and it's a true lover's, too. It does your heart as much honor as your head," and Wade gave him his hand now, with no mental reservation.

"Do you really think so, Caryl? That makes me very happy! I was afraid it might look calculating and self-interested"—

"You self interested, Matt!"

"Oh, I know! But is it considering my duty too much, my love too little? If I love her, hasn't she the first claim upon me, before father and mother, brother and sister, before all the world?"

"If you are sure she loves you, yes."

Matt laughed. "Ah, that's true; I hadn't thought of that little condition! Perhaps it changes the whole situation. Well, I must go, now. I've just run over from the farm to see you"—

"I inferred that from your peasant garb," said Wade with a smile at the rough farm suit Matt had on: his face refined it and made it look mildly improbable. "Besides," said Wade, as if the notion he recurred to were immediately relevant to

Matt's dress, "unless you are perfectly sure of yourself beyond any chance of change, you owe it to her as well as yourself to take time before speaking."

"I am perfectly sure, and I shall never change," said Matt with a shade of displeasure at the suggestion. "If there were nothing but that I should not take a moment of time." He relented and smiled again in adding, "but I have decided now, and I shall wait. And I'm very much obliged to you, old fellow, for talking the matter over with me, and helping me to see it in the right light."

"Oh, my dear Matt!" said Wade, in deprecation.

"Yes. And oh, by the way! I've got hold of a young fellow that I think you could do something for, Wade. Do you happen to remember the article on the defalcation in the *Boston Abstract?*"

"Yes, I do remember that. Didn't it treat the matter, if I recall it, very humanely—too humanely, perhaps?"

"Perhaps, from one point of view, too humanely. Well, it's the writer of that article—a young fellow, not twenty-five, yet, as completely at odds with life, as any one I ever saw. He has a great deal of talent, and no health or money; so he's toiling feebly for a living on a daily newspaper, instead of making literature. He was a reporter up to the time he wrote that article, but the managing editor is a man who recognizes quality; he's fond of Maxwell,—that's the fellow's name—and since then he's given him a chance in the office, at social topics. But he hasn't done very well; the fact is, the boy's too literary, and he's out of health, and he needs rest, and the comfort of appreciative friendship. I want you to meet him. I've got him up at my place out of the east winds. You'll be interested in him as a type—the artistic type cynicised by the hard conditions of life—newspaper conditions, and then economic conditions."

Matt smiled with satisfaction in what he felt to be his very successful formulation of Maxwell. Wade said he should be very glad to meet him; and if he could be of any use to him he should be even more glad. But his mind was still upon Matt's love affair, and as they wrung each other's hands, once more he said, "I think you've decided *so* wisely, Matt; and justly and unselfishly."

"It's involuntary unselfishness, if it's unselfishness at all," said Matt. He did not go; Wade stood bareheaded with him at the outer door of his study. After a while he said with embarrassment, "Wade! Do you think it would seem unfeeling —or out of taste, at all—if I went to see her at such a time?"

"Why, I can't imagine *your* doing anything out of taste, Matt."

"Don't be so smooth, Caryl! You know what I mean. Louise sent some messages by me to her. Will you take them, or"—

"I certainly see no reason why you shouldn't deliver Miss Hilary's messages yourself."

"Well, I do," said Matt. "But you needn't be afraid."

MATT took the lower road that wound away from Wade's church toward the Northwick place; but as he went, he kept thinking that he must not really try to see Suzette. It would be monstrous, at such a time; out of all propriety, of all decency; it would be taking advantage of her helplessness to intrude upon her the offer of help and of kindness which every instinct of her nature must revolt from. There was only one thing that could justify his coming, and that was impossible. Unless he came to tell her that he loved her and to ask her to let him take her burden upon him, to share her shame and her sorrow for his love's sake, he had no right to see her. At moments it seemed as if that were right and he could do it, no matter how impossible, and then he almost ran forward; but only to check himself, to stop short, and doubt whether not to turn back altogether. By such faltering progresses, he found himself in the Northwick avenue at last, and keeping doggedly on from the mansion, which the farm road had brought him to, until he reached the cottage at the avenue gate. On the threshold drooped a figure that the sight of set his heart beating with a stifling pulse in his throat, and he floundered on till he made out that this languid figure was Adeline. He could have laughed at the irony, the mockery of the anticlimax, if it had not been for the face that the old maid turned upon him at the approach of his footfalls, and the pleasure that lighted up its pathos when she recognized him.

"*Oh*, Mr. Hilary!" she said; and then she could not speak, for the twitching of her lips and the trembling of her chin.

He took her hand in silence, and it seemed natural for him to do that reverent and tender thing which is no longer a part of our custom; he bent over it and kissed the chill, bony knuckles.

She drew her hand away to find her handkerchief and wipe her tears. "I suppose you've come to see Suzette; but she's gone up to the village to talk with Mr. Putney; he's our lawyer."

"Yes," said Matt.

"I presume I don't need to talk to you about that—letter. I think,—and I believe Suzette will think so too, in the end,— that his mind is affected, and he just accuses himself of all those things because they've been burnt into it so. How are your father and mother? And your sister?"

She broke off with these questions, he could see, to stay herself in what she wished to say. "They are all well. Father is still in Boston; but mother and Louise are at the farm with me. They sent their love, and they are anxious to know if there is anything"—

"Thank you. Will you sit down here? It's so close indoors." She made room for him on the threshold; but he took the step below.

"I hope Miss Suzette is well?"

"Why, thank you, not very well. There isn't anything really the matter; but we didn't either of us sleep very well, last night; we were excited. I don't know as I ought to tell you," she began; "I don't suppose it's a thing you would know about, any way; but I've got to talk to somebody"—

"Miss Northwick," said Matt, "if there is anything in the world that I can do for you; or that you even hope I can do, I *beg* you to let me hear it. I should be glad beyond all words to help you."

"Oh, I don't know as anything can be done," she began after the fresh gush of tears which were her thanks, "but

Suzette and I have been talking it over a good deal, and we thought we would like to see your father about it. You see, Suzette can't feel right about our keeping the place here, if father's really done what he says he's done. We don't believe he has; but if he has, he has got to be found somewhere, and made to give up the money he says he has got. Suzette thinks we ought to give up the money we have got in the bank—fifteen hundred or two thousand dollars—and she wanted I should let her give up her half of the place here; and at first I *did* say she might. But come to find out from Mr. Putney, the whole place would have to be sold before it could be divided, and I couldn't seem to let it. That was what we—disputed about. Yes! We had a dispute; but it's all right now, or it will be, when we get the company to say they will stop the lawsuit against father, if he will give up the money he's got, and we will give up the place. Mr. Putney seemed to think the company couldn't stop it; but I don't see why a rich corporation like that couldn't do almost anything it wanted to with its money."

Her innocent corruption did not shock Matt, nor her scheme for defeating justice; but he smiled forlornly at the hopelessness of it. "I'm afraid Mr. Putney is right." He was silent, and then at the despair that came into her face, he hurried on to say, "But I will see my father, Miss Northwick; I will go down to see him at once; and if anything can be honorably and fairly done to save your father, I am sure he will try to do it for your sake. But don't expect anything," he said getting to his feet, and putting out his hand to her.

"No, no; I won't," she said, with gratitude that wrung his heart. "And—wont you wait and see Suzette?"

Matt reddened. "No; I think not, now. But, perhaps, I will come back; and—and—I will come soon again. Good-bye!"

"Mr. Hilary!" she called after him. He went back to her. "If—if your father don't think anything can be done, I don't want he should say anything about it."

"Oh, no; certainly not."

"And Mr. Hilary! Don't *you* let Suzette know I spoke to you. *I'll* tell her."

"Why of course."

On his way to Boston the affair seemed to grow less and less impossible to Matt; but he really knew nothing of the legal complications; and when he proposed it to his father, old Hilary shook his head. "I don't believe it could be done. The man's regularly indicted, and he's in contempt of court as long as he doesn't present himself for trial. That's the way I understand it. But I'll see our counsel. Whose scheme is this?"

"I don't know. Miss Northwick told me of it; but I fancied Miss Suzette"—

"Yes," said Hilary. "It must have cost her almost her life to give up her faith in that pitiful rascal."

"But after she had done that, it would cost her nothing to give up the property, and as I understood Miss Northwick, that was her sister's first impulse. She wished to give up her half of the estate unconditionally; but Miss Northwick wouldn't consent, and they compromised on the conditions she told me of."

"Well," said Hilary, "I think Miss Northwick showed the most sense. But, of course, Sue's a noble girl. She almost transfigures that old scoundrel of a father of hers. That fellow—Jack Wilmington—ought to come forward now and show himself a man if he *is* one. *Any* man might be proud of such a girl's love—and they say she was in love with him. But he seems to have preferred to dangle after his uncle's wife. He isn't good enough for her, and probably he always knew it."

Matt profitted by the musing fit that came upon his father, to go and look at the picture over the mantel. It was not a new picture; but he did not feel that he was using his father quite frankly; and he kept looking at it for that reason.

"If those poor creatures gave up their property what would they do? They've absolutely nothing else in the world!"

"I fancy," said Matt, "that isn't a consideration that would weigh with Suzette Northwick."

"No. If there's anything in heredity, the father of such a girl must have some good in him. Of course they wouldn't be allowed to suffer."

"Do you mean that the company would regard the fact that it had no legal claim on the property, and would recognize it in their behalf?"

"The company!" Hilary roared. "The company has no right to that property, moral *or* legal. But we should act as if we had. If it were unconditionally offered to us, we ought to acknowledge it as an act of charity to us, and not of restitution. But every man Jack of us would hold out for a right to it that didn't exist, and we should take it as part of our due; and I should be such a coward that I couldn't tell the Board what I thought of our pusillanimity."

"It seems rather hard for men to act magnanimously in a corporate capacity, or even humanly," said Matt. "But I don't know but there would be an obscure and negative justice in such action. It would be right for the company to accept the property if it was right for Northwick's daughter to offer it, and I think it is most unquestionably right for her to do that."

"Do you, Matt? Well, well," said Hilary, willing to be comforted, "perhaps you're right. You must send Louise and your mother over to see her."

"Well, perhaps not just now. She's proud, and sensitive, and perhaps it might seem intrusive, at this juncture?"

"Intrusive? Nonsense! She'll be glad to see them. Send them right over!"

Matt knew this was his father's way of yielding the point, and he went away with his promise to say nothing of the matter they had talked of till he heard from Putney. After that, it would be time enough to ascertain the whereabouts of Northwick, which no one knew yet, not even his own children.

What his father had said in praise of Suzette gave his love for her unconscious approval; but at the same time it created a sort of comedy situation, and Matt was as far from the comic as he hoped he was from the romantic in his mood. When he thought of going direct to her, he hated to be going, like the hero of a novel, to offer himself to the heroine at the moment her fortunes were darkest; but he knew that he was only like that outwardly, and inwardly was simply and humbly her lover, who wished in any way or any measure he might, to be her friend and helper. He thought he might put his offer in some such form as would leave her free to avail herself a little if not much of his longing to comfort and support her in her trial. But at last he saw that he could do nothing for the present, and that it would be cruel and useless to give her more than the tacit help of a faithful friend. He did not go back to Hatboro' as he longed to do. He went back to his farm, and possessed his soul in such patience as he could.

XII

Suzette came back from Putney's office with such a disheartened look that Adeline had not the courage to tell her of Matt's visit and the errand he had undertaken for her. The lawyer had said no more than that he did not believe anything could be done. He was glad they had decided not to transfer their property to the company, without first trying to make interest for their father with it; that was their right and their duty; and he would try what could be done; but he warned Suzette that he should probably fail.

"And then what did he think we ought to do?" Adeline asked.

"He didn't say," Suzette answered.

"I presume," Adeline went on after a little pause, "that you would like to give up the property any way. Well, you can do it, Suzette." The joy she might have expected did not show itself in her sister's face, and she added, "I've thought it all over, and I see it as you do, now. Only," she quavered, "I do want to do all I can for poor father, first."

"Yes," said Suzette spiritlessly, "Mr. Putney said we ought."

"Sue," said Adeline after another little pause, "I don't know what you'll think of me, for what I've done. Mr. Hilary has been here"—

"Mr. Hilary!"

"Yes. He came over from his farm"—

"Oh! I thought you meant his father." The color began to mount into the girl's cheeks.

240

"Louise and Mrs. Hilary sent their love and they all want to do anything they can; and—and—I told Mr. Hilary what we were going to try; and—he said he would speak to his father about it; and— Oh, Suzette, I'm afraid I've done more than I ought!"

Suzette was silent, and then, "No," she said, "I can't see what harm there could be in it."

"He said," Adeline pursued, with joyful relief, "he wouldn't let his father speak to the rest about it, till we were ready; and I know he'll do all he can for us. Don't you?"

Sue answered, "I don't see what harm it can do for him to speak to his father. I hope, Adeline," she added with the severity Adeline had dreaded, "you didn't ask it as a favor from him?"

"No, no! I didn't indeed, Sue! It came naturally. He offered to do it."

"Well," said Suzette, with a sort of relaxation, and she fell back in the chair where she had been sitting.

"I don't see," said Adeline with an anxious look at the girl's worn face, "but what we'd both better have the doctor."

"Oh, the doctor!" cried Suzette. "What can the doctor do for troubles like ours?" She put up her hands to her face, and bowed herself on them, and sobbed, with the first tears she had shed since the worst had come upon them.

The company's counsel submitted Putney's overtures as he expected, to the State's attorney in hypothetical form and the State's attorney, as Putney expected, dealt with the actuality. He said that when Northwick's friends communicated with him and ascertained his readiness to surrender the money he had with him, and to make restitution in every possible way, it would be time to talk of a *nolle prosequi*. In the meantime by the fact of absconding he was in contempt of court. He must return and submit himself for trial, and take the chance of a merciful sentence.

There could be no other answer, he said, and he could give none for Putney to carry back to the defaulter's daughters.

Suzette received it in silence, as if she had nerved herself up to bear it so. Adeline had faltered between her hopes and fears, but she apparently decided how she should receive the worst, if the worst came.

"Well, then," she said, "we must give up the place. You can get the papers ready, Mr. Putney."

"I will do whatever you say, Miss Northwick."

"Yes, and I don't want you to think, that I don't want to do it. It's my doing, now; and if my sister was all against it, I should wish to do it all the same."

Matt Hilary learned from his father the result of the conference with the State's attorney, and he came up to Hatboro' the next day, to see Putney on his father's behalf, and to express the wish of his family that Mr. Putney would let them do anything he could think of for his clients. He got his message out bunglingly, with embarrassed circumlocution and repetition; but this was what it came to in the end.

Putney listened with sarcastic patience, shifting the tobacco in his mouth from one thin cheek to the other, and letting his fierce blue eyes burn on Matt's kindly face.

"Well, sir," he said, "what do *you* think can be done for two women, brought up as ladies, who choose to beggar themselves?"

"Is it so bad as that?" Matt asked.

"Why, you can judge for yourself. My present instructions are to make their whole estate over to the Ponkwasset Mills company"—

"But I thought—I thought they might have something besides—something"—

"There was a little money in the bank that Northwick placed there to their credit when he went away; but I've had their instructions to pay that over to your company, too. I suppose they will accept it?"

"It isn't my company," said Matt. "I've nothing whatever to do with it—or any company. But I've no doubt they'll accept it."

"They can't do otherwise," said the lawyer with a humorous sense of the predicament twinkling in his eyes. "And that will leave my clients just nothing in the world—until Mr. Northwick comes home with that fortune he proposes to make. In the meantime they have their choice of starving to death, or living on charity. And I don't believe," said Putney, breaking down with a laugh, "they've the slightest notion of doing either."

Matt stood appalled at the prospect which the brute terms brought before him. He realized that after all there is no misery like that of want, and that yonder poor girl had chosen something heavier to bear than her father's shame.

"Of course," he said, "they mustn't be allowed to suffer. We shall count upon you to see that nothing of that kind happens. You can contrive somehow not to let them know that they are destitute."

"Why," said Putney, putting his leg over the back of a chair into its seat, for his greater ease in conversation, "I could, if I were a lawyer in a novel. But what do you think I can do with two women like these, who follow me up every inch of the way, and want to know just what I mean by every step I take? You're acquainted with Miss Suzette, I suppose?"

"Yes," said Matt, consciously.

"Well, do you suppose that such a girl as that, when she had made up her mind to starve, wouldn't know what you were up to if you pretended to have found a lot of money belonging to her under the cupboard?"

"The company must do something," said Matt desperately. "They have no claim on the property, none whatever!"

"Now you're shouting." Putney put a comfortable mass of tobacco in his mouth, and began to work his jaws vigorously upon it.

"They mustn't take it—they won't take it!" cried Matt.

Putney laughed scornfully.

XIII

Matt made his way home to his farm, by a tiresome series of circuitous railroad connections across country. He told his mother of the new shape the trouble of the Northwicks had taken, and asked her if she could not go to see them, and find out some way to help them.

Louise wished to go instantly to see them. She cried out over the noble action that Suzette wished to do; she knew it was all Suzette.

"Yes, it is noble," said Mrs. Hilary. "But I almost wish she wouldn't do it."

"Why, mamma!"

"It complicates matters. They could have gone on living there very well as they were; and the company doesn't need it; but now, where will they go? What will become of them?" Louise had not thought of that, and she found it shocking.

"I suppose," Matt said, "that the company would let them stay where they are, for the present, and that they wont be actually houseless. But they propose now to give up the money that their father left for their support till he could carry out the crazy schemes for retrieving himself that he speaks of in his letter; and then they will have nothing to live on."

"I *knew* Suzette would do that!" said Louise. "Before that letter came out she always said that her father never did what the papers said. But that cut the ground from under her feet, and such a girl could have no peace till she had given up every-thing—everything!"

"Something must be done," said Mrs. Hilary. "Have they—has Suzette—any plans?"

"None, but that of giving up the little money they have left in the bank," said Matt, forlornly.

"Well," Mrs. Hilary commented with a sort of magisterial authority, "they've all managed as badly as they could."

"Well, mother, they hadn't a very hopeful case, to begin with," said Matt, and Louise smiled.

"I suppose your poor father is worried almost to death about it," Mrs. Hilary pursued.

"He was annoyed, but I couldn't see that he had lost his appetite. I don't think that even his worriment is the first thing to be considered, though."

"No; of course not, Matt. I was merely trying to think. I don't know just what we can offer to do; but we must find out. Yes, we must go and see them. They don't seem to have any-one else. It is very strange that they should have no relations they can go to!" Mrs. Hilary meditated upon a hardship which she seemed to find personal. "Well, we must try what we can do," she said relentingly after a moment's pause.

They talked the question of what she could do futilely over, and at the end Mrs. Hilary said, "I will go there in the morn-ing. And I think I shall go from there to Boston, and try to get your father off to the shore."

"Oh!" said Louise.

"Yes; I don't like his being in town so late."

"Poor papa! Did he look very much wasted away, Matt? Why don't you get him to come up here?"

"He's been asked," said Matt.

"Yes, I know he hates the country," Louise assented. She rose and went to the glass door standing open on the piazza, where a syringa bush was filling the dull, warm air with its breath. "We must all try to think what we can do for Suzette."

Her mother looked at the doorway after she had vanished through it; and listened a moment to her voice in talk with some one outside. The two voices retreated together, and

Louise's laugh made itself heard farther off. "She is a light nature," sighed Mrs. Hilary.

"Yes," Matt admitted, thinking he would rather like to be of a light nature himself at that moment. "But I don't know that there is anything wrong in it. It would do no good if she took the matter heavily."

"Oh, I don't mean the Northwicks entirely," said Mrs. Hilary. "But she is so in regard to everything. I know she is a good child, but I'm afraid she doesn't feel things deeply. Matt, I don't believe I like this protégé of yours."

"Maxwell?"

"Yes. He's too intense!"

"Aren't you a little difficult, mother?" Matt asked. "You don't like Louise's lightness, and you don't like Maxwell's intensity. I think he'll get over that. He's sick, poor fellow; he wont be so intense when he gets better."

"Oh, yes; very likely." Mrs. Hilary paused, and then she added abruptly, "I hope Louise's sympathies will be concentrated on Sue Northwick for a while, now."

"I thought they were that, already," said Matt. "I'm sure Louise has shown herself anxious to be her friend ever since her troubles began. I hadn't supposed she was so attached to her—so constant"—

"She's romantic; but she's worldly; she likes the world and its ways. There never was a girl who liked better the pleasure, the interest of the moment. I don't say she's fickle; but one thing drives another out of her mind. She likes to live in a dream; she likes to make-believe. Just now she's all taken up with an idyllic notion of country life, because she's here in June, with that sick young reporter to patronize. But she's the creature of her surroundings, and as soon as she gets away she'll be a different person altogether. She's a strange contradiction!" Mrs. Hilary sighed. "If she would only be *entirely* worldly, it wouldn't be so difficult; but when her mixture of unworldliness comes in, it's quite distracting." She waited a moment as if to let Matt ask her what she meant; but he did not, and she went on: "She's certainly not a simple character—like Sue Northwick, for instance."

Matt now roused himself. "Is *she* a simple character?" he asked, with a show of indifference.

"Perfectly," said his mother. "She always acts from pride. That explains everything she does."

"I know she is proud," Matt admitted, finding a certain comfort in openly recognizing traits in Sue Northwick that he had never deceived himself about. He had a feeling, too, that he was behaving with something like the candor due his mother in saying, "I could imagine her being imperious, even arrogant at times; and certainly she is a wilful person. But I don't see," he added, "why we shouldn't credit her with something better than pride in what she proposes to do, now."

"She has behaved very well," said Mrs. Hilary, "and much better than could have been expected of her father's daughter."

Matt felt himself getting angry at this scanty justice but he tried to answer calmly, "Surely, mother, there must be a point where the blame of the innocent ends! I should be very sorry if you went to Miss Northwick with the idea that we were conferring a favor in any way. It seems to me that she is indirectly putting us under an obligation which we shall find it difficult to discharge with delicacy."

"Aren't you rather fantastic, Matt?"

"I'm merely trying to be just. The company has no right to the property which she is going to give up."

"We are not the company."

"Father is the president."

"Well, and he got Mr. Northwick a chance to save himself and he abused it and ran away. And if she is not responsible for her father, why should you feel so for yours? But I think you may trust me, Matt, to do what is right and proper—even what is delicate—with Miss Northwick."

"Oh, yes! I didn't mean that."

"You said something like it, my dear."

"Then I beg your pardon, mother. I certainly wasn't thinking of her alone. But she *is* proud, and I hoped you would let her feel that *we* realize all that she is doing."

"I'm afraid," said Mrs. Hilary, with a final sigh, "that if I were quite frank with her, I should tell her she was a silly, headstrong girl, and I wished she wouldn't do it."

XIV

THE MORNING which followed was that of a warm, lulling, luxurious June day, whose high tides of life spread to everything. Maxwell felt them in his weak pulses where he sat writing at an open window of the farm house, and early in the forenoon he came out on the piazza of the farm house, with a cushion clutched in one of his lean hands; his soft hat brim was pulled down over his dull, dreamy eyes, where the far off look of his thinking still lingered. Louise was in the hammock, and she lifted herself alertly out of it at sight of him, with a smile for his absent gaze.

"Have you got through?"

"I've got tired; or rather, I've got bored. I thought I would go up to the camp."

"You're not going to lie on the ground, there?" she asked with the importance and authority of a woman who puts herself in charge of a sick man, as a woman always must when there is such a man near her.

"I would be willing to lie under it, such a day as this," he said. "But I'll take the shawl, if that's what you mean. I thought it was here?"

"I'll get it for you," said Louise; and he let her go into the parlor, and bring it out to him. She laid it in a narrow fold over his shoulder; he thanked her carelessly, and she watched him sweep languidly across the buttercupped and dandelioned grass of the meadow land about the house, to the dark shelter of the pine grove at the north. The sun struck full upon

249

the long levels of the boughs, and kindled their needles to a glistening mass; underneath, the ground was red, and through the warm-looking twilight of the sparse wood, the gray canvas of a tent showed; Matt often slept there in the summer, and so the place was called the camp. There was a hammock between two of the trees, just beyond the low stone wall, and Louise saw Maxwell get into it.

Matt came out on the piazza in his blue woollen shirt and overalls and high boots, and his cork helmet topping all.

"You look like a cultivated cowboy that had gobbled an English tourist, Matt," said his sister. "Have you got anything for me?"

Matt had some letters in his hands which the man had just brought up from the postoffice. "No; but there are two for Maxwell"—

"I will carry them to him, if you're busy. He's just gone over to the camp."

"Well, do," said Matt. He gave them to her, and he asked, "How do you think he is, this morning?"

"He must be pretty well; he's been writing ever since breakfast."

"I wish he hadn't," said Matt. "He ought really to be got away somewhere out of the reach of newspapers. I'll see. Louise, how do you think a girl like Sue Northwick would feel about an outright offer of help at such a time as this?"

"How, help? It's very difficult to help people," said Louise wisely. "Especially, when they're not able to help themselves. Poor Sue! I don't know what she *will* do. If Jack Wilmington— but he never really cared for her, and now I don't believe she cares for him. No, it couldn't be."

"No; the idea of love would be sickening to her now."

Louise opened her eyes. "Why, I don't know what you mean, Matt. If she still cared for him, I can't imagine any time when she would rather know that he cared for her."

"But her pride—wouldn't she feel that she couldn't meet him on equal terms"—

"Oh, pride! Stuff! Do you suppose that a girl who really

cared for a person would think of the terms she met them on?
When it comes to such a thing as that there *is* no pride; and
proud girls and meek girls are just alike—like cats in the dark."

"Do you think so?" asked Matt; the sunny glisten, which
had been wanting to them before, came into his eyes.

"I *know* so," said Louise. "Why, do you think that Jack
Wilmington still"—

"No; no. I was just wondering. I think I shall run down
to Boston to-morrow and see father— Or, no! Mother wont be
back till tomorrow evening. Well, I will talk with you at dinner, about it."

Matt went off to his mowing, and Louise heard the cackle
of his machine before she reached the camp with Maxwell's
letters.

"Don't get up!" she called to him, when he lifted himself
with one arm at the stir of her gown over the pine needles.
"Merely two letters that I thought perhaps you might want
to see at once."

He took them, and glancing at one of them threw it out on
the ground. "This is from Ricker," he said, opening the other.
"If you'll excuse me," and he began to read it. "Well, that is
all right," he said when he had run it through. "He can manage without me a little while longer; but a few more days like
this will put an end to my loafing. I begin to feel like work for
the first time since I came up here."

"The good air is beginning to tell," said Louise, sitting
down on the board which formed a bench between two of the
trees fronting the hammock. "But if you hurry back to town,
now, you will spoil everything. You must stay the whole summer."

"You rich people are amusing," said Maxwell, turning himself on his side, and facing her. "You think poor people can
do what they like."

"I think they can do what other people like," said the girl,
"if they will try. What is to prevent your staying here till you
get perfectly well?"

"The uncertainty whether I shall ever get perfectly well,

for one thing," said Maxwell, watching with curious interest the play of the light and shade flecks on her face and figure.

"I *know* you will get well, if you stay," she interrupted.

"And for another thing," he went on, "the high and holy duty we poor people feel not to stop working for a living as long as we live. It's a caste pride. Poverty obliges, as well as nobility."

"Oh, pshaw. Pride obliges, too. It's your wicked pride. You're worse than rich people, as you call us; a great deal prouder. Rich people will let you help them."

"So would poor people, if they didn't need help. You can take a gift if you don't need it. You can accept an invitation to dinner, if you're surfeited to loathing, but you can't let any one give you a meal if you're hungry. You rich people are like children, compared with us poor folks. You don't know life; you don't know the world. I should like to do a girl brought up like you in the ignorance and helplessness of riches."

"You would make me hateful."

"I would make you charming."

"Well, do me, then!"

"Ah, you wouldn't like it."

"Why?"

"Because—I found it out in my newspaper work, when I had to interview people, and write them up—people don't like to have the good points they have, recognized; they want you to celebrate the good points they haven't got. If a man is amiable and kind and has something about him that wins everybody's heart, he wants to be portrayed as a very dignified and commanding character, full of inflexible purpose and indomitable will."

"I don't see," said Louise, "why you think I'm weak, and low minded and undignified."

Maxwell laughed. "Did I say something of that kind?"

"You meant it."

"If ever I have to interview you I shall say that under a mask of apparent incoherency and irrelevance, Miss Hilary conceals a profound knowledge of human nature and a gift of divination which explores the most unconscious opinions and motives of her interlocutor. How would you like that?"

"Pretty well, because I think it's true. But I shouldn't like to be interviewed."

"Well, you're safe from me. My interviewing days are over. I believe if I keep on getting better at the rate I've been going the last week, I shall be able to write a play this summer, besides doing my work for the *Abstract*. If I could do that, and it succeeded, the riddle would be read for me."

"What do you mean?"

"I mean that I should have a handsome income, and could give up newspaper work altogether."

"Could you? How glorious!" said Louise, with the sort of maternal sympathy she permitted herself to feel for the sick youth. "How much could you get for your play?"

"If it was only reasonably successful, it would be worth five or six thousand dollars a year."

"And is that a handsome income?" she asked, with mounting earnestness.

He pulled himself up in the hammock to get her face fully in view, and asked, "How much do you think I've been able to average up to this time?"

"I don't know. I'm afraid I don't know at all about such things. But I should *like* to."

Maxwell let himself drop back into the hammock. "I think I wont humiliate myself by giving the figures. I'd better leave it to your imagination. You'll be sure to make it enough."

"Why should you be ashamed of it, if it's ever so little?" she asked. "But *I* know. It's your pride. It's like Sue Northwick's wanting to give up all her property because her father wrote that letter, and said he had used the company's money. And Matt says it isn't his property at all, and the company has no right to it. If she gives it up, she and her sister will have nothing to live on. And they *wont* let themselves be helped—anymore than—than—*you* will!"

"No. We began with that: people who need help can't let

you help them. Don't they know where their father is?"

"No. But of course they must, now, before long."

Maxwell said after the silence that followed upon this: "I should like to have a peep into that man's soul."

"Horrors! Why should you?" asked Louise.

"It would be such splendid material. If he is fond of his children"—

"He and Sue doat upon each other. I don't see how she can endure him: he always made me feel creepy."

"Then he must have written that letter to conciliate public feeling, and to make his children easier about him and his future. And now if you could see him when he realizes that he's only brought more shame on them, and forced them to beggar themselves—it would be a tremendous situation."

"But I shouldn't *like* to see him at such a time. It seems to me that's worse than interviewing, Mr. Maxwell."

There was a sort of recoil from him in her tone, which perhaps he felt. It seemed to interest, rather than offend him. "You don't get the artistic point of view."

"I don't want to get it, if that's it. And if your play is going to be about any such thing as that"—

"It isn't," said Maxwell. "I failed on that. I shall try a comic motive."

"Oh!" said Louise, in the concessive tone people use when they do not know but they have wronged some one. She spiritually came back to him, but materially she rose to go away and leave him. She stooped for the letter he had dropped out of the hammock and gave it him. "Don't you want this?"

"Oh, thank you! I'd forgotten it." He glanced at the superscription. "It's from Pinney. You ought to know Pinney, Miss Hilary, if you want the *true* artistic point of view."

"Is he a literary man?"

"Pinney? Did you read the account of the defalcation in the *Events*—when it first came out? All illustrations?"

"*That?* I don't wonder you didn't care to read his letter! Or perhaps he's your friend"—

"Pinney's everybody's friend," said Maxwell, with an odd sort of relish. "He's delightful. I should like to do Pinney. He's a type." Louise stood frowning at the mere notion of Pinney. "He's not a bad fellow, Miss Hilary, though he *is* a remorseless interviewer. He would be very good material. He is a mixture of motives, like everybody else, but he has only one ambition: he wants to be the greatest newspaper man of his generation. The ladies nearly always like him. He never lets five minutes pass without speaking of his wife; he's so proud of her he can't keep still."

"I should think she would detest him."

"She doesn't. She's quite as proud of him as he is of her. It's' affecting to witness their devotion—or it would be if it were not such a bore."

"I can't understand you," said Louise, leaving him to his letter.

XV

———

PART of Matt Hilary's protest against the status in which he found himself a swell was to wash his face for dinner in a tin basin on the back porch, like the farm hands. When he was alone at the farm he had the hands eat with him; when his mother and sister were visiting him he pretended that the table was too small for them all at dinner and tea, though he continued to breakfast with the hands because the ladies were never up at his hour; the hands knew well enough what it meant, but they liked Matt.

Louise found him at the roller towel, after his emblematic ablutions. "Oh, is it so near dinner?" she asked.

"Yes. Where is Maxwell?"

"I left him up at the camp." She walked a little way out into the ground-ivy that matted the back-yard under the scattering spruce trees.

Matt followed, and watched the homing and departing bees around the hives in the deep red clovered grass near the wall.

"Those fellows will be swarming, before long," he said with a measure of the good comradeship he felt for all living things.

"I don't see," said Louise plucking a tender green shoot from one of the fir boughs overhead, "why Mr. Maxwell is so hard."

"Is he hard?" asked Matt. "Well, perhaps he is."

"He is very sneering and bitter," said the girl. "I don't like it."

"Ah, he's to blame for that," Matt said. "But as for his hardness, that probably comes from his having had to make such

256

a hard fight for what he wants to be in life. That hardens people, and brutalizes them, but somehow we mostly admire them and applaud them for their success against odds. If we had a true civilization a man wouldn't have to fight for the chance to do the thing he is fittest for, that is, to be himself. But I'm glad you don't like Maxwell's hardness; I don't, myself."

"He seems to look upon the whole world as material, as he calls it; he doesn't seem to regard people as fellow beings, as you do, Matt, or even as servants or inferiors; he hasn't so much kindness for them as that."

"Well, that's the odious side of the artistic nature," said Matt, smiling tolerantly. "But he'll probably get over that; he's very young; he thinks he has to be relentlessly literary, now."

"He's older than I am!" said Louise.

"He hasn't seen so much of the world."

"He thinks he's seen a great deal more. I don't think he's half so nice as we supposed. I should call him dangerous."

"Oh, I shouldn't say *that*, exactly," Matt returned. "But he certainly hasn't our traditions. I'll just step over and call him to dinner."

"Oh, no! Let me try if I can blow the horn." She ran to where the long tin tube hung on the porch, and coming out with it again, set it to her lips and evoked some stertorous and crumby notes from it. "Do you suppose he saw me?" she asked, running back with the horn.

Matt could not say; but Maxwell had seen her, and had thought of a poem which he imagined illustrated with the figure of a tall, beautiful girl lifting a long tin horn to her lips with outstretched arms. He did not know whether to name it simply The Dinner Horn, or grotesquely, Hebe Calling the Gods to Nectar. He debated the question as he came lagging over the grass with his cushion in one hand and Pinney's letter, still opened, in the other. He said to Matt, who came out to get the cushion of him, "Here's something I'd like to talk over with you, when you've the time."

"Well, after dinner," said Matt.

Pinney's letter was a long one, written in pencil on one side of long slips of paper, like printer's copy; the slips were each carefully folioed in the upper right hand corner; but the language was the language of Pinney's life and not the decorative diction which he usually addressed to the public on such slips of paper.

"I guess," it began, "I've got onto the biggest thing yet, Maxwell. The *Events* is going to send me to do the Social Science Congress which meets in Quebec this year, and I'm going to take Mrs. Pinney along and have a good time. She's got so she can travel first-rate, now; and the change will do her and the baby both good. I shall interview the social science wiseacres, and do their proceedings, of course, but the thing that I'm onto is Northwick. I've always felt that Northwick kind of belonged to yours truly, anyway; I was the only man that worked him up in any sort of shape, at the time the defalcation came out, and I've got a little idea that I think will simply clean out all competition. That letter of his set me to thinking, as soon as I read it, and my wife and I both happened on the idea at the same time: clear case of telepathy. Our idea is that Northwick didn't go to Europe—of course he didn't!—but he's just holding out for terms with the company. I don't believe he's got off with much money; but if he was going into business with it in Canada, he would have laid low till he'd made his investments. So my theory is that he's got all the money he took with him except his living expenses. I believe I can find Northwick, and I am not going to come home without trying hard. I am going to have a detective's legal outfit, and I flatter myself I can get Northwick over the frontier somehow, and restore him to the arms of his anxious friends of the Ponkwasset Company. I don't know yet just how I shall do it, but I guess I shall do it. I shall have Mrs. Pinney's advice and counsel, and she's a team; but I shall have to leave her and the baby at Quebec, while I'm roaming round in Rimouski and the wilderness generally, and I shall need active help.

"Now, I liked some things in that *Abstract* article of yours;

it was snappy, and literary, and all that, and it showed grasp of the subject. It showed a humane and merciful spirit toward our honored friend that could be made to tell in my little game if I could get the use of it. So I've concluded to let you in on the ground floor, if you want to go into the enterprise with me; if you don't, don't give it away; that's all. My idea is that Northwick can be got at quicker by two than by one; but we have not only got to get *at* him, but we have got to *get* him; and get him on this side of Jordan. I guess we shall have to do that by moral suasion mostly, and that's where your massive and penetrating intellect will be right on deck. You wont have to play a part, either; if you believe that his only chance of happiness on earth is to come home and spend the rest of his life in State's prison, you can conscientiously work him from that point of view. Seriously, Maxwell, I think this is a great chance. If there's any of that money he speaks of we shall have our pickings; and then as a mere scoop, if we get at Northwick at all, whether we can coax him over the line or not, we will knock out the fellow that fired the Ephesian dome so that he'll never come to time in all eternity.

"I mean business, Maxwell; I haven't mentioned this to anybody else but my wife, yet; and if you don't go in with me, nobody shall. *I want you, old boy, and I'm willing to pay for you.* If this thing goes through, I shall be in a position to name my own place and price on the *Events.* I expect to be managing editor before the year's out, and then I shall secure the best talent as leading writer, which his name is Brice E. Maxwell, and don't you forget it.

"Now, you think it over, Maxwell. There's no hurry. Take time. We've got to wait till the Soc. Sci. Congress meets, anyway, and we've got to let the professional pursuit die out. This letter of Northwick's will set a lot of detectives after him, and if they can't find him, or can't work him, after they've found him, they'll get tired, and give him up for a bad job. Then will be the time for the gifted amateur to step in and show what a free and untrammeled press can do to punish vice and reward virtue."

———

MAXWELL explained to Matt, as he had explained to Louise, that Pinney was the reporter who had written up the Northwick case for *The Events*. He said, after Matt had finished reading the letter, "I thought you would like to know about this. I don't regard Pinney's claim on my silence where you're concerned; in fact, I don't feel bound to him, anyway."

"Thank you," said Matt. "Then I suppose his proposal doesn't tempt you?"

"Why, yes it does. But not as he imagines. I should like such an adventure, well enough, because it would give me a glimpse of life and character that I should like to know something about. But the reporter business and the detective business wouldn't attract me."

"No, I should suppose not," said Matt. "What sort of fellow personally is this—Pinney?"

"Oh, he isn't bad. He is a regular type," said Maxwell, with tacit enjoyment of the typicality of Pinney. "He hasn't the least chance in the world of working up into any controlling place in the paper. They don't know much in the *Events* office; but they do know Pinney. He's a great liar and a braggart, and he has no more notion of the immunities of private life than— Well, perhaps it's because he would as soon turn his own life inside out as not, and in fact would rather. But he's very domestic, and very kind-hearted to his wife; it seems they have a baby, now, and I've no doubt Pinney is a pattern to parents. He's always advising you to get married; but he's a born Bohemian. He's the most harmless creature in the world, as far as intentions go, and quite softhearted, but he wouldn't spare his dearest friend if he could make copy of him; it would be impossible. I should say he was first a newspaper man, and then a man. He's an awfully common nature, and hasn't the first literary instinct. If I had any mystery, or mere privacy that I wanted to guard, and I thought Pinney was on the scent of it, I shouldn't have any more scruple in setting my foot on him than I would on that snake."

A little reptile, allured by their immobility, had crept out of the stone wall which they were standing near, and lay flashing its keen eyes at them, and running out its tongue, a forked thread of tremulous scarlet. Maxwell brought his heel down upon its head as he spoke, and ground it into the earth.

Matt winced at the anguish of the twisting and writhing thing. "Ah, I don't think I should have killed it!"

"I should," said Maxwell.

"Then you think we couldn't trust him?"

"Yes. If you put your foot on him in some sort of agreement, and keep it there. Why, of course! Any man can be held. But don't let Pinney have room to wriggle."

They turned, and walked away, Matt keeping the image of the tormented snake in his mind; it somehow mixed there with the idea of Pinney, and unconsciously softened him toward the reporter.

"Would there be any harm," he asked, after a while, "in my acting on a knowledge of this letter in behalf of Mr. Northwick's family?"

"Not a bit," said Maxwell. "I make you perfectly free of it, as far as I'm concerned; and it can't hurt Pinney, even if he ought to be spared. *He* wouldn't spare *you*."

"I don't know," said Matt, "that I could justify myself in hurting him on that ground. I shall be careful about him. I don't at all know that I shall want to use it; but it has just struck me that perhaps— But I don't know! I should have to talk with their attorney— I will see about it! And I thank you very much, Mr. Maxwell."

"Look here, Mr. Hilary!" said Maxwell. "Use Pinney all

you please, and all you can; but I warn you he is a dangerous tool. He doesn't mean any harm till he's tempted, and when it's done he doesn't think it's any harm. He isn't to be trusted an instant beyond his self-interest; and yet he has flashes of unselfishness that would deceive the very elect. Good heavens!" cried Maxwell, "if I could get such a character as Pinney's into a story or a play, I wouldn't take odds from any man living!"

His notion, whatever it was, grew upon Matt, so that he waited more and more impatiently for his mother's return, in order to act upon it. When she did get back to the farm she could only report from the Northwicks that she had said pretty much what she thought she would like to say to Suzette concerning her wilfulness and obstinacy in wishing to give up her property; but Matt inferred that she had at the same time been able to infuse so much motherly comfort into her scolding that it had left the girl consoled and encouraged. She had found out from Adeline that their great distress was not knowing yet where their father was. Apparently, he thought that his published letter was sufficient reassurance for the time being. Perhaps he did not wish them to get at him in any way, or to have his purposes affected by any appeal from them. Perhaps, as Adeline firmly believed, his mind had been warped by his suffering—he must have suffered greatly —and he was not able to reason quite sanely about the situation. Mrs. Hilary spoke of the dignity and strength which both the sisters showed in their trial and present stress. She praised Suzette, especially; she said her trouble seemed to have softened and chastened her; she was really a noble girl, and she had sent her love to Louise; they had both wished to be remembered to everyone. "Adeline especially wished to be remembered to you, Matt; she said they should never forget your kindness."

Matt got over to Hatboro' the next day, and went to see Putney, who received him with some ironical politeness, when Matt said he had come hoping to be useful to his clients, the

Miss Northwicks. "Well, we all hope something of that kind, Mr. Hilary. You were here on a mission of that kind, before. But may I ask why you think I should believe you wish to be useful to them?"

"Why?"

"Yes. Your father is the president of the company Mr. Northwick had his little embarrassment with, and the natural presumption would be that you could not really be friendly toward his family."

"But we *are* friendly! All of us! My father would do them any service in his power, consistent with his duty to—to—his business associates."

"Ah, that's just the point. And you would all do anything you could, for them, consistent with your duty to him. That's perfectly right—perfectly natural. But you must see that it doesn't form a ground of common interest for us. I talked with you about the Miss Northwicks' affairs the other day—too much, I think. But I can't, to-day. I shall be glad to converse with you on any other topic—discuss the ways of God to man, or any little interest of that kind. But unless I can see my way clearer to confidence between us in regard to my clients' affairs than I do at present, I must avoid them."

It was absurd; but in his high good-will toward Adeline, and in his latent tenderness for Suzette, Matt was hurt by the lawyer's distrust, somewhat as you are hurt when the cashier of a strange bank turns over your check and says you must bring some one to recognize you. It cost Matt a pang; it took him a moment, to own that Putney was right. Then he said, "Of course I must offer you proof somehow that I've come to you in good faith. I don't know exactly how I shall be able to do it— Would the assurance of my friend, Mr. Wade, the rector of St. Michael's"—

The name seemed to affect Putney pleasantly; he smiled, and then he said, "Brother Wade is a good man, and his words usually carry conviction, but this is a serious subject, Mr. Hilary." He laughed, and concluded earnestly, "You *must* know that I can't talk with you on any such authority. I couldn't talk with Mr. Wade himself."

"No, no; of course not," Matt assented; and he took himself off crestfallen, ashamed of his own shortsightedness.

There was only one way out of the trouble, and now he blamed himself for not having tried to take that way at the outset. He had justified himself in shrinking from it by many plausible excuses, but he could justify himself no longer. He rejoiced in feeling compelled, as it were, to take it. At least now he should not be acting from any selfish impulse, and if there were anything unseemly in what he was going to do, he should have no regrets on that score, even in the shame of failure.

XVII

MATT HILARY gave himself time, on his way to the North-wick place, or at least as much time as would pass between walking and driving, but that was because he was impatient, and his own going seemed faster to his nerves than that of the swiftest horse could have seemed. At the crest of the up-land which divides Hatboro' from South Hatboro' and just beyond the avenue leading to Dr. Morrell's house, he met Sue Northwick; she was walking quickly, too. She was in mourning, but she had put aside her long, crape veil, and she came towards him with her proud face framed in the black, and looking the paler for it; a little of her yellow hair showed under her bonnet. She moved imperiously, and Matt was afraid to think what he was thinking at sight of her. She seemed not to know him at first, or rather not to realize that it was he; when she did, a joyful light, which she did not try to hide from him flashed over her visage; and "Mr. Hilary!" she said as simply and hospitably as if their last parting had not been on terms of enmity that nothing could clear up or explain away.

He ran forward and caught her hand. "Oh, I am so glad," he said, "I was going out to see you about something—very important; and I might have missed you."

"No. I was just coming to the doctor's, and then I was going back. My sister isn't at all well, and I thought she'd better see the doctor."

"It's nothing serious, I hope?"

"Oh, no. I think she's a little worn out."

"I know!" said Matt, with intelligence, and nothing more was said between them as to the cause or nature of Adeline's sickness. Matt asked if he might go up the doctor's avenue with her, and they walked along together under the mingling elm and maple tops, but he deferred the matter he wished to speak of. They found a little girl playing in the road near the house, and Sue asked, "Is your father at home, Idella?"

"Mamma is at home," said the child; she ran forward calling toward the open doors and windows, "Mamma! Mamma! There's a lady!"

"It isn't their child," Sue explained. "It's the daughter of the minister who was killed on the railroad, here, a year or two ago—a very strange man; Mr. Peck."

"I have heard Wade speak of him," said Matt.

A handsome and very happy looking woman came to the door, and stilled the little one's boisterous proclamation to the hoarse whisper of "A lady! A lady!" as she took her hand; but she did not rebuke or correct her.

"How do you do, Mrs. Morrell," said Suzette, with rather a haughty distance; but Matt felt that she kept aloof with the pride of a person who comes from an infected house, and will not put herself at the risk of avoidance. "I wished to see Doctor Morrell about my sister. She isn't well. Will you kindly ask him to call?"

"I will send him as soon as he comes," said Mrs. Morrell, giving Matt that glance of liking which no good woman could withhold. "Unless," she added, "you would like to come in and wait for him."

"Thank you, no," said Suzette. "I must go back to her. Goodbye."

"Goodbye!" said Mrs. Morrell.

Matt raised his hat and silently bowed; but as they turned away, he said to Suzette, "What a happy face! What a lovely face! What a *good* face!"

"She is a very good woman," said the girl. "She has been

very kind to us. But so has everybody. I couldn't have believed it." In fact it was only the kindness of their neighbors
that had come near the defaulter's daughters; the harshness
and the hate had kept away.

"Why shouldn't they be kind?" Matt demanded, with his
heart instantly in his throat. "I can't imagine—at such a time—
Don't you know that I love you?" he entreated as if that exactly followed; there was perhaps a subtle spiritual sequence,
transcending all order of logic in the expression of his passion.

She looked at him over her shoulder as he walked by her
side, and said with neither surprise nor joy, "How can you
say such a thing to me?"

"Because it is true! Because I can't help it! Because I wish
to be everything to you, and I have to begin by saying that.
But don't answer me now; you need never answer me. I only
wish you to use me as you would use some one who loved you
beyond anything on earth,—as freely as that, and yet not be
bound or hampered by me in the least. Can you do that? I
mean, can you feel, 'This is my best friend, the truest friend
that any one can have, and I will let him do anything and
everything he wishes for me.' Can you do that,—say that?"

"But how could I do that? I don't understand you!" she
said faintly.

"Don't you? I am so glad you don't drive me from you"—

"I? *You!*"

"I was afraid— But now we can speak reasonably about it;
I don't see why people shouldn't. I know it is shocking to speak
to you of such a thing at such a time— It's dreadful; and yet
I can't feel wrong to have done it! No! If it's as sacred as it
seems to me when I think of it, then it couldn't be wrong in
the presence of death itself. I do love you; and I want you
some day for my wife. Yes! But don't answer that now! If you
never answer me, or if you deny me at last, still I want you
to let me be your true lover, while I can, and to do everything
that your accepted lover could, whether you ever look at me
again or not. Couldn't you do that?"

"You know I couldn't," she answered simply.

"Couldn't you?" he asked, and he fell into a forlorn silence, as if he could not say anything more. He forced her to take the word by asking, "Then you are offended with me?"

"How could I be?"

"Oh"—

"It's what any girl might be glad of"—

"Oh, my"—

"And I am not so silly as to think there can be a wrong time for it. If there were, you would make it right, if you chose it. You couldn't do anything I should think wrong. And I—I—love you, too"—

"Suzette! Suzette!" he called wildly, as if she were a great way off. It seemed to him his heart would burst. He got awkwardly before her, and tried to seize her hand.

She slipped by him, with a pathetic "Don't! But you know I never could be your wife. You *know* that."

"I don't know it. Why shouldn't you?"

"Because I couldn't bring my father's shame on my husband."

"It wouldn't touch me, any more than it touches you!"

"It would touch your father and mother,—and Louise."

"They all admire you and honor you. They think you're everything that's true and grand."

"Yes, while I keep to myself. And I shall keep to myself. I know how; and I shall not give way. Don't think it!"

"You will do what is right. I shall think that."

"Don't praise me! I can't bear it."

"But I love you, and how can I help praising you? And if you love me"—

"I do. I do, with all my heart." She turned and gave him an impassioned look from the height of her inapproachability.

"Then I won't ask you to be my wife, Suzette! I know how you feel; I wont be such a liar as to pretend I don't. And I will respect your feeling, as the holiest thing on earth. And if you wish we will be engaged as no other lovers ever were. You shall promise nothing but to let me help you all I can, for our love's sake, and I will promise never to speak to you of our love again. That shall be our secret—our engagement. Will you promise?"

"It will be hard for you," she said with a pitying look, which perhaps tried him as sorely as anything could.

"Not if I can believe I am making it easy for you."

They walked along, and she said with averted eyes, that he knew had tears in them, "I promise."

"And I promise, too," he said.

She impulsively put out her left hand toward him, and he held its slim fingers in his right a moment, and then let it drop. They both honestly thought they had got the better of that which laughs from its innumerable disguises at all stratagems and all devices to escape it.

"And now," he said. "I want to talk to you about what brought me over here to-day. I thought at first that I was only going to see your lawyer."

XVIII

Matt felt that he need now no longer practice those reserves in speaking to Sue of her father which he had observed so painfully hitherto. Neither did she shrink from the fact they had to deal with. In the trust established between them they spoke of it all openly, and if there was any difference in them concerning it, the difference was in his greater forbearance toward the unhappy man. They both spoke of his wrong-doing as if it were his infirmity; they could not do otherwise; and they both insensibly assumed his irresponsibility in a measure; they dwelt in the fiction or the persuasion of a mental obliquity which would account for otherwise unaccountable things.

"It is what my sister has always said," Sue eagerly assented to his suggestion of this theory. "I suppose it's what I've always believed, too, somehow, or I couldn't have lived."

"Yes; yes, it *must* be so," Matt insisted. "But now the question is how to reach him, and make some beginning of the end with him. I suppose it's the suspense and the uncertainty that is breaking your sister down?"

"Yes—that, and what we ought to do about giving up the property. We—quarreled about that at first; we couldn't see it alike; but now I've yielded; we've both yielded; and we don't know what to do."

"We must talk all that over with your lawyer, in connection with something I've just heard of." He told her of Pinney's scheme, and he said, "We must see if we can turn it to account."

270

They agreed not to talk of her father with Adeline, but she began it herself. She looked very old and frail, as she sat nervously rocking herself in a corner of the cottage parlor, and her voice had a sharp, anxious note. "What I think is that now we know father is alive, we oughtn't to do anything about the property without hearing from him. It stands to reason, don't you think it does, Mr. Hilary, that he would know better than anybody else, what we ought to do. Any rate, I think we ought to wait and consult with him about it, and see what he says. The property belonged to mother in the first place, and he mightn't like to have us part with it."

"I don't think you need trouble about that, now, Miss Northwick," said Matt. "Nothing need be done about the property at present."

"But I keep thinking about it. I want to do what Sue thinks is right, and to see it just in the light she does; and I've told her I would do exactly as she said about it; but now she wont say; and so I think we've *got* to wait and hear from father. Don't you?"

"Decidedly, I think you ought to do nothing now till you hear from him," said Matt.

"I knew you would," said the old maid, "and if Sue will be ruled by me, she'll see that it will all turn out right. I know father, and I know he'll want to do what is sensible and at the same time honorable. He is a person who could never bear to wrong any one out of a cent."

"Well," said Sue, "we will do what Mr. Hilary says; and now, try not to worry about it any more," she coaxed.

"Oh, yes! It's well enough to say not to worry *now*, when my mind's got going on it," said the old maid, querulously; she flung her weak frame against the chair back, and she began to wipe the gathering tears. "But if you'd agreed with me in the first place, it wouldn't have come to this. Now I'm all broken down, and I don't know *when* I shall be well again."

It was a painful moment; Sue patiently adjusted the cushion to her sister's shoulders, while Adeline's tongue ran helplessly on. "You were so headstrong and stubborn, I thought you would kill me. You were just like a rock, and I could beat myself to pieces against you, and you wouldn't move."

"I was wrong," said the proud girl, meekly.

"I'm sure," Adeline whimpered, "I hate to make an exhibition before Mr. Hilary, as much as any one, but I can't help it; no, I can't. My nerves are *all* gone."

The doctor came, and Sue followed Matt out of doors, to leave her, for the first few confidential moments, sacred to the flow of symptoms, alone with the physician. There was a little sequestered space among the avenue firs beside the lodge, with a bench toward which he led the way, but the girl would not sit down. She stood with her arms fallen at her side, and looked him steadily in the face.

"It is all true that she said of me. I set myself like a rock against her. I have made her sick, and if she died, I should be her murderer!"

He put his arms round her, and folded her to his heart. "Oh, my love, my love, my love!" he lamented and exulted over her.

She did not try to resist; she let her arms hang at her side; she said, "Is *this* the way we keep our word?— Already!"

"Our word was made to be broken; we must have meant it so. I'm glad we could break it so soon. Now I can truly help you; now that you are to be my wife."

She did not gainsay him, but she asked, "What will you think when you know—you must have known—that I used to care for some one else; and he never cared for me? It ought to make you despise me; it made me despise myself! But it is true. I did care all the world for him, once. *Now* will you say"—

"Now, more than ever," said the young man, silencing her lips with his own, and in their trance of love the world seemed to reel away from under their feet, with all its sorrows and shames, and leave them in mid-heaven.

"Suzette!" Adeline's voice called from within. "Suzette! Where are you?"

Sue released herself, and ran into the cottage. She came

out again in a little while, and said that the doctor thought
Adeline had better go to bed for a day or two and have a
thorough rest, and relief from all excitement. "We mustn't
talk before her any more, and you mustn't stay any longer."

He accepted the authority she instinctively assumed over
him, and found his dismissal already of the order of things.
He said, "Yes, I'll go at once. But about"—

She put a card into his hand. "You can see Mr. Putney, and
whatever you and he think best, will *be* best. Haven't you
been our good angel ever since— Oh, I'm not half good enough
for you, and I wouldn't be, even if there were no stain"—

"Stop!" he said; he caught her hand, and pulled her towards
him.

The doctor came out, and said in a low voice, "There's
nothing to be anxious about, but she really must have quiet.
I'll send Mrs. Morrell down to see you, after tea. She's quiet
itself."

Suzette submitted, and let Matt take her hand again in parting. "Will you give me a lift, doctor, if you're going toward
town?"

"Get in," said the doctor.

Sue went indoors and the two men drove off together.

Matt looked at the card in his hand, and read: "Mr. Putney: Please talk to Mr. Hilary as you would to my sister or
me." Suzette's printed name served for signature. Matt put
the card in his pocket-book, and then he said, "What sort of
man is Mr. Putney, doctor?"

"Mr. Putney?" said the doctor, with a twinkle of his blue
eyes, "is one of those uncommon people who have enemies.
He has a good many, because he's a man that thinks, and then
says what he thinks. But he's his own worst enemy, because
from time to time he gets drunk."

"A character," said Matt. "Do you think he's a safe one?
Doesn't his getting drunk from time to time interfere with
his usefulness?"

"Well, of course," said the doctor. "It's bad for him; but I
think it's slowly getting better. Yes, decidedly. It's very ex-

traordinary, but ever since he's been in charge of the Miss Northwicks' interests"—

"Yes; that's what I was thinking of."

"He's kept perfectly straight. It's as if the responsibilities had steadied him."

"But if he goes on sprees, he may be on the verge of one that's gathering violence from its postponement," Matt suggested.

"I think not," said the doctor after a moment. "But of course I can't tell."

"They trust him so implicitly," said Matt.

"I know," said the doctor. "And I know that he's entirely devoted to them. The fact is, Putney's a very dear friend of mine."

"Oh, excuse me"—

"No, no!" The doctor stayed Matt's apologies. "I understand just what you mean. He disliked their father very much. He was principled against him as a merely rich man, with a mischievous influence on the imaginations of all the poor people about him who wanted to be like him"—

"Oh, that's rather good," said Matt.

"Do you think so?" asked the doctor looking round at him. "Well! I supposed you would be all the other way. Well! What I was saying was that Putney looks upon those poor girls as their father's chief victims. I think he was touched by their coming to him, and he pitied them. The impression is that he's managed their affairs very well; I don't know about such things; but I know he's managed them honorably; I would stake my life on it; and I believe he'll hold out straight to the last. I suppose," the doctor conjectured, at the end, "that they will try to get at Northwick now, and arrange with his creditors for his return?"

"I don't mind telling you," said Matt, "that it's been tried and failed. The State's attorney insists that he shall come back and stand his trial, first of all."

"Oh!" said the doctor.

"Of course, that's right from the legal point of view. But in the meantime, nobody knows where Mr. Northwick is."

"I suppose," said the doctor, "it would have been better for him not to have written that letter."

"It's hard to say," Matt answered. "I thought so, too, at first. I thought it was cowardly and selfish of him to take away his children's superstition about his honesty— You knew that they held to that through all?"

"Most touching thing in the world," said the doctor, leaning forward to push a fly off his horse with the limp point of his whip. "That poor old maid has talked it into me till I almost believed it myself."

"I don't know that I should hold him severely accountable. And I'm not sure now that I should condemn him for writing that letter. It must have been a great relief to him. In a way you may say he *had* to do it. It's conceivable that if he had kept it on his mind any longer, his mind would have given way. As it is, they have now the comfort of another superstition—if it *is* a superstition. What do you think, doctor? Do you believe that there was a mental twist in him?"

"There seems to be in nearly all these defaulters. What they do is so senseless—so insane. I suppose that's the true theory of all crime. But it wont do to act upon it, yet awhile."

"No."

The doctor went on after a pause, with a laugh of enjoyment at the notion. "Above all, it wont do to let the defaulters act upon that theory, and apply for admission to the insane asylums instead of taking the express for Canada, when they're found out."

"Oh, no," said Matt. He wondered at himself for being able to analyze the offence of Suzette's father so cold-bloodedly. But in fact, he could not relate the thought of her to the thought of him in his sin at all; he could only realize their kindred in her share of his suffering.

XIX

PUTNEY accepted Suzette's authorization of Matt with apparent unconsciousness of anything but its immediate meaning, and they talked Pinney's scheme intimately over together. In the end it still remained a question whether the energies of such an investigator could be confined to the discovery of Northwick's whereabouts; whether his newspaper instincts would not be too strong for any sense of personal advantage that could be appealed to in him. They both believed that it would not be long before Northwick followed up the publication of his letter by some communication with his family.

But time began to go by again, and Northwick made no further sign; the flurry of activity which his letter had called out in the detectives came to nothing. Their search was not very strenuous; Northwick's creditors were of various minds as to the amount of money he had carried away with him. Every one knew that if he chose to stay in Canada, he could not be molested there; and it seemed very improbable that he could be persuaded to put himself within reach of the law. The law had no terms to offer him, and there was really nothing to be done.

Putney forecast all this in his talk with Matt, when he held that they must wait Northwick's motion. He professed himself willing to wait as long as Northwick chose, though he thought they would not have to wait long, and he contended for a theory of the man's whole performance which he said he should like to have tested before a jury. Matt could not make

276

out how much he really meant by saying that Northwick could be defended very fairly on the ground of insanity; and that he would enjoy managing such a defence. It was a common thing to show that a murderer was insane; why not a defaulter? Tilted back in his chair, with one leg over the corner of his table, and changing the tobacco in his mouth from one cheek to the other as he talked, the lawyer outlined the argument which he said could be made very effective. There was the fact, to begin with, that Northwick was a very wealthy man, and had no need of more money when he began to speculate; Putney held that this want of motive could be made a strong point; and that the reckless, almost open, way in which Northwick used the company's money, when he began to borrow, was proof in itself of unsound mind: apparently he had no sense whatever of *meum* and *tuum,* especially *tuum.* Then, the total collapse of the man when he was found out; his flight without an effort to retrieve himself, although his shortage was by no means hopelessly vast, and could have been almost made up by skilful use of the credit that Northwick could command, was another evidence of shaken reason. But besides all this, there was his behavior since he left home. He had been absent nearly five months, and in that time he had made no attempt whatever to communicate with his family, although he must have known that it was perfectly safe for him to do so. He was a father who was almost dotingly fond of his children, and singularly attached to his home; yet he had remained all that time in voluntary exile, and he had left them in entire uncertainty as to his fate except so far as they could accept the probability of his death by a horrible casualty. This inversion of the natural character of a man was one of the most striking phenomena of insanity, and Putney, for the purposes of argument, maintained that it could be made to tell tremendously with a jury.

Matt was unable to enjoy the sardonic metaphysics of the case with Putney. He said gravely that he had been talking of the matter with Dr. Morrell, and he had no doubt that there was a taint of insanity in every wrong-doer; some day he believed the law would take cognizance of the fact.

"I don't suppose the time is quite ripe yet, though I think I could make out a strong case for Brother Northwick," said Putney. He seemed to enter into it more fully, as if he had a mischievous perception of Matt's uneasiness, and chose to torment him; but then apparently he changed his mind, and dealt with other aspects of their common interest so seriously and sympathetically that Matt parted from him with a regret that he could not remove the last barrier between them, and tell the lawyer that he concerned himself so anxiously in the affairs of that wretched defaulter because his dearest hope was that the daughter of the criminal would some day be his wife.

But Matt felt that this fact must first be confided to those who were nearest him; and how to shape it in terms that would convey the fact and yet hide the repulsiveness he knew in it, was the question that teased him all the way back to Vardley like some tiresome riddle. He understood why his love for Suzette Northwick must be grievous to his father and mother; how embarrassing, how disappointing, how really in some sort disastrous; and yet he felt that if there was anything more sacred than another in the world for him, it was that love. He must be true to it at whatever cost, and in every event, and he must begin by being perfectly frank with those whom it would afflict, and confessing to himself all its difficulties and drawbacks. He was not much afraid of dealing with his father; they were both men, and they could look at it from the man's point of view. Besides, his father really cared little what people would say; after the first fever of disgust, if he did not change wholly and favor it vehemently, he would see so much good in it that he would be promptly and finally reconciled.

But Matt knew that his mother was of another make, and that the blow would be much harder for her to bear; his problem was how to lighten it. Sometimes he thought he had bet-

ter not try to lighten it, but let it fall at once, and trust to her
affection and good sense for the rest. But when he found himself alone wih her that night he began by making play, and
keeping her beyond reach. He was so lost in this perverse
effort that he was not aware of some such effort on her part,
till she suddenly dropped it, and said, "Matt, there is something I wish to speak to you about—very seriously."

His heart jumped into his throat, but he said "Well?" and
she went on.

"Louise tells me that you think of bringing this young man
down to the shore with you when you come to see us next
week."

"Maxwell? I thought the change might do him good; yes,"
said Matt, with a cowardly joy in his escape from the worst
he feared. He thought she was going to speak to him of Suzette.

She said, "I don't wish you to bring him. I don't wish Louise
to see him again after she leaves this place—ever again. She is
fascinated with him."

"Fascinated?"

"I can't call it anything else. I don't say that she's in love;
but there's no question but she's allowed her curiosity to run
wild, and her fancy to be taken: the two strongest things in
her—in most girls. I want to break it all up."

"But do you think"—

"I *know*. It isn't that she's with him at every moment, but
that her thoughts are with him when they're apart. He puzzles
her, he piques her; she's always talking and asking about him.
It's their difference in everything that does it. I don't mean to
say that her heart is touched, and I don't intend it shall be.
So, you mustn't ask him to the shore with you, and if you've
asked him already, you must get out of it. If you think he
needs sea air, you can get him board at some of the resorts.
But not near us." She asked, in default of any response from
her son, "You *don't* think, Matt, it would be well for the acquaintance to go on?"

"No, I don't, mother; you're quite right as to that," said Matt, "if you're not mistaken in supposing"—

"I'm not; you may depend upon it. And I'm glad you can see the matter from my point of view. It is all very well for you to have your queer opinions, and even to live them. I think it's all ridiculous; but your father and I both respect you for your sincerity though your course has been a great disappointment to us."

"I know that, mother," said Matt, groaning in spirit to think how much worse the disappointment he was meditating must be, and feeling himself dishonest and cowardly, through and through.

"But I feel sure," Mrs. Hilary went on, "that when it's a question of your sister, you would wish her life to be continued on the same plane, and in the surroundings she had always been used to."

"I should think that best, certainly, for a girl of Louise's ideas," said Matt, trying to get his own to the surface.

"Ideas!" cried his mother. "She *has* no ideas. She merely has impulses, and her impulses are to do what people wish. But her education and breeding have been different from those of such a young man, and she would be very unhappy with him. They never could quite understand each other, no matter how much they were in love. I know he is very talented, and all that; and I shouldn't at all mind his being poor. I never minded Caryl Wade's being poor, when I thought he had taken her fancy, because he was one of ourselves; and this young man— Matt, you *can't* pretend that with all his intellectual qualities he's what one calls a gentleman. With his origin, and bringing up; his coarse experiences; all his trials and struggles; even with his successes, he couldn't be; and Louise could not be happy with him for that very reason. He might have all the gifts, all the virtues under the sun; I don't deny that he has"—

"He has some very serious faults," Matt interrupted.

"We all have," said Mrs. Hilary, tolerantly. "But he might

be a perfect saint—a hero—a martyr; and if he wasn't what one calls a gentleman, don't you see? We can't be frank about such things, here, because we live in a republic; but"—

"We get there, just the same," said Matt, with unwonted slang.

"Yes," said his mother. "That is what I mean."

"And you're quite right, as to the facts, mother." He got up and began to walk about the long, low living-room of the farmhouse, where they were sitting. Louise had gone to direct her maid in packing for her flitting to the seaside in the morning; Matt could see a light in the ell-chamber where Maxwell was probably writing. "The self-made man can never be the social equal of the society-made man. He may have more brains, more money, more virtue, but he's a kind of inferior, and he betrays his inferiority in every worldly exigency. And if he's successful, he's so because he's been stronger, fiercer, harder than others, in the battle of life. That's one reason why I say that there oughtn't to *be* any battle of life. Maxwell has the defects of his disadvantages—I see that. He's often bitter, and cynical, and cruel because he has had to fight for his bread. He isn't Louise's social equal; I quite agree with you there, mother; and if she wants to live for society, he would be always in danger of wounding her by his inferiority to other people of her sort. I'm sorry for Maxwell; but I don't pity him, especially. He bears the penalty of his misfortunes; but he is strong enough to bear it. Let him stand it! But there are others—weaker, unhappier— Mother! You haven't asked me yet about—the Northwicks." Matt stopped in front of her chair, and looked down into her lifted face, where the satisfaction with his acquiescence in her views concerning Louise was scarcely marred by her perception that he had not changed his mind at all, on other points. She was used to his way of thinking, and she gratefully resolved to be more and more patient with it and give him time for the change that was sure to come. She interpreted the look of stormy wistfulness he wore as an expression of his perplexity in the presence of the

contradictory facts and theories. "No," she said, "I expected
to do that. You know I've seen them so very lately, and with
this about Louise on my mind— How are they? That poor
Adeline— I'm afraid it's killing her. Were you able to do anything for them?"

"Ah, I don't know," the young man sighed. "They have to
suffer for their misfortunes, too."

"It seems to be the order of Providence," said Mrs. Hilary
with the resignation of the philosophical spectator.

"No!" Matt protested. "It's the disorder of improvidence.
There's nothing of the Divine will in consequences so unjust
and oppressive. Those women are perfectly innocent; they've
only wished to do right, and tried to do it; but they're under
a ban the same as if they had shared their father's guilt. They
have no friends"—

"Well, Matt," said his mother, with dignity, "I think you
can hardly say that. I'm sure that as far as *we* are concerned,
we have nothing to reproach ourselves with. I think we've
gone to the extreme to show our good will. How much further do you want us to go? Come; I don't like your saying
this!"

"I beg your pardon. I certainly don't blame you, or Louise,
or father. I blame myself—for cowardice—for—for unworthi-
ness in being afraid to say—to tell you— Mother," he burst
out suddenly, after a halt, "I've asked Suzette Northwick to
marry me."

Matt had tried to imagine himself saying this to his mother,
and the effect it would have, ever since he had left Suzette's
absorbing presence; all through his talk with Putney, and
all the way home, and now throughout what he and his mother had been saying of Maxwell and Louise. But it always
seemed impossible, and more and more impossible, so that
when he heard the words spoken in his own voice, it seemed
wholly incredible.

XX

THE EFFECT of a thing is never quite what we have forecast. Mrs. Hilary heard Matt's confession without apparently anything of his tumult in making it. Women, after all, dwell mainly in the region of the affections; even the most worldly women, have their likes and dislikes and the question of the sort Matt had sprung upon his mother, is first a personal question with them. She was not a very worldly woman; but she liked her place in the world, and she preferred conformity and similarity; the people she was born of and bred with, were the nicest kind of people, and she did not see how any one could differ from them to advantage. Their ideas were the best, or they would not have had them; she herself did not wish to have other ideas. But her family was more, far more, to her than her world was. She knew that in his time her husband had not had the ideas of her world concerning slavery, but she had always contrived to honor the ideas of both. Since her son had begun to disagree with her world concerning what he called the industrial slavery, she contrived without the sense of inconsistency to suffer him and yet remain with the world. She represented in her maternal tolerance the principle actuating the church which includes the facts as fast as they accomplish themselves, without changing any point of doctrine.

"Then you mean, Matt," she asked, "that you are going to marry her?"

"Yes," said Matt, "that is what I mean," and then, something in his mother's way of taking it, nettled him on Sue's

283

behalf. "But I don't know that my marrying her necessarily followed from my asking her. I expected her to refuse me."

"Men always do; I don't know why," said Mrs. Hilary. "But in this case, I can't imagine it."

"Can't imagine it? *I* can imagine it!" Matt retorted; but his mother did not seem to notice his resentment.

"Then, if it's quite settled, you dont wish me to say anything?"

"I wish you to say everything, mother—all that you feel and think—about her, and the whole affair. But I don't wish you to think—I can't *let* you think—that she has ever, by one look or word, allowed me to suppose that my offer would be welcome."

"Oh, I didn't mean that," said Mrs. Hilary. "She would be too proud for that. But I've no doubt it was welcome." Matt fretted in silence, but he allowed his mother to go on. "She is a very proud girl, and I've no doubt that what she's been through has intensified her pride."

"I don't suppose she's perfect," said Matt. "I'm not perfect, myself. But I don't conceal her faults from myself any more than I do my own. I know she's proud. I don't admire pride; but I suppose that with her it can't be helped."

"I don't know that I object to it," said Mrs. Hilary. "It doesn't always imply hardness; it goes with very good things, sometimes. That hauteur of hers is very effective. I've seen it carry her through with people who might have been disposed to look down on her for some reasons."

"I shouldn't value it, for that," Matt interposed.

"No. But she's made it serve her in stead of her want of those family connections that every one else has"—

"She will have all of ours, I hope, mother!" Matt broke in with a smile; but his mother would not be diverted from the point she was making.

"And that it always seemed so odd she shouldn't have. I'm sure that to see her come into a room, you would think half Boston, or all the princes of the blood, were her cousins. She's certainly a magnificent creature."

Matt differed with his mother from the ground up, in all her worldly reasons for admiring Suzette, but her praises filled his heart to overflowing. Tears stood in his eyes, and his voice trembled.

"She is—she *is*—angelically!"

"Well, not just that type, perhaps," said Mrs. Hilary. "But she is a good girl. No one can help respecting her; and I think she's even more to be respected for yielding to that poor old maid sister of hers about their property, than for wishing to give it up."

"Yes," Matt breathed gratefully.

"But there, *there* is the real skeleton, Matt! Suzette would grace the highest position. But her father! What will people say?"

"Need we mind that, mother?"

"Not, perhaps, so much if things had remained as they were—if he had never been heard from again. But that letter of his! And what will he do next? He may come home, and offer to stand his trial!"

"I would respect him for that!" cried Matt, passionately.

"Matt!"

"It isn't a thing I should urge him to do. He may not have the strength for it. But if he had, it would be the best thing he could do, and I should be glad to stand by him!"

"And drag us all through the mire? Surely, my son, whatever you feel about your mother and sister, you can't wish your poor father to suffer anything more on that wretch's account?"

"Wish? No. And heaven knows how deeply anxious I am about the effect my engagement may have on father. I'm afraid it will embarrass him—compromise him, even"—

"As to that, I can't say," said Mrs. Hilary. "You and he ought to know best. One thing is certain. There wont be any opposition on his part or mine, my son, that you wont see yourself is reasonable"—

"Oh, I am sure of that, mother! And I can't tell you how deeply I feel"—

"Your father appreciates Suzette as fully as I do; but I don't believe he could stand any more Quixotism from you, Matt, and if you intend to make your marriage a preliminary to getting your father-in-law into State's prison, you may be very sure your father wont approve of your marriage."

Matt laughed at the humor of a proposition which his mother did not perceive so keenly.

"I don't intend that, exactly."

"And I'm satisfied, as it is, he wont be easy about it till the thing is hushed up, or dies out of itself, if it's let alone."

"But father can't let it alone!" said Matt. "It's his duty to follow it up at every opportunity. I don't want you to deceive yourself about the matter. I want you to understand just how it will be. I have tried to face it squarely, and I know how it looks. I shall try to make Suzette see it as I do, and I'm sure she will. I don't think her father is guiltier than a great many other people who haven't been found out. But he has been found out, and he ought, for the sake of the community, to be willing to bear the penalty the law inflicts. That is his only hope, his salvation, his duty. Father's duty is to make him bear it whether he's willing or not. It's a much more odious duty"—

"I don't understand you, Matt, saying your father's part is more odious than a self-confessed defaulter's."

"No, I don't say"—

"Then I think you'd better go to your father, and reconcile your duty with his, if you can. I wash my hands of the affair. It seems to me, though, that you've quite lost your head. The world will look very differently, I can assure you, at a woman whose father died in Canada, nobody could remember just why, from what it will on one whose father was sent to State's prison for taking money that didn't belong to him."

Matt flung up his arms. "Oh, the world, the world! I wont let the world enter! I will never let Suzette face its mean and cruel prejudices. She will come here to the farm with me, and we will live down the memory of what she has innocently suffered; and we will let the world go its way."

"And don't you think the world will follow you here? Don't you suppose it *is* here, ready to welcome you home with all those prejudices you hope you can shun? Every old gossip of the neighborhood will point Suzette out, as the daughter of a man who is serving his term in jail for fraud. The great world forgets, but this little world around you here would remember it as long as either of you lived. No; the day you marry Suzette Northwick, you must make up your mind to follow her father into exile, or else to share his shame with her at home."

"I've made up my mind to share that shame at home. I never would ask her to run from it."

"Then for pity's sake let that miserable man alone, wherever he is. Or if you can get at him, beg him to stay away, and keep still till he dies. Good-night."

Mrs. Hilary rose from her own chair, and stooped over Matt, where he had sunk in his, and kissed his troubled forehead. He thought he had solved one part of his problem; but her words showed him that he had not rightly seen it in that light of love, which had really hid it in dazzling illusions.

The difficulty had not yielded, at all, when he met his father with it; he thought it had only grown tougher and knottier; and he hardly knew how to present it. His mother had not only promised not to speak to his father of the affair; she had utterly refused to speak of it, and Matt instantly perceived that the fact he announced was somehow far more unexpected to his father than it had seemed to his mother.

But Hilary received it with a patience, a tenderness for his son, in all his amazement, that touched Matt more keenly than any other fashion of meeting it could have done. He asked if it were something that Matt had done, or had merely made up his mind sometime to do; and when Matt said it was something he had done, his father was silent a moment. Then he said, "I shall have to take some action about it."

"How, action?"

"Why, you must see, my dear boy, that as soon as this thing becomes known—and you wish it to be known, of course"—

"Of course!"

"It will be impossible for me to continue holding my present relation to Northwick."

"To Northwick?"

"As president of the Board I'm ex-officio, his enemy and persecutor. It wouldn't be right, it wouldn't be decent, for me to continue that after it was known that you were going to marry his daughter. It wouldn't be possible. I must resign; I must withdraw from the Board altogether. I haven't the stuff in me to do my official duty at such a cost; so I'd better give up my office, and get rid of my duty."

"That will be a great sacrifice for you, father," said Matt.

"It wont bring me to want, exactly, if you mean moneywise."

"I didn't mean moneywise. But I know you've always enjoyed the position so much."

Hilary laughed uneasily. "Well, it hasn't been a bed of roses since we discovered Northwick's obliquities—excuse me!"

Matt blushed. "Oh, I know he's oblique, as such things go."

"In fact," his father resumed, "I shall be glad to be out of it, and I don't think there'll be much opposition to my going out. I know that there's a growing feeling against me, in the Board. I *have* tried to carry water on both shoulders. I've made the effort honestly; but the effect hasn't been good. I couldn't keep my heart out of it; from the very first, I pitied that poor devil's children so that I got him and gave him all the chance I could"—

"That was perfectly right. It was the only business-like"—

"It wasn't business-like to hope that even if justice were defeated he might somehow, anyhow, escape the consequences of his crime; and I'm afraid this is what I've hoped, in spite of myself," said Hilary.

This was so probably true that Matt could not help his father deny it. He could only say, "I don't believe you've ever allowed that hope to interfere with the strict performance of your duty, at any moment."

"No; but I've had the hope; and others have had the suspicion that I've had it. I've felt that; and I'm glad that it's coming to an end. I'm not ashamed of your choice, Matt; I'm proud of it. The thing gave me a shock at first, because I had to face the part I must take. But she's all kinds of a splendid girl. The Board knows what she wished to do, and why she hasn't done it. No one can help honoring her. And I don't believe people will think the less of any of us for your wanting to marry her. But if they do, they may do it and be damned."

Hilary shook himself together with greater comfort than he had yet felt, upon this conclusion; but he lapsed again after the long hand pressure that he exchanged with his son.

"We must make it our business, now, to see that no man loses anything by that— We must get at him, somehow. Of course they have no more notion where he is than we have."

"No; not the least," said Matt. "I think it's the uncertainty that's preying upon Miss Northwick."

"The man's behaving like a confounded lunatic," said Hilary.

The word reminded Matt of Putney, and he said, "That's their lawyer's theory of him"—

"Oh, you've *seen* him, have you? Odd chap."

"Yes; I saw him, when I was up there, after—after—at the request of Suzette. I wished to talk with him about the scheme that Maxwell's heard of from a brother-reporter," and Matt now unfolded Pinney's plan to his father, and showed his letter.

Hilary looked from it at his son. "You don't mean that this is the blackguard who wrote that account of the defalcation in the *Events?*"

"Yes; the same fellow. But as to blackguard"—

"Well, then, Matt, I don't see how we can employ him. It seems to me it would be a kind of insult to those poor girls."

"I had thought of that. I felt that. But after all, I don't think he knew how much of a blackguard he was making of himself. Maxwell says he wouldn't know. And besides we can't help ourselves. If he doesn't go for us, he will go for himself. We *must* employ him. He's a species of *condottiere*; we can buy his allegiance with his service: and we must forego the sentimental objection. I've gone all over it, and that's the only conclusion." Hilary fumed and rebelled; but he saw that they could not help themselves, that they could not do better. He asked, "And what did their lawyer think of it?"

"He seemed to think we had better let it alone, for the present; better wait and see if Mr. Northwick would not try to communicate with his family."

"I'm not so sure of that," said Hilary. "If this fellow is such a fellow as you say, I don't see why we shouldn't make use of him at once."

"Make use of him to get Mr. Northwick back?" said Matt. "I think it would be well for him to come back, but voluntarily"—

"Come back?" said Hilary, whose civic morality flew much lower than this. "Nonsense! And stir the whole filthy mess up in the courts? I mean, make use of this fellow to find him, and enable us to find out just how much money he has left, and how much we have got to supply, in order to make up his shortage."

Matt now perceived the extent of his father's purpose, and on its plane he honored it.

"Father, you're splendid."

"Stuff! I'm in a corner. What else is there to do? What less could we do? What's the money for, if it isn't to"— Hilary choked with the emotion that filled him at the sight of his son's face. Every father likes to have his grown up son think him a good man; it is the sweetest thing that can come to him in life, far sweeter than a daughter's faith in him; for a son *knows* whether his father is good or not. At the bottom of his soul Hilary cared more for his son's opinion than most fathers; Matt was a crank, but because he was a crank, Hilary valued his judgment as something ideal.

After a moment he asked, "Can this fellow be got at?"

"Oh, I imagine very readily."

"What did Maxwell say about him, generally?"

"Generally, that he's not at all a bad kind of fellow. He's a reporter by nature, and he's a detective upon instinct. He's done some amateur detective work, as many reporters do—according to Maxwell's account. The two things run together—and he's very shrewd and capable in his way. He's going into it as a speculation, and of course he wants it to be worth his while. Maxwell says his expectation of newspaper promotion is mere brag; they know him too well to put him in any position of control. He's a mixture, like every body else. He's devotedly fond of his wife, and he wants to give her and the baby a change of air"—

"My idea," Hilary interrupted, "would be not to wait for the Social Science convention, but to send this"—

"Pinney."

"Pinney at once. Will you see him?"

"If you have made up your mind."

"I've made up my mind. But handle the wretch carefully, and for heaven's sake bind him by all that's sacred—if there's anything sacred to him—not to give the matter away. Let him fix his price, and offer him a pension for his widow afterwards."

XXI

Mrs. Hilary was a large woman, of portly frame, the prophecy in amplitude of what her son might come to be if he did not carry the activities of youth into his later life. She, for her part, was long past such activities; and yet she was not a woman to let the grass grow upon any path she had taken. She appointed the afternoon of the day following her talk with Matt for leaving the farm and going to the shore; Louise was to go with her, and upon the whole she judged it best to tell her why, when the girl came to say goodnight, and to announce that her packing was finished.

"But what in the world are we in such a hurry for, mamma, all of a sudden?"

"We are in a hurry because— Don't you really know, Louise? —because in the crazy atmosphere of this house, one loses the sense of—of proportion—of differences."

"Aren't you rather—Emersonian, mamma?"

"Do you think so, my dear? Matt's queer notions infect everybody; I don't blame *you*, particularly; and the simple life he makes people lead—by leading it himself, more than anything else—makes you think that you could keep on living just as simply if you wished, everywhere."

"It's very sweet—it's so restful," sighed the girl. "It makes you sick of dinners and ashamed of dances."

"But you must go back to them; you must go back to the world you belong to; and you'd better not carry any queer habits back with you."

"You *are* rather sphinx-like, mamma! Such habits, for instance, as?"

"As Mr. Maxwell." The girl's face changed; her mother had touched the quick. She went on, looking steadily at her daughter, "You know he wouldn't do, there."

"No; he wouldn't," said Louise promptly; so mournfully, though, that her mother's heart relented.

"I've seen that you've become interested in him, Louise; that your fancy is excited; he stimulates your curiosity. I don't wonder at it! He *is* very interesting. He makes you feel his power more than any young man I've met. He charms your imagination even when he shocks your taste."

"Yes; all that," said Louise desolately.

"But he does shock your taste?"

"Sometimes—not always."

"Often enough, though, to make the difference that I'm afraid you'll lose the sense of. Louise, I should be very sorry if I thought you were at all—in love with that young man!"

It seemed a question; Louise let her head droop, and answered with another. "How should I know? He hasn't asked me."

This vexed her mother. "Don't be trivial, don't be childish, my dear. You don't need to be asked, though I'm exceedingly glad he *hasn't* asked you, for now you can get away with a good conscience."

"I'm not sure, yet, that I want to get away," said the girl dreamily.

"Yes, you are, my dear!" her mother retorted. "You know it wouldn't do at all. It isn't a question of his poverty; your father has money enough; it's a question of his social quality, and of all those little nothings that make up the whole of happiness in marriage. He would be different enough, being merely a man; but being a man born and reared in as different world from yours, as if it were another planet— I want you to think over all the girls you know—all the *people* you know —and see how many of them have married out of their own set, their own circle—we might almost say, their own family. There isn't one!"

"I've not said I wished to marry him, mamma."

"No. But I wish you to realize just what it would be."

"It would be something rather distinguished, if his dreams came true," Louise suggested.

"Well, of course," Mrs. Hilary admitted. She wished to be very, very reasonable; very, very just; it was the only thing with a girl like Louise; perhaps with any girl. "It would be distinguished, in a way. But it wouldn't be distinguished in the society way; the only way you've professed to care for. I know that we've always been an intellectual community, and New Yorkers, and that kind of people, think or profess to think, that we make a great deal of literary men. We do invite them somewhat, but I pass whole seasons without meeting them; and I don't know that you could say that they are *of* society, even when they are *in* it. If such a man has society connections, he's in society; but he's there on account of his connections, not on account of his achievements. This young man may become very distinguished, but he'll always be rather queer; and he would put a society girl at odds with society. His distinction would be public; it wouldn't be social."

"Matt doesn't think society is worth minding," Louise said, casually.

"But *you* do," returned her mother. "And Matt says that a man of this young man's traditions might mortify you before society people."

"Did Matt say that?" Louise demanded, angrily. "I will *speak* to Matt about that! I should like to know what he means by it. I should like to hear what he would say."

"Very likely he would say that the society people were not worth minding. You know his nonsense. If you agree with Matt, I've nothing more to say, Louise; not a word. You can marry a mechanic or a day laborer, in that case, without loss of self-respect. I've only been talking to you on the plane where I've always understood you wished to be taken. But if you don't, then I can't help it. You must understand, though, and understand distinctly, that you can't live on two levels; the world wont let you. Either you must be in the world and of it entirely; or you must discard its criterions, and form your own, and hover about in a sort of Bohemian limbo on its outskirts; or, you must give it up altogether." Mrs. Hilary rose from the lounge where she had been sitting, and said, "Now I'm going to bed. And I want you to think this all carefully over, Louise. I don't blame you for it; and I wish nothing but your good and happiness—yours and Matt's both. But I must say you've been pretty difficult children to provide for. Do you know what Matt has been doing?" Mrs. Hilary had not meant to speak of it, but she felt an invincible necessity of doing so, at last.

"Something more about the Northwicks?"

"Very decidedly—or about one of them. He's offered himself to Suzette."

"How grand! How perfectly magnificent! Then she can give up her property at once, and Matt can take care of her and Adeline both."

"Or, your father can, for him. Matt has not the crime of being a capitalist on his conscience. His idea seems to be to get Suzette to live here on the farm with him."

"I don't believe she'd be satisfied with that," said Louise. "But could she bear to face the world? Wouldn't she always be thinking what people thought?"

"I felt that I ought to suggest that to Matt; though, really, when it comes to the practical side of the matter, people wouldn't care much, what her father had been—that is, society people wouldn't, *as* society people. She would have the education and the traditions of a lady, and she would have Matt's name. It's nonsense to suppose there wouldn't be talk; but I don't believe there would be anything that couldn't be lived down. The fact is," said Mrs. Hilary, giving her daughter the advantage of a species of soliloquy, "I think we ought to be glad Matt has let us off so easily. I've been afraid that he would end by marrying some farmer's daughter, and bringing somebody into the family who would say 'Want to know,' and 'How?' and 'What-say?' through her nose. Suzette is indefinitely better than that, no matter what her father is. But I must confess that it was a shock when Matt told me they were engaged."

"Why, *were* you surprised, mamma?" said Louise. "I thought all along that it would come to that. I knew that in the first place, Matt's sympathy would be roused; and you know that's the strongest thing in him. And then, Suzette *is* a beautiful girl. She's perfectly regal; and she's just Matt's opposite, every way; and of *course* he would be taken with her. I'm not a *bit* surprised. Why, it's the most natural thing in the world."

"It might be very much worse," sighed Mrs. Hilary. "As soon as he has seen your father, we must announce it, and face it out with people. Fortunately, it's summer; and a great many have gone abroad, this year."

Louise began to laugh. "Even Mr. Northwick is abroad."

"Yes, and I hope he'll stay there," said Mrs. Hilary, wincing.

"It would be quite like Matt, wouldn't it, to have him brought home in chains, long enough to give away the bride?"

"Louise!" said her mother.

Louise began to cry. "Oh, you think it's nothing," she said stormily, "for Matt to marry a girl whose father ran away with other people's money; but a man, who has fought his way honestly, is disgraceful, no matter how gifted he is, because he hasn't the traditions of a society man"—

"I wont condescend to answer your unjust nonsense, my dear," said Mrs. Hilary. "I will merely ask you if you wish to marry Mr. Maxwell"—

"I will take care of myself!" cried the girl, in open if not definite rebellion. She flung from the room, and ran up stairs to her chamber, which looked across at the chamber where Maxwell's light was burning. She dropped on her knees beside the window and bowed herself to the light, that swam on her tears, a golden mist, and pitied and entreated it, and remained there, till the lamp was suddenly quenched, and the moon possessed itself of the night in unbroken splendor.

After breakfast, which she made late, the next morning, she found Maxwell waiting for her on the piazza.

"Are you going over to the camp?" she asked.

"I was, after I had said good bye," he answered.

"Oh, we're not going for several hours, yet. We shall take the noon train, mamma's decided." She possessed herself of the cushion, stuffed with spruce sprays, that lay on the piazza-steps, and added, "I will go over with you." They had hitherto made some pretence, one to the other, for being together at the camp; but this morning neither feigned any reason for it. Louise stopped, when she found he was not keeping up with her, and turned to him, and waited for him to reach her. "I wanted to speak with you, Mr. Maxwell, and I expect you to be very patient and tractable." She said this very authoritatively; she ended by asking, "Will you?"

"It depends upon what it is. I am always docile if I like a thing."

"Well, you ought to like this."

"Oh, that's different. That's often infuriating."

They went on and then paused at the low stone wall between the pasture and the pines.

"Before I say it, you must *promise* to take it in the right way," she said.

He asked, teasingly, "Why do you think I wont?"

"Because—because I wish you to so much!"

"And am I such a contrary-minded person that you can't trust me to behave myself, under ordinary provocation?"

"You may think the provocation is extraordinary."

"Well, let's see." He got himself over the wall, and allowed her to scramble after him. She asked herself whether, if he had the traditions of a society man he would have done that; but somehow, when she looked at his dreamy face, rapt in remote

thought that beautified it from afar, she did not care for hi
neglect of small attentions. She said to herself that if a woman
could be the companion of his thoughts that would be enough,
she did not go into the detail of arranging association with
thoughts so far off as Maxwell's; she did not ask herself whethe
it would be easy or possible. She put the cushion into the
hammock for a pillow, but he chose to sit beside her on the
bench between the pine tree boles, and the hammock swayed
empty in the light breeze that woke the sea-song of the boughs
over them.

"I don't know exactly how to begin," she said, after a little
silence.

"If you'll tell me what you want to say," he suggested, "I'll
begin for you."

"No, thank you, I'll begin myself. Do you remember, the
other day, when we were here, and were talking of the difference in people's pride?"

"Purse pride and poverty-pride? Yes, I remember that."

"I didn't like what you said, then; or, rather, what you
were."

"Have you begun now? Why didn't you?"

"Because—because you seemed very worldly."

"And do you object to the world? I didn't make it," said
Maxwell, with his scornful smile. "But I've no criticism of the
creator to offer. I take the world as I find it, and as soon as I
get a little stronger, I'm going back to it. But I thought you
were rather worldly yourself, Miss Hilary."

"I don't know. I don't believe I am, very. Don't you think
the kind of life Matt's trying to live is better?"

"Your brother is the best man I ever knew—"

"Oh, isn't he? Magnificent!"

"But life means business. Even literary life, as I understand
it, means business."

"And can't you think—can't you wish—for anything better
than the life that means business?" she asked, she almost entreated. "Why should you ever wish to go back to the world?

If you could live in the country away from society, and all its vanity and vexation of spirit, why wouldn't you rather lead a literary life that didn't mean business?"

"But how? Are you proposing a public subscription, or a fairy godmother?" asked Maxwell.

"No; merely the golden age. I'm just supposing the case," said Louise. "You were born in Arcady, you know," she added with a wistful smile.

"Arcady is a good place to emigrate from," said Maxwell, with a smile that was not wistful. "It's like Vermont, where I was born, too. And if I owned the whole of Arcady, I should have no use for it till I had seen what the world had to offer. Then I might like it for a few months in the summer."

"Yes," she sighed faintly, and suddenly she rose, and said, "I must go and put the finishing touches. Good-by, Mr. Maxwell"—she mechanically gave him her hand. "I hope you will soon be well enough to get back to the world again."

"Thank you," he said, in surprise. "But the great trial you were going to make of my patience, my docility"—

She caught away her hand. "Oh, that wasn't anything. I've decided not. Good by! Don't go through the empty form of coming back to the house with me. I'll take your adieux to mamma." She put the cushion into the hammock. "You had better stay and try to get a nap, and gather strength for the battle of life as fast as you can."

She spoke so gayly and lightly, that Maxwell, with all his subtlety, felt no other mood in her. He did not even notice, till afterwards, that she had said nothing about their meeting again. He got into the hammock, and after a while he drowsed with a delicious, poetic sense of her capricious charm, as she drifted back to the farmhouse over the sloping meadow. He visioned a future in which fame had given him courage to tell her his love.

Mrs. Hilary knew from her daughter's face that something had happened; but she knew also that it was not what she dreaded.

Part Third

I

_____

MATT HILARY saw Pinney, and easily got at the truth of his hopes and possibilities concerning Northwick. He found that the reporter really expected to do little more than to find his man, and make a newspaper sensation out of his discovery. He was willing to forego this in the interest of Northwick's family, if it could be made worth his while; he said he had always sympathized with his family, and Mrs. Pinney had, and he would be glad to be of use to them. He was so far from conceiving that his account of the defalcation in the *Events* could have been displeasing to them, that he bore them none of an offender's malice. He referred to his masterpiece in proof of his interest, and he promptly agreed with Matt as to the terms of his visit to Canada, and its object.

It was in fact the more practicable because, since he had written to Maxwell, there had been a change in his plans and expectations. Pinney was disappointed in the *Events* people; they had not seen his proposed excursion as he had; the failure of Northwick's letter, as an enterprise, had dashed their interest in him; and they did not care to invest in Pinney's scheme even so far as to guarantee his expenses. This disgusted Pinney, and turned his thoughts strongly toward another calling. It was not altogether strange to him; he had already done some minor pieces of amateur detective work; and acquitted himself with gratifying success; and he had lately seen a private detective who attested his appreciation of Pinney's skill by offering him a partnership. His wife was not

in favor of his undertaking the work, though she could not
deny that he had some distinct qualifications for it. The air
of confidence which he diffused about him unconsciously, and
which often served him so well in newspaper life was in itself
the most valuable property that a detective could have. She
said this, and she did not object to the profession itself, except for the dangers that she believed it involved. She did not
wish Pinney to incur these, and she would not be laughed out
of her fears when he told her that there were lines of detective
work that were not half so dangerous in the long run as that
of a reporter subject to assignment. She only answered that
she would much rather he kept along on the newspaper. But
this offer to look up Northwick in behalf of his family, was a
different affair. That would give them a chance for their out-
ing in Canada, and pay them better than any newspaper enterprise. They agreed to this, and upon how much good it
would do the baby, and they imagined how Mrs. Pinney should
stay quietly at Quebec while Pinney went about looking up
his man, if that was necessary.

"And then," he said, "if I find him, and all goes well, and
I can get him to come home with me, by moral suasion, I
can butter my bread on both sides. There's a reward out for
him; and I guess I will just qualify as a detective before we
start, so as to be prepared for emergencies"—

"Lorenzo Pinney!" screamed his wife. "Don't you think
of such a wicked thing! So dishonorable!"

"How wicked? How dishonorable?" demanded Pinney.

"I'm ashamed to have to tell you, if you don't see; and I
wont. But if you go as a detective, *go* as a detective; and if you
go as their friend, to help them and serve them, then go that
way. But don't you try to carry water on both shoulders. If
you do, I wont stir a step with you. So there!"

"Oh!" said Pinney. "I understand. I didn't catch on, at first.
Well, you needn't be afraid of my mixing drinks. I'll just use
the old fellow for practice. Very likely he may lead to something else in the defaulter line. You wont object to that?"

"No; I wont object to that."

They had the light preparations of young house-keepers to make, and they were off to the field of Pinney's work in a very few days after he had seen Matt, and told him that he would talk it over with his wife. At Quebec he found board for his family at the same hotel where Northwick had stopped in the winter, but it had kept no recognizable trace of him in the name of Warwick on its register. Pinney passed a week of search in the city, where he had to carry on his investigations with an eye not only to Northwick's discovery, but to his concealment as well. If he could find him he must hide him from the pursuit of others, and he went about his work in the journalistic rather than the legal way. He had not wholly "severed his connection" as the newspaper phrase is, with the *Events*. He had a fast and loose relation with it, pending a closer tie with his friend, the detective, which authorized him to keep its name on his card; and he was soon friends with all the gentlemen of the local press. They did not understand, in their old fashioned, quiet ideal of newspaper work, the vigor with which Pinney proposed to enjoy the leisure of his vacation in exploiting all the journalistic material relating to the financial exiles resident in their city. But they had a sort of local pride in their presence, and with their help Pinney came to know all that was to be known of them. The colony was not large, but it had its differences, its distinctions, which the citizens were very well aware of. There are defaulters and defaulters, and the blame is not in all cases the same, nor the breeding of the offenders. Pinney learned that there were defaulters who were in society, and not merely because they were defaulters for large sums and were of good social standing at home, but because there were circumstances that attenuated their offence in the eyes of the people of their city of refuge; they judged them by their known intentions and their exigencies, as the justice they had fled from could not judge them. There were other defaulters of a different type and condition whose status followed them: embezzlers who had deliberately

planned their misdeeds, and who had fallen from no domestic
dignity in their exclusion from respectable association abroad
These Pinney saw in their walks about the town; and he was
not too proud, for the purposes of art, to make their acquaint
ance, and to study in their vacancy and solitude the dullness
and wearisomeness of exile. They did not consort together,
but held aloof from one another, and professed to be ignorant,
each of the affairs of the rest. Pinney sympathized in tone if
not in sentiment with them, but he did not lure them to the
confidence he so often enjoyed; they proved to be men of
reticent temper; when frankly invited to speak of their history and their hopes in the interest of the reputations they
had left behind them, they said they had no statement to make.

It was not from them that Pinney could hope to learn anything of the man he was seeking; Northwick was not of their
order, morally or socially; and from the polite circles where
the more elect of the exiles moved, Pinney was himself ex-
cluded by the habit of his life and by the choice of the people
who formed those circles. This seemed to Pinney rather comi-
cal, and it might have led him to say some satirical things
of the local society, if it had been in him to say bitter things at
all. As it was, it amused his inexhaustible amiability that an
honest man like himself should not be admitted to the company of even the swellest defaulters when he was willing to
seek it. He regretted that it should be so mainly because
Northwick could have been heard of among them, if at all; and
when all his other efforts to trace him at Quebec failed, he
did not linger there. In fact he had not expected to find him
there, but he had begun his search at that point because he
must stop there on his way to Rimouski, where Northwick's
letter to the *Events* was posted. This postmark was the only
real clue he had; but he left no stone unturned at Quebec
lest Northwick should be under it. By the time he came to the
end of his endeavors, Mrs. Pinney and the baby were on such
friendly terms with the landlady of the hotel where they were
staying that Pinney felt as easy at parting from them as he could

ever hope to feel. His soft heart of husband and father was torn at leaving them behind; but he did not think it well to take them with him, not knowing what Rimouski might be like, or how long he might be kept remote from an English-speaking, or English practising doctor. He got a passage down the river on one of the steamers for Liverpool; and with many vows in compliance with his wife's charges that he would not let the vessel by any chance carry him on to Europe, he rent himself away. She wagged the baby's hand at him from the window where she stood to watch him getting into the calash, and the vision of her there shone in his tears as the calash dashed wildly down Mountain Hill Street, and whirled him through the Lower Town on to the steamer's landing. He went to his stateroom as soon as he got aboard that he might give free course to his heartache; and form resolutions to be morally worthy of getting back alive to them, and of finding them well. He would, if he could, have given up his whole enterprise; and he was only supported in it by remembering what she had said in praise of its object. She had said that if he could be the means of finding their father for those two poor women, she should think it the greatest thing that ever was; and more to be glad of than if he could restore him to his creditors. Pinney had laughed at this womanish view of it; he had said that in either case it would be business, and nothing else; but now his heart warmed with acceptance of it as the only right view. He pledged himself to it in anticipative requital of the Providence that was to bring them all together again, alive and well; good as he had felt himself to be when he thought of the love in which he and his wife were bound, he had never experienced so deep and thorough a sense of desert as in this moment. He must succeed, if only to crown so meritorious a marriage with the glory of success, and found it in lasting prosperity.

THESE emotions still filled Pinney to the throat when at last he left his cabin, and went forward to the smoking room where he found a number of veteran voyagers enjoying their cigars over the cards which they had already drawn against the tedium of the ocean passage. Some were not playing, but merely smoking and talking, with glasses of clear pale straw colored liquid before them. In a group of these the principal speaker seemed to be an American; the two men who chorussed him were Canadians; they laughed and applauded with enjoyment of what was national as well as what was individual in his talk.

"Well, I never saw a man as mad as old Oiseau when he told about that fellow, and how he tried to start him out every day to visit his soap-mine in the 'ill, as he called it, and how the fellow would slip out of it, day after day, week after week, till at last Oiseau got tired, and gave him the bounce when the first boat came up in the spring. He tried to make him believe it would be good for his health, to go out prospecting with him, let alone making his everlasting fortune; but it was no good; and all the time Oiseau was afraid he would fall into my hands and invest with me. 'I make you a present of 'im, Mr. Markham,' says he. 'I 'ave no more use for him, if you find him.' "

One of the Canadians said, "I don't suppose he really had anything to invest."

"Why, yes, that was the curious thing about it; he had a

306

belt full of thousand dollar bills round him. They found it when he was sick; and old Oiseau was so afraid that something would happen to him, and *he* would be suspected of it that he nursed him like a brother till he got well, and as soon as he was able to get away he bounced him."

"And what do you suppose was the matter with him, that he wouldn't even go to look at Oiseau's soap mine?"

"Well," said the American, closing his eyes for the better enjoyment of the analysis, and giving a long, slow pull at his cigar, "there might have been any one of several things. My idea is that he was a defaulter, and the thousand dollar bills— there were forty or fifty of them, Oiseau says—were part of the money he got away with. Then, very likely he had no faith in Oiseau—knew it was probably a soap-mine, and was just putting him off till he could get away himself. Or, maybe his fever left him a little cracked, and he didn't know exactly what he was about. Then, again, if my theory of what the man was is true, I think that kind of fellow gets a twist simply from what he's done. A good many of them must bring money away with them, and there are business openings everywhere; but you never hear of their going into anything over here."

"That *is* odd," said the Canadian.

"Or would be if it were not so common. It's the rule, here, and I don't know an exception. The defaulter never does anything with his money, except live on it. Meigs, who built those railroads in the Andes, is the only one who ever showed enterprise; and I never understood that it was a private enterprise with him. Any way, the American defaulter that goes to Canada never makes any effort to grow up with the country. He simply rests on his laurels, or else employs his little savings to negotiate a safe return. No, sir; there's something in defalcation that saps a man's business energies, and I don't suppose that old fellow would have been able to invest in Oiseau's gold mine if it had opened at his feet, and he could have seen the sovereigns ready coined in it. He just *couldn't*. I can understand that state of mind, though I don't pretend to respect it.

I can imagine just how the man *trembled* to go into some speculation, and didn't dare to. Must have been an old hand at it, too. But it seems as if the money he steals becomes sacred to a man when he gets away with it, and he can't risk it."

"I rather think you could have overcome his scruples, Markham, if you could have got at him," said the Canadian.

"Perhaps," Markham assented. "But I guess I can do better with our stock in England."

Pinney had let his cigar go out, in his excitement. He asked Markham for a light, though there were plenty of matches, and Markham accepted the request as an overture to his acquaintance.

"Brother Yank?" he suggested.

"Boston."

"Going over?"

"Only to Rimouski. You don't happen to know the name of that defaulter, do you?"

"No; I don't," said Markham.

"I had an idea I knew who it was," said Pinney.

Markham looked sharply at him. "After somebody in Rimouski?"

"Well, not just in that sense, exactly, if you mean as a detective. But I'm a newspaper man, and this is my holiday, and I'm working up a little article about our financiers in exile while I'm resting. My name's Pinney."

"Markham can fill you up with the latest facts," said the Canadian going out; "and he's got a gold mine that beats Oiseau's hollow. But don't trust him too far. I know him; he's a partner of mine."

"That accounts for me," said Markham, with the tolerant light of a much joked joker in his eye. With Pinney alone he ceased to talk the American which seemed to please his Canadian friends, and was willing soberly to tell all he knew about Oiseau's capitalist, whom he merely conjectured to be a defaulter. He said the man called himself Warwick, and professed to be from Chicago; and then Pinney recalled the name and address in the register of his Quebec hotel, and the date, which was about that of Northwick's escape. "But I never dreamt of this using half of his real name," and he told Markham what the real name was; and then he thought it safe to trust him with the nature of his special mission concerning Northwick.

"Is there any place, on board, where a man could go and kick himself?" he asked.

"Do it here, as well as anywhere," said Markham, breaking his cigar-ash off. But Pinney's alluring confidence, and his simple-hearted acknowledgment of his lack of perspicacity had told upon him; he felt the fascinating need of helping Pinney which Pinney was able to inspire in those who respected him least, and he said, "There was a priest who knew this man when he was at Ha-ha Bay, and I believe he has a parish now—yes, he has! I remember Oiseau told me—at Rimouski. You'd better look him up."

"Look him up!" said Pinney in a frenzy. "I'll *live* with him before I'm in Rimouski twenty seconds!"

He had no trouble in finding Père Étienne, but after the first hopeful encounter with the sunny surface sweetness of the young priest, he found him disposed to be reserved concerning the Mr. Warwick he had known at Ha-ha Bay. It became evident that Père Étienne took Pinney for a detective; and however willing he might have been to save a soul for Paradise in the person of the man whose unhappiness he had witnessed he was clearly not eager to help hunt a fugitive down for State's Prison. Even when Pinney declared his true character and mission, the priest's caution exacted all the proofs he could give, and made him submit his authorization to an English-speaking notary of the priest's acquaintance. Then he owned that he had seen Mr. Warwick since their parting at Ha-ha Bay; Mr. Warwick had followed him to Rimouski, after several weeks, and Père Étienne knew where he was then living. But he was still so anxious to respect the secrecy of a man who had trusted him as far as Northwick had, that it required all the logic and all the learning of the notary to convince him that Mr. Warwick, if he were the largest defaulter ever self-banished, was in no danger of extradition at Pinney's hands. It was with many injunctions, and upon many promises that at last, he told Pinney where Mr. Warwick was living, and furnished him with a letter which was at once warrant and warning to the exile.

Pinney took the first train back toward Quebec; he left it at St. André, and crossed the St. Lawrence to Malbaie. He had no trouble, there, in finding the little hostelry where Mr. Warwick lodged. But Pinney's spirit, though not of the greatest delicacy, had become sensitized toward the defaulter through the scrupulous regard for him shown by Père Étienne no less than by the sense of holding almost a filial relation to him in virtue of his children's authorization. So, his heart smote him at the ghastly look he got, when he advanced upon Warwick, where he sat at the inn door, in the morning sun, and cheerily addressed him, "Mr. Northwick, I believe."

It was the first time Northwick had heard his real name spoken since Putney had threatened him in the station, the dark February morning when he fled from home. The name he had worn for the last five months was suddenly no part of him, though till that moment it had seemed as much so as the white beard which he had suffered to hide his face.

"I don't expect you to answer me," said Pinney, feeling the need of taking as well as giving time, "till you've looked at this letter, and of course I've no wish to hurry you. If I'm mistaken, and it isn't Mr. Northwick, you wont open the letter."

He handed him not the letter which Père Étienne had given him, but the letter Suzette Northwick had written her father; and Pinney saw that he recognized the hand-writing of the superscription. He saw the letter tremble in the old man's hand, and heard its crisp rustle as he clutched it to keep it from falling to the ground. He could not bear the sight of the longing and fear that came into his face: "No hurry; no hurry," he said kindly, and turned away.

III

WHEN Pinney came back from the little turn he took, Northwick was still holding the unopened letter in his hand. He stood looking at it in a kind of daze, and he was pale and seemed faint.

"Why, Mr. Northwick," said Pinney, "why don't you read your letter? If it hadn't been yours, don't I know that you'd have given it back to me at once?"

"It isn't that," said the man, who was so much older and frailer than Pinney had expected to find him. "But—are they well? Is it—bad news?"

"No!" Pinney exulted. "They're first-rate. You needn't be afraid to read the letter!" Pinney's exulation came partly from his certainty that it was really Northwick, and partly from the pleasure he felt in reassuring him; he sympathized with him as a father. His pleasure was not marred by the fact that he knew nothing of the state of Northwick's family, and built his assertion upon the probability that the letter would contain nothing to alarm or afflict him. "Like a glass of water?" he suggested, seeing Northwick sit inert and helpless on the steps of the inn-porch, apparently without the force to break the seal of the letter. "Or a little brandy?" Pinney handed him the neat leather-covered flask his wife had reproached him for buying when they came away from home; she said he could not afford it; but he was glad he had got it, now, and he unscrewed the stopple with pride in handing it to Northwick. "You look sick."

"I haven't been very well," Northwick admitted, and he touched the bottle with his lips. It revived him, and Pinney now saw that if he would leave him again, he would open the letter. There was little in it but the tender assurance Suzette gave him of their love, and the anxiety of Adeline and herself to know how and where he was. She told him that he was not to feel troubled about them; that they were well, and unhappy only for him; but that he must not think they blamed him, or had ever done so. As soon as they were sure they could reach him, she said, they would write to him again. Adeline wrote a few lines with her name, to say that for some days past she had not been quite well; but that she was better, and had nothing to wish for but to hear from him.

When Pinney came back a second time, he found Northwick with the letter open in his hand.

"Well, sir," he said with the easy respectfulness toward Northwick that had been replacing, ever since he talked with Matt Hilary, the hail fellow manner he used with most men, and that had now fully established itself, "You've got some noble scenery, about here." He meant to compliment Northwick on the beauty of the landscape, as people ascribe merit to the inhabitant of a flourishing city.

Northwick, by his silence, neither accepted nor disclaimed the credit of the local picturesqueness; and Pinney ventured to add, "But you seem to take it out in nature, Mr. Northwick. The place is pretty quiet, sir."

Northwick paid no heed to this observation, either; but after sitting mute so long that Pinney began to doubt whether he was ever going to speak at all, he began to ask some guarded and chary questions as to how Pinney had happened to find him. Pinney had no unwillingness to tell, and now he gave him the letter of Père Étienne, with a eulogy of the priest's regard for Northwick's interest and safety. He told him how Markham's talk had caught his attention, and Northwick tacitly recognized the speculator. But when Pinney explained that it was the postmark on his letter to the *Events* that gave him the notion of going to Rimouski, he could see that North-wick was curious to know the effect of that letter with the public. At first he thought he would let him ask; but he perceived that this would be impossible for Northwick, and he decided to say, "That letter was a great sensation, Mr. Northwick." The satisfaction that lighted up Northwick's eyes caused Pinney to add, "I guess it set a good many people thinking about you in a different way. It showed that there was something to be said on both sides, and I believe it made friends for you, sir. Yes, sir." Pinney had never believed this till the moment he spoke, but then it seemed so probable he had that he easily affirmed it. "I don't believe, Mr. Northwick," he went on, "but what this trouble could be patched up, somehow, so that you could come back, if you wanted to; give 'em time to think it over, a little."

As soon as he said this the poison of that ulterior purpose which his wife had forbidden him, began to work in Pinney's soul. He could not help feeling what a grand thing it would be if he could go back with Northwick in his train, and deliver him over a captive of moral suasion to his country's courts. Whatever the result was, whether the conviction or the acquittal of Northwick, the process would be the making of Pinney. It would carry him to such a height in the esteem of those who knew him that he could choose either career and whether as a reporter or a detective, it would give his future the distinction of one of the most brilliant pieces of work in both sorts. Pinney tried his best to counteract the influence of these ideas by remembering his promises to his wife; but it was difficult to recall his promises with accuracy in his wife's absence; and he probably owed his safety in this matter more to Northwick's temperament than to any virtue of his own.

"I think I understand how that would be," said the defaulter coldly; and he began very cautiously to ask Pinney the precise effect of his letter as Pinney had gathered it from print and hearsay. It was not in Pinney's nature to give any but a rose-colored and illusory report of this; but he felt that

Northwick was sizing him up while he listened, and knew just when and how much he was lying. This heightened Pinney's respect for him, and apparently his divination of Pinney's character had nothing to do with Northwick's feeling toward him. So far as Pinney could make out it was friendly enough, and as their talk went on, he imagined a growing trustfulness in it. Northwick kept his inferences and conclusions to himself. His natural reticence had been intensified by the solitude of his exile; it stopped him short of any expression concerning Pinney's answers; and Pinney had to construct Northwick's opinions from his questions. His own cunning was restlessly at work exploring Northwick's motives in each of these, and it was not at fault in the belief it brought him that Northwick clearly understood the situation at home. He knew that the sensation of his offence and flight was past, and that so far as any public impulse to punish him was concerned, he might safely go back. But he knew that the involuntary machinery of the law must begin to operate upon him as soon as he came within its reach; and he could not learn from Pinney that anything had been done to block its wheels. The letter from his daughters threw no light upon this point; it was an appeal for some sign of life and love from him; nothing more. They or the friends who were advising them had not thought it best to tell him more than that they were well, and anxious to hear from him; and Pinney really knew nothing more about them. He had not been asked to Hatboro' to see them before he started, and with all the will he had to invent comfortable and attractive circumstance for them, he was at a disadvantage for want of material. The most that he could conjecture was that Mr. Hilary's family had not broken off their friendly relations with them. He had heard old Hilary criticised for it, and he told Northwick so.

"I guess he's been standing by you, Mr. Northwick, as far as he consistently could," he said; and Northwick ventured to reply that he expected that. "It was young Hilary who brought me the letter, and talked the whole thing up with me," Pinney added.

Northwick had apparently not expected this; but he let no more than the fact appear. He kept silent for a time; then he said, "And you don't know anything about the way they're living?"

"No, I don't," said Pinney with final candor. "But I should say they were living along there about as usual. Mr. Hilary didn't say but what they were. I guess you haven't got any cause to be uneasy on that score. My idea is, Mr. Northwick, that they wanted to leave you just as free as they could about themselves. They wanted to find out your whereabouts, in the land of the living first of all. You know that till that letter of yours came out, there were a good many that thought you were killed in that accident at Wellwater, the day you left home."

Northwick started. "What accident? What do you mean?" he demanded.

"Why, didn't you know about it? Didn't you see the accounts? They had a name like yours amongst the missing, and people who thought you were not in it, said it was a little job you had put up. There was a despatch engaging a Pullman seat signed T. W. Northwick"—

"Ah! I knew it!" said Northwick. "I knew that I must have signed my real name!"

"Well, of course," said Pinney, soothingly, "a man is apt to do that, when he first takes another. It's natural."

"I never heard of the accident. I saw no papers for months. I wouldn't; and then I was sick— They must have believed I was dead!"

"Well, sir," said Pinney, "I don't know that that follows. My wife and myself talked that up a good deal at the time, and we concluded that it was about an even thing. You see it's pretty hard to believe that a friend is dead, even when you've seen him die; and I don't understand how people that lose friends at a distance can ever quite realize that they're gone. I guess that even if the ladies went upon the theory of the accident, there was always a kind of a merciful uncertainty about it, and that was my wife's notion, too. But that's neither here nor there, now, Mr. Northwick. Here you are, alive and well, in spite of all theories to the contrary—though *they* must have been pretty well exploded by your letter to the *Events*—and the question is what answer are you going to let me take back to your family? You want to send some word, don't you? My instructions were not to urge you at all, and I wont. But if I was in your place, I know what *I* would do."

Northwick did not ask him what it was he would do. He fell into a deep silence which it seemed to Pinney he would never break; and his face became such a blank that all Pinney's subtlety was at fault. It is doubtful indeed if there was anything definite or directed in the mute misery of Northwick's soul. It was not a sharp anguish, such as a finer soul's might have been, but it was a real misery, of a measure and a quality that he had not felt before. Now he realized how much he must have made his children suffer. Perhaps it wrung him the more keenly because it seemed to be an expression of the divine displeasure, which he flattered himself he had appeased, and was a fatal consequence of his guilt. It was a terrible suggestion of the possibility that, after all, providence might not have been a party to the understanding between them, and that his goodwill toward those he had wronged had gone for nothing. He had blamed himself for not having tried to retrieve himself and make their losses good. It was no small part of his misery now to perceive that anything he might have done would have gone for nothing in this one-sided understanding. He fetched a long, unconscious sigh.

"Why, it's all over, now, Mr. Northwick," said Pinney, with a certain amusement at the simple heartedness of the sigh whose cause he did not misinterpret. "The question is now about your getting back to them."

"Getting back? You know I can't go back," said Northwick, with bitter despair, and an openness that he had not shown before.

Far beneath and within the senses that apprehend the obvious things, Pinney felt the unhappy man beginning to cling to him. He returned joyously, "I don't know about that. Now see here, Mr. Northwick: you believe that I'm here as your friend, don't you? That I want to deal in good faith with you?" Northwick hesitated, and Pinney pursued, "Your daughter's letter ought to be a guaranty of that!"

"Yes," Northwick admitted, after another hesitation.

"Well, then, what I'm going to say is in your interest, and you've got to believe that I have some authority for saying it. I can't tell you just how much, for I don't know as I know myself exactly. But *I* think you can get back if you work it right. Of course you can't get back for nothing. It's going to cost you something. It's going to cost you all you've brought with you"— Pinney watched Northwick's impassive face for the next change that should pass upon it; he caught it, and added—"and more. But I happen to know that the balance will be forthcoming when it's needed. I can't say *how* I know it, for I don't exactly *know* how I know it. But I do know it; and you know that it's for you to take the first step. You must say how much money you brought with you, and where it is, and how it can be got at. I should think," said Pinney, with a drop in his earnestness, and as if the notion had just occurred to him, "you would want to see that place of yours again."

Northwick gave a gasp in the anguish of homesickness the words brought upon him. In a flash of what was like a luminous pang, he saw it all as it looked the night he left it in the white landscape under the high, bare winter sky. "You don't know what you're talking about," he said with a kind of severity.

"No," Pinney admitted, "I don't suppose any one can begin to appreciate it as you do. But I was there, just after you skipped"—

"Then I *was* the kind of man who would skip," Northwick swiftly reflected—

"And I must say I would take almost any chance of getting

back to a place like that. Why," he said, with an easy, caressing cordiality, "you can't have any idea how completely the thing's blown over. Why, sir, I'll bet you could go back to Hatboro', now, and be there twenty-four hours before anybody would wake up enough to make trouble for you. Mind, I don't say that's what we want you to do. We couldn't make terms for you half as well, with you on the ground. We want you to keep your distance for the present, and let your friends work for you. Like a candidate for the presidency," Pinney added with a smile. "Hello! Who's this?"

A little French maid, barefooted, blackeyed, curly-headed, shyly approached Northwick, and said, "Dîner, Monsieur."

"That means dinner," Northwick gravely interpreted. "I will ask you to join me."

"Oh, thank you, I shall be very glad," said Pinney rising with him. They had been sitting on the steps of a structure that Pinney now noticed was an oddity among the bark-sheathed cabins of the little hamlet. "Why, what's this?"

"It's the studio of an American painter who used to come here. He hasn't been here for several years."

"I suppose you expect to light out if he comes," Pinney suggested, in the spirit of good fellowship towards Northwick now thoroughly established in him.

"He couldn't do me any harm, if he wanted to," answered Northwick with unresentful dignity.

"No," Pinney readily acquiesced, "and I presume you'd be glad to hear a little English, after all the French you have around."

"The landlord speaks a little; and the priest. He is a friend of Father Étienne."

"Oh, I see," said Pinney. He noticed that Northwick walked slowly and weakly; he ventured to put his hand under his elbow, and Northwick did not resent the help offered him.

"I had a very severe sickness during the latter part of the winter," he explained, "and it pulled me down a good deal."

"At Rimouski, I presume," said Pinney.

"No," said Northwick, briefly.

IV

Over the simple dinner, which Pinney praised for the delicacy of the local lamb, and Northwick ate of so sparingly, Northwick talked more freely. He told Pinney all about his flight, and his winter journey up toward the northern verge of the civilized world. The picturesque details of this narrative, and their capability of distribution under attractive catch-heads almost maddened the reporter's soul in Pinney with longing to make newspaper material of Northwick on the spot. But he took his honor in both hands, and held fast to it; only, he promised him that if the time ever came when that story could be told, it should be both fortune and fame to him.

They sat long over their dinner. At last Pinney pulled out his watch. "What time did you say the boat for Quebec got along here?"

Northwick had not said, of course, but he now told Pinney. He knew the time well in the homesickness which mounted to a paroxysm as that hour each day came and went.

"We must get there some time in the night, then," said Pinney, still looking at his watch. "Then let's understand each other about this: Am I to tell your family where you are? Or what? Look here!" he broke off suddenly, "why don't you come up to Quebec with me? You'll be just as safe there as you are here; you know that; and now that your whereabouts are bound to be known to your friends, you might as well be where they can get at you by telegraph in case of emergency. Come! What do you say?"

Northwick said simply, "Yes, I will go with you."

"Well, now, you're shouting," said Pinney. "Can't I help you to put your traps together? I want to introduce you to my wife. She takes as much interest in this thing, as I do; and she'll know how to look after you a great deal better, get you to Quebec, once. She's the greatest little nurse in *this* world; and as you *say*, you don't seem over and above strong. I hope you don't object to children. We've got a baby, but it's the *best* baby! I've heard that child cry just *once*, since it was born, and that was when it first realized that it was in this vale of tears; I believe we all do that; but *our* baby finished up the whole crying-business on that occasion."

With Pinney these statements led to others until he had possessed Northwick of his whole autobiography. He was in high content with himself, and his joy overflowed in all manner of affectionate services to Northwick which Northwick accepted as the mourner entrusts his helplessness to the ghastly kindness of the undertaker, and finds in it a sort of human sympathy. If Northwick had been his own father, Pinney could not have looked after him with tenderer care, in putting his things together for him, and getting on board the boat, and making interest with the clerk for the best stateroom. He did not hesitate to describe him as an American financier; he enjoyed saying that he was in Canada for his health; and that he must have an extra room. The clerk gave up the captain's, as all the others were taken, and Pinney occupied it with Northwick. It was larger and pleasanter than the other rooms, and after Pinney got Northwick to bed, he sat beside him and talked. Northwick said that he slept badly, and liked to have Pinney talk; Pinney could see that he was uneasy when he left the room, and glad when he got back; he made up his mind that Northwick was somehow a very sick man. He lay quite motionless in the lower berth, where Pinney made him comfortable; his hands were folded on his breast, and his eyes were closed. Sometimes Pinney, as he talked on, thought the man was dead; and there were times when he invented questions that Northwick had to answer yes or no, before he felt sure that he was still alive; his breath went and came so softly Pinney could not hear it.

Pinney told him all about his courtship and married life, and what a prize he had drawn in Mrs. Pinney. He said she had been the making of him, and if he ever did amount to anything he should owe it to her. They had their eye on a little place out of town, out Wollaston way, and Pinney was going to try to get hold of it. He was tired of being mewed up in a flat, and he wanted the baby to get its feet on the ground, when it began to walk. He wanted to make his rent pay part of his purchase. He considered that it was every man's duty to provide a permanent home for his family, as soon as he began to have a family; and he asked Northwick if he did not think a permanent home was the thing.

Northwick said he thought it was, and after he said that, he sighed so deeply that Pinney said, "Oh, I beg your pardon." He had in fact lost the sense of Northwick's situation, and now he recurred to it with a fresh impulse of compassion. If his compassion was mixed with interest, with business, as he would have said, it was none the less a genuine emotion, and Pinney was sincere enough in saying he wished it could be fixed so that Northwick could get back to his home; at his time of life he needed it.

"And I don't believe but what it *could* be fixed," he said. "I don't know much about the points of the case; but I should say that with the friends you've got, you wouldn't have a great deal of trouble. I presume there are some legal forms you would have to go through with; but those things can always be appealed and continued and *nolle prossed*, and all that, till there isn't anything of them, in the end. Of course, it would have been different if they could have got hold of you in the beginning. But now," said Pinney, forgetting what he had already said of it, "the whole thing has blown over so that that letter of yours from Rimouski hardly started a ripple in Boston; I can't say how it was in Hatboro'. No, sir, I don't believe that if you went back now, and your friends stood by you as they ought to,—I don't believe you'd get more than a mere nominal sentence, if you got that."

Northwick made no reply, but Pinney fancied that his words were having weight with him, and he went on: "I don't know whether you've ever kept the run of these kind of things; but a friend of mine has, and he says there isn't one case in ten where the law carries straight. You see, public feeling has got a good deal to do with it, and when the people get to feeling that a man has suffered enough, the courts are not going to be hard on him. No, sir. I've seen it time and again, in my newspaper experience. The public respects a man's sufferings, and if public opinion can't work the courts, it can work the governor's council. Fact is, I looked into that business of yours, a little, after you left, Mr. Northwick, and I couldn't see, exactly, why you didn't stay, and try to fix it up with the company. I believe you could have done it, and that was the impression of a good many other newspaper men; and they're pretty good judges; they've seen a lot of life. It's exciting, and it's pleasant, newspaper work is," said Pinney straying back again into the paths of autobiography, "but I've got about enough of it, myself. The worst of it is, there ain't any outcome to it. The chances of promotion are about as good as they are in the U.S. Army when the Reservations are quiet. So I'm going into something else. I'd like to tell you about it, if you ain't too sleepy?"

"I *am* rather tired," said Northwick with affecting patience.

"Oh, well, then, I guess we'll postpone it till tomorrow. It'll keep. My! It don't seem as I *was* going back to my wife and baby. It seems too good to be true. Every time I leave 'em, I just bet myself I sha'n't get back alive; or if I do that I sha'n't find 'em safe and sound; and I'm just as sure I'll win every time as if I'd never lost the bet, yet."

Pinney undressed rapidly, and before he climbed into the berth over Northwick's he locked the door, and put the key under his pillow. Northwick did not seem to notice him, but a feeling of compunction made him put the key back in the door. "I guess I'd better leave it there, after all," he said. "It'll stop a key from the outside. Well, sir, good-night," he added to Northwick, and climbed to his berth with a light heart. Toward morning he was wakened by a groaning from the lower berth, and he found Northwick in great pain. He wished to call for help; but Northwick said the pain would pass, and asked him to get him some medicine he had in his hand-bag; and when he had taken that he was easier. But he held fast to Pinney's hand, which he had gripped in one of his spasms, and he did not loose it till Pinney heard him drawing his breath in the long respirations of sleep. Then Pinney got back to his berth and fell heavily asleep.

He knew it was late when he woke. The boat was at rest and must be lying at her landing in Quebec. He heard the passengers outside hurrying down the cabin to go ashore. When he had collected himself, and recalled the events of the night he was almost afraid to look down at Northwick lest he should find him lying dead in his berth; but when he summoned courage to look, he found the berth empty.

He leaped out upon the floor, and began to throw himself into his clothes. He was reassured, for a moment by seeing Northwick's travelling bag in the corner with his own; but the hand bag was gone. He rushed out as soon as he could make himself decent, and searched every part of the boat where Northwick might probably be; but he was not to be seen.

He asked a steward how long the boat had been in; and the steward said since six o'clock. It was then eight.

Northwick was not waiting for Pinney on the wharf, and he climbed disconsolately to his hotel in the Upper Town. He bet, as a last resource, that Northwick would not be waiting there for him, to give him a pleasant surprise, and he won his disastrous wager. It did not take his wife so long to understand what had happened as Pinney thought it would. She went straight to the heart of the mystery.

"Did you say anything about his going back?"

"Why—in a general way," Pinney admitted ruefully.

"Then, of course, that made him afraid of you. You broke your word, Ren, and it's served you right."

His wife was walking to and fro with the baby in her arms; and she said it was sick, and she had been up all night with it. She told Pinney he had better go out and get a doctor.

It was all as different from the return Pinney had planned, as it could be.

"I believe the old fool is crazy," he said, and he felt that this was putting the mildest possible construction upon Northwick's behavior.

"He seems to have known what he was about, anyway," said Mrs. Pinney coldly. The baby began to cry. "Oh, *do* go for the doctor!"

V

THE DAY was still far from dawning when Northwick crept up the silent avenue, in the dark of its firs, toward his empty house, and stealthily began to seek for that home in it which had haunted his sleeping and waking dreams so long. He had a kind of extasy in the risk he ran; a wild pleasure mixed with the terror he felt in being what and where he was. He wanted to laugh when he thought of the perfect ease and safety of his return. At the same time a thrilling anxiety pierced him through and through, and made him take all the precautions of a thief in the night.

A thief in the night: that was the phrase which kept repeating itself to him, till he said it over under his breath, as he put off his shoes, and stole up the piazza steps, and began to peer into the long windows, at the blackness within. He did not at once notice that the shutters were open, with an effect of reckless security or indifference, which struck a pang to his heart when he realized it. He felt the evil omen of this faltering in the vigilance which had once guarded his home, and which he had been himself the first to break down, and lay it open to spoil and waste. He tried the windows; he must get in, somehow, and he did not dare to ring at the door, or to call out. He must steal into his house, as he had stolen out of it.

One of the windows yielded; the long glass door gave inward, and he stepped on the carpetless floor of the library. Then the fact of the change that must have passed upon the whole house enforced itself, and he felt a passionate desire to face and appropriate the change in every detail. He lit one of the little taper matches that he had with him and hollowing his hands around it, let its glimmer show him the desolation of the dismantled and abandoned rooms. He passed through the doors set wide between library and drawing room and dining room and hall; and then from his dying taper he lit another, and mounted the stairs. He had no need to seek his daughters' rooms to satisfy himself that the whole place was empty; they were gone; but he had a fantastic expectation that in his own room he might find himself. There was nothing there, either; it was as if he were a ghost come back in search of the body it had left behind; any one that met him, he thought, might well be more frightened than he; and yet he did not lose the sense of risk to himself.

He had an expectation, born of long custom, and persisting in spite of the nakedness of the place otherwise, that he should see the pictured face of his wife, where it had looked so mercifully at him that last night from the portrait above the mantel. He sighed lightly to find it gone; her chair was gone from the bay window, where he had stood to gaze his last over the possessions he was abandoning. He let his little taper die out by the hearth, and then crept toward the glimmer of the window, and looked out again. The conservatories and the dairies and the barns showed plain in the gray of the moonless, starless night; in the coachman's quarters a little point of light appeared for a moment through the window, and then vanished.

Northwick knew from this that the place was inhabited; unless some homeless tramp like himself was haunting it, and it went through his confusion that he must speak to Newton, and caution him about tramps sleeping in the barns anywhere; they might set them on fire. His mind reverted to his actual condition, and he wondered how long he could come and go as a vagrant, without being detected. If it were not for the action against vagrants which he had urged upon the selectmen the summer before he might now come and go indefinitely. But he was not to blame; it was because Mrs. Morrell had encouraged the tramps by her reckless charity that something had to be done; and now it was working against him. It was hard: he remembered reading of a man who had left his family, one day, and taken a room across the street, and lived there in sight of them unknown till he died; and now he could not have passed his own door without danger of arrest as a vagrant. He struck another match and looked at himself in the mirror framed as a window at one side of the bay; he believed that with the long white beard he wore, and his hair, which he had let grow, his own children would not have known him.

It was bitter; but his mind suddenly turned from the thought, with a lightness it had, and he remembered that now he did not know where his children lived. He must find out, somehow; he had come to see them; and he could not go back without. He must hurry to find them, and be gone again before daylight.

He crept out to the stairs, and struck a match to light himself down, and he carried it still burning toward the window he had left open behind him in the library. As soon as he stepped out on the piazza he found himself gripped fast in the arms of a man.

"I've got you! What you doing in here, I'd like to know? Who are you, anyway, you thief? Just hold that lantern up to his face, a minute, 'Lectra."

Northwick had not tried to resist; he had not struggled; he had known Elbridge Newton's voice at the first word. He saw the figure of a woman beside him stooping over the lantern, and he knew that it was Mrs. Newton; but he made no sort of appeal to either. He did not make the least sound or movement. The habit of his whole life was reticence, especially in emergencies; and this habit had been strengthened and deepened by the solitude in which he had passed the last half year. If a knife had been put to his throat he would not have uttered a cry for mercy. But his silence was so involuntary that it seemed to him he did not breathe while Mrs. Newton was turning up the wick of the lantern for a good look at him. When the light was lifted to his face, Northwick felt that they both knew him through the disguise of his white beard. Elbridge's grip fell from him, and let him stand free. "Well, I'll be dumned," said Elbridge.

His wife remained holding the lantern to Northwick's face. "What are you going to do with him?" she asked at last, as if Northwick were not present; he stood so dumb and impassive.

"I d'know as I know," said Newton, overpowered by the peculiar complications of the case. He escaped from them for the moment in the probable inference: "I presume he was lookin' for his daughters. Didn't you know," he turned to Northwick, with a sort of apologetic reproach, "lightin' matches that way in the house, here, you might set it on fire, and you'd be sure to make people think there was somebody there, anyhow?"

Northwick made no answer to this question, and Newton looked him carefully over in the light of the lantern. "I swear, he's in his stockin' feet. You look round and see if you can find his shoes, anywhere, 'Lectra. You got the light." Newton seemed to insist upon this because it relieved him to delegate any step in this difficult matter to another.

His wife cast the light of her lantern about, and found the shoes by the piazza steps, and as Northwick appeared no more able to move than to speak, Elbridge stooped down, and put on his shoes for him where he stood. When he lifted himself he stared again at Northwick, as if to make perfectly sure of him, and then he said with a sigh of perplexity, "You go ahead a little ways, 'Lectra, with the lantern. I presume we've got to take him to 'em," and his wife, usually voluble and wilful, silently obeyed. "Want to see your daughters?" he asked Northwick, and at the silence which was his only response, Newton said, "Well, I don't know as I blame him any, for not

wantin' to commit himself. You don't want to be afraid," he
added to Northwick, "that anybody's goin' to keep you against
your will, you know."

"Well, I *guess* not," said Mrs. Newton finding her tongue,
at last. "If they was to double and treble the reward, I'd slap
'em in the face first. Bring him along, Elbridge."

As Northwick no more moved than spoke, Newton took
him by the arm, and helped him down the piazza steps and
into the dark of the avenue, tunneled about their feet by the
light of the lantern, as they led and pushed their helpless
capture toward the lodge at the avenue gate.

Northwick had heard and understood them; he did not
know what secret purpose their pretence of taking him to
his children might not cover; but he was not capable of offering any resistance, and when he reached the cottage he sank
passively on the steps. He shook in every nerve while Elbridge pounded on the door, till a window above was lifted,
and Adeline's frightened voice quavered out: "Who is it?
What is it?"

Mrs. Newton took the words out of her husband's mouth.
"It's us, Miss Northwick. If you're sure you're awake"—

"Oh, yes. I haven't been asleep!"

"Then listen!" said Mrs. Newton, in a lowered tone. "And
don't be scared. Don't call out—don't speak loud. There's
somebody here— Come down, and let him in."

Northwick stood up. He heard the fluttered rush of steps
on the stairs inside. The door opened, and Adeline caught
him in her arms, with choking, joyful sobs. "Oh father! Oh,
father! Oh, I knew it! I knew it! Oh, oh, oh! Where was he?
How did you find him?"

She did not heed their answers. She did not realize that
she was shutting them out when she shut herself in with her
father; but they understood.

————

VI

Northwick stared round him in the light of the lamp which Adeline turned up. He held fast by one of her hands. "What's he going to do? Has he gone for the officers? Is he going to give me up?"

"Who? Elbridge Newton? Well, I guess his wife hasn't forgot what you did for them when their little boy died, if *he* has, and I *guess* he hasn't gone for any officer! Where did you see him."

"In the house. I was there."

"But how did he know it?"

"I had to have a light to see by."

"Oh, my goodness! If anybody else had caught you, I don't know what I *should* have done. I don't see how you could be so venturesome!"

"I thought you were there. I had to come back. I couldn't stand it any longer, when that fellow came with your letter."

"Oh he *found* you!" she cried, joyfully. "I *knew* he would find you, and I said so— Sit down, father; do." She pushed him gently into a cushioned rocking chair. "It's mother's chair; don't you remember, it always stood in the bay window in your room, where she put it? Louise Hilary bought it at the sale—I know she bought it—and gave it to me. It was because the place was mother's that I wouldn't let Suzette give it up to the company."

He did not seem to understand what she was saying. He stared at her piteously, and he said with an effort, "Adeline,

I didn't know about that accident. I didn't know you thought
I was dead, or I"—

"No! Of *course* you didn't! I always told Suzette you didn't.
Don't you suppose I always believed in you, father? We both
believed in you, through it all; and when that letter of yours
came out in the paper I knew you were just overwrought."

Northwick rose and looked fearfully round him again, and
then came closer to her, with his hand in his breast. He drew
it out with the roll of bank notes in it. "Here's that money I
took away with me. I always kept it in my belt; but it hurt me
there. I want you should take care of it for me, and we can
make terms with them to let me stay"—

"Oh, they *wont* let you stay! We've tried it over and over;
and the court wont let you. They say you will have to be tried,
and they will put you in prison."

Northwick mechanically put the money back. "Well, let
them," said the broken man. "I can't stand it, any longer. I
have got to stay." He sank into the chair, and Adeline broke
into tears.

"Oh, I can't let you! You must go back! Think of your
good name, that there's never been any disgrace on!"

"What—what's that?" Northwick quavered, at the sound of
footsteps overhead.

"Why it's Suzette, of course! And I hadn't called her," said
Adeline breaking off from her weeping. She ran to the foot
of the stairs, and called huskily, "Suzette, Suzette! Come down
this instant! Come down, come down, come down!" She
bustled back to her father. "You must be hungry, ain't you,
father? I'll get you a cup of tea over my lamp here; the water
heats as quick! And you'll feel stronger after that. Don't you
be afraid of anything; there's nobody here but Suzette; Mrs.
Newton comes to do the work in the morning; they used to
stay with us, but we don't mind it a bit, being alone here. I *did*
want to go into the farmhouse, when we left our own, but
Suzette couldn't bear to live right in sight of our home, all
the time; she said it would be worse than being afraid; but

we haven't *been* afraid; and the Newtons come all the time to see if we want anything. And now that you've got back"— She stopped, and stared at him in a daze, and then turned to her lamp again, as if unable to cope with the situation. "I haven't been very well lately, but I'm getting better; and if only we could get the court to let you come back I should be as well as ever. I don't believe but what Mr. Hilary will make it out yet. Father!" She dropped her voice, and glanced round, "Suzette's engaged to young Mr. Hilary—oh, he's the *best* young man!—and I guess they're going to be married just as soon as we can arrange it about you. I thought I'd tell you before she came down."

Northwick did not seem to have taken the fact in, or else he could not appreciate it rightly. "Do you suppose," he whispered back, "that she'll speak to me?"

"*Speak* to you!"

"I didn't know. She was always so proud. But now I've brought back the money, all but the little I've had to use"—

There was a rustle of skirts on the stairs. Suzette stood a moment in the doorway, looking at her father, as if not sure he was real; then she flung herself upon him, and buried her face in his white beard, and kissed him with a passion of grief and love. She sank into his lap, with a long sigh, and let her head fall on his shoulder. All that was not simply father and daughter was for the moment annulled between them.

Adeline looked on admiring, while she kept about heating the water over her lamp; and they all took up fitfully the broken threads of their lives, and tried to piece them again into some sort of unity.

Adeline did most of the talking. She told her father how friends seemed to have been raised up for them in their need, when it was greatest. She praised herself for the inspiration she had in going to Putney for advice because she remembered how her father had spoken of him that last night, and for refusing to give up the property to the company. She praised Putney for justifying and confirming her at every step, and for doing everything that could be done about the court. She praised the Hilarys, all of them, for their constancy to her father throughout, and she said she believed that if Mr. Hilary could have had his way there never would have been any trouble at all about the accounts, and she wanted her father to understand just how the best people felt about him.

He listened vaguely to it all. A clock in the next room struck four, and Northwick started to his feet. "I must go!"

"Go?" Adeline echoed.

"Why must you go?" said Suzette, clinging about him.

They were all silent in view of the necessity that stared them in the face.

Then Adeline roused herself from the false dream of safety in which her own words had lulled her. She wailed out, "He's *got* to go! Oh, Suzette, let him go! He's got to go to prison if he stays!"

"It's prison, *there*," said Northwick. "Let me stay!"

"No, no! I can't let you stay! Oh how hard I am to make you go! What makes you leave it all to me, Suzette? It's for you, as much as anything I do it."

"Then, don't do it! If father wants to stay; if he thinks he had better, or if he will feel easier; he shall stay; and you needn't think of me. I wont *let* you think of me!"

"But what would they say—Mr. Hilary say—if they sent father to prison?"

Suzette's eyes glowed. "Let them say what they will. I know I can trust *him*, but if he wants to give me up for that, he may. If father wishes to stay, he shall, and nothing that they can do to him will ever make him different to us. If he tells us that he didn't mean anything wrong, that will be enough; and people may say what they please, and think what they please."

Northwick listened with a confused air. He looked from one to the other, as if beaten back and forth between them; he started violently when Adeline almost screamed out:

"Oh, you don't know what you're talking about! Father, tell her you don't *wish* to stay!"

"I must go, Suzette; I had better go"—

"Here, drink this tea, now, and it will give you a little strength." Adeline pressed the cup on him that she had been getting ready through all, and made him drain it. "Now, then, hurry, hurry, hurry, father! Say good bye! You've got to go, now,—yes, you've *got* to!—but it wont be for long. You've seen us, and you've found out we're alive and well, and now we can write—be sure you write, father, when you get back there—or, you'd better telegraph—and we can arrange,—I know we can—for you to come home, and stay home."

"Home! Home!" Northwick murmured.

"It seems as if he wanted to *kill* me!" Adeline sobbed into her hands. She took them away. "Well, *stay*, then!" she said.

"No, no! I'll go," said Northwick. "You're not to blame, Adeline. It's all right—all for the best. I'll go"—

"And let us know where you are, when you get there, this time, father!" said Adeline.

"Yes; I will."

"And we will come to you, there," Suzette put in. "We can live together in Canada, as well as here."

Northwick shook his head. "It's not the same. I can't get used to it; their business methods are different. I couldn't put my capital into any of their enterprises. I've looked the whole ground over. And—and I want to get back into our place."

He said these things vaguely, almost dryly, but with an air of final conviction, as after much sober reflection. He sat down, but Adeline would not let him be. "Well, then, we'll help you to think out some way of getting back, after we're all there together. Go; it'll soon begin to be light, and I'm afraid somebody'll see you, and stop you! But oh, my goodness! How are you going? You can't walk! And if you try to start from our depot, they'll know you, some one, and they'll arrest you. What shall we do?"

"I came over from East Hatboro' tonight," said Northwick. "I am going back there to get the morning train." This was the way he had planned, and he felt the strength of a fixed purpose in returning to his plan in words.

"But it's three miles!" Adeline shrieked. "You can never get there in the world in time for the train. Oh, why didn't I tell Elbridge to come for you! I must go and tell him to get ready right away."

"No, I'll go!" said Suzette. "Adeline!"

Adeline flung the door open, and started back with a cry from the dark van-like vehicle before the door, which looked like the Black Maria, or an undertaker's wagon in the pale light.

"It's me," said Elbridge's voice from the front of it, and Elbridge's head dimly showed itself. "I got to thinkin' maybe you'd want the carryall, and I didn't know but what I'd better go and hitch up, anyway."

"Oh, well, we *did!*" cried Adeline, with an hysterical laugh. "Here, now, father, get right in! Don't lose a second. Kiss Suzette; good bye! Be sure you get him to East Hatboro' in time for the four forty, Elbridge!" She helped her father, shaking and stumbling, into the shelter of the curtained carryall. "If anybody tries to stop you"—

"I'd like to see anybody try to stop me," said Elbridge, and he whipped up his horse. Then he leaned back toward Northwick and said, "I'm going to get the black colt's time out of the old mare."

"Which mare is it?" Northwick asked.

VII

ON HIS WAY home from the station, Elbridge Newton began to have some anxieties. He had no longer occasion for any about Northwick, he was safe on his way back to Canada; and Elbridge's anxieties were for himself. He was in the cold fit after his act of ardent generosity. He had no desire to entangle himself with the law by his act of incivism in helping Northwick to escape, and he thought it might be well to put himself on the safe side by seeing Putney about it; and locking the stable after the horse was stolen.

He drove round by the lawyer's house, and stopped at his gate just as Putney pushed his lawn-mower up to it, in his exercise of the instrument before breakfast.

Elbridge leaned out of the carryall, and asked, in a low confidential voice, "If J. Milton Northwick was to come back here, on the sly, say, to see his family, and I was to help him git off ag'in, would I be li'ble?"

"Why?" asked Putney.

"Because I just done it," said Elbridge, desperately.

"Just done it?" shouted Putney. "Why confound you!" He suddenly brought his voice down. "Do you mean to tell me the fellow's been back here, and you didn't let me know?"

"I hadn't any orders to do it," Elbridge weakly urged.

"Orders, the devil!" Putney retorted. "I'd 'a' given a hundred dollars to see that man and talk with him. Come, now; tell me all you know about it! Don't miss a thing!" After a few words from Newton, he broke out: "Found him in the house!

And I was down there prowling round the place myself not three hours before! Go on! Great Scott! Just think of it!"

Putney was at one of those crises of his life when his drink-devil was besetting him with sore temptation, and for the last twenty-four hours he had been fighting it with the ruses and pretences which he had learned to employ against it, but he felt that he was losing the game, though he was playing for much greater stakes than usual. He had held out so long since his last spree, that if he lost now he would defeat hopes that were singularly precious and sacred to him: the hopes that those who loved him best, and distrusted him most, and forgave him soonest, had begun to cherish. It would not break his wife's heart; she was used to his lapses; but it would wring it more cruelly than usual if he gave way, now.

When the fiend thrust him out of his house the night before, he knew that she knew of it; though she let him go in that fearful company, and made no effort to keep him. He was so strait an agnostic that, as he boasted, he had no superstitions, even; but his relation to the Northwicks covered the period of his longest resistance of temptation, and by a sort of instinctive, brute impulse, he turned his step towards the place where they lived, as if there might be rescue for him in the mere vicinity of those women who had appealed to him in their distress, as to a faithful enemy. His professional pride, his personal honor, were both involved in the feeling that he must not fail them; their implicit reliance had been a source of strength to him. He was always hoping for some turn of affairs which would enable him to serve them, or rather to serve Adeline; for he cared little for Suzette, or only secondarily; and since Pinney had gone upon his mission to Canada he was daily looking for this chance to happen. He must keep himself for that, and not because of them alone, but because those dearest to him had come tacitly to connect his resistance of the tempter with his zeal for the interests of his clients. With no more reasoned motives than these he had walked over the Northwick place, calling himself a fool for supposing that some virtue should enter into him out of the ground there, and yet finding a sort of relief, in the mere mechanical exercise, the novelty of exploring by night the property grown so familiar to him by day, and so strangely mixed up with the great trial and problem of his own usefulness.

He listened by turns with a sinking and a rising heart, as Newton now dug the particulars of his adventure out of himself. At the end he turned to go into the house.

"Well, what do you say, Squire Putney?" Elbridge called softly after him.

"Say?"

"You know: about what I done."

"Keep your mouth shut about what you 'done.' I should like to see you sent to jail, though, for what you didn't do."

Elbridge felt a consolatory quality in Putney's resentment, and Putney, already busy with the potentialities of the future, was buoyed up by the strong excitement of what had actually happened rather than finally cast down by what he had missed. He took three cups of the blackest coffee at breakfast and he said to the mute anxious face of his wife, "Well, Ellen, I seem to be pulling through, somehow."

VIII

Adeline was in a flutter of voluble foreboding till Elbridge came back. She asked Suzette whether she believed their father would get away; she said she knew that Elbridge would miss the train, with that slow, old mare, and their father would be arrested. Weak as she was from the sick bed she had left to welcome him, she dressed herself carefully, so as to be ready for the worst; she was going to jail with him if they brought him back; she had made up her mind to that. From time to time she went out and looked up the road to see if Elbridge was coming back alone, or whether the officers were bringing her father; she expected they would bring him first to his family; she did not know why. Suzette tried to keep her indoors; to make her lie down. She refused, with wild upbraidings. She declared that Suzette had never cared anything for her father; she had wanted to give their mother's property away, to please the Hilarys; and now that she was going to marry Matt Hilary, she was perfectly indifferent to everything else. She asked Suzette what had come over her.

Elbridge drove first to the stable and put up his horse when he came back. Then he walked to the lodge to report.

"Is he safe? Did he get away? Where is he?" Adeline shrieked at him before he could get a word out.

"He's all right, Miss Northwick," Elbridge answered soothingly. "He's on his way back to Canady, again."

"Then I've driven him away!" she lamented. "I've hunted him out of his home, and I shall never see him any more. Send for him! *Send* for him! Bring him *back*, I tell you! Go right straight after him, and tell him I said to come back! What are you standing there, for?"

She fell fainting. Elbridge helped Suzette carry her up stairs to her bed, and then ran to get his wife, to stay with them while he went for the doctor.

Matt Hilary had been spending the night at the rectory with Wade, and he walked out to take leave of Suzette once more before he went home. He found the doctor just driving away. "Miss Northwick seems not so well," said the doctor. "I'm very glad you happen to be here, on all accounts. I shall come again later in the day."

Matt turned from the shadow of mystery the doctor's manner left, and knocked at the door. It was opened by Suzette almost before he touched it. "Come in," she said, in a low voice whose quality fended him from her almost as much as the conditional look she gave him. The excited babble of the sick woman overhead, mixed with Mrs. Newton's nasal attempts to quiet her broke in upon their talk.

"Mr. Hilary," said Suzette formally, "are you willing my father should come back, no matter what happens?"

"If he wishes to come back. You know what I have always said."

"And you would not care if they put him in prison?"

"I should care very much"—

"You would be ashamed of me!"

"No! Never! What has it to do with you?"

"Then," she pursued, "he has come back. He has been here." She flashed all the fact upon him in vivid, rapid phrases, and he listened with an intelligent silence that stayed and comforted her as no words could have done. Before she had finished, his arms were round her, and she felt how inalienably faithful he was. "And now Adeline is raving to have him come back again, and stay. She thinks she drove him away; she will die if something can't be done. She says that she would not let him stay because—because you would be ashamed of us. She says I would be ashamed"—

"Suzette! Sue!" Adeline called down from the chamber above, "don't you let Mr. Hilary go before I get there. I want to speak to him," and while they stared helplessly at each other they heard her saying to Mrs. Newton, "Yes, I shall, too! I'm perfectly rested, now; and I shall go down. I should think I knew how I felt. I don't care what the doctor said; and if you try to stop me"— She came clattering down the stairs in the boots which she had pulled loosely on, and as soon as she showed her excited face at the door, she began: "I've thought out a plan, Mr. Hilary, and I want you should go and see Mr. Putney about it. You ask him if it wont do. They can get father let out on bail, when he comes back, and I can be his bail, and then, when there's a trial, they can take me instead of him: it won't matter to the court which they have, as long as they have somebody. Now, you go and ask Mr. Putney. I know he'll say so, for he's thought just as I have about father's case, all along. Will you go?"

"Will you go up and lie down again, Adeline, if Mr. Hilary will go?" Suzette asked, like one dealing with a capricious child.

"What do you all want me to lie down for?" Adeline turned upon her. "I'm perfectly well. And do you suppose I can rest, with such a thing on my mind? If you want me to rest, you'd better let him go and find out what Mr. Putney says. I think we'd better all go to Canada, and bring father back with us. He isn't fit to travel alone, or with strangers; he needs some one that understands his ways; and I'm going to him, just as soon as Mr. Putney approves of my plan, and I know he will. But I don't want Mr. Hilary to lose any time, now. I want to be in Quebec about as soon as father is. Will you go?"

"Yes, Miss Northwick," said Matt, taking her tremulous hand, "I'll go to Mr. Putney; and I'll see my father again; and whatever can be done to save your father any further suffering or yourself"—

"I don't care for myself," she said, plucking her hand away. "I'm young and strong, and I can bear it. But it's father I'm so anxious about."

She began to cry, and at a look from Suzette, Matt left them. As he walked along up toward the village in mechanical compliance with Adeline's crazy wish, he felt more and more the deepening tragedy of the case, and the inadequacy of all compromises and palliatives. There seemed indeed but one remedy for the trouble, and that was for Northwick to surrender himself and for them all to meet the consequences together. He realized how desperately homesick the man must have been to take the risks he had run in stealing back for a look upon the places and the faces so dear to him; his heart was heavy with pity for him. One might call him coward and egotist all one would; at the end remained the fact of a love which if it could not endure heroically, was still a deep and strong affection, doubtless the deepest and strongest thing in the man's weak and shallow nature. It might be his truest inspiration, and if it prompted him to venture everything and to abide by whatever might befall him, for the sake of being near those he loved, and enjoying the convict's wretched privilege of looking on them now and then, who should gainsay him?

Matt took Wade in on his way to Putney's office, to lay this question before him, and he answered it for him in the same breath: "Certainly no one less deeply concerned than the man's own flesh and blood, could forbid him."

"I'm not sure," said Wade, "that even his own flesh and blood would have supreme rights there. It may be that love, and not duty, is the highest thing in life. Oh, I know how we reason it away, and say that *true* love is unselfish and can find its fruition in the very sacrifice of our impulses; and we are fond of calling our impulses blind, but God alone knows whether they are blind. The reasoned sacrifice may satisfy the higher soul, but what about the simple and primitive natures which it wont satisfy?"

For answer, Matt told how Northwick had come back, at the risk of arrest, for an hour with his children, and was found in the empty house that had been their home, and brought to them; how he had besought them to let him stay, but they had driven him back to his exile. Matt explained how he was on his way to the lawyer, at Adeline's frantic demand, to go all over the case again, and see if something could not be done to bring Northwick safely home to them. He had himself no hope of finding any loophole in the law through which the fugitive could come and go; if he returned, Matt felt sure that he would be arrested and convicted, but he was not sure that this might not be the best thing for all. "You know," he said, "I've always believed that if he could voluntarily submit himself to the penalty of his offence, the penalty would be the greatest blessing for him on earth; the only blessing for his ruined life."

"Yes," Wade answered, "we have always thought alike about that, and perhaps this torment of longing for his home and children, may be the divine means of leading him to accept the only mercy possible with God for such a sufferer. If there were no one but him concerned, we could not hesitate in urging him to return. But the innocent who must endure the shame of his penalty—with him"—

"They are ready for that. Would it be worse than what they have learned to endure?"

"Perhaps not. But I was not thinking of his children alone. You, yourself, Matt—your family"—

Matt threw up his arms impatiently, and made for the door. "There's no question of *me*. And if *they* could not endure their portion,—the mere annoyance of knowing the slight for them in the minds of vulgar people,—I should be ashamed of them."

"Well, you are right, Matt," said his friend. "God bless you and guide you!" added the priest.

The lawyer had not yet come to his office, and Matt went to find him at his house. Putney had just finished his breakfast, and they met at his gate, and he turned back indoors with Matt. "Well, you know what's happened, I see," he said after the first glance at Matt's face.

"Yes, I know; and now what can be done? Are you sure we've considered every point? Isn't there some chance"—

Putney shook his head, and then bit off a piece of tobacco

before he began to talk. "I've been over the whole case in my mind this morning, and I'm perfectly certain there isn't the shadow of a chance of his escaping trial if he gives himself up. That's what you mean, I suppose?"

"Yes; that's what I mean," said Matt, with a certain disappointment. He supposed he had nerved himself for the worst, but he found he had been willing to accept something short of it.

"At times I'm almost sorry he got off," said Putney. "If we could have kept him, and surrendered him to the law, I believe we could have staved off the trial, though we couldn't have prevented it, and I believe we could have kept him out of State's prison on the ground of insanity." Matt started impatiently. "Oh, I don't mean that it could be shown that he was of unsound mind when he used the company's funds and tampered with their books, though I have my own opinion about that. But I feel sure that he's of unsound mind at present; and I believe we could show it so clearly in court that the prosecution would find it impossible to convict. We could have him sent to the Insane Asylum, and that would be a creditable exit from the affair in the public eye; it would have a retroactive effect that would popularly acquit him of the charges against him."

Putney could not forego a mischievous enjoyment of Matt's obvious discomfort, at this suggestion. His fierce eyes blazed; but he added seriously, "Why shouldn't he have the advantage of the truth, if that is the truth about him? And I believe it is. I think it could be honestly and satisfactorily proved from his history, ever since the defalcation came out, that his reason is affected. His whole conduct, so far as I know it, shows it; and I should like a chance to argue the case in court. And I feel pretty sure I shall, yet. I'm just as certain as I sit here that he will come back again. He can't keep away, and another time he may not fall into the hands of friends. It will be a good while before any rumor of last night's visit gets out; but it will get out at last, and then the detectives will be on the watch for him. Perhaps it will be just as well for us if he falls into their hands. If we produced him in court it might be more difficult to work the plea of insanity. But I do think the man's insane, and I should go into the case with a full and thorough persuasion on that point. Did he tell them where to find him in Canada?"

"He promised to let them know."

"I doubt if he does," said Putney. "He means to try coming back again. The secrecy he's kept as to his whereabouts—the perfectly needless and motiveless secrecy, as far as his children are concerned—would be a strong point in favor of the theory of insanity. Yes, sir; I believe the thing could be done; and I should like to do it. If the pressure of our life produces insanity of the homicidal and suicidal type, there's no reason why it shouldn't produce insanity of the defalcational type. The conditions tend to produce it in a proportion that is simply incalculable, and I think it's time that jurisprudence recognized the fact of such a mental disease, say, as defalcomania. If the fight for money, and material success goes on, with the opportunities that the accumulation of vast sums in a few hands afford, what is to be the end?"

Matt had no heart for the question, of metaphysics or of economics, whichever it was, that would have attracted him in another mood. He went back to Suzette and addressed himself with her to the task of quieting her sister. Adeline would be satisfied with nothing less than the assurance that Putney agreed with her that her father would be acquitted if he merely came back and gave himself up; she had changed to this notion in Matt's absence; and with the mental reservation which he permitted himself he was able to give the assurance she asked. Then at last, she consented to go to bed, and wait for the doctor's coming, before she began her preparations for joining her father in Canada. She did not relinquish that purpose; she felt sure that he never could get home without her; and Suzette must come, too.

IX

THE FOURTH morning, when Pinney went down into the hotel office at Quebec, after a trying night with his sick child and its anxious mother, he found Northwick sitting there. He seemed to Pinney a part of the troubled dream he had waked from.

"Well, where under the sun, moon and stars have *you* been?" he demanded, taking the chance that this phantasm might be flesh and blood.

A gleam of gratified slyness lit up the haggardness of Northwick's face. "I've been at home—at Hatboro'."

"Come off!" said Pinney, astounded out of the last remnant of deference he had tried to keep for Northwick. He stood looking incredulously at him a moment. "Come in to breakfast, and tell me about it. If I could only have it for a scoop"-

Northwick ate with wolfish greed, and as the victual refreshed and fortified him, he came out with his story, slowly bit by bit. Pinney listened with mute admiration.

"Well, sir," he said, "it's the biggest thing I ever heard of." But his face darkened. "I suppose you know it leaves me out in the cold. I came up here," he explained, "as the agent of your friends, to find you, and I did find you. But if you've gone and given the whole thing away, *I* can't ask anything for my services."

Northwick seemed interested and even touched by the

346

ardship he had worked to Pinney. "They don't know where
am now," he suggested.

"Are you willing I should take charge of the case from this
on?" asked Pinney.

"Yes. Only—don't leave me," said Northwick, with tremu-
ous dependance.

"You may be sure I wont let you out of my sight again,"
said Pinney. He took a telegraphic blank from his breastpocket, and addressed it to Matt Hilary: "Our friend here
all right with me at Murdock's Hotel." He counted the words
to see that there were no more than ten; then he called a
waiter, and sent the despatch to the office. "Tell 'em to pay
it, and set it down against me. Tell 'em to rush it."

Pinney showed himself only less devoted to Northwick than
to his own wife and child. His walks and talks were all with
him; and as the baby got better he gave himself more and
more to the intimacy established with him; and Northwick
seemed to grow more and more reliant on Pinney's filial cares.
Mrs. Pinney shared these, as far as the baby would permit;
and she made the silent refugee at home with her. She had her
opinion of his daughters, who did not come to him, now that
they knew where he was; but she concealed it from him, and
helped him answer Suzette's letters when he said he was not
feeling quite well enough to write himself. Adeline did not
write; Suzette always said she was not quite well, but was getting better. Then in one of Suzette's letters there came a tardy
confession that Adeline was confined to her bed. She was
tormented with the thought of having driven him away; and
Suzette said she wished her to write and tell him to come back,
or to let them come to him. She asked him to express some
wish in the matter, so that she could show his answer to Adeline. Suzette wrote that Mr. Hilary had come over from his
farm, and was staying at Elbridge Newton's, to be constantly
near them; and in fact Matt was with them when Adeline
suddenly died; they had not thought her dangerously sick,
till the very day of her death, when she began to sink rapidly.

In the letter that brought this news, Suzette said that if they had dreamed of present danger they would have sent for their father to come back at any hazard, and she lamented that they had all been so blind. The Newtons would stay with her, till she could join him in Quebec; or, if he wished to return, she and Matt were both of the same mind about it. They were ready for any event; but Matt felt that he ought to know that there was no hope of his escaping a trial if he returned, and that he ought to be left perfectly free to decide. Adeline would be laid beside her mother.

The old man broke into a feeble whimper as Mrs. Pinney read him the last words. Pinney, walking softly up and down with the baby in his arms, whimpered too.

"I believe he *could* be got off, if he went back," he said to his wife, in a burst of sympathy when Northwick had taken his letter away to his own room.

The belief, generous in itself, began to mix with self-interest in Pinney's soul. He conscientiously forebore to urge Northwick to return, but he could not help portraying the flattering possibilities of such a course. Before they parted for Pinney's own return he confided his ambition for the future to Northwick, and, as delicately as he could, suggested that if Northwick ever did make up his mind to go back, he could not find a more interested and attentive travelling-companion. Northwick seemed to take the right view of the matter, the business view, and Pinney thought he had managed a difficult point with great tact; but he modestly concealed his success from his wife. They both took leave of the exile with affection; and Mrs. Pinney put her arms round his neck and kissed him; he promised her that he would take good care of himself in her absence. Pinney put a business address in his hand at the last moment.

Northwick seemed to have got back something of his moral force after these people, who had so strangely become his friends, left him to his own resources. Once more he began to dream of employing the money he had with him for making more, and paying back the Ponkwasset company's forced loans. He positively forbade Suzette's coming to him, as she proposed, after Adeline's funeral. He telegraphed to prevent her undertaking the journey, and he wrote saying that he wished to be alone for a while, and to decide for himself the question of his fate. He approved of Matt's wish that they should be married at once, and he replied to Matt with a letter decently observant of the peculiar circumstances, recognizing the reluctance his father and mother might well feel, and expressing the hope that he was acting with their full and free consent. If this letter could have been produced in court it would have told heavily against Putney's theory of a defence on the ground of insanity. It was so clear, and just and reasonable, though perhaps an expert might have recognized a mental obliquity in its affirmation of Northwick's belief that Matt's father would yet come to see his conduct in its true light, and to regard him as the victim of circumstances which he really was.

Among the friends of the Hilarys there was misgiving on the point of their approval of Matt's marriage. Some of them thought that the parents' hands had been forced in the blessing they gave it. Old Bromfield Corey expressed a general feeling to Hilary with senile frankness. "Hilary, you seem to have disappointed the expectation of the admirers of your iron firmness. I tell 'em that's what you keep for your enemies. But they seem to think that in Matt's case you ought to have been more of a Roman father."

"I'm just going to become one," said Hilary, with the good temper proper to that moment of the dinner. "Mrs. Hilary and Louise are taking me over to Rome for the winter."

"You don't say so, you don't say!" said Corey. "I wish my family would take me. Boston is gradually making an old man of me. I'm afraid it will end by killing me."

X

_____

Northwick, after the Pinneys went home, lapsed into a solitude relieved only by the daily letters that Suzette sent him. He shrank from the offers of friendly kindness on the part of people in the hotel, who pitied his loneliness; and he began to live in a dream of his home again. He had relinquished that notion of attempting a new business life, which had briefly revived in his mind; the same causes that had operated against it in the beginning, controlled and defeated it now. He felt himself too old to begin life over; his energies were spent. Such as he had been, he had made himself very slowly and cautiously, in familiar conditions; he had never been a man of business dash, and he could not pick himself up and launch himself in a new career, as a man of different make might have done, even at his age. Perhaps there had been some lesion of the will in that fever of his at Ha-ha Bay, which disabled him from forming any distinct purpose, or from trying to carry out any such purpose as he did form. Perhaps he was, in his helplessness, merely of that refugee-type which exile moulds men to: a thing of memories and hopes, without definite aims or plans.

As the days passed, he dwelt in an outward inertness, while his dreams and longings incessantly rehabilitated the home whose desolation he had seen with his own eyes. It would be better to go back and suffer the sentence of the law, and then go to live again in the place which, in spite of his senses he could only imagine clothed in the comfort and state that had been stripped from it. Elbridge's talk, on the way to East Hatboro' about the sale, and what had become of the horses and cattle, and the plants, went for no more than the evidence of his own eyes that they were all gone. He did not realize, except in the shocks that the fact imparted at times, that death as well as disaster had invaded his home. Adeline was, for the most part, still alive; in his fond reveries she was present and part of that home as she had always been.

He began to flatter himself that if he went back he could contrive that compromise with the court which his friends had failed to bring about; he persuaded himself that if it came to a trial, he could offer evidence that would result in his acquittal. But if he must undergo some punishment for the offence of being caught in transactions which were all the time carried on with impunity, he told himself that interest could be used to make his punishment light. In these hopeful moods it was a necessity of his drama that his transgression of the law should seem venial to him. It was only when he feared the worst that he felt guilty of wrong.

It could not be said that these moments of a consciousness of guilt were so frequent as ever to become confluent, and to form a mood. They came and went; perhaps toward the last they were more frequent. What seems certain is that in the end there began to mix with his longing for home a desire, feeble and formless enough, for expiation. There began to be suggested to him from somewhere, somehow, something like the thought that if he had really done wrong, there might be rest and help in accepting the legal penalty, disproportionate and excessive as it might be. He tried to make this notion appreciable to Pinney when they first met after he summoned Pinney to Quebec; he offered it as an explanation of his action.

In making up his mind to return at all hazards and to take all the chances, he remembered what Pinney had said to him about his willingness to bear him company. It was not wholly a generous impulse that prompted him to send for Pinney

or the self-sacrificing desire to make Pinney's fortune in his
new quality of detective; he simply dreaded the long journey
alone; he wanted the comfort of Pinney's society. He liked
Pinney, and he longed for the vulgar cheerfulness of his
buoyant spirit. He felt that he could rest upon it in the fate
he was bringing himself to face; he instinctively desired the
kindly, lying sympathy of a soul that had so much affinity with
his own. He telegraphed Pinney to come for him, and he was
impatient till he came.

Pinney started the instant he received Northwick's telegram, and met him with an enthusiasm of congratulation.
"Well, Mr. Northwick, this is a great thing. It's the right
thing, and it's the wise thing. It's going to have a tremendous
effect.— I suppose," he added a little tremulously, "that you've
thought it all thoroughly over?"

"Yes; I'm prepared for the worst," said Northwick.

"Oh, there wont be any *worst*," Pinney returned gayly.
"There'll be legal means of delaying the trial; your lawyer
can manage that; or if he can't, and you have to face the music
at once, we can have you brought into court without the least
publicity, and the judge will go through the forms, and it'll
be all over before anybody knows anything about it. I'll see
that there's no *interviewing*, and that there are no *reporters*
present. There'll probably be a brief announcement among
the cases in court; but there wont be anything painful. You
needn't be afraid. But what I'm anxious about now is not to
bring any influence to bear on you. I promised my wife I
wouldn't urge you, and I wont; I know I'm a little optimistic,
and if you don't see this thing exactly *couleur de rose*, don't
you do it from anything *I* say." Pinney apparently put great
stress upon himself to get this out.

"I've looked it in the face," said Northwick.

"And your friends know you're coming back?"

"They expect me at any time. You can notify them."

Pinney drew a long, anxious breath. "Well," he said with
a sort of desperation, "then I don't see why we don"t start at
once."

"Have you got your papers all right?" Northwick asked.

"Yes," said Pinney, with a blush. "But you know," he added, respectfully, "I can't touch you till we get over the line, Mr. Northwick."

"I understand that. Let me see your warrant."

Pinney reluctantly produced the paper and Northwick read it carefully over. He folded it up with a deep sigh, and took a long stiff envelope from his breastpocket, and handed it to Pinney, with the warrant. "Here is the money I brought with me."

"Mr. Northwick! It isn't necessary yet! Indeed it isn't. I've every confidence in your honor as a gentleman." Pinney's eyes glowed with joy, and his fingers closed upon the envelope convulsively. "But if you mean business"—

"I mean business," said Northwick. "Count it."

Pinney took the notes out and ran them over. "Forty one thousand six hundred and forty."

"That is right," said Northwick. "Now, another matter: Have you got handcuffs?"

"Why, Mr. Northwick! What are you giving me?" demanded Pinney. "I'd as soon put them on my own father."

"I want you to put them on *me*," said Northwick. "I intend to go back as your prisoner. If I have anything to expiate"— and he seemed to indulge question of the fact for the last time—"I want the atonement to begin as soon as possible. If you haven't brought those things with you, you'd better go out to the police station and get them, while I attend to the tickets."

"Oh, I needn't go," said Pinney, and his face burned.

He was full of nervous trepidation at the start, and throughout the journey he was anxious and perturbed, while on Northwick, after the first excitement, a deep quiet, a stupor or a spiritual peace, seemed to have fallen. "By George!" said Pinney, when they started, "anybody to see us would think *you* were taking *me* back." He was tenderly watchful of Northwick's comfort; he left him free to come and go at the stations; from the restaurants he brought him things to tempt his appetite; but Northwick said he did not care to eat.

They had a long night in a day-car, for they found there was no sleeper on their train. In the morning, when the day broke, Northwick asked Pinney what the next station was.

Pinney said he did not know. He looked at Northwick as if the possession of him gave him very little pleasure, and asked him how he had slept.

"I haven't slept," said Northwick. "I suppose I'm rather excited. My nerves seem disordered."

"Well, of course," said Pinney soothingly.

They were silent a moment, and then Northwick asked, "What did you say the next station was?"

"I'll ask the brakeman." They could see the brakeman on the platform. Pinney went out to him, and returned. "It's Wellwater, he says. We get breakfast there."

"Then we're over the line, now!" said Northwick.

"Why, yes," Pinney admitted reluctantly. He added in a livelier note, "You get a mighty good breakfast at Wellwater, and I'm ready to meet it half way." He turned and looked hard at Northwick. "If I should happen to get left there, what would you do? Would you keep on, anyway? Is your mind still made up on that point? I ask, because all kinds of accidents happen, and"— Pinney stopped, and regarded his captive fixedly. "Or if you don't feel quite able to travel"—

"Let me see your warrant again," said Northwick.

Pinney relaxed his gaze with a shrug, and produced the paper. Northwick read it all once more. "I'm your prisoner," he said, returning the paper. "You can put the handcuffs on me now."

"No, no, Mr. Northwick!" Pinney pleaded. "I don't want to do that. I'm not afraid of your trying to get away. I assure you, it isn't necessary, between gentlemen"—

Northwick held out his wrists. "Put them on, please."

"Oh, well, if I *must!*" protested Pinney. "But I *swear* I wont lock 'em." He glanced round to find whether any of the other passengers were noticing. "You can slip 'em off when-

ever you get tired of 'em." He pushed Northwick's sleeves
down over them with shame-faced anxiety. "Don't let people
see the damned things, for God's sake!"

"That's good!" murmured Northwick as if the feel of the
iron pleased him.

The incident turned Pinney rather sick. He went out on
the platform of the car for a little breath of air, and some
restorative conversation with the brakeman. When he came
back, Northwick was sitting where he left him. His head had
fallen on his breast. "Poor old fellow, he's asleep," Pinney
thought. He put his hand gently on Northwick's shoulder.
"I'll have to wake you, here," he said. "We'll be in, now, in a
minute."

Northwick tumbled forward at his touch, and Pinney
caught him round the neck and lifted his face.

"Oh, my God! He's dead!"

The loosened handcuffs fell on the floor.

XI

AFTER they were married Suzette and Matt went to live on his farm; and it was then that she accomplished a purpose she had never really given up. She surrendered the whole place at Hatboro' to the company her father had defrauded. She had no sentiment about the place such as had made the act impossible to Adeline, and must have prevented the sacrifice on Suzette's part as long as her sister lived. But suffering from that and from all other earthly troubles was past for Adeline; she was dead; and Suzette felt it no wrong to her memory to put out of her own hands the property which something higher than the logic of the case forbade her to keep. As far as her father was concerned she took his last act as a sign that he wished to make atonement for the wrong he had committed; and she felt that the surrender of this property to his creditors was in the line of his endeavor. She had strengthened herself to bear his conviction and punishment, if he came back, and since he was dead this surrender of possessions tainted for her with the dishonesty in which the unhappy man had lived, was nothing like loss; it was rather a joyful relief.

Yet it was a real sacrifice, and she was destined to feel it in the narrowed conditions of her life. But she had become used to narrow conditions; she had learned how little people could live with when they had apparently nothing to live for, and now that in Matt she had everything to live for, the surrender of all she had in the world left her incalculably rich.

Matt rejoiced with her in her decision, though he had carefully kept himself from influencing it. He was poor, too, except for the comfortable certainty that his father could not let him want; but so far as he had been able, he had renounced his expectations from his father's estate in order that he might seem to be paying Northwick's indebtedness to the company. Doubtless it was only an appearance; in the end the money his father left would come equally to himself and Louise; but in the meantime the restitution for Northwick did cramp Eben Hilary more for the moment than he let his son know. So he thought it well to allow Matt to go seriously to work on account of it, and to test his economic theories in the attempt to make his farm yield him a living. It must be said that the prospect dismayed neither Matt nor Suzette: there was that in her life which enabled her to dispense with the world and its pleasures and favors; and he had long ceased to desire them.

The Ponkwasset directors had no hesitation in accepting the assignment of property made them by Northwick's daughter. As a corporate body they had nothing to do with the finer question of right involved. They looked at the plain fact that they had been heavily defrauded by the former owner of the property, who had inferably put it out of his hands in view of some such contingency as he had finally reached; and as it had remained in the possession of his family ever since, they took no account of the length of time that had elapsed since he was actually the owner. They recognized the propriety of his daughter's action in surrendering it, and no member of the Board was quixotic enough to suggest that the company had no more claim upon the property she conveyed to them than upon any other piece of real estate in the commonwealth.

"They considered," said Putney, who had completed the affair on the part of Suzette, and was afterwards talking it over with his crony Dr. Morrell in something of the bitterness of defeat, "that their first duty was to care for the interests of their stockholders, who seemed to turn out all widows and orphans, as nearly as I could understand. It appears as if nobody but innocents of that kind live on the Ponkwasset dividends, and it would have been inhuman not to look after their interests. Well," he went on, breaking from this grievance, "there's this satisfactory thing about it: somebody has done something at last that he intended to do; and, of course, the *he* in question is a *she*. 'She that was' Miss Suzette is the only person connected with the whole affair, that's had her way. Everybody else's way has come to nothing, beginning with my own. *I* can look back to the time when I meant to have the late J. Milton Northwick's blood. I was lying low for years, waiting for him to do just what he did do, at last, and I expected somehow by the blessing of God to help run him down, or bring him to justice, as we say. The first thing I knew, I turned up his daughters' counsel, and was devoting myself to the interests of a pair of grass-orphans with the high and holy zeal of a Board of Directors. All I wanted was to have J. Milton brought to trial, not so I could help send him to State's prison with a band of music, but so I could get him off on the plea of insanity. But I wasn't allowed to have my way, even in a little thing like that; and of all the things that were planned for and against, and round about Northwick, just one has been accomplished. The Directors failed to be in at the death; and old Hilary has had to resign from the Board and pay the defaulter's debts. Pinney, I understand, considers himself a ruined man: he's left off detecting for a living and gone back to interviewing. Poor old Adeline lived in the pious hope of making Northwick's old age comfortable in their beautiful home on the money he had stolen; and now that she's dead it goes to his creditors. Why, even Billy Gerrish, a highminded, public spirited man like William B. Gerrish—couldn't have his way about Northwick. No, sir: Northwick himself couldn't! Look how he fooled away his time there in Canada after he got off, with money enough to start him on the high road to fortune again! He couldn't budge of his own motion; and the only thing he really tried to do he failed in disgracefully. Adeline wouldn't let him stay when he came back to buy himself off; and that killed *her*. Then, when he started home again to take his punishment, the first thing he did was to drop dead. Justice herself couldn't have her way with Northwick. But I'm not sorry he slipped through her fingers. There wasn't the stuff for an example in Northwick; I don't know that he's much of a warning. He just seems to be a kind of—incident; and a pretty common kind. He was a mere creature of circumstance—like the rest of us! His environment made him rich, and his environment made him a rogue. Sometimes I think there *was* nothing to Northwick, except what happened to him. He's a puzzle. But what do you say, Doc, to a world where we fellows keep fuming and fizzing away, with our little aims and purposes, and the great ball of life seems to roll calmly along, and get where it's going without the slightest reference to what we do or don't do? I suppose it's wicked to be a fatalist, but I'll go a few æons of eternal punishment more, and keep my private opinion that it's all Fate."

"Why not call it Law?" the doctor suggested.

"Well, I don't like to be too bold. But taking it by and large, and seeing that most things seem to turn out pretty well in the end, I'll split the difference with you and call it Mercy."

Note to the Text

———

327.5–7   he remembered reading of a man . . . : Howells is probably referring to Hawthorne's short story "Wakefield."

TEXTUAL APPARATUS

Textual Commentary

Twelve different published forms of *The Quality of Mercy* were produced during Howells' lifetime. The novel made its first printed appearance during the fall of 1891 and spring of 1892 as a weekly serial in eight American newspapers—the only one of Howells' novels ever to be serialized in this way. During this same period it also appeared in the small weekly London journal *Wit and Wisdom*. David Douglas, Howells' British publisher, issued the first British book edition in February 1892, and in late March 1892 Harper and Brothers published their first edition. The only other printed form of the novel was a new edition by Harper and Brothers, bearing only the copyright date 1891 and set in the typography of the aborted "Library Edition" of Howells' works; the finished volumes of the "Library Edition" were issued in 1911, and *The Quality of Mercy* was presumably reset in anticipation of its inclusion in that series.

In addition to these printed forms, there exists a complete manuscript of the novel, consisting of 1,900 leaves of Howells' holograph and 111 typescript leaves also prepared by him and bearing his holograph revisions and corrections. The leaves are numbered in a fairly consecutive sequence and form a coherent final draft of the novel.[1] Shop marks indicating compositorial stints and line breaks in the manuscript correspond to line breaks in the first Harper and Brothers edition,[2] and verify that the manuscript was used as setting copy by S. J. Parkhill & Co. of Boston when that firm set type and made the electrotype plates used by Harper.

Howells' correspondence provides a good deal of information

---

1. For a complete description of the manuscript, see A Note on the Manuscript, pp. 379–384.
2. A further description of these line breaks and their significance can be found in A Note on the Manuscript, pp. 382–383.

useful in establishing the details of the transmission of the text. On 28 May 1891 he wrote to Harper and Brothers, "I hope by the end of next month to have the story I am writing for *The Sun* ready for the printers. I wish to stereotype it first in book form, and let The Sun [sic] use the sheets for copy."[3] Howells apparently submitted his manuscript in sections as he finished revising them. All of the text had been turned over to Parkhill by early July,[4] and Howells spent the rest of that month and part of August proofreading the novel. He wrote to his father on 26 July that "I am stereotyping the *Sun* story in book-form before beginning to print it in the paper, so as to not to [sic] have to do proof-reading for the serial. When the book is all cast, I hope to come out to you, some time between the middle of August and the beginning of September." Even as late as 5 August, when he had begun work on his next novel, *The World of Chance*, Howells wrote to Sylvester Baxter that he was "proof-reading my 'Sun'-myth."[5] Finally, on 31 August, he "cashed up" the sheets of the novel at the New York *Sun* office and as per contract collected ten thousand dollars from the newspaper's editor, William M. Laffan.[6] On 11 September S. S. McClure, who had over a year before arranged with the *Sun* for the distribution of the novel through his Newspaper Syndicate,[7] announced in a syndicate circular that he had "secured

---

3. The manuscripts of all letters by Howells cited in this commentary are in the Houghton Library, Harvard University, unless otherwise identified. Permission to quote from the Harvard and other unpublished Howells materials has been granted by William White Howells for the heirs of the Howells estate, and for the Harvard materials by the Harvard College Library. Republication of these materials requires the same permissions.

4. On 5 July Howells wrote to his father, William Cooper Howells, "Tomorrow, if I have luck, I shall finish my *Sun* novel . . . ." It was only the end of an early draft, however, as the date of "July 6 1891" in Howells' hand at the end of Part Third, chapter X, attests; he did more internal revision in the final section of the book after this date and added the chapters eventually numbered VII, VIII, and XI to Part Third.

5. MS in the Huntington Library.

6. See letters of 2 September 1891 to William Cooper Howells and 6 September 1891 to Aurelia Howells.

7. It is not clear whether McClure subsidized the $10,000 the *Sun* paid Howells or whether McClure paid the *Sun* for distribution rights to the novel, although details in the correspondence suggest the latter. On 11 October 1891 Howells informed his father that the story "was sold to the N.Y. Sun, which is publishing it simultaneously with several other papers, to which it had the right to sub-let it"; and in the draft of a syndicate circular dated 20 October

the complete copy of probably the most important novel I have ever offered to the newspaper press."[8] The serial publication of the novel began in the New York *Sun* on 4 October 1891 and ran in fourteen Sunday installments through 3 January 1892.[9] The McClure Syndicate also sold the serial to seven other newspapers —the Boston *Herald*, the Buffalo *Express*, the Cleveland *Leader*, the Chicago *Inter-Ocean*, the Cincinnati *Commercial-Gazette*, the Philadelphia *Inquirer*, and the Toronto *Globe*.[10]

1891, S. S. McClure wrote that "Mr [sic] Laffan of the *Sun* consented to let me sell the novel to other papers" (MS in the McClure Papers, Lilly Library, Indiana University). In any event, in 1890 McClure acted as intermediary between Howells and the *Sun*, which frequently subscribed to his syndicate, and the plan to serialize a Howells novel in newspapers probably originated with him.

8. A typescript carbon of what is evidently the copy for the circular contains McClure's holograph revisions and is pasted into one of the McClure Syndicate Scrapbooks in the McClure Papers, Lilly Library, Indiana University.

9. The fourteen installments of the New York *Sun* publication of *The Quality of Mercy* were divided thus: 4 October 1891 (Part First, I–V), 11 October (VI–X), 18 October (XI–XII), 25 October (XIII–XVI), 1 November (XVII–XX), 8 November (XXI–Part Second, I), 15 November (II–VI), 22 November (VII–X), 29 November (XI–XVI), 6 December (XVII–XX), 13 December (XXI–Part Third, I–II), 20 December (III–IV), 27 December (V–VII), 3 January 1892 (VII–XI).

10. In a syndicate circular dated 20 October 1891 McClure mentioned that the serial would appear in these seven newspapers besides the New York *Sun*, "at an average price of $600 each." The installments of the seven serializations are as follows:

Boston *Herald* (thirteen installments): 4 October 1891 (Part First, I–IV), 11 October (VI–X), 18 October (X[cont.]–[XII]), 25 October (XIII–[XV]), 1 November (XVI–XIX), 8 November (XX–XXIV), 15 November (Part Second, I–IV), 22 November (V–VIII), 29 November (IX–XII), 6 December (XIII–XIX), 13 December (XIX[cont.]–Part Third, III), 20 December ([IV]–VII), 27 December (VIII–XI);

Buffalo *Express* (thirteen installments): 4 October 1891 (Part First, I–IV), 11 October (IV[cont.]–IX), 18 October ([X]–XII), 25 October (XIII–XVI), 1 November (XVII–XX), 8 November (XXI–Part Second, I), 15 November (II–VI), 22 November (VII–X), 29 November (XI–XVI), 6 December (XVII–XX), 13 December (XXI–Part Third, III), 20 December (IV–VII), 27 December (VIII–XI);

Chicago *Inter-Ocean* (thirteen installments): 4 October 1891 (Part First, I–V), 11 October (VI–X), 18 October (XI–XII), 25 October (XIII–XVI), 26 October (Supplement: Part First, I–XVI), 1 November (XVII–XX), 8 November (XXI–Part Second, I), 15 November (II–VI), 22 November (VII–X), 29 November (XI–XVI), 6 December (XVII–XX), 13 December (XXI–Part Third, III), 20 December (IV–VII), 27 December (VIII–XI);

Cincinnati *Commercial-Gazette* (twelve installments): 11 October 1891 (Part First, I–X), 18 October (XI–XII), 25 October (XIII–XVI), 1 November (XVII–

The conditions surrounding the serial publication of *The Quality of Mercy* in the weekly London journal *Wit and Wisdom*, where it was entitled *John Northwick, Defaulter*, are unknown.[11] No mention of this serialization appears in Howells' correspondence or in the extant publishing records of Harper and Brothers, McClure, or Douglas. The McClure Syndicate, however, might have sold some form of the novel to this journal. "I have a fully equipped office in London in charge of my brother," McClure wrote in an advertising circular dated 4 December 1891, "who both purchases features for American newspapers and sells matter in England."[12] Whatever the contractual arrangements, printer's copy for each of the serial texts seems to have been some form of the Parkhill setting rather than *Sun* galleys or sheets or typescript

XX), 8 November (XXI–Part Second, I), 15 November (II–VI), 22 November (VII–X), 29 November (XI–XVI), 6 December (XVII–XX), 13 December (XXI–Part Third, III), 20 December (IV–VII), 27 December (VIII–XI);

Cleveland *Leader* (ten installments): 25 October 1891 (Part First, I–XVI), 1 November (XVII–XX), 8 November (XXI–Part Second, I), 15 November (II–VI), 22 November (VII–X), 29 November (XI–XVI), 6 December (XVII–XX), 13 December (XXI–Part Third, III), 20 December (IV–VII), 27 December (VIII–XI);

Philadelphia *Inquirer* (thirteen installments): 9 October 1891 (Part First, I–V), 11 October (VI–X), 18 October (XI–XII), 25 October (XIII–XVI), 1 November (XVII–XX), 8 November (XXI–Part Second, I), 15 November (II–V), 22 November (VI–IX), 29 November (X–XIV), 6 December (XV–XX), 13 December (XX[cont.]–Part Third, III), 20 December (IV–VIII), 27 December (IX–XI);

Toronto *Globe* (twenty-one installments): 10 October 1891 (Part First, I–III), 17 October (III[cont.]–VI), 24 October (VII–IX), 31 October (X–XII), 7 November (XII[cont.]), 14 November (XIII–XIV), 21 November (XIV[cont.]–XVI), 28 November (XVII–XVIII), 5 December (XIX), 12 December (XX–XXI), 19 December (XXII–XXIII), 26 December (XXIV–Part Second, II), 2 January 1892 (III–VII), 9 January (VIII–XI), 16 January (XII–XVI), 23 January ([XVII]–XIX), 30 January (XIX[cont.]–[XXI]), 6 February (Part Third, I–III), 13 February (III[cont.]–V), 20 February (V[cont.]–VIII), 27 February (IX–XI).

11. The twenty-three installments of the *Wit and Wisdom* serialization of *The Quality of Mercy* divided the novel as follows: 7 November 1891 (Part First, I–IV), 14 November (V–VII), 21 November (VIII–X), 28 November (XI–XII), 5 December (XII[cont.]), 12 December (XIII–XIV), 19 December (XIV[cont.]–XVI), 26 December (XVII–XVIII), 2 January 1892 (XIX–XX), 9 January (XXI–XXII), 16 January (XXIV–Part Second, II), 23 January (III–V), 30 January (VI–VIII), 6 February (VIII[cont.]–IX), 13 February (X–XI), 20 February (XII–XIV), 27 February (XV–XVII), 5 March (XVIII–XIX), 12 March (XVIII[i.e. XX]–XXI), 19 March (Part Third, I–III), 26 March (IV–V), 2 April (VI–VIII), 9 April (IX–XI).

12. Typescript in McClure Papers, Lilly Library, Indiana University.

copy provided by McClure's office (see below, pages 373–374).
Howells himself provided David Douglas with copy for the
novel. In the eight-year period before 1891 Douglas had usually
set type from galleys or sheets of the American serializations and
printed copyright deposit parts from his setting. Then, after making stereotype plates from this type and using the plates for his
own edition, Douglas shipped them to Howells. By this method
Howells could secure British copyright for his novels while gain-
ing possession of the plates, giving him a better bargaining position for royalties with his American publisher.[13] But the new copyright laws of 1891 stipulated that a book had to be set in type in
America in order to secure American copyright. The Douglas edition of *The Quality of Mercy* thus becomes of secondary concern
to the printing history of the novel because it is derived from the
American edition rather than being the basis of it. Douglas mentioned to Howells on 5 January 1892 that "the book was all set up
in America when you sent me the sheets"; Howells evidently already had or secured from Parkhill a set of sheets of the novel
which he sent to Douglas solely for Douglas' own use.

In the same letter Douglas told Howells that Howells' letter of
21 December 1891 (which is not extant) "arrived in time to prevent the delivery of 'Mercy' to the trade though not the publication of the book which I understood was intended to be issued in
the States on January 1st & to secure your copyright here I put on
all pressure & had the book printed, bound & issued to the Stationers' Hall on the last day of the year." The curious combination
of haste and delay in the arrangements between Howells and
Douglas was probably occasioned by the details of the new copyright law; Douglas was proceeding according to his older understanding with Howells, getting the full text registered for copyright before any other available form (e.g. full English serial
publication without copyright) could be pirated; Howells, on the
other hand, was intent on protecting the Harper American copy-

---

13. For a fuller description of Douglas' role in the publication of Howells'
works prior to the copyright laws of 1891, see the Textual Commentary to *The
Rise of Silas Lapham* (Bloomington and London: Indiana University Press,
1971), pp. 375–378; the Textual Commentary to *An Imperative Duty* (Bloomington and London: Indiana University Press, 1969), pp. 104–105; and Scott
Bennett, "David Douglas and the British Publication of W. D. Howells' Works,"
SB, XXV (1972), 107–124.

right by arranging that the American book edition be published first. In any case, the Douglas edition, set from sheets deriving from the Parkhill plates which Harper and Brothers used for their first edition of the novel, was actually published earlier than the first impression of the Harper first edition. This Douglas edition, entitled *Mercy* and bearing the title-page date of 1892 (BAL 9665), was registered at the British Museum on 1 January and was listed as published on 6 February 1892.[14] There was evidently only one impression printed from the Douglas plates; no information concerning the size of the impression is available.

Contrary to Douglas' original understanding that the Harper first edition of the novel was to be issued on 1 January 1892, Harper and Brothers told Howells on 18 January that they had "just received the plates from Messrs. Parkhill & Co., and have ordered the book to press. We shall endeavor to publish as soon as possible. The date fixed by Mr. Douglas for the regular publication of his edition—February 1st—is satisfactory to us, although we can hardly get our edition ready by that time." More than two months later, on 26 March 1892, the first impression of this Harper and Brothers edition, entitled *The Quality of Mercy* and bearing a title-page date of 1892 (BAL 9666), was announced and deposited at the Library of Congress; 3,000 copies were printed.[15] The plates were used later in the year for the volume numbered 726 in the "Franklin Square Library, New Series," dated 1892 and deposited on 1 October 1892. Subsequent re-impressions in the format of the first impression were made in 1893, 1899, 1900, and 1903.[16] One re-

14. See the Introduction, p. xix, footnote 21, for an explanation of the alternate title of the Douglas edition.

15. See Harper Memorandum Book, 1892–1896. This Harper material is surveyed by Edwin and Virginia Price Barber in "A Description of Old Harper and Brothers Publishing Records Recently Come to Light," *Bulletin of Bibliography*, XXV (1967), 1–6, 29–34, 39–40.
The first page of the manuscript bears the pencilled notation "1891/Jan. 1"; the date may be a reminder to the Parkhill office of Harper's deadline for completion of all work on the book text.

16. *Publishers' Weekly*, LXII (1893), 78, announced in a list of already published Howells works that *The Quality of Mercy* had appeared in the Harper "Black and White Series" format, numbered 726. But no such volume in the "Black and White Series"—another Harper program—has been located, and the announcement is probably an erroneous reference to the "Franklin Square Library" volume, published in October 1892 and announced correctly at that time in *Publishers' Weekly*, LXI (1892), 587.

impression—either the "Franklin Square Library" or the regular 1893 impression—totalled 2,000 copies,[17] but no further information is available concerning the size of the other re-impressions.

A new Harper edition of the novel bearing only a copyright date of 1891 was set in the typography of the "Library Edition" of Howells' works. According to the plans between Harper and Howells for this edition, Harper and Brothers was to reset Howells' works in a consistent format, and Howells was to furnish a short "Bibliographical" preface for each volume. But unlike the titles actually published in 1911 in the full "Library Edition" format, the copies of this new edition of *The Quality of Mercy* which have been examined lack the distinctive "Library Edition" title-page and frontispiece, and no "Bibliographical" essay is known to exist. The Harper plans proceeded far enough for a new edition of the work to be set, but it was not included in the "Library Edition."[18] No information concerning date of publication or the size of the edition has been located.

Because the manuscript is the text representing Howells' most complete control over both the substance and form of the novel, it has been selected copy-text for the present edition. The major editorial task is then to determine which of the many substantive revisions appearing in the printed versions based on the manuscript have Howells' authority.[19] That Howells revised the Park-

---

17. Harper Memorandum Book, 1892–1896.

18. Since this new edition is not cited or described in Jacob Blanck, comp., *Bibliography of American Literature*, IV (New Haven, Conn., 1963), a full bibliographical description follows:
THE/QUALITY OF MERCY/[Gothic] A Novel/BY/W. D. HOWELLS/ [Publisher's Ornament]/Harper & Brothers Publishers/New York and London [i–vi], [1]–423, [424–425]. 7 11/16 in. x 5 1/16 in.
1–27⁸. Signed.
Green cloth stamped black.
On copyright page: *Copyright, 1891, by William Dean Howells.*

19. The following copies of the books described as relevant to the establishment of the text of the present edition, including at least earliest and latest known impressions, have been collated in the preparation of the critical text of *The Quality of Mercy*: xerox copy of the New York *Sun* from the New York Public Library and microfilm copy from the Center for Research Libraries, Chicago; xerox copies of the Douglas edition, BAL 9665, from the British Museum (012705.h.26) and Harvard University Library (*AC85 H8395.892q); copies of the Harper first edition, first impression, BAL 9666, in the Indiana University (PS2025.Q1), Lilly (PS2025.M3 1892), Northwestern University (813.4 H85q, copy 3), and University of Chicago (PS2025.Q2 1892) libraries and the

hill proof set from his manuscript is suggested by references to proofreading in his correspondence of July and August 1891 and verified by the quality and extent of the substantive readings variant from the manuscript in the printed texts. The earliest actual publication of the majority of the readings accepted as authorial in the present edition was the New York *Sun* serial. But the printing history indicates that the typesetting of the serial in the *Sun* shop was based upon some form of the Parkhill setting. Despite its later publication, the Harper first edition, printed from the Parkhill plates prepared from the manuscript, is thus more directly derived from revised Parkhill proofs, and is therefore the true historical source for those emendations.

Less crucial than decisions about the authority of substantive variants from the manuscript that appear in the Harper first edition are questions of the authority and source of variants unique to the other texts, including the *Sun* and other serializations. There are no substantive variants from the manuscript unique to the Harper first edition alone, for all such readings appearing for the first time in it are also present in the Douglas edition and the Harper second edition. Nor are there any significant differences, beyond the normal type wear and batter, between the first impression of the Harper first edition and subsequent re-impressions. There are, however, some ninety readings unique to the New York *Sun* serial (excluding substantive differences which appear to involve styling only; see page 377, below); twenty-six readings unique to the Douglas edition; and nineteen readings unique to the Harper second edition. Some compositorial error and nonauthorial sophistication must be expected in all three of these texts, given their indirect derivation from the manuscript; and indeed none of the unique variants suggests Howells as its source.[20] Except for the Harper first edition, the printed forms of *The*

Howells Edition Center (HE9666.1.1); copy of the "Franklin Square Library" impression in the Rutherford B. Hayes Memorial Library, Fremont, Ohio; copy of the Harper 1900 impression in the Harvard University Library (AL1783.345); copies of the Harper 1903 impression in the University of Chicago (PS2025.Q2 1903) and Indiana University (PS2025.Q1 1903) libraries; copies of the Harper second [c1891] edition (format of the Harper "Library Edition") in the University of Illinois (813.H83q, copy 2) and University of Chicago (PS2025.Q2 1891) libraries and the Howells Edition Center (HEc1891.1).

20. Howells generally paid little attention to the "Library Edition" texts of his works; Harper and Brothers probably used an earlier BAL 9666 impression of *The Quality of Mercy* as printer's copy for new edition in that format.

Quality of Mercy are textually significant only insofar as they corroborate or fail to corroborate the emendations made to the Parkhill plates as exhibited in the Harper first edition. Thus only one substantive reading from these other texts ("East" at 351.2, from the newspaper serialization), which appears to be a correction of an error in the manuscript and Harper first edition, is accepted in the present edition. All other unique readings in the printed texts are considered to lack final authority and are recorded in the Rejected Substantives list.

Nineteen further readings need to be considered. The New York *Sun* serial agrees substantively with the manuscript against a different Harper first-edition reading at fifteen points: 80.15, 85.7, 87.13, 108.16–17, 251.20, 274.30, 298.17, 327.8–9, 327.11, 329.23, 332.24, 338.20, 342.4–5, 359.3, and 359.6 in the present text. And each of the three texts has a substantive reading different from the other two at 25.28, 124.4, 354.27, and 359.7. Since Howells' revision of the Parkhill proof is best exhibited in the Harper first edition, the best policy for the present edition ought to be generally to accept its readings at these points as Howells' final intention. The first-edition readings at 108.16–17, 274.30, and 354.27 (listed in Emendations), which appear to be appropriate corrections in their context, support this decision. For example, at 108.16–17 the manuscript and the *Sun* serial read, "Maxwell rose from the place where he had been sitting." During internal revision of the manuscript Howells had inserted a new page before this point, containing a sentence (at 107.16–17 in the present edition) which indicates that Maxwell remains standing during his interview of Eben Hilary. The resulting aberration between this passage and that at 108.16–17 was probably not discovered until some point in the proofreading of the Parkhill setting. The sheets which Howells turned over to the New York *Sun* apparently did not contain this and possibly the other final readings at these points; the *Sun* copy might have been a set of proofs run off before Parkhill made the final revisions and corrections in the set type, and would therefore exhibit an earlier stage of revision at these points. The fact that the Parkhill plates were not received by Harper and Brothers until 18 January offers evidence of continued work on the text after the delivery of copy to the New York *Sun* on 31 August.

A check of these same serial-Harper first-edition variants in the other serializations reveals an interesting situation: except for 108.16–17, mentioned above—for which all the other newspapers agree with the *Sun*—the Buffalo *Express*, the Cleveland *Leader*, the Chicago *Inter-Ocean*, and the Cincinnati *Commercial-Gazette* generally follow the New York *Sun* readings, while the Boston *Herald*, the Philadelphia *Inquirer*, the Toronto *Globe*, and *Wit and Wisdom* serials generally follow the Harper first edition.

One possible explanation of these discrepancies involves McClure's manner of obtaining the copy that he sent to his subscribing newspapers and, presumably, to *Wit and Wisdom*. Unfortunately, no evidence exists which provides the crucial details of McClure's relationship to the New York *Sun* or to Parkhill, and the explanation must remain conjectural. But McClure's announcement on 11 September 1891 that he had "complete copy" of the novel and the fact of the differing lengths and divisions of the installments in the various serializations suggest that the syndicate sent a complete text of the novel rather than individual installments to the newspapers. Also, since newspapers tried to avoid holding standing type and did not usually anticipate publication by preparing boiler plate which might have to be altered for the demands of the edition in which the plate was finally used, the *Sun* would not have set the whole novel at one time. Thus it is unlikely that the copy sent to the other newspapers would be galleys or proofs of the *Sun* setting. McClure did not know on 11 September how many sets of copy he would need, and he probably had Parkhill send duplicates of the book galleys or proofs to him or directly to the subscribing newspapers. Since Howells would have had no control over the form of the text Parkhill delivered, it is possible that Parkhill gave out sets of copy incorporating various states of revision or mixtures of earlier and later states. The *Express*, the *Leader*, the *Inter-Ocean*, and the *Commercial-Gazette* might have received earlier sets similar to the *Sun's* with most of the penultimate readings at the nineteen points, and the *Herald*, the *Inquirer*, the *Globe*, and *Wit and Wisdom*, sets with most of the final readings. Even the remote possibility that Howells made revisions for the Parkhill plates some time during late fall does not invalidate this conjecture; he would still have had no control over the sets of galleys or proofs which were distributed, though obviously his authoritative revisions could be incorporated into them.

Whatever the explanation for the variance among the newspapers and the journal, the preparation of their texts did not involve Howells' direct authority. The Harper first edition, printed from the Parkhill plates, reflects most coherently Howells' demonstrable control over the revision of the substance of his original manuscript text. The general lack of authority of the newspaper and journal texts is the principal reason that only the readings of the New York *Sun* serial are fully recorded in the Emendations and Rejected Substantives lists: the *Sun's* independent resetting, like that of the other serializations, reduces even the potential authority of its readings, but the record of its substantive variants may be useful as an historical example of the amount of transformation a literary text undergoes in newspaper publication.

When he adopts the manuscript of *The Quality of Mercy* as copy-text for the present edition, the editor must address himself to its difficulties: some almost illegible words which probably caused compositorial misreadings in the printed texts; inconsistent spelling and hyphenation; the occasional absence of necessary words or punctuation; and inconsistent or repeated internal revision of the manuscript, often yielding anomalous readings.

There are several points in the manuscript at which Howells' hand makes the manuscript word closely resemble a different word which appears at the same point in the printed texts. Here compositorial misreading must be suspected in the preparation of the Parkhill plates. Such errors Howells would not discover in proof because he generally did not read proof against his manuscripts. On the basis of a knowledge of Howells' hand and the sense that the manuscript word better suits the context, the present edition has retained the manuscript readings at these points and recorded the variant forms in the Rejected Substantives list.

Because Howells' preference for the spelling of some words is often difficult to ascertain, the present edition has not attempted to regularize all the variant spellings in the manuscript (for example, "Good-by" and "Good-bye"). The present edition has followed the manuscript form for all words except those which Howells consistently misspelled in unacceptable ways and which are corrected in the Harper first edition.

For word-division and word-hyphenation the present edition has also followed Howells' inconsistent manuscript forms. Howells apparently did not address himself to the consistency of his hyphenation in this manuscript, but the occurrence of words in both hyphenated and unhyphenated forms with equal frequency (for example, "dining-room" and "dining room") does not detract from the readability of the text. The present edition has made only one exception to this procedure—the hyphenation of the name "Ha-ha Bay." The manuscript overwhelmingly exhibits the hyphenated form, and the present edition has therefore supplied or adopted hyphenation in the few unhyphenated occurrences (see the Emendations list at 172.11–12 and the accompanying Textual Note).

Howells also neglected to furnish an obviously necessary word or mark of punctuation at several points in the manuscript; for example, the manuscript text at 4.18 is missing a necessary quotation mark, and the pronoun "one" is an obvious omission at 70.11. The adoption of possibly non-authorial corrections is necessary to the preparation of a clear and readable text. That a correction was furnished by a Parkhill compositor or by Howells in proof is not a crucial question here; in all cases the addition is required by the sense of the text and has been incorporated.

The present edition has adopted the Harper first-edition corrections of anomalous manuscript readings resulting from internal revision. These forms are recorded in the Emendations list and involve one or more of the following errors made during Howells' revision of the manuscript text: uncancelled mistyping; uncancelled false starts or incomplete cancelling of passages; doubling of punctuation caused by deletion or interlineation; word duplication resulting from the rewriting of the same word on a new line or a new manuscript page; missing terminal letters when a word extends beyond the right margin of the manuscript page; Howells' failure to insert necessary hyphens at line breaks; mistakenly capitalized words following semicolons or commas; transposed words or phrases with unadjusted punctuation; and carets occurring at the wrong place in the line to indicate interlined words or phrases. All such corrections are recorded, and by using the Emendations entries the reader can reconstruct the text of the finished manuscript, including its inconsistencies.

In incorporating authorial revisions in the Harper first edition into the copy-text, the present edition has consistently made one emendation of punctuation. Without exception in the manuscript, Howells uses a quotation mark-dash construction which the printed texts render as dash-quotation mark. Therefore, in accepting the substantive revisions recorded in the Emendations list at 66.17, 66.34–35, 109.23, and 153.4, the present edition has rejected the printed texts' dash-quotation mark construction and retained Howells' manuscript usage.

The styling of the New York *Sun* is not relevant to the establishment of the text of the present edition. In the interest of historical accuracy, however, three consistent types of variants caused by the styling of the serialization should be mentioned: first, the *Sun* printed many numerals in arabic form; second, the *Sun* did not use italic type at those points where the manuscript and the Harper first edition italicize words for emphasis (see the Rejected Substantives list at 9.4 and the accompanying Textual Note), though the *Sun* did use an italic font for book and newspaper titles and some foreign words; third, the *Sun* began all chapters with the heading "Chapter" followed by a roman numeral instead of the simple roman numeral common to the manuscript and the Harper first edition.

The arrangement of the apparatus to this edition follows the sequence of textual derivation rather than the chronology of publication. Specifically, even though the New York *Sun* serial installments had all appeared before the Harper first edition was released, and though the Douglas edition was printed and officially registered before that date as well, both those texts were derived from some typeset form of what was eventually published as the Harper first edition. The sequence of the textual record in Emendations and Rejected Substantives follows this sequence of derivation and places the readings of the Harper first edition first after the manuscript, and then in their chronological order the *Sun* readings, the Douglas edition, and the Harper second edition. Though this arrangement may tend to obscure the complex patterns of derivation of the serial text from the pre-publication materials of the Harper edition which lay between the manuscript and that published text, the readings significant to this relationship have already been identified. The greater advantage to this system lies in the clear identification of the authorial revisions recorded in the Emendations list as having been made for and historically first incorporated into the materials of the Parkhill typesetting for the Harper first edition.

No attempt has been made in the present edition to preserve the purely visual appurtenances of the copy-text: type style, format of part, chapter, and paragraph openings (including the nineteenth-century use of a period after roman numerals in headings), the spacing of indentations, and the normalization of italic punctuation.[21]

J.P.E.

21. The present edition has normalized the use of italic punctuation after italic letters. Question marks and exclamation points are set in italics after italicized words, and all other punctuation in roman; the manuscript copy-text contains no italic punctuation at all.

A Note on the Manuscript

The complete manuscript of *The Quality of Mercy*, owned by the Houghton Library, Harvard University, was one of twenty-nine manuscripts purchased by the library from Miss Mildred Howells in July 1959. They had earlier been stored in a tin bread-box in the vault of a Boston bank.[1]

The manuscript consists of 1,900 leaves of holograph and 111 leaves of typescript, a total of 2,011 leaves on eight different kinds of paper, all measuring approximately 5¼ in. x 8¼ in. The typescript portions evidence four distinct typefaces. Howells assigned page numbers to and wrote across the short dimension of one side of the manuscript leaves.[2] Holograph and typescript are interleaved and numbered consecutively to form a final coherent draft which is in good condition and has no apparent missing leaves. With the manuscript is a small slip of brown wrapping paper 1 in. x 5 in. bearing in Howells' hand the words "Quality of Mercy./ Mostly MS. but some typewriting."

The pagination of the manuscript is as follows (a hyphen signifies inclusive numbering, an equal sign a single page marked by Howells with that full set of numbers or combination of letters and numbers): [1]-85, 2=35-3=35, 87-89, 2=89, 90, 91 to 97[*single leaf*], 98-109, 110=113, 114-153, 154 & 155 [*single leaf*], 156-159, 159 [*bis*]-160, 2=160-3=160, 161-167, 167[*bis*]-172, 172[*bis*]-188, 190-220, 2=220, 221-244, 243-261, 263-285, A=285, 286-311, 311[*bis*]-

---

1. John K. Reeves, "The Literary Manuscripts of W. D. Howells: A Supplement to the Descriptive Finding List," *Bulletin of the New York Public Library*, LXV (1961), 465.

2. The following manuscript leaves also have Howells' holograph on the verso, which is unnumbered except where noted: 158, 168, 174, 175, 322(cancelled), 383, 399, 412(cancelled), 423, 426, 447, 499, 539, 2=574, 637, 796(cancelled), 895, 929, 973, 995, 1034, 1060, 1075, 1087, 1092, 1136, 1157, 1324 (numbered 1237, cancelled), 1405, 1409, 1652, 1660, 1685, 1881, 1974(cancelled), and 1992. These passages are intended for insertion at points indicated on the rectoes.

321, 321=2, 322, 2=322-6=322, 323-324, 326-399, 400 to 402[*single leaf*], 403-434, 434=438, 439-450, 452-453, 453=2, 454 to 462[*single leaf*], 463-466, 4??[*sheet torn*], 467-470, 471 & 472[*single leaf*], 473, 474 to 483[*single leaf*], 484-487, 488 to 495[*single leaf*], 496-501, 2= 501, 502-504, 506-514, 516-522, 2=522-3=522, 523-524, 2=524-10= 524, 12=524-26=524, 527-530, 2=530, 532-552, 555-571, A571, 572, 574, 574[*bis*], 2=574, 575-585, 586=587, 588-593, A=593, 594-606, 2=606, 607-621, 2=621-3=621, 622-625, 2=625, 626-632, 634-636, 2=637, 637-657, 656-668, 668[*bis*]-672, 2=671, 672[*bis*]-683, 684,685 [*two numbers on single leaf*], 686–687, 670-705, 706 to 732[*single leaf*], 734-746, 746[*bis*]-749, 749[*bis*]-750, 751 & 752[*single leaf*], 753-756, 757 to 560[*sic; single leaf*], 761-790, 790[*bis*]-794, 2=794, 795-797, 788, 799-808, 809 to 821[*single leaf*], 822-826, 2=826, 827-903, 905-908, 2=908-5=908, 909-968, 970-1001, 1001[*bis*]-1061, A1061= B1061, 1062-1082, 1183, 1084, 1086-1133, 2=1132, 2=1133, 1134-1150, 2=1150, 1151, 1153-1166, 2=1166, 1167-1209, 1211-1246, 2= 1246, 1247-1248, 1250-1287, 1290-1310, 1312-1325, 1329-1539, 1540 & 1541[*single leaf*], 1542-1591, 2=1592-4=1592, 1592-1812, 2=1812, 1813-1825, 1826 & 1827[*single leaf*], 1828-1831, 2=1831, 1832-1834, 1834[*bis*]-1847, 1848 & 1849[*single leaf*], 1850, 2=1850, 1851-1859, 2=1859, 1860-1870, 2=1870-3=1870, 1871-1874, 2=1874-3=1874, 1875-1884, 2=1885, 2=1884, 1885-1891, 1892 & 1895[*single leaf*], 1896-1917, 1918,1919,1920[*three numbers on single leaf*], 1921-1967, 2=1967, 1968-1969, 2=1969, 1970-1973, 2=1973-4=1973, 1974, 2=1974, 1975-1977, 2=1977-3=1977, 1978, 2=1978, 1979, 2=1979, 1980-1985, A1985, B=1985, 1986-1989, 2=1989-3=1989, 1990, 2=1990-3=1990, 1991-2008, 2=2008, 2009-2020.

The complexity of the final numbering sequence results from Howells' extensive rearrangement, insertion, and cancellation of leaves. The first nine hundred leaves of the manuscript in particular have many sections which were rearranged, necessitating the cancellation of an original numbering sequence in favor of a second one. Some of these altered sections were then further rearranged, and for these a third numbering sequence replaced the revised one. Howells also discarded two versions of Part Third, chapter VII; altering their numbering sequences, however, he reincorporated them into the manuscript after he had written the final chapter VII. The general numbering of the material is further complicated by several practices of Howells': expansions of the manuscript, including insertions into the text of manuscript leaves, are often numbered by using the original manuscript page numbers and adding A and B or 1, 2, 3 to them to indicate the location of the new material (285, A=285; 220, 2=220); on the other hand, when leaves are discarded, a leaf which precedes or follows that gap usually is given the numbers of the discarded leaves (91 to 97; 1848 & 1849).

Eight distinct kinds of paper appear in the manuscript of *The Quality of Mercy*. The papers, in the order of their first appearance, are as follows: light-weight, wove, unlined white paper, torn, watermarked "Lacroix Frères"; unlined white wove tissue, cut, unwatermarked; heavy-weight, wove, unlined white paper, cut, watermarked "LACROIX FRÈRES"; medium-weight white wove paper lined in blue in 3/16 in. squares, cut, watermarked with the open block figures "LA [gothic cross]-F"; heavy-weight, wove, unlined gray-green deckle stationery, uncut, unwatermarked; light-weight, laid, unlined white paper with heavy wire lines forming rectangles enclosing six lighter wire lines per rectangle, cut, unwatermarked; light-weight, laid, unlined white paper with chain and wire lines forming ½ in. squares, cut, watermarked "LACROIX FRÈRES"; and light-weight, wove, unlined pale blue paper, cut, watermarked "LACROIX FRÈRES." With the exception of the blue stationery, the 5¼ in. x 8¼ in. dimensions of the manuscript leaves are the result of the even tearing or cutting in half of 8¼ in. x 10½ in. sheets. The exact dimensions of the leaves therefore vary slightly, but the dimensions are consistent to a tolerance of one-eighth of an inch. Reconstructing the original 8¼ in. x 10½ in. sheets reveals an indiscriminate use of both sides of the original sheets. For example, manuscript leaves 21 and 18 form the top and bottom of an original 8¼ in. x 10½ in. sheet, but the text on leaf 21 is written on what was one side of the full sheet, and the text on leaf 18 on the other.

Howells generally used black ink for the holograph text and for his revision; only a few revisions are in pencil. The holograph pages average seventeen lines of text for the first half of the novel, but the average falls to thirteen and fourteen as Howells nears the end and his handwriting becomes larger. The typescript leaves average twenty lines per manuscript page.

Howells' internal revisions of the manuscript range from the alteration of single words, adjustment of punctuation, and careted words or phrases, to addition or deletion of full sentences and paragraphs. No attempt has been made in the present edition to offer a full record of these internal alterations; cancellations, self-editings, interlinings, careted insertions, and so on have been accepted as pre-copy-text alterations and thus integral parts of the copy-text.

Nine of the manuscript leaves bear traces of pencil writing in Howells' hand. These passages are lightly written or partially erased, and Howells' black ink holograph is written over them. Transcriptions appear below of the legible portions of the passages, keyed to the final overwritten text. The manuscript reading cited at 298.19–23 was further revised in proof and can be reconstructed from the Emendations list. A word enclosed in brackets is a doubtful transcription.

22.13–15	for all . . . strong herself] *Very faint passage written underneath these words is illegible.*
24.1–2	Northwick . . . he had] *Underneath is written:* Experience of life so often [teaches] us to doubt the moral govt of the universe
26.5	"My . . . stairs] *Underneath is written:* [My] God and nonsense [would] Providence finally on his side.
34.11	He told] Feb. 1. *written at center top of page and partially cancelled in ink.*
181.22	When from time to time] *Underneath is written:* As if [nothing] wisdom to if He gave up the money
200.16	his convalescence] *Beneath the line is written:* (he intended restore all the [mon].
201.36–202.1	he would . . . excused him] *Underneath is written:* , he would have accounted for Northwick and excused him to himself.
298.19–23	"If I were . . . I should, too] *Underneath is written:* If I were a man I would In the folly of it.
313.16–17	As soon . . . forbidden] *Underneath is written:* and as soon as he had said this a poison began to work in Pinney's soul. He [had] not the [evil] to say it.

Some non-authorial marks appear in the manuscript; the bulk of these, which are in pencil and originated in the Parkhill printing shop, are compositors' signatures, of limited textual importance. They divide the manuscript into irregular compositorial stints that average approximately one hundred and twenty lines (or four pages) of the Harper first-edition text. Three compositors' names—Collins, Hiler, and Swinton—appear regularly, usually written between two parallel lines slanting upward and beginning at a new paragraph. No discernible order in the alternation of the compositors is apparent.

Other non-authorial pencil marks in the manuscript, however, are of greater textual importance. These include the date "1891/ Jan. 1." at the top of the first page of the manuscript, correction or clarification of Howells' manuscript page numbers, printers' brackets and lines indicating line breaks, one galley number, duplication of a paragraph sign originally written by Howells, and the insertion of a phrase inadvertently omitted from the manuscript—the only non-authorial marking which actually affects the meaning of the text (see below, page 384, for details). Not written in Howells' hand, the date "1891/Jan. 1." on the first page of the manuscript is probably a reminder to the Parkhill office of the date by which Harper wanted the completed plates.[3] The compositorial signatures indicate a minimum of one hundred and twenty-two stints to set the novel. It is not likely that the stints took up whole or even half days, since in that case setting would have taken place at the very slow rate of one page an hour. Probably the compositors worked at the material as the schedules of other jobs required, and fast enough to meet a pre-determined deadline fitting Howells' arrangements with the New York *Sun*.

The Parkhill shop evidently altered some of Howells' misnumbered manuscript pages. The manuscript sequence 85, 2=35, 3= 35 is changed to read 1=85, 2=85, 3=85 or 86, for example. In the heavily revised early portion of the manuscript, Howells' mistaken numbering of the leaves probably results from his addition of material to leaf 85; in numbering the two later leaves he may have misread 85 as 35. The Parkhill alteration of the leaf numbers reflects the fact that the texts of the three leaves follow an obvious and intended sequence.

At locations corresponding to readings at 9.18, 19.16, 27.14, 67.10, 70.13, 97.25, 209.26, 212.29, 287.4, and 290.24 in the present text, printer's lines and brackets indicating a line break occurring

---

3. See the Introduction, pp. xix–xx, for details of the proposed and actual dates of publication of the Harper edition printed from the Parkhill plates.

in the middle of a manuscript sentence or word rather than at the end of a paragraph correspond to line breaks in the Harper first edition. (The only line break of this kind which does not correspond to the Harper first edition is at 160.2–3, but the two-line insertion in proof at 159.26–160.1 probably caused the displacement of the original line break in the first edition.) This evidence, along with the galley number 42 in the manuscript at the paragraph break at 144.35–36, is evidence that the manuscript was actual fair copy for the preparation of the plate type; there was no typed transcription of the manuscript prepared in the Parkhill shop for use as the setting copy.

At 166.16 a paragraph sign pencilled in the right margin of the manuscript leaf duplicates Howells' own paragraph sign above the manuscript line; someone in the Parkhill shop evidently wanted to be certain that the compositor was aware of the beginning of a new paragraph at that point.

The only non-authorial material which bears on an actual textual reading occurs at 161.15 (manuscript leaf 795), where the phrase "would not let it worry other people." accompanies the word "Query" in the manuscript. Close examination reveals that "Query" was written first and that it was then overwritten with the phrase. The manuscript page is a late insertion, and Howells evidently did not notice that he had left the sentence incomplete. Someone at Parkhill detected the omission and wrote "Query" on the page to insure that Howells be asked to furnish copy. The phrase supplied in the manuscript, though not in Howells' hand, can therefore be assumed to have his authority, and has been accepted in the present edition as an integral part of the copy-text.

J.P.E.

Textual Notes

3.19   Here and at 86.14, 93.18, 215.24, 224.18, 263.31, 265.16, 272.5, 296.32, 333.24, 347.32, 353.11, and 354.30 in the present text, Howells failed to follow his usual practice and place a period after the abbreviated form "Mr." At all the later points the punctuation is provided without further citation in the Emendations list.

4.33   Howells originally wrote "highland" in the manuscript, but then drew a vertical line between the two parts to indicate that they should be set as separate words; the present edition accepts the revised manuscript reading as more reflective of Howells' intention.

6.34   The replacement of the manuscript reading "luring" by "having" in all the printed texts is one of a number of examples of apparent compositorial misinterpretation of the manuscript in the setting of the Harper book edition (A), and the perpetuation of such errors in the other printed texts derived from it. In addition to the reading at this point, other such misreadings— all recorded in the Rejected Substantives list—occur at 14.19, 16.27, 16.28, 38.6–7, 49.5, 60.3, 70.31, 79.19, 109.35, 120.5, 133.18, 143.29, 163.6, 207.27, 219.22, 230.23, 239.11, 243.5, 249.18, 261.17, 295.16, 314.15, 316.30, and 348.26–27.

9.4   The newspaper text usually failed to print in italics words italicized for emphasis in the manuscript and American book edition. The following list notes the locations in the present text of italicized words which are not italicized in the serial (these items are not

cited further in the Rejected Substantives list): 9.7,
9.15, 22.7, 30.1, 33.4, 33.6, 45.8, 48.17, 49.7, 49.12, 49.28
(*like, that, No*), 49.29, 51.21, 52.5, 53.33, 54.2, 60.6,
60.23, 66.28, 69.28, 71.11, 71.13, 72.7, 72.26, 73.15, 74.15
(*You, less*), 74.18, 75.10, 75.13, 76.18, 77.15, 82.6 (*The*),
82.24, 82.25, 83.3, 83.5, 83.16, 83.17, 83.29 (*have, my*),
85.4 (*is*), 85.18, 85.24, 85.28, 85.31, 86.13, 86.26, 86.33,
87.7, 87.13, 87.20, 88.1, 88.5, 93.12 (*Representing the*),
94.1, 95.19, 98.6, 100.11, 101.5, 101.26, 104.13, 104.23,
105.4, 105.34, 109.1, 109.2, 109.9, 109.33, 109.37, 110.22,
110.24 (*no, think*), 114.16, 114.17 (*any, us*), 122.2, 122.8
(*I, didn't*), 122.29, 129.7, 131.18, 131.20, 131.23, 131.24,
132.9, 132.10, 132.21, 132.22, 133.11, 133.35, 137.19,
137.20, 137.32, 138.14, 140.26, 140.34, 143.35, 144.9,
144.26 (*Intrusive, brother*), 144.29, 145.18, 145.20,
149.26, 149.36, 150.29, 151.33, 151.34, 157.5, 158.3,
158.13, 158.15, 195.24, 199.11, 209.22, 209.24, 211.1,
211.21, 215.10, 215.27, 216.2, 216.26 (*I, you*), 217.9,
217.14, 217.21, 217.25, 217.28, 217.31, 217.34, 219.5,
219.11, 219.32, 220.6, 220.16, 220.34, 221.7, 221.35,
225.5, 226.3, 226.15, 226.16, 226.19, 227.4, 228.18 (*you,
you*), 228.20, 228.21, 229.25, 230.35, 233.3, 233.10, 235.1,
235.33, 236.10, 237.1, 237.2, 237.25 (*is, Any*), 238.7,
238.8, 242.21, 244.22, 246.33–34, 247.3, 248.1, 248.2,
250.28, 251.2, 251.6, 252.3, 253.25, 253.30, 253.35,
253.36, 254.15, 254.31, 254.35, 255.4, 257.19, 259.8 (*at,
get*), 259.23–24 (*I want you, old boy, and I'm willing
to pay for you*), 263.10, 263.36, 266.35, 267.25, 268.17,
270.16, 271.18, 271.29, 271.34, 272.6, 272.21, 272.29,
273.9, 275.16, 275.19, 279.26, 279.35, 280.19, 280.28,
281.18, 282.17, 284.5, 284.11, 285.5, 285.12, 287.2,
288.23, 289.23, 290.3 (*must*), 290.33, 292.18, 293.1,
293.10, 293.24, 293.35, 294.16, 294.17, 294.26, 294.30,
295.31, 296.8, 296.11, 296.13, 296.14, 297.26, 302.29
(*wont, go*), 307.3, 307.22, 307.35, 308.1, 309.17, 316.2,
316.7, 317.11, 317.17, 317.18, 317.34, 320.6, 320.7, 320.9
(*best, once*), 320.11, 321.25, 322.27, 322.29, 324.12,
329.4, 330.6, 330.7, 330.13, 330.17 (*found, knew*), 331.3,
331.13, 331.33, 332.1, 332.10, 332.16, 333.15, 333.17,

333.23, 333.27, 333.36, 334.6, 334.12, 334.13, 335.14, 340.1(*Send, back*), 342.27, 343.24 (*me, they*), 346.6, 346.22, 348.14, 352.17, 352.23 (*interviewing, reporters*), 352.30, 353.22, 353.35 (*you, me*), 354.34 (*must, swear*), 358.7, 358.8, 358.11, 359.4, and 359.12.

9.5   Here and at the other points listed below, Howells spaced verbal contractions in the manuscript. Since such usage was not deliberate, and was often the result of incomplete revision or failure to supply hyphens at line breaks, the present edition adopts unspaced forms. Besides the contraction in this entry, the other instances—none of them further recorded in the Emendations list—occur at 22.8(mustn't), 39.5(shouldn't), 43.25(shouldn't), 45.3(hadn't), 45.12(he's), 47.24 (shouldn't), 56.26(wouldn't), 62.24(haven't), 66.9 (wouldn't), 70.16(couldn't), 71.22(isn't), 73.36(mustn't), 74.2(mustn't), 100.23(hasn't), 105.18(couldn't), 121.13(didn't), 130.30(didn't), 132.8(Didn't), 133.12 (couldn't), 213.7(isn't), 214.7(Hasn't), 219.8(isn't), 226.13(didn't), 231.9(isn't), 233.14(shouldn't), 238.2 (wouldn't), 261.5(hasn't), 268.11(couldn't), 280.31 (couldn't), 282.18(we've), 289.7(hasn't), 293.29(isn't), 296.29(hasn't), 322.16(didn't), 330.7(hasn't), 331.24 (hadn't), 331.35(couldn't), 332.5(haven't), and 353.11 (isn't).

9.17   A line like a long dash appears between "shoe-brushes." and "But" in the manuscript reading. The mark was one typically employed by Howells throughout the manuscript to indicate text to be continued on the next line or leaf without a paragraph break, even though the preceding line or page was not filled out. All such marks were correctly interpreted thus by the book compositors. Though these marks are not reproduced in the body of the text of the present edition, they are significant details in the manuscript, and are recorded here. In the following list, the location of the mark is given by page and line numbers in the

present text followed by the manuscript reading; to
suggest how Howells used these marks in relation to
page and line breaks, the transcriptions include a single virgule to indicate a manuscript line break and a
double virgule a break between leaves. Since the readings cited here are those of the manuscript, they may
not agree with the readings of the present text because
of Howells' later revision of the material; readings of
this kind are prefaced by an asterisk, indicating that
the final reading of the present edition can be found
in the Emendations list.

26.2	it.——//He
*30.10–11	room.——/Northwick
41.21	honesty.——//The
68.29	words./——/"Well,
72.33	there——//I've
73.30	go.——//¶"She
87.10	generally.——/Poor
98.34	clerks.——//At
99.26	other.——//They
127.9	o'clock.——//Several
135.26	wife.——//She
143.1	stay——//stay
145.11	what.——//Matt
147.3	him,——//"Wade
209.10	owning.——/In
230.32	moment.——//Then
244.18	houseless.——//But
246.18	abruptly,——//"I
246.25	ways.——//There
247.1	on:——//She's
267.36	not.——/Couldn't
294.26	mother.——/"And
*298.19–23	escape.——//This
313.27	sorts.——/Pinney
315.15	started.——/"What
327.29	word./——He
328.1	mercy.——/But
330.15	back.——//I
337.27	him.——//He

337.35	clients.——/With
341.7	me"—/——She
348.30	him;——//he
353.18	matter:——//Have
354.15	says.——//We

18.27　The terminal *s* of the interlined word "stairs" is ill-formed in the manuscript and was probably misread as a hyphen by the Parkhill compositor.

20.30　Perhaps because Howells found using the hyphen key on the typewriter at which he composed this portion of *The Quality of Mercy* inconvenient, he typed ellipses to indicate the interruption of dialogue in contexts where he normally used dashes in his handwriting. That the two typographical variants were essentially identical in his usage is clear from an internal revision in the manuscript: at 58.8–9, Howells had originally typed "hosses' . . ."; at some later stage of revision, he added the word "there" after "hosses" and at the same time replaced the typed ellipses with a handwritten dash.

Given Howells' customary usage of the dash rather than ellipses in such contexts in this and other manuscripts (the only exception occurs at 71.2, where the ellipses indicate speech trailing off rather than being interrupted; in this instance the ellipses have been retained), the present edition emends the ellipsized forms of the typed portions of the manuscript to the long dash, preserving the order of the replaced form in relationship to other marks of punctuation. The original forms and their locations by page and line number in the present edition are recorded here and not repeated in the Emendations list:

20.30	that" . . . .
40.2	term" . . .
48.7	get" . . . .
53.2	and" . . .
53.35	fun'al" . . .
54.1–2	back. . . Why,

54.14   when" . .
57.1   only" . . .
57.5   see" . . .
57.14   name" . . .
57.24   when" . . .
57.28   been" . . .
57.32   we" . . .
58.12   yet" . . .
58.22   and" . . .
59.28   or" . . .
59.34   and" . . .
70.37   you" . . .
76.20   plans" . . .
96.1   to . . . it's
96.2   you . . . I
96.2   you" . . .

36.11   In the manuscript the paragraph sign which Howells
         originally wrote before "He" is imperfectly cancelled
         and was probably considered part of the standing text
         by the Parkhill compositor.

36.35   Here and at 55.7(sho'd), 55.9(c'd), 64.15(thro'), 72.13
         (c'd), 75.27(w'd), and 95.27(sh'd), Howells wrote or
         typed the contracted form of the word, apparently be-
         cause he did not have enough space at the right margin
         on the manuscript leaf to write the full form; since
         the contracted forms were chosen out of necessity rath-
         er than preference, the present edition adopts the ex-
         panded forms at these points (they are not recorded
         further in Emendations). The printed texts correctly
         rendered all these expanded forms except "c'd" at
         55.9, which was printed as "would," and "sh'd" at
         95.27, where the contraction at the end of the line was
         retained in the book texts and corrupted in the serial
         to "she'd."

38.6   The Parkhill compositor probably mistook the line
         which italicized "speak" in the manuscript for the

crossing of the *t* in the word "agricultural" immediately below it on the leaf.

44.3 Here and at 51.18, 105.7, 129.21, 238.26, 290.19, 294.33, 295.33, and 296.30, Howells' manuscript uses the incorrect spelling "nonesense." None of the further corrections of this spelling are recorded in the Emendations list.

65.29 Howells cancelled "winding" in the manuscript at some point, but later reinstated it by placing stet-mark dots beneath. Since the word is appropriate to the context and could have been missed by a compositor working from the manuscript, it has been retained.

82.6–7 Here and at 84.34, 96.20, 104.5, 117.30, 118.24, 118.34, 119.6, 119.14, 119.14–15, 119.21, 119.22, 120.8, 120.31, 123.17, 127.4, 127.6, 129.4, 129.28, 145.15, 208.2, 208.6, 208.10, 208.12, 211.4, 211.10, 232.14–15, 258.8, 260.19, 289.31, 301.9, 303.14, and 304.31, Howells failed to underline the titles of newspapers in the manuscript, inconsistent with his italicized usage elsewhere. The present edition adopts the italic form of the titles at these points; the normalization is not further recorded in the Emendations list.

82.20 The word "breath" ends only halfway across the manuscript line, and "Baked" is flush with the left margin, a situation which probably led the compositor to set a new paragraph.

85.32 Howells' caret indicating the interlining of the clause following this word is placed to the right of the period which follows the word in the manuscript. Since he makes no indication that a comma should make the clause unrestrictive, the present edition adopts the reading without the comma supplied in the Harper second edition.

94.31 The underlining which italicizes "anything" in the manuscript resembles the crossing of the *t* in the word "it's" directly underneath on the leaf, and was probably misinterpreted thus in typesetting.

107.4 The final manuscript reading "extanding" resulted from incomplete revision: Howells had originally written "standing," then placed *ex* over the *s* but failed to change *a* to *e*.

130.1 Since Howells customarily used the abbreviation "Mrs." with a period, the present edition provides one where he failed to do so here and at 130.15, 131.23, 133.30, 216.1, 216.35, 217.8, 217.14, 217.34, 241.1, 246.33, 296.31, 324.12, 348.11, and 348.29. At all the later points the punctuation is provided without citation in the Emendations list.

132.21–22 The erroneous reading "is! I—" introduced in the first Harper book edition and repeated in the other printed texts apparently resulted from the typesetter's interpretation of Howells' combined page number "2—606," which immediately follows "is!" on the first line of the manuscript leaf, as capital *I*, dash, and number.

148.4–5 The word "What" begins a one-sentence paragraph obviously spoken by Matt; the printed texts erroneously assign it to Wade.

172.2 The present edition provides a period in accordance with Howells' ordinary usage following the abbreviation "St" here and at 172.7 (twice), 177.21, 178.8, 178.13, 179.13, 179.14, 181.3, 181.8, 183.9, 205.7, and 263.32. At all the later points the punctuation is provided without citation in the Emendations list.

172.11–12 Here and at 309.22, 309.31, and 350.15, Howells writes the name of the bay as one word, and at 309.14 as two; without further citation of the forms in the Emendations list, the present edition adopts the hyphenated form at these points to accord with Howells' usage in all other instances of the word in the text.

174.17 Here and at 179.10, 180.3, 180.30, 183.36–184.1, 184.13, 185.22, and 186.36, Howells incorrectly spells "carriole" in both singular and plural with a single *r*; the present edition corrects the spelling without further citation in the Emendations list.

179.23 The apparent terminal apostrophe in the manuscript here is caused by a comma in the previous manuscript line placed in the position of an apostrophe following this word. The serial evidently attempted to regularize the form by adding a terminal apostrophe to another occurrence of the word at 179.14.

192.26 Here and at 192.31, 195.30, 198.2, 203.20, 204.6, 204.11, 204.16, 204.25, 204.35, 205.20, 205.23, 205.26, 205.30, 205.32, 206.2, 206.11, 206.36, 208.1 (*accent grave*), 309.19, and 309.33, Howells wrote the French priest's name without a necessary *accent aigu* over the initial letter; the present edition provides the correct accent without further citation in the Emendations list.

272.27 The word "one" is necessary in the context of the passage, but it was somehow deleted from all of the printed texts except the Douglas edition.

280.26 The citation of Mr. Wade's first name is made consistent with earlier references to him as "Caryl" (see, for example, 64.20 and 67.6 in the present text).

333.6–7 The sentence beginning with "He" is an interlineation joined to a sentence beginning a new paragraph, but because the interlined sentence follows immediately upon the word "him," the last word of the preceding paragraph, it is likely that the Parkhill compositor misinterpreted the manuscript instructions.

351.2   The correct location here should be "East Hatboro' "; the incorrect manuscript reading "West Hatboro' " was perpetuated in all the printed texts except the newspapers.

Emendations

The following list records all changes in substantives and accidentals introduced into the copy-text, with the exception of the normalizations specified in the Textual Commentary. The reading of the present edition appears to the left of the bracket; the source of that reading, followed by a semicolon, the copy-text reading and the copy-text symbol, as well as intermediate variant readings when such exist, appear to the right of the bracket. The readings of texts which fall between the copy-text and the source cited for the reading of the present edition may be assumed to agree substantively with the copy-text reading if not listed; accidental variants in these intermediate texts have not been recorded here. Readings of texts subsequent to the source of the adopted reading may be presumed to agree with the adopted reading unless recorded in Rejected Substantives. Texts are listed in the chronological order described in the Textual Commentary, page 377.

Within an entry, the curved dash ~ represents the same word that appears before the bracket and is used in recording punctuation and paragraphing variants. The abbreviation HE indicates emendation made for the first time in the present edition and not found in any of the editions examined in the preparation of this text. If the corrected form adopted here has appeared in an earlier state of the text, that text is cited for historical interest, even though it may have no textual authority. *Om.* means that the reading to the left of the bracket does not appear in the text or texts cited to the right of the semicolon. An asterisk indicates that the reading is discussed in the Textual Notes.

The following texts are referred to:

AMS   Printer's copy manuscript of *The Quality of Mercy*
A   Harper and Brothers, 1892; First Edition

S   New York *Sun*, 4 October 1891–3 January 1892
B   David Douglas, 1892
C   Harper and Brothers, [c 1891]

3.7	the bursts] A; these bursts AMS
3.8	evoked] A; rose from the soliloquies [evo]ked AMS
3.8	pace] A; pace, and then AMS
3.8	in] A; into those monologues with AMS
3.9	falling] A; failing AMS
*3.19	Mr.] A; Mr AMS
3.24	Elbridge's),] A; ~) AMS
3.25	himself,] A; ~ AMS
4.18	you?"] A; ~? AMS
4.25	Northwick] A; Northway AMS
5.12	He] A; He who AMS
5.18	Here] A; Then he Here AMS
5.21–22	tears again,"] A; ~, ~" AMS
5.34	that] A; that mere AMS
6.18	I'll] A; Ill AMS
6.29	had] A; had had AMS
6.29	herself] A; herself to AMS
7.21	At such times] A; Once or twice AMS
8.5	dead] A; dead his AMS
8.6–7	thief. ¶ The] A; thief./II/¶ The AMS
8.7	so filled his mind] A; filled his his mind so AMS
*9.5	hadn't] A; had n't AMS
*9.17	shoe-brushes. But] A; shoe-brushes.—— But AMS
9.26	and the] A; and just the AMS
9.27	just] A; *om.* AMS
9.37–10.1	flicker./II/¶ If] A; flicker. ¶ If AMS
10.1	of the] A; of that AMS
11.9	his behavior] A; hi/ behavior AMS
12.21	type.] A; ~AMS
14.24	Northwick's] A; Northway's AMS
15.16	dowry] A; money AMS
16.1	daughters] A; daughter's AMS
16.21	moon's] A; moon AMS
16.29	beyond] A; Beyond AMS
17.5	moonlight] A; ~. AMS

17.16	it to] A; it AMS
17.19	and he] A; he AMS
17.20–21	house ... were] A; house and the furniture, all but the pictures, were AMS
17.26	all,] A; all, and AMS
17.28	for] A; fo/for AMS
18.5	said] A; ~, AMS
19.20	of] A; of flimsy AMS
20.6	on] A; of on AMS
20.26	Superintendent] A; Superintendant AMS
*20.30	that"–] HE; ~" .... AMS; ~–" A, S, B–C
21.18	I] A; But I AMS
21.22	tolerant!"] A; ~! AMS
22.14	she] A; Sue AMS
25.20	most.] A; ~ AMS
25.28	leave] A; leave her AMS
26.33–34	belonged] A; belonging AMS
27.36	stood] A; stood where he stood AMS
29.7	desk,] A; desk, and compromised with his personal dignity, affected by having to stand while Northwick sat; he put one leg partly up on the desk, AMS
30.10–11	away. ¶ Northwick] A; away with no more ceremony than he had entered the room. Northwick AMS
31.7	Newtons'; their] A; Elbridges', whose AMS
31.23	taking] A; stealing AMS
31.29	case] A; ~, AMS
33.7	that.] A; that—and you can't drive *away* from the Law. AMS
34	VII] A; VI AMS
34.21	Board] A; directors AMS
34.25	honor] A; ho/or AMS
35.3	community] A; conpmunity AMS
35.6	points.] A; points. There were so many of these that he sometimes felt like a monument erected to the things that he seemed to stand almost alone for. He was at all times able to hold his head high, and to carry it through with a bold, bluff, hearty

defiance in a world where he flourished in univer-
sal esteem. AMS

35.8   more] A; mone AMS

35.24   seemed] A; seeemed AMS

35.26   justice] A; j/justice AMS

35.32   Northwick] A; ~, AMS

36.8   but] A; But AMS

36.17   principles.] A; ~.. AMS

36.18–19   disappointed] A; diappointed AMS

36.22–25   begun . . . company.] A; grown to think it immoral
            to make a profit on the earnings of other people,
            and he could not go back to the mills; he gave up
            his interest in the business. AMS

36.34   that] A; *om.* AMS

*36.35   would] A; w'd AMS

37.1   work and wages in Europe] A; *The Life of Labor
            in Europe* AMS

37.4–5   nothing. ¶ Eben] A; nothing. Matt went to live the
            greater part of the year on a farm in Vardley, left
            him by one of his father's sisters, who was very
            much such a crank as Matt himself, and who died
            while he was abroad. His family visited him there
            in the late spring and fall, and agreed not to dis-
            parage his theories or practices, on condition that
            he would spend the winter-months in town with
            them; he divided his time there between the un-
            deserving poor of the North End, and the meri-
            torious fair on the Back Bay; he really went out a
            good deal with his sister. Eben AMS

37.29   'shut] A; "~ AMS

37.29   again.'] A; ~." AMS

38.2–5   Hilary . . . farming it.] A; *om.* AMS

38.15   with] A; with frog-mouth, and AMS

38.16   that had no] A; without AMS

38.17   them] A; her this AMS

38.25   throat] A; neck AMS

39.11   must] A; had must AMS

39.11   scuffling] A; skuffling AMS

39.21   you're] A; you r'e AMS

39.33	of the] A; of th/ AMS
39.34–35	his . . . hide] A; in its clean shaven distinction showed AMS
39.36	father. "If] A; ~ ~ AMS
40.4	girl] A; ~, AMS
40.5	a little] A; alittle AMS
40.7	Then,] A; and then AMS
40.10	somewhere] A; somew/where AMS
41	VIII] A; XIV AMS
41.5	cloak] A; claak AMS
42.1	reasonable] A; reasoned AMS
42.11	all of the] A; the other AMS
42.13–14	for the moment] A; *om.* AMS
42.36	Northwick] A; ~, AMS
43.8	than] A; tha/than AMS
43.19	fraud] A; thief AMS
43.31	isn't] A; is'nt AMS
43.31	criminal.] A; ~; AMS
*44.3	nonsense] A; nonesense AMS
44.17	away."] A; ~.' AMS
44.30	he had] A; *om.* AMS
45.12	abroad.] A; ~.. AMS
45.17	well] A; wall AMS
45.22	as] A; a/as AMS
45.34	guess] A; juess AMS
45.35	Yes,"] A; ~." AMS
46	IX] A; VII AMS
46.16	gayeties] A; gayities AMS
47.36	Wilmington."] A; ~" AMS
47.37	her] A; he/her AMS
48.5	quarrel."] A; ~.." AMS
48.22	a moment] A; moment AMS
48.29	explained] A; explained and forgiven AMS
51	X] A; VIII AMS
51.16	stuff.] A; stuff. Is God so good to his creatures here that you think Arty's goin' to be any better off *there*? AMS
52.13	morning?"] A; ~.?" AMS
52.14	ma'am,] A; ma'am AMS

52.27	heart.] A; ~ .. AMS
52.34	wouldn't] A; would't AMS
52.36	account] A; a/account AMS
54.6	went] A; went out AMS
54.9	what] A; uhat AMS
54.9	take] A; a take AMS
54.11	it] A; i/it AMS
54.15	needn't] A; need't AMS
54.19	anxiety,] A; ~., AMS
54.21	know] A; know he AMS
54.22	train] terain AMS
54.28	his] A; him AMS
56	XI] A; VIII AMS
56.6	calamity] A; calamitny AMS
56.21	itself,] A; ~ AMS
57.7	it and ran] A; and ran it AMS
57.15	Wade] A; Wade a AMS
57.27	station] A; statiou AMS
57.28	answer] A; nswer AMS
57.30	Elbridge. But] A; Elbridge "but— AMS
58.16	library] A; libraray AMS
58.17	happened] A; heppened AMS
58.23	cried] A; said AMS
58.23–24	the door] A; door AMS
58.28	severely,] A; ~ AMS
58.34	about,] A; ~ AMS
58.34	of the] A; of th/the AMS
60.6	have] A; have is AMS
60.37	untasted] A; half-full AMS
61.9	elder] A; eldest AMS
61.16	she'd—] A; ~"— AMS
61.37	the pair] A; this pair AMS
62.15	Nordeck] A; Nordick AMS
62.20	hasn't] A; has't AMS
62.24	Louise] A; Miss Hilary AMS
62.27	reins.] A; ~ AMS
64	XII] A; IX AMS
64.15	saw] A; discovered AMS
66.7–8	generally] A; *om.* AMS

66.16	subjected] A; educated AMS
66.17	suspicion on no kind of"—] HE; suspicion. AMS; suspicion on no kind of—" A, S, B–C
66.17	juncture Matt] A; ~"— ¶ ~ AMS
66.30	Matt. "But] A; ~. ¶ "~, AMS
66.32	her."] A; her. Her misfortune is all that even a woman who hated her could wish!" AMS
66.34–35	besides"— ¶ "Yes." Matt] HE; besides"— ¶ "Matt! ¶ Matt AMS; besides—" ¶ "Yes." Matt A, S, B–C
67.4	suspicions."] A; ~. AMS
67.12	mercifullest] A; meercifullest AMS
67.13	first] A; firs AMS
67.14	just] A; the day night AMS
67.16	powers] A; pouers AMS
67.31	morning,] A; ~,, AMS
68.3	don't suppose] A; d/don't suppose AMS
68.6	way] A; way way AMS
68.16	to] A; *om.* AMS
68.16	cruelty] A; ~, AMS
68.17	when it] A; when it when it AMS
68.18	know that] A; know that that AMS
68.24	know] A; *om.* AMS
68.28	again] A; *om.* AMS
69.1	up] A; up again AMS
69.5	When Louise] A; When she AMS
69.8	But] A; Why, AMS
69.8	have its] A; have have it's AMS
69.17	itself] A; *om.* AMS
70.3	same class] A; sane class AMS
70.7	manufacturing] A; business AMS
70.11	one] A; *om.* AMS
70.13	Northwick's] A; Northwicks AMS
70.22	away] A; off AMS
70.29	friend's] A; f/friend's AMS
71.5	projected] A; projected/ed AMS
71.21	Wellwater.] A; ~ AMS
71.25	comforting] A; comfort/ng AMS
71.29	Michael's,"] A; ~" AMS
71.30	station.] A; ~ AMS

71.33	snow.] A; ~; AMS
73.1	said] A; spoke AMS
73.3	it] A; the answer AMS
73.4	the answer] A; it AMS
73.6	his hand] A; hishand AMS
73.15	alone."] A; alone."/X AMS
73.18	lounge] A; bed AMS
73.19	explained] A; then explained AMS
73.30	go. She] A; ~. ¶ "~ AMS
73.33–34	the accident] A; her accident AMS
73.37	lounge] A; bed AMS
74.5	not? I] A; ~?" "~ AMS
74.5	four or five] A; five or six AMS
74.37	here—whether] A; ~— —~ AMS
75.4	lounge] A; bed AMS
75.5	knot] A; high French knot AMS
75.6	said,] A; ~ AMS
75.15	him] A; his AMS
75.20	it.] A; it. Women of her class are brought up so that they cannot imagine such things. AMS
76.1	alone,] A; ~. AMS
76.5	Wellwater] A; Ethan AMS
76.23	at the] A; at her the AMS
76.23	self-discouragement] A; sef-discouragement AMS
76.26	Wellwater] A; Ethan AMS
76.31	Boston.] A; ~.. AMS
77.5	when] A; When AMS
78.16	sort] A; s/sort AMS
78.20	poor] A; p/poor AMS
78.20	ugly."] A; ugly. How soon," he mused aloud, "we begin to talk of people in the preterites, after their death. And it isn't certain yet that he's dead." AMS
79.34	Northwick's,] A; ~. AMS
80.5	intervals] A; intervalis AMS
80.5	punging.] A; ~.. AMS
80.12	telegram."] A; ~".. AMS
80.14	what it] A; what AMS
80.18	Well,"] A; ~, AMS
80.25	Me.] A; Me. he must AMS

80.26	to Wellwater] A; there AMS
80.27	Come;] A; Come; you must AMS
80.33	borne] A; b/borne AMS
80.36	wouldn't] A; would't AMS
81.2	you!"] A; ~.!" AMS
81.6	other] A; o/other AMS
82	XIII] A; XI AMS
*82.6–7	*The Boston Events*] A; The Boston Events AMS
82.11	conversable] A; converseble AMS
83.9	hot mince-pie] A; hot-mince pie AMS
83.36	Newton] A; Gerry AMS
84.2–3	much as] A; much as as AMS
84.3	dependence] A; dependance AMS
85.6	wrong.] A; ~,. AMS
85.7	Putneys] A; Putney's AMS
85.9–10	but not] A; but with not AMS
85.15	than] A; thah AMS
85.17	I d'] A; I'd' AMS
85.23	any lawyer] A; anybody AMS
85.29	man] A; ~, AMS
*85.32	pie] C; ~. AMS; ~, A, S, B
85.33	brought.] A; ~ AMS
86.6	Northwick] A; ~, AMS
86.36	he] A; the landlady AMS
87.9	the] A; the. AMS
87.11	when,"] A; ~" AMS
87.14	Ponkwasset] A; "~ AMS
87.17–18	Union and Dominion] A; Connecticut River AMS
87.21	that's . . . winter] A; *om.* AMS
87.26	the kitchen, and] A; her kitchen, & AMS
88.7	If] A; No, AMS
88.7	hain't,] hain't; but AMS
89.7	"I'd] A; ~ AMS
89.9	between] A; beetween AMS
89.11	sympathy] A; sympat/thy AMS
89.15	other] A; ~, AMS
90.2	two.] A; ~." AMS
90.3	exclusive?"] A; exclusive? Dear little isle—ile-will —of yours, ours?" AMS

92	XIV] A; XII AMS
92.9	copy.] A; copy. a work of art. AMS
92.16	intelligence.] A; ~ AMS
93.16	sorry] A; sorry not AMS
93.16	you,] A; ~ AMS
93.21	Adeline.] A; ~ AMS
93.30	this] A; the AMS
93.34	some] A; several AMS
94.19–20	Union and Dominion] A; Connecticut AMS
95.15	troubles."] A; ~. AMS
95.25	I] A; I I AMS
95.25	as] A; as as AMS
95.31	Pinney] A; Purdy AMS
96.3–4	people,] A; ~. AMS
96.4	interview.] A; ~, AMS
96.8	to publish] A; to to publish AMS
96.22	"This] A; ~ AMS
96.29	Manton] A; Maxwell AMS
96.31	Manton] A; Maxwell AMS
97.2	Manton. ¶ "We] HE; Maxwell. ¶ "We AMS; Manton. "We A, S, B–C
97.4	it] A; *om.* AMS
97.8	coat,] A; coat, to AMS
97.20	his] A; his his AMS
98.5	if] A; if if AMS
98.6	take] A; take all AMS
98.14	Wellwater] A; Newport AMS
98.15	myself,] A; ~ AMS
98.16	wasn't] A; was AMS
98.24	fellow himself,] A; ~, ~ AMS
98.25	women] A; woman AMS
98.31	brought in] A; brought AMS
99.14	tendency] A; tendeacy AMS
99.27	Pinney's] A; Purdy's AMS
99.29	without] A; with out AMS
100	XV] A; XIII AMS
100.1	Maxwell's] A; Meredith's AMS
101.19	you] A; ~, AMS
102.26	merely] A; merley AMS

102.31	she said,] A; *om.* AMS
102.34	her] A; hir AMS
102.34	this] A; that AMS
102.35	sense of] A; sense o/of AMS
103.9	on mischief] A; o/on miachief AMS
103.13–14	Before he knew] A; He did not know AMS
103.14	he had] A; but he AMS
103.20–21	direction,] A; ~ AMS
103.23	a] A; a a AMS
103.34	at a] A; at at AMS
103.37	picture,] A; ~. AMS
104.24	Maxwell] A; Meredith AMS
104.25	experience] A; experence AMS
105.1	eyes] A; eyss AMS
105.5	to. I] A; ~,. "~ AMS
105.7	nonsense.] A; ~ AMS
105.14	Matt] A; he AMS
105.15	Wellwater] A; Newport AMS
105.16	involve] A; i/involve AMS
105.17	how he] A; how Matt AMS
105.19	Hilary,] A; ~; AMS
105.21	Maxwell] A; Meredith AMS
105.27	Louise] A; "~ AMS
105.27–28	intelligent,] A; ~ AMS
105.28	in] A; ~, AMS
106.3	Maxwell] A; Meredith AMS
107	XVI] A; XIV AMS
*107.4	extending] A; extanding AMS
107.7	your] A; you' AMS
107.8	I–] A; I–I AMS
107.9	I–I–] A; ~–~ AMS
107.14	use] A; *om.* AMS
107.16	invitation] A; invi/tion AMS
107.21	Wellwater] A; Newport AMS
107.21	ground.] A; ~ AMS
108.4	what] A; *om.* AMS
108.5	annoyances] A; annoyances/ances AMS
108.16–17	did . . . conversation] A; rose from the place where he had been sitting AMS

108.24	him?"] A; ~? AMS
108.28	"You] A; ~ AMS
109.13	was a] A; was AMS
109.23	time in"—] HE; time in your stocking-feet?" AMS; time in—" A, S, B–C
109.25	I] A; "~ AMS
109.28	in] A; ~, AMS
110.3	papa!"] A; ~! AMS
110.5	seem much impressed even after] A; exactly leap for joy when AMS
110.6	had] A; *om.* AMS
110.14	father,"] A; ~, AMS
111	XVII] A; XV AMS
111.1	on him] A; of the Board AMS
111.24	monster] A; mon/ter AMS
112.4	and] A; *om.* AMS
112.5	conductor;] A; conductor and AMS
112.5–6	with the operator] A; *om.* AMS
112.6–7	asking to . . . Wellwater, and] A; *om.* AMS
112.9	death.] A; death. The dispatch was dated at White River, and asked to have a chair reserved in the Pullman from Wellwater. AMS
112.10	definite] A; only definite AMS
112.36	her] A; his AMS
113.5	her father] A; he AMS
113.12	them] A; her AMS
113.13	their] A; her AMS
113.13	they were] A; she was AMS
113.31	proudly,] A; ~ AMS
115.6	upon] A; into AMS
115.7	strange] A; wild AMS
115.10	were] A; were theirs, AMS
115.10	to them] A; *om.* AMS
115.11	was] A; seemed AMS
115.15	stain of a] A; stain as of AMS
115.17	Against] A; But against AMS
116	XVIII] A; XVI AMS
117.2	Boston. ¶ In] A; ~. ~ AMS
117.14	behavior] A; character AMS

117.16	him.] A; him. Pinney employed the gossip and conjecture he had picked up in the village to paint an imaginary figure of Suzette, whose hopes in life were blighted by her father's crime, and he left it to be supposed that he had met both the ladies in the visit which the Events young man had paid to the Home of the Defaulter. AMS
118.19	The report] A; It AMS
118.26–27	temperament] A; tempeament AMS
118.27	from the] A; from th/the AMS
118.30	temperaments] A; temperamenwts AMS
118.34	of the] A; of th/the AMS
119.21	journalism;] A; journalism, and AMS
119.21	a] A; such a AMS
119.21	and it] A; that it AMS
120.7	'onto'] A; "~" AMS
120.7	thing?"] A; ~"? AMS
120.15	do the work] A; go ahead AMS
120.18	fact] A; affair AMS
120.21	morning to begin,] A; ~, ~ ~ AMS
120.22	Hilarys'] A; Hilary's AMS
120.23	the house] A; his mother AMS
121.30	began] A; ~, AMS
121.34–35	sometimes] A; ometimes AMS
122.1	boldness] A; b/boldness AMS
122.19	emptiness] A; e/emptiness AMS
122.25	Maxwell] A; Meredith AMS
122.25	mother] A; mother with a kiss of simple hearted rapture AMS
122.26	going] A; going/ing AMS
122.30	was] A; *om.* AMS
122.35	slept] A; sleep AMS
123.23	Maxwell] A; Meredith AMS
123.32	were] A; was AMS
124.4	when . . . together] A; while they were at dinner AMS
124.14	his] A; *om.* AMS
124.23	to the reader] A; *om.* AMS
124.24	offence] A; offence to the reader AMS

124.30	evident] A; tedious AMS
125.28	this] A; one AMS
125.29	that] A; another AMS
127	XIX] A; XVII AMS
127.3	last. They] A; ~. ¶ ~ AMS
127.19	duty.] A; ~, AMS
127.23	but] A; and AMS
128.1	them] A; them them AMS
128.15	out,] A; ~. AMS
129.7	willing] A; willing and eager AMS
129.33	doesn't begin] A; doesn't began AMS
*130.1	Mrs.] A; Mrs AMS
130.15	and Mrs.] A; and would more pitilessly exact eye for eye and tooth for tooth than a man would. Mrs AMS
131.4	rest] A; bless AMS
131.4	C] A; ~. AMS
131.8	A's] A; As AMS
131.35	Hilary?] A; ~?. AMS
132.2	him,] A; *om.* AMS
132.10	dishonest] A; a thief AMS
132.16	needn't] A; mustn't AMS
132.34	what] A; what all AMS
134.22	both;] A; both: the one to say it and the other to think it, AMS
135	XX] A; XVIII AMS
135.7	possible] A; possible only AMS
135.14	Northwick's] A; Northwicks AMS
135.20	encouraged] A; recognized AMS
135.24	through] A; though AMS
136.8–9	behind. ¶ Day] A; ~. ~ AMS
137.16	morning] A; evening AMS
137.34	spree] A; last spree AMS
137.34	past] A; long past AMS
138.6	circus-clothes."] A; her night-clothes. AMS
138.12	Northwicks, personally,] A; Northwicks AMS
138.13	part] A; parts AMS
138.24	strikers] A; ~, AMS
138.25	shops] A; ~. AMS

139.27	was eager] A; desired it AMS
140.1	and, reflecting] A; and when they reflected AMS
140.2	many of them] A; they AMS
140.14	as] A; *om.* AMS
140.14	Dominion] A; Dom/ion AMS
140.33	him.] A; ~ AMS
141	XXI] A; XIX AMS
141.11	the masks we wear to] A; all the shows and masks of AMS
142.10	he allowed] A; and allow AMS
142.11–12	regrets and . . . lawyer.] A; regrets. AMS
142.15	to the deuce] A; the devil AMS
142.37	but] A; *om.* AMS
143.1	stay] A; stay/stay AMS
143.1	so badly] A; badly AMS
143.7	was the] A; *om.* AMS
144.2	hopelessly] A; hoplessly AMS
144.7	friend:] A; ~. AMS
144.17	to] A; to to AMS
144.28	her voice] A; them AMS
145.25	you,] A; you, you, AMS
145.37	parted] A; parted parted AMS
146.6	Northwicks] A; Northwick's AMS
146.7	he] A; He AMS
146.9	Northwicks, though] A; Northwick's; but AMS
146.12	her.] A; her. ¶ Louise was a worlding, on principle and from the reasoned conviction that the world was lovely, and that there was no wrong in it that could not be set right. She saw very little that seemed to her evil. There were some things that were mistaken, and uncomfortable, and askew, like this whole affair of poor Mr. Northwick's; but they could be got over, or got round, if one used a little tact or patience with them; and they were not what one would call wicked. ¶ Her optimism was a family joke, but perhaps in dealing, as it did, with ends rather than means, it was not optimism of a peculiarly ridiculous type. AMS
147	XXII] A; XIX AMS

148.24	personal] A; ~. AMS
150.11	desire] A; desire he felt AMS
150.14	were] A; *om.* AMS
150.15	Poor] A; Even AMS
150.34	it, both] A; ~ ~, AMS
151.6	perfect] A; heroic AMS
151.12	will] A; will all AMS
151.14	will be] A; *om.* AMS
151.25	good] A; *om.* AMS
152.4	how] A; why AMS
152.11	them. We] A; them, and now *we* will pay them. But we AMS
152.28	wished] A; meant AMS
153.4	or"—] HE; or affect you in my eyes." AMS; or—" A, S, B–C
154	XXIII] A; XXI AMS
154.22	agreed to ask] A; asked AMS
155.15	was the] A; was one of the AMS
155.16	lawyer] A; lawyers AMS
155.20	father,] A; father, and talked against him; AMS
155.33	this noon] A; last week AMS
155.35	Putney, "that] A; ~ ~ AMS
157.36	you] A; *om.* AMS
158.5	Northwicks] A; Northwick's AMS
158.15	him.] A ~ AMS
159	XXIV] A; XXII AMS
159.1–2	had to avail] A; availed AMS
159.26–160.1	and she lived . . . . He] A; *om.* AMS
160.29	sojourn] A; ~, AMS
160.33	decidedly.] A; ~., AMS
161.1	proposing to become] A; becoming AMS
161.3	concerning] A; concerning the AMS
161.3	land-values] A; increment AMS
161.4	these] A; it AMS
161.8	Hatboro'] A; Hatboro AMS
161.9	working] A; honest AMS
161.10	get] A; make AMS
161.12	any] A; in any case a AMS
161.16	To] A; *om.* AMS

161.16	Gerrish] A; ~; AMS
161.26	citizens] A; citizens and citizenesses AMS
162.25	was] A; is was AMS
162.31	Adeline's] A; her AMS
165.12	pursuit.] A; pursuit. Perhaps the part had its own charm for him. AMS
165.23	Wellwater] A; Newport AMS
165.34	Hilary had] A; ~, ~ AMS
166.7	ship was] A; ships were AMS
166.9	twelve] A; fifteen AMS
166.22	seemed] A; would be AMS
166.23	own] A; real AMS
167.16	this] A; his AMS
171.1	region] A; hills AMS
171.2	found] A; found in the hills, AMS
171.10	utilize] A; utilizi AMS
171.20	go] A; go go AMS
*172.2	St.] A; St AMS
172.5	stages,] A; ~. AMS
172.6	between.] A; ~ AMS
*172.11–12	Ha-ha] HE; Haha AMS, A, B–C; Ha! ha! S
172.12	miles;] A; ~.; AMS
172.22	alone] A; *om.* AMS
172.22	worth] A; alone worth AMS
172.29	Work] A; Working AMS
172.29	set] A; setting AMS
173.22	was] A; seemed AMS
173.31	hung;] A; ~,; AMS
174.4	blue] A; blue of AMS
*174.17	carrioles] A; carioles AMS
174.24	to house-front] A; to house front AMS
174.33	days] A; life AMS
176.9	Northwick's] A; Northwicks AMS
176.15	the broker] A; broker AMS
176.17	caps in] A; caps AMS
176.21	about him in it] A; in it about home AMS
176.24	offence] A; frauds AMS
177.10	forty-two] A; forty four AMS
177.10	bulk,] A; ~ AMS

177.14–15	expected,] A; ~ AMS
177.16–17	logging camps. Some took a] A; logging. Some of them took AMS
177.22	was curiously] A; felt curiously AMS
177.33	he was] A; he meant AMS
178.12	pains] A; frauds AMS
178.13	pilgrimage] A; pilgrim AMS
178.23	hurts] A; hurt AMS
178.27	district,] A; *om.* AMS
178.27	be] A; *om.* AMS
179.1	be] A; *om.* AMS
179.4	to go] A; go AMS
181.11–12	farther and farther] A; further and farther AMS
181.23	as if] A; if AMS
181.24	restored] A; gave back AMS
182.10	contour] A; countour AMS
182.16	about] A; abut AMS
182.19	used to be] A; was AMS
182.34	States.] A; ~ AMS
183.7	soon as] A; *om.* AMS
184.1	lightly] A; swiftly AMS
185.1–2	not go back to them] A; let them mourn him dead AMS
185.3	live,] A; live again, AMS
185.3	die] A; really die AMS
185.21	pleasure.] A; pleasure. Then Hilary laid his hand on his shoulder, and said he had a warrant for him, and one of the directors began feeling for his belt. AMS
185.33	face] A; ~; AMS
186.11	to see] A; see AMS
186.32	accomplishment] A; accomplish- AMS
187.8	Canadian] A; ~, AMS
188.15	gayety,] A; ~ AMS
188.18	opened] A; gave AMS
188.25	weak] A; worn, and beaten AMS
190.16	place.] A; ~ AMS
190.19	and then] A; an/and then AMS
190.28	right, and] A; right— AMS

190.31	through the vagary] A; through all the vagueness AMS
190.36	gate?] A; gate? Damn fool! AMS
191.22	and] A; an/and AMS
191.23	aid.] A; aid. "I helped to undress a great many of your countrymen, when I used to go into the bush with them." AMS
192.5	efforts,] A; ~ AMS
192.18	nature] A; ~; AMS
192.20	voices of women] A; women's voices AMS
192.21	daughters'] A; daughter's AMS
192.22	let] A; be let AMS
*192.26	Étienne] A; Etienne AMS
193.2	hands] A; heads AMS
193.23	fact.] A; fact, and AMS
194.23	seaside, at] A; seaside— AMS
194.32	too."] A; ~. AMS
195.4	railroad stocks] A; railroads AMS
195.10	earn?] A; earn, or only enough to leave themselves a profit? AMS
195.11	miserable.] A; miserable; that they rebel against their hard conditions, and then they have to be shot. AMS
195.13	questions] A; ~; AMS
195.15	he] A; Northwick AMS
197.5	not] A; not not AMS
197.22	Bird's] A; his AMS
199.1	once.] A; once, as if he had risen suddenly out of some gulf of deep waters into the full light of day. AMS
199.36	blew] A; seemed to blow AMS
199.36	birds] A; summer birds, AMS
200.1	woods] A; woods; he heard the blackbirds drifting over head AMS
200.13	where] A; that AMS
200.14	go] A; go in AMS
201.6	come through safely] A; escaped AMS
201.6	Their] A; Their congratulations and AMS
201.7	as] A; and AMS

201.8	visits] A; visit AMS
201.9	begun] A; began AMS
201.18	develop] A; develope AMS
202.4	have] A; have have AMS
203.18	accidents] A; accidents that he had AMS
204.5	share] A; take part in AMS
204.14	different men] A; all classes AMS
204.15	suggestion,] A; interest and suggestion, inflaming the fancy and corrupting the will of the ignorant with dreams of sudden gains, AMS
204.28	delicately] A; delecately AMS
205.4	and] A; and then AMS
205.6	bateau] A; batteau AMS
205.7	was] A; was now AMS
205.7	the St. Lawrence.] A; the the St Lawrence, and that the first steamboat of the season had already come down from Quebec. AMS
205.9	steamboats] A; boats AMS
205.23	came to] A; came a AMS
205.26	Rimouski] A; Rimourski AMS
205.26	Père] A; Pére AMS
205.34	Rimouski] A; Rimourski AMS
206.11	pressed] A; pushed AMS
206.12	are."] A; ~" AMS
206.28	Northwick's] A; Northwick AMS
206.32	Rimouski] A; Rimourski AMS
207.6	which] A; which might so well be stolen money, and which AMS
207.7	way; at once] A; way: AMS
207.7	danger] A; danger to them all AMS
207.8	known.] A; known. It made Bird afraid of himself, of the doctor who shared the secret with him, and of the whole community ignorant of it. AMS
207.8	poor, who] A; poor AMS
207.15	about] A; about his cabin AMS
207.15–16	alms that kind people leave out-doors] A; alms left out AMS
207.16	sleep.] A; sleep. If Northwick died or were killed, suspicion would first fall upon the house of Bird. AMS

207.18	neglect; but] A; neglect. He lost his appetite and AMS
207.21	thought] A; *om.* AMS
207.22	believed] A; thought AMS
208.2	Rimouski] A; Rimourski AMS
208.5	trying] A; then trying AMS
208.10	of the] A; to come from AMS
209.8	sufficient] A; possible woman in the case, as the AMS
209.9	peculations; its] A; speculations; her AMS
209.37	Hilary's] A; Hilarys AMS
210.7	spoons] A; spoons spoons AMS
211.26	farm."] A; farm. He's mother, is the relict of a country AMS
211.31	him,] A; *om.* AMS
213.3	or five] A; *om.* AMS
213.31	restitution] A; making restitution AMS
214.14	here] A; there AMS
214.22	Hilary] A; Hilary's AMS
214.31	for] A; *om.* AMS
216.3	clean] A; clear AMS
216.7	opinions] A; views AMS
216.7	subject] A; topic AMS
216.16	inconsistent] A; inconsastent AMS
216.21	Mrs. Munger] A; Mr Munger AMS
216.23	it.] A; ~ AMS
217.3	man] A; man in him AMS
217.4	does.] A; ~." AMS
217.5	they don't] A; it doesn't AMS
217.5–6	every one . . . woman] A; the women AMS
217.23	Dr.] A; Dr AMS
217.29	was burned] A; had been killed AMS
218.2	homœopathy] A; homeopathy AMS
218.7	pass] A; surround AMS
218.23	help] A; help against it AMS
219.7	he'd] A; and AMS
219.29	dismay.] A; ~ AMS
220.32	now] A; now, if AMS
220.35	needn't] A; needed AMS
221.22	please] A; choose AMS

222.25	Your] A; You're AMS
222.32	it has] A; it has it has AMS
223.5	wares.] A; wares. Abstractly, a thing like that can't *have* a moral claim. AMS
223.8	Putney] A; ~, AMS
227.20	just] A; right AMS
227.28	wrong; and] A; wrong; she did not know that it always did, and so AMS
227.32–33	church, and] A; church. Wade was AMS
227.33	letter.] A; letter, but Matt showed himself impatient of the discussion. AMS
228.5	speak] A; talk AMS
228.25	preference] A; happiness AMS
228.31	him] A; him laxly, and AMS
228.32	air, at first] A; air AMS
228.34	cold] A; selfishly cold AMS
228.35	sometimes] A; *om.* AMS
229.7	final] A; electrical AMS
229.9	hand] A; hand without loss of time AMS
229.15	really] A; possibly AMS
231.2	out, sometimes he] A; out and sometimes him AMS
231.31	true;] A; ~,; AMS
232.26	social] A; literary and social AMS
232.27–28	he . . . he's] A; the boy's AMS
234.21	figure] A; presence AMS
235.18	well.] A; ~." AMS
235.33	should] A; am truly your friend, and would AMS
236.6	thinks] A; wants AMS
236.7	ought to] A; should AMS
236.7	bank] A; bank here AMS
236.10	say] A; say say AMS
236.15	lawsuit] A; ~. AMS
236.19	money."] A; money. The papers say the corporations own the courts; and in such a good cause"— AMS
237.14	rascal] A; scoundrel AMS
237.16–20	property, and as . . . told me of."] A; property." AMS

237.21–23	Hilary, "I . . . . hers.] A; Hilary "she's a fine girl. AMS
237.25	one.] A; one. She's a magnificent creature. She would make him a noble wife—or any one. AMS
238.15	It] A; It's AMS
238.19	daughter] A; children AMS
238.20	her to] A; them AMS
238.22	right. You] A; right." ¶ "Yes, and as I understood Miss Northwick, that was her sister's first impulse. She wished to give up her half of the estate unconditionally; but Miss Northwick wouldn't consent, and they compromised on the conditions she told me of." ¶ "Well," said Hilary "I think Miss Northwick showed the most sense. But of course that's a noble girl. She almost transfigures that old scoundrel of a father of hers. Matt, you AMS
238.36	mood.] A; ~ AMS
239.7	herself a] A; herself AMS
240.13	pause, "that] A; ~ ~ AMS
241.31	*nolle prosequi*] A; nolle prosequi AMS
241.32	the fact of absconding] A; absconding beyond its jurisdiction AMS
241.32	court] A; the court before which he was indicted AMS
242.2	it] A; ~. AMS
242.5	said,] A; said, with a sort of tetanic force, AMS
242.10	all the] A; just the AMS
242.10	same."] A; same." ¶ Suzette remained looking down, and made no sign of leaving. AMS
243.16	destitute] A; distitute AMS
244.3	Northwicks] A; Northwick's AMS
244.6	go] A; *om.* AMS
244.13	doesn't] A; doesnt AMS
245.14–15	I don't] A; "~ ~ AMS
245.20	pause] A; silence AMS
245.22	there] A; over AMS
246.24	romantic;] A; ~.; AMS
247.1	"She's] A; ~ AMS
247.3	himself. "Is] A; ~. ¶ "~ AMS

247.4   asked,] A; ~. AMS
248.2   all that] A; what AMS
250.9   cork helmet topping] A; a cork helmet over AMS
250.31   sickening] A; shocking AMS
251.23   little] A; *om.* AMS
252.6–7   Poverty obliges, as well as nobility.] A; *Pauvreté oblige.* AMS
252.8   Pride obliges, too.] A; *Fiereté oblige.* AMS
252.30   inflexible] A; lofty AMS
253.33   isn't] A; wasn't AMS
254.3   this:] S; ~. AMS, A
254.15   see . . . time] A; know what his feelings were AMS
256.26   to] A; too AMS
257.18   dangerous."] A; dangerous." ¶ This is what the moth probably says of the candle, when it tacitly decides to look into it farther. AMS
257.32   Nectar.] A; ~.. AMS
258.7   "I've] A; ~ AMS
258.34–35   Rimouski] A; Rimourski AMS
259.32   Northwick's] A; Northwicks AMS
260.14   Matt.] A; Matt, thoughtfully. He was asking himself whether the artistic use of life, which Maxwell evidently prided himself on was so much higher, or so very different from those businesses, which he scorned. But he asked Maxwell, AMS
260.17   "He] A; " "~ AMS
260.24   kind-hearted] A; devoted AMS
261.25   after a] A; after AMS
261.36   Mr.] A; *om.* AMS
262.14   obstinacy] A; obstinacey AMS
262.27   present] A; its present AMS
262.34   next] A; same AMS
263.33   pleasantly;] A; ~,; AMS
264.12   no] A; no no AMS
265.16   visage;] A; ~,; AMS
265.19–20   away. ¶ He] A; ~. ~ AMS
266.20   do,] A; ~," AMS
267.33–34   you to let me] A; to AMS
267.36   not. Couldn't] A; ~."–~ AMS

268.11	do] A; *om.* AMS
268.24	true] A; noble AMS
269.3	again] A; *om.* AMS
270	XVIII] A; XVII AMS
270.22	yielded ... yielded] A; given up ... given up AMS
270.25–26	something I've ... said, "We] A; this reporter's enterprise. We AMS
270.26	it] A; him AMS
271.1	of her father with] A; it over before AMS
271.2	began] A; began with AMS
271.12	trouble] A; be troubled AMS
271.15	it.] A; it. I want to do what's right. AMS
271.19	you?"] A; ~." AMS
271.24	and I] A; and I I AMS
271.33	wouldn't] A; needn't AMS
272.29	him, once] A; him AMS
273.14	came] A; *om.* AMS
273.36	Well, of course] A; Not to others AMS
274.7	its] A; its' AMS
274.16	apologies.] A; ~ AMS
274.21	good] A; nice AMS
274.30	last] A; end AMS
274.33	"that] A; ~ AMS
276	XIX] A; XVIII AMS
277.35–36	been ... had] A; *om.* AMS
278.1	wrong-doer;] A; wrong-doer, and that AMS
278.23	more sacred] A; higher or sacreder AMS
279.29	It's] A; Its AMS
279.35	Matt,] A; Matt, that AMS
279.36	on?"] A; ~? AMS
280.5	queer] A; radical AMS
280.7	course has] A; career AMS
*280.26	Caryl] HE; Cyril AMS, A, S, B–C
280.27	one of ourselves] A; a gentleman AMS
280.29	what one calls a gentleman. With] A; a gentleman? He hasn't the feelings of a gentleman, you must see that," Mrs. Hilary urged. ¶ "Very few men have the feelings of a gentleman," Matt conceded. ¶ "With AMS

280.30	experiences; all] A; companionships; AMS
280.31	be] A; be a gentleman AMS
280.33	gifts,] A; gifts, he might have AMS
281.2	don't you see?] A; it would go for nothing. AMS
281.12	writing. "The] A; writing. "There is no doubt but we have talked all sorts of lying nonesense about self made men. The AMS
281.14	kind of inferior,] A; social inferior AMS
281.16	successful] A; self-made AMS
281.16	fiercer] A; greedier AMS
281.17	one] A; the AMS
281.21	bread] A; life AMS
281.22–24	mother; and if . . . of her sort.] A; mother. It's atrocious that a man naturally so fine and rare as Maxwell cannot have the feelings of a gentleman; but I admit that he can't. They are the birthright of every one, but long before most men were born the share they ought to have had was bartered for a mess of pottage. AMS
281.35	come] A; come some time AMS
282.4	Adeline] A; old maid AMS
282.12	Those women are] A; They're AMS
282.34–283.1	incredible./XX/ ¶ The] A; incredible. the AMS
283.1–2	forecast. Mrs.] A; forecast./XIX/ ¶ Mrs. AMS
283.19	suffer] A; follow AMS
283.21	includes] A; includes and adopts AMS
284.21	proud. I] A; proud. ¶ I AMS
284.29	instead] A; in stead AMS
284.37	She's] A; She's a AMS
285.7	good] A; noble AMS
285.12	Suzette] A; Suzette is a splendid girl, and AMS
286.20	hope, his] A; hope, his his AMS
287.7	either] A; you either AMS
287.8	Northwick] A; Northway AMS
287.11	that] A; her AMS
288.18	obliquities] A; rascalities AMS
288.19	oblique] A; a rascal AMS
289.5	she's] A; she's a noble creature—she's AMS
289.7	help] A; help respecting her, AMS

289.15	that—] A; that—infernal scoundrel. AMS
290.3	him.] A; him. Maxwell says he'll be faithful to us if we employ him. AMS
290.4	service:] A; service. He's entirely safe; AMS
290.13	why we shouldn't] A; but we should AMS
290.15	back?] A; ~. AMS
290.25	he] A; he recognized and AMS
291.23–24	afterwards] A; *om.* AMS
292	XXI] A; XX AMS
292.5	taken.] A; taken. She had set out to break off the growing affair between Maxwell and Louise and she did not pause from the moment she resolved upon it. AMS
293.6	promptly;] A; ~;, AMS
294.11	society] A; social AMS
294.12	community, and] A; community, and people outside think we're very literary, and all that; and I dare say we *do* care more for literature than most people; but you've only to look over your acquaintance, Louise, and see whether there are any literary men who have the first place. I know that AMS
294.17	it. If such] A; it." ¶ "That's partly their own fault; they wont come, often." ¶ "Yes, that's true," said Mrs. Hilary. "If AMS
294.27–28	might . . . people] A; can't have the feelings of a gentleman, as we understand it AMS
294.32–33	society . . . minding] A; feelings of a gentleman were not worth what they cost other people AMS
294.33	nonsense.] A; nonesense. He believes that if we lived rightly everybody could have them at no expense to anybody else. AMS
295.2–3	though, and] A; though, and you must AMS
295.3	understand distinctly] A; ~, ~ AMS
295.10	Louise. I] A; Louise. Whatever your feeling is in regard to this young man, there's no doubt of his toward you"— ¶ "No; I suppose not," murmured Louise. ¶ "I AMS
295.16	Northwicks] A; Northwick's AMS

295.20–21   her and Adeline] A; them AMS
295.31   wouldn't,] A; ~. AMS
296.3   'Want] A; "~ AMS
296.3   know,'] A; ~", AMS
296.4   How?'] A; ~?,' AMS
296.24   said] A; cried AMS
296.26   ran] A; has run AMS
296.29   society man] A; gentleman AMS
297.3   there,] A; there weeping AMS
297.12   you."] A; you," and she tripped down the steps and swept across the grassy slope with a pace that left Maxwell's invalid languor behind. AMS
297.16   turned] A; turned round AMS
297.35   society man] A; gentleman AMS
298.2   small attentions] A; the *convenances* AMS
298.6   possible.] A; possible. Perhaps she was so intent upon what she wished to say that she could not look closely into the matter. But through all she felt herself above him, and she was now, as always, piqued that he seemed not to know their social difference. AMS
298.19–23   "I . . . . make it,"] A; "And you remember what I said of Sue Northwick?" ¶ "Yes—partially." ¶ "Well, now, we are all going to know how she feels, and to understand how hard it is to be forgiven for disgrace we didn't bring on ourselves. My brother is going to marry her." ¶ Maxwell puckered his mouth to the whistle he did not permit to escape. This could not be what she wished him to be patient with, to take in the right way. He had nothing whatever to do with it. But apparently she expected him to say something, and he said: "I should think the fact that your brother was going to do it was sufficient to transmute any disgrace there was into honor." That sounded rather fine; Maxwell was not ashamed of it as literature. ¶ The tears flashed into the girl's eyes. "Oh, you *do* appreciate Matt, don't you? Don't you think he's glorious? Magnificent?" ¶ "I never

saw any one like him," said Maxwell, with sincerity. ¶ Her heart thrilled toward him in thankfulness for his generous praise. "Matt knows just how it will be looked at, but he doesn't care for anything but our feeling about it, and I shall take what you say as a good omen: you are the first one to know of it out of our own family. Of course, there is something Quixotic, I suppose, about Matt, and a good many people consider him a crank for trying to live the kind of life he believes in; but its a question whether they are not the cranks, trying to live a life that nobody believes in." ¶ "The life of the world?" Maxwell asked. ¶ "Yes; the life of the world. Perfectly hollow, and false. It makes me sick to think how vulgar it really is! Matt has chosen the true life, and I honor him for doing it," she ended passionately. ¶ "Then, why don't you choose it, too?" ¶ "If I were a man, I would." ¶ "Perhaps if I were a saint, I should, too," said Maxwell. ¶ "But you are very happy, here, away from the world; and yet you are not"— ¶ "A saint? No. But I'm sick. If I were well, I should want to be in the thick of the fight. I suppose that's because all my life has been a fight. I'm used to it; I suppose like it. Yes, and I like the world. It's a good enough world for me; I should like to be at the top of it; I'm miserable away from it. I think your brother is the finest fellow I ever knew; but I don't agree with him. He believes that the race can get on with a diet of vegetables and dumb animals. I don't believe it can. Men must eat men. The only way not to be eaten is to eat." ¶ "Yes," said Louise, sadly, absently. That was the way in the world, even as she had seen it. "But don't you think it's horrible?" ¶ "I didn't make the race," AMS

298.24   But I've] A; I've AMS
298.26-33   But I . . . . business."] A; I don't expect to give or to be given quarter. I'm not afraid but I shall

get on; and I'm not going to stop till I've seen the folly of it. I shall use every advantage I can get, and I shall expect others to do the same. Life means business." ¶ "Yes," she said vaguely again. She had found that society meant business, too; it certainly did not mean beauty. She felt a great soreness of heart, like the weight of a crushing disappointment. AMS

298.36–299.7   "Why . . . . Louise.] A; *om.* AMS

299.10–13   Vermont, where . . . . summer."] A; Vermont." AMS

299.14   faintly] A; lightly AMS

299.14   suddenly] A; *om.* AMS

299.26   so gayly] A; gayly, so gayly AMS

299.26   Maxwell] A; Maxwell self centred as he was AMS

299.30   capricious] A; *om.* AMS

299.36   dreaded.] A; dreaded. ¶ Louise broke out fiercely, "Well, he is hard and ambitious and selfish! It's over, quite over! You needn't be afraid of his interesting me too much, any more. He wont interest me at all; I understand him! Do you know what I had made up my mind to do, mamma? If I found he was really high and noble, I was going to offer him that money Aunt Martha left me, so that he could have a chance to write the things he wants to, and I was going to take the consequences! But I found him a mere egotist at heart! Talk about giving up the world! If he had been brought up in the worldiest society, he could be more worldly. It's everything to him; I can see that; and his literature is only a means to an end! Oh, what a happy girl Sue Northwick is, to have a man like Matt—a man, *not* a tiger! And I would done everything for him!" ¶ "If you were really going to do what you say, my dear, "I'm heartily glad you found Mr. Maxwell out in time," said her mother with no great coherency, but sufficient clearness. "It would have been the most ridiculous thing in the world." AMS

303.13	than] A; *om.* AMS
303.24	all . . . them] A; all of them that was to be known AMS
303.32	people] A; citizens AMS
303.36	embezzlers] A; embezzlirs AMS
304.30	Rimouski] A; Rimourski AMS
304.31	*Events*] A; events AMS
305.3	Rimouski] A; Rimourski AMS
306.19	making] A; make AMS
306.21	'I] A; "∼ AMS
306.22	Markham,'] A; ∼," AMS
306.22	'I] A; "∼ AMS
306.23	him.' "] A; ∼." AMS
308.16	Rimouski] A; Rimourski AMS
308.21	Rimouski] A; Rimourski AMS
309.8	well as] A; well as well as AMS
309.16	Rimouski] A; Rimourski AMS
309.18	Rimouski] A; Rimourski AMS
309.29	made him submit] A; the submission of AMS
309.32	Rimouski] A; Rimourski AMS
309.34–35	who had . . . Northwick had] A; whom at the worst he knew nothing bad of AMS
310.8	there] A; here AMS
310.9	though] A; *om.* AMS
310.9–10	greatest] A; greatest native AMS
310.30	superscription.] A; superscription, and the seal stamped with the ring he had given her on her last birthday. AMS
311.20	apparently without] A; without apparently AMS
312.10	she] A; Sue had AMS
312.13	but] A; so much as AMS
313.1	Rimouski] A; Rimourski AMS
313.33	cautiously] A; guardedly AMS
314.34	ventured] A; went so far as AMS
314.37	Pinney] A; he AMS
315.5	don't,"] A; ∼"AMS
315.11	of the] A; of AMS
315.12	were] A; were were AMS
315.22	it!] A; it! I knew it! AMS

316.16	suffer.] A; suffer. The sophistry that had sustained when he tried to imagine the effect of his crime upon them, could not avail him in this stress. AMS
316.27	this one-sided] A; the absence of this AMS
316.34	not] A; *om.* AMS
317.5	with] A; *om.* AMS
317.12	It's] A; Its AMS
317.15	next] A; secret AMS
318.18	Why,] A; ~" AMS
318.36	Rimouski] A; Rimourski AMS
319.18	hour] A; time AMS
320.25	have] A; give him AMS
320.34	comfortable] A; comfortable with the affectionate care of a son AMS
321.3	Pinney] A; that he AMS
321.4	him] A; him all about himself, and AMS
321.33	now,"] A; ~", AMS
321.35	Rimouski] A; Rimourski AMS
323.14–15	the passengers] A; the the passengers AMS
323.28	said] A; *om.* AMS
323.32	for] A; *om.* AMS
324.1	course, . . . you.] A; course he thought you were a detective. AMS
324.11	known . . . about,] A; had some method in his madness AMS
325.19	he had] A; he AMS
326.2	the change in every detail] A; this change before he met his children AMS
326.15	of] A; of peril and AMS
327.8–9	have . . . vagrant.] A; pass his daughters' door as a vagrant, without danger of arrest. AMS
327.11	he believed] A; and he saw AMS
327.23	found] A; felt AMS
328.5	both] A; both both AMS
328.9	face. "What] A; ~. ¶ "~ AMS
328.9	are you] A; we AMS
328.12	d'know] A; d'now, AMS
328.15	Didn't] A; "~ AMS
328.21	"I] A; "Where your shoes. I AMS

328.35	only] A; sole AMS
329.5	treble] A; trebble AMS
329.10	lantern,] A; lantern. Neither Elbridge nor his wife spoke, AMS
329.12	them;] A; them; but AMS
330.3	gone] A; give AMS
330.11	see] A; see it AMS
331.22	at] A; in at AMS
331.23	footsteps] A; steps AMS
332.19	rustle of] A; rush of feet and AMS
332.23	sigh,] A; ~ AMS
332.24	All] A; She was his pet again; she was like a little child on his knee; all AMS
332.29	unity.] A; unity. Perhaps they were shocked too wholly out of custom to feel what was strange in one another; they lived in this moment of the present as if nothing had gone before or could come after. AMS
333.13	herself] A; her self AMS
333.15	go! He's] A; ~!" "~ AMS
333.21	wants] A; want's AMS
333.28–29	do to] A; do AMS
334.4	it. "Now] A; ~. ¶ "~ AMS
334.8	write,] A; ~ AMS
334.14	blame,] A; ~ AMS
335.16	Hatboro'] A; Hatboro AMS
337.11	distrusted] A; ~. AMS
337.13	would] A; *om.* AMS
337.15	night] A; ~, AMS
337.18	boasted,] A; ~ AMS
337.25	were] A; ware AMS
337.36	had] A; had he AMS
338.3	mechanical] A; mechanic AMS
338.4	him] A; *om.* AMS
338.14	'done.'] A; "~." AMS
338.16	resentment] A; extravagance AMS
338.20	blackest] A; strongest AMS
338.21	I seem] A; I I AMS
339	VIII] A; VII AMS

339.1	foreboding] A; anxiety AMS
340.5	get] A; send AMS
340.5	to stay with them] A; *om.* AMS
340.7	rectory] A; parsonage AMS
340.10	away.] A; away, and they met with grave faces. AMS
340.19	to quiet] A; at quieting AMS
340.33	Adeline] A; Adline AMS
341.5	and I] A; and I I AMS
341.31	her] A; her cold, AMS
342.4–5	compromises and] A; the conventional AMS
342.28	our] A; its AMS
342.29	our] A; its AMS
342.33	For answer, Matt told] A; He went on to tell AMS
343.3	himself] A; *om.* AMS
343.10	only] A; only possible AMS
343.13	this] A; this this AMS
334.9	At times] A; *om.* AMS
344.9	off] A; off, though AMS
346	IX] A; VIII AMS
346.13	in to] A; into AMS
346.24	seemed] A; semed AMS
347.3	Are] A; And are AMS
347.31	the] A; *om.* AMS
347.31–32	Adeline. Suzette] A; ~. ¶ ~ AMS
347.36	day] A; hour AMS
348.22	as he] A; he AMS
348.24	interested] A; sympathetic AMS
348.25	to] A; to to AMS
348.28	success] A; triumph AMS
349.11	been] A; *om.* AMS
349.21	the parents'] A; their AMS
349.27	been] A; been rather AMS
350	X] A; IX AMS
350.22	his] A; he AMS
350.25	again in] A; again AMS
*351.2	East] S; West AMS, A
352.28	little] A; little too AMS
352.36	start] A; ~. AMS

353.1	Northwick] A; Northway AMS
353.27	out] A; *om.* AMS
354.3	day] A; day/-wick AMS
354.25	again,"] A; ~," " AMS
354.27	all once more. "I'm] A; carefully over. "Then I'm AMS
355.4	Northwick] A; ~. AMS
356	XI] A; X AMS
358.7	*he*] A; he AMS
358.8	Suzette] A; Suzette that AMS
359.6	But] A; *om.* AMS
359.7	slipped] A; slipped out of AMS
359.21	Law] A; Providence AMS
359.25	Mercy."] A; Mercy."/*End.* AMS

Rejected Substantives

The following list records all substantive variants subsequent to the reading accepted at each point in the present edition which have been rejected as nonauthorial. The reading of the present edition appears to the left of the bracket; the source of that reading, followed by a semicolon, the subsequent variant reading or readings and their sources appear to the right of the bracket. The curved dash ∼ represents the same word that appears before the bracket and is used in recording punctuation and paragraphing variants. An asterisk indicates that the reading is discussed in the Textual Notes. *Om.* means that the reading to the left of the bracket does not appear in the text or texts cited to the right of the semicolon. Texts are listed here in the chronological order described in the Textual Commentary, page 377. If the authority for the present reading is other than copy-text, the copy-text reading is recorded in Emendations. The reading of any relevant text other than copy-text, if not listed here, may be presumed to agree with the reading to the left of the bracket, unless recorded in Emendations.

The following texts are referred to:

AMS   Printer's copy manuscript of *The Quality of Mercy*
A   Harper and Brothers, 1892: First Edition
S   New York *Sun*, 4 October 1891–3 January 1892
B   David Douglas, 1892
C   Harper and Brothers, [c 1891]

4.13	gi'] AMS; give A, S, B–C
*4.33	high land] AMS; highland A, S, B–C
6.28	woods] AMS; wood B
*6.34	luring] AMS; having A, S, B–C
8.25	proofs] AMS; proof A, S, B–C

*9.4   *mind*] AMS; mind S
10.23   wrong in] AMS; wrong to S
11.29   and then] AMS; *om.* S
12.35   sometimes] AMS; sometime S
14.17   was a] AMS; was a a S
14.19   determined] AMS; believed A, S, B–C
16.1   up into] AMS; up in S
16.14   scheme] AMS; schemes A, S, B–C
16.25–26   diaphanous] AMS; a diaphanous S
16.27   were] AMS; rose A, S, B–C
16.28   their] AMS; this A, S, B–C
*18.27   stairs landing] AMS; stair-landing A, B–C; stair landing S
19.5   self-repression] AMS; self-possession A, S, B–C
19.5–6   seated and silent] AMS; silent and seated A, S, B–C
19.18   simple] AMS; single A, S, B–C
20.5   face] AMS; fact C
21.30   you'd] AMS; you S
25.27   and whom] AMS; to whom S
25.28   leave to] A; leave S
26.30   that Northwick] AMS; when Northwick S
28.11   shake] AMS; to shake B
30.17   in there] AMS; there S
32.23   you're] AMS; you've A, S, B–C
35.33   were given] AMS; should get S
*36.11   on. He] AMS; ~. ¶ ~ A, S, B–C
37.3   book] AMS; books C
37.8   radicalism] AMS; radicalism had A, S, B–C
37.26   time] AMS; a time A, S, B–C
*38.6   *speak*] AMS; speak A, S, B–C
38.6–7   pulling] AMS; putting A, S, B–C
43.5   be easily] AMS; easily be S
49.5   resumed] AMS; returned A, S, B–C
49.14–15   room!" ¶ She] AMS; ~." ~ A, S, B–C
49.24–25   slowly. ¶ "You] AMS; ~. "~ A, S, B–C
51.2   to] AMS; into B
51.25   each other] AMS; one another C
53.12–13   had . . . Junction.] AMS; had, just after leaving the Junction, run off the track. A, S, B–C

55.9	could] HE; would A, S, B–C
58.8	talkin'] AMS; talking S
59.1	sufficiently recovered] AMS; recovered sufficiently A, S, B–C
60.3	guilty] AMS; quietly A, S, B–C
60.12	reappeared] AMS; appeared A, S, B–C
62.11–12	steam. ¶ Suzette] AMS; ~. ~ A, S, B–C
62.16	telephone and telegraph] AMS; telegraph and telephone A, S, B–C
64.24–25	rhythmical, free handed] AMS; free handed rhythmical A, S, B–C
*65.29	winding] AMS; *om.* A, S, B–C
69.36	alike on] AMS; alike in A, S, B–C
70.9	were the] AMS; were A, S, B–C
70.12	ignored as forgot] AMS; forgot as ignored A, S, B–C
70.31	sinuous] AMS; serious S
74.24	that] AMS; the B
74.26	had] AMS; *om.* A, S, B–C
76.36	surprise] AMS; surprise that S
78.9	was] AMS; is A, S, B–C
79.10	her jacket] AMS; the jacket A, S, B–C
79.19	could] AMS; should A, S, B–C
79.26–27	he was] AMS; eh was S
79.27–28	gone. ¶ The] AMS; ~. ~ A, S, B–C
79.30–31	Northwick. She] AMS; ~. ¶ ~ A, S, B–C
79.31	waitin'] AMS; waiting A, S, B–C
80.3	and which] AMS; which S
80.15	if it] AMS; if A
80.15	expected] AMS; expect C
82.2	the] AMS; *om.* A, S, B–C
*82.20	breath. "Baked] AMS; ~. ¶ "~ A, S, B–C
83.11–12	want?" ¶ She] AMS; ~?" ~ A, S, B–C
84.23	*Events*] AMS; *Events'* A, S, B–C
84.34	*Events*] AMS; *Events'* A, S, B–C
85.4	*Events*] AMS; *Events'* A, S, B–C
85.7	Putneys] A; Putney's S
85.19	see him] AMS; see S
86.36	*was*] AMS; was A, S, B–C
87.13	That] AMS; That's A, B–C

87.37	they's] AMS; they'd A, S, B–C
88.28–29	it. He] AMS; ~. ¶ ~ A, S, B–C
90.20	burnt] AMS; burned C
90.22	you're] AMS; you are S
90.34	you're] AMS; you are A, S, B–C
92.11	flat at] AMS; flat in A, S, B–C
93.3	know] AMS; knew A, S, B–C
94.1	one] AMS; but one S
*94.31	*anything*] AMS; anything A, S, B–C
95.27	should] HE; sh'd AMS, A, B–C; she'd S
97.7–8	you." ¶ He] AMS; ~." ~ A, S, B–C
98.14	should] AMS; should have S, C
98.34	clerks. At] AMS; ~. ¶ ~ A, S, B–C
101.33	began] AMS; begin S
102.4	him] AMS; him that A, S, B–C
102.13	them] AMS; him A, S, B–C
102.17	in Hatboro'] AMS; at Hatboro' S
102.31	he] AMS; he's A, S
104.27	gentleman] AMS; gentlemen S
104.34	didn't] AMS; don't S
105.15	on] AMS; in A, S, B–C
107.6	arm] AMS; door A, S, B–C
107.17	on. "I] AMS; ~. ¶ "~ A, S, B–C
108.16–17	did . . . conversation] A; rose from the place where he had been sitting S
109.1	would] AMS; could A, S, B–C
109.7	too] AMS; to S
109.35	mock-imploring] AMS; meek imploring A, S, B–C
110.4	amiability. She] AMS; ~. ¶ ~ A, S, B–C
110.7	grumped] AMS; grumbled A, S, B–C
111.14	have] AMS; *om.* S
111.20	burnt] AMS; burned C
112.17	were] AMS; was A, S, B–C
112.20	were] AMS; was A, S, B–C
113.17	off of] AMS; off A, S, B–C
115.1	that] AMS; which A, S, B–C
115.15	as of] AMS; of a A, S, B–C
117.9	reluctances] AMS; reluctance S
117.25	*Events*] AMS; *Events*' A, S, B–C

117.30	*Events*] AMS; *Events'* A, S, B–C
118.5	patrons." People] AMS; ~." ¶ ~ A, S, B–C
118.15	indulged] AMS; indulged in A, S, B–C
118.37	and who] AMS; and S
119.3	ideals] AMS; ideas B
119.16	press, and] AMS; press, S
119.37	Ricker] AMS; Rickers B
120.5	almost] AMS; about A, S, B–C
120.30	sensation] AMS; senation S
121.22	you've] AMS; you're A, S, B–C
122.13	knew] AMS; know A, S, B–C
123.3	again. He] AMS; ~. ¶ ~ A, S, B–C
123.10	corporate] AMS; private S
123.23–24	gathered in] AMS; gathered on A, S, B–C
124.4	when . . . together] A; *om.* S
125.28	educated to] AMS; educated in C
125.30	the struggle] AMS; this struggle S, B
129.1	to him] AMS; to them S
129.5	we can] AMS; can we A, S, B–C
129.36	State's] AMS; State S
*132.21–22	is! You] AMS; is! I— You A, S, B–C
133.14	discussion] AMS; discution A
133.18	duly] AMS; truly A, S, B–C
135.22	and especially] AMS; especially A, S, B–C
136.27	merchant of] AMS; merchant in A, S, B–C
137.31	soldiers'] AMS; soldier's A, S, B–C
137.32	soldiers'] AMS; soldier's A, S, B–C
138.7	soldiers'] AMS; soldier's A, S, B–C
139.35–36	Mahomet] AMS; Mohammed S
140.25	't] AMS; that A, S, B–C
142.34	pity of] AMS; pity for A, S, B–C
143.9	were] AMS; was A, S, B–C
143.20	arms'] AMS; arm's A, S, B–C
143.29	futile] AMS; feeble A, S, B–C
145.1	intonation] AMS; intimation A, S, B–C
145.5	He is] AMS; He's S
145.15	This] AMS; His A, S, B–C
145.28	this] AMS; the A, S, B–C
147.3–4	Miss Northwicks] AMS; Misses Northwick C

*148.4–5   worse." ¶ "What] AMS; ~. ~ A, S, B–C
149.14   I'd] AMS; I had S
150.24   would] AMS; could A, S, B–C
152.14   this] AMS; the A, S, B–C
160.14   gentlemen] AMS; gentleman A, S, B–C
160.35   land] AMS; lands A, S, B–C
161.1   on] AMS; in A, S, B–C
163.6   stop] AMS; step A, S, B–C
164.9   accident] AMS; accidents S
166.6   risks] AMS; risk A, S, B–C
167.1   rearrange] AMS; arrange A, S, B–C
171.4   this] AMS; his A, S, B–C
171.8   that] AMS; which A, S, B–C
171.9   which] AMS; om. S
171.33   we] AMS; he S
172.2   Anne's] AMS; Anne S
172.5   there's] AMS; there is A, S, B–C
172.11   new] AMS; the new A, S, B–C
174.6   and that] AMS; om. S
174.12   expanses] AMS; expanse A, S, B–C
174.21   ice] AMS; ice which was A, S, B–C
174.36   finally fail] AMS; fail finally S
176.12   for all] AMS; in A, S, B–C
177.4   the changes] AMS; changes A, S, B–C
178.34–35   mail carrier] AMS; mail-carriers A, S, B–C
179.14   You] AMS; You' S
179.20   dreamed that] AMS; dreamed A, S, B–C
*179.23   You] AMS; You' A, S, B–C
180.17   he went] AMS; went S
182.11   village] AMS; villages A, S, B–C
182.21   were] AMS; was A, S, B–C
183.10   he must go] AMS; must go A, S, B–C
184.2–3   a photograph] AMS; the photograph A, S, B–C
184.23   or] AMS; of S
188.7   Hall] AMS; All B
190.36   gate] AMS; gates B
191.5   hout] AMS; out A, S, B–C
191.19   mile] AMS; miles S
192.27   heat] AMS; eat C

192.27	'e] AMS; he B
193.15	at] AMS; at the A, S, B–C
193.20	meat. Bird] AMS; ~. ¶ ~ A, S, B–C
193.33	believe] AMS; believe that A, S, B–C
194.11	Northwick. "Tell] AMS; ~. ¶ "~ S
195.34–35	is." ¶ He] AMS; ~." ~ A, S, B–C
198.35	where and what] AMS; what and where A, S, B–C
201.1	and which] AMS; which S
205.2	and which] AMS; which S
205.22	joint] AMS; *om.* S
205.29–30	superiors] AMS; superior A, S, B–C
206.19	For] AMS; In A, S, B–C
207.27	that] AMS; the A, S, B–C
207.31	to] AMS; *om.* A, S, B–C
207.33	hon] AMS; on A, S, B–C
208.3	scare-heading] AMS; care-heading B
208.20	fully] AMS; *om.* S
209.8	of] AMS; for A, S, B–C
209.31	egoist] AMS; egotist A, S, B–C
210.2	must] AMS; had to S
210.8	knew] AMS; know B
210.32–33	What is] AMS; What's S
213.35	that] AMS; *om.* A, S, B–C
214.30	those] AMS; these A, S, B–C
214.33	on] AMS; in A, S, B–C
215.1	at] AMS; at the A, S, B–C
216.5	bolt] AMS; roll A, S, B–C
216.6	rejoined, "I] AMS; ~: ¶ "~ S
216.14	bluntly, "What] AMS; ~: ¶ "~ S
217.14–15	man!" She] AMS; ~!" ¶ ~ A, S, B–C
217.15	for the] AMS; for a A, S, B–C
217.18	Doctor] AMS; Dr. A, S, B–C
217.23	Dr.] AMS; Doctor A, S, B–C
218.1	her husband] AMS; a husband B
218.19	paper] AMS; paper that A, S, B–C
219.22	quavered] AMS; groaned A, S, B–C
220.6	*now*] AMS; now C
222.4	that] AMS; *om.* A, S, B–C
222.27	his] AMS; *om.* A, S, B–C

223.26	morning] AMS; *om.* C
224.29	think] AMS; thing B
226.2–3	her. ¶ "I] AMS; ~. "~ A, S, B–C
226.19	*Do*] AMS; Do C
226.24–25	breakfast. ¶ Suzette] AMS; ~. ~ A, S, B–C
227.21	herself] AMS; *om.* S
228.27	hope] AMS; hopes A, S, B–C
228.30	*all*] AMS; all A, S, B–C
229.35–36	purposes] AMS; purpose A, S, B–C
230.12	belief] AMS; believe S
230.17	Northwick] AMS; Northwicks' A, S, B–C
230.23	honor] AMS; know A, S, B–C
232.35	Maxwell. Wade] AMS; ~. ¶ ~ A, S, B–C
235.15	those] AMS; these A, S, B–C
235.18	say. "They] AMS; ~. ¶ "~ S
236.33	went] AMS; ran A, S, B–C
238.16	humanly] AMS; humanely A, S, B–C
238.30–31	that, it] AMS; that A, S, B–C
239.11	tacit] AMS; tried A, S, B–C
239.13	in] AMS; with S
241.21	Oh] AMS; Ah A, S, B–C
241.26	in] AMS; in the A, S, B–C
242.3	she] AMS; she had A, S, B–C
242.3	should] AMS; would S
243.5	choice] AMS; chance A, S, B–C
243.9	brute] AMS; brutal S
243.12	heavier] AMS; harder A, S, B–C
244.14–15	them?" Louise] AMS; ~?" ¶ ~ A, S, B–C
245.21	futilely over] AMS; over futilely S
246.24	she's] AMS; she S
248.1	hoped] AMS; hope B
249.2	luxurious] AMS; luxuriant A, S, B–C
249.18	lie] AMS; be A, S, B–C
251.20	Ricker] AMS; Riker S
251.20	he] AMS; he he A
253.16	could] AMS; would A, S, B–C
253.30	Northwick's] AMS; Northwick A, S, B–C
254.28	him] AMS; to him C
257.19	shouldn't] AMS; wouldn't S

257.19	returned] AMS; replied S
257.33–34	letter, still opened,] AMS; letter open S
259.22	else] AMS; *om.* A, S, B–C
260.23	own] AMS; *om.* A, S, B–C
261.1	as far] AMS; so far A, S, B–C
261.17	we] AMS; one A, S, B–C
261.19	keep] AMS; kept A, S, B–C
261.29	I'm] AMS; I am B
263.1	Miss Northwicks. "Well] AMS; Miss **Northwicks.** ¶ "Well A, S, B; Misses Northwick. ¶ "Well C
266.11	There's] AMS; Here's A, S, B–C
267.27	it is] AMS; it's A, S, B–C
270.19	is] AMS; are S
270.26	can] AMS; can't A, S, B–C
272.4	whimpered] AMS; whispered B
272.10	avenue] AMS; avenue of C
272.14	It is] AMS; It's A, S, B–C
*272.27	one] AMS; *om.* A, S, C
272.27	and he] AMS; but he A, S, B–C
273.11	wouldn't] AMS; shouldn't A, S, B–C
273.18–19	parting. "Will] AMS; ~. ¶ "~ A, S, B–C
273.23	read: "Mr.] AMS; read: ¶ "Mr. A, S, B–C
274.18	with a] AMS; with A, S, B–C
274.24	those] AMS; these A, S, B–C
274.26	and he] AMS; and has A, S, B–C
274.30	last] A; end S
276.5	investigator] AMS; investigation S
276.6	instincts] AMS; instinct C
276.26	jury. Matt] AMS; ~. ¶ ~ A, S, B–C
277.1	he] AMS; she B
277.17	without] AMS; withought S
277.32	purposes] AMS; purpose A, S, B–C
280.30	all] A; *om.* S
281.13	social] AMS; society A, S, B–C
281.20	he has] AMS; he's B
281.26	he is] AMS; he's B
281.30	with] AMS; *om.* A, S, B–C
282.1	theories. "No] AMS; ~. ¶ "~ A, S, B–C
282.33	heard] AMS; found A, S, B–C

284.28	interposed] AMS; interrupted A, S, B–C
284.29	she's] AMS; she A, S, B–C
284.29	in stead] AMS; instead A, S, B–C
284.29	of her want] AMS; *om.* S
286.6	a proposition] AMS; the proposition A, S, B–C
287.12	would] AMS; could A, S, B–C
289.18	preying] AMS; playing S
290.6	conclusion." Hilary] AMS; ~." ¶ ~ A, S, B–C
290.30	face. Every] AMS; ~. ¶ ~ A, S, B–C
293.11	any young] AMS; any other young A, S, B–C
294.11	the society] A; a society S
295.6	about] AMS; about it C
295.15	at] AMS; at at S
295.16	more] AMS; new A, S, B–C
296.4–5	indefinitely] AMS; infinitely C
296.9	knew that] AMS; knew A, S, B–C
297.34	him. She] AMS; ~. ¶ ~ A, S, B–C
298.4	detail] AMS; details A, S, B–C
298.17	people's] AMS; peoples' A, B–C
298.24	criticism] AMS; criticisms A, S, B–C
301.16	*Events*] AMS; *Events'* A, S, B–C
302.2	qualifications] AMS; qualification A, S, B–C
302.3	and] AMS; *om.* S
302.33	Oh] AMS; Ah A, S, B–C
304.6	wearisomeness] AMS; weariness A, S, B–C
304.18	habit] AMS; habits A, S, B–C
304.25	mainly] AMS; merely B
304.26	Northwick] AMS; Northwich C
306.7	liquid] AMS; liquor B
307.26	railroads in] AMS; railroads on A, S, B–C
307.28	that] AMS; who A, S, B–C
308.31	eye] AMS; eyes A, S, B–C
308.33	friends] AMS; friend A, S, B–C
309.27	Prison. Even] AMS; ~. ¶ ~ A, S, B–C
310.33	fear] AMS; the fears A, S, B–C
312.8	that] AMS; *om.* A, S, B–C
312.22	inhabitant] AMS; inhabitants A, S, B–C
314.15	was] AMS; were A, S, B–C
314.28	circumstance] AMS; circumstances A, S, B–C

316.7	would] AMS; should A, S, B–C
316.30	of the] AMS; of this A, S, B–C
317.28	winter] AMS; wintry A, S, B–C
318.17–18	bark-sheathed] AMS; black-sheathed S
319.4	and] AMS; and of S
320.3	your] AMS; you're B
322.16	couldn't] AMS; didn't S
322.29	as] AMS; as if S
323.18	but] AMS; *om.* A, S, B–C
323.25	probably] AMS; *om.* S
323.33	wager. It] AMS; ~. ¶ ~ A, S, B–C
324.2	it's] AMS; it S
324.3	in her arms] AMS; *om.* S
325.19	himself] AMS; *om.* A, S, B–C
326.9	daughters'] AMS; daughter's A, S, B
327.8–9	have . . . vagrant] A; pass his daughters' door as a vagrant, without danger of arrest S
327.11	he believed] A; and he saw S
327.19–20	daylight. ¶ He] AMS; ~. ~ A, S, B–C
328.34	obeyed. "Want] AMS; ~. ¶ "~ A, S, B–C
329.23	Mrs.] AMS; Mr. A, B–C
330.3	officers] AMS; officer A, S, B–C
331.16	back. "Well] AMS; ~. ¶ "~ A, S, B–C
332.24	All] A; She was his pet again; she was like a little child on his knee; all S
*333.6–7	him. ¶ He] AMS; ~. ~ A, S, B–C
333.14	own] AMS; *om.* A, S, B–C
333.34–35	out: ¶ "Oh] AMS; ~: "~ A, S, B–C
336.16	ag'in] AMS; again A, S, B–C
338.20	blackest] A; strongest S
339.12	she] AMS; sh B
339.24	back] AMS; *om.* B
339.24	Canady] AMS; Canada B
340.15	it. "Come] AMS; ~. ¶ "~ A, S, B–C
340.35	that] AMS; *om.* A, S, B–C
340.37	says I] AMS; says that I A, S, B–C
342.4–5	compromises and] A; the conventional S
342.25	have supreme rights] AMS; have a supreme right A, S, B–C

343.3	to them] AMS; *om.* A, S, B–C
343.29	priest] AMS; minister C
344.13	State's] AMS; State S
345.8–9	coming] AMS; to come S
346.15	victual] AMS; victuals A, S, B–C
346.17–18	admiration. ¶ "Well] AMS; ~. "~ A, S, B–C
347.34	near] AMS; with S
348.7	know that] AMS; know A, S, B–C
348.22	suggested] AMS; he suggested A, S, B–C
348.26–27	managed] AMS; arranged A, S, B–C
349.4	that] AMS; *om.* A, S, B–C
349.20	the point] AMS; this point A, S, B–C
349.23	frankness. "Hilary] AMS; ~: ¶ "~ S
350.4	people in] AMS; people at A, S, B–C
351.2	East] S; West B–C
352.21	through] AMS; through with A, S, B–C
352.23	*reporters*] AMS; reporters A, S, B–C
352.35	drew] AMS; draws S
353.24	indulge] AMS; indulge a A, S, B–C
353.33	fallen. "By] AMS; ~. ¶ "~ A, S, B–C
353.37	brought] AMS; bought A, S, B–C
354.27	all once more. "I'm] A; carefully over. ¶ "I'm S
355.8	brakeman] AMS; brakesman B
358.7	*he*] A; he S
358.16	daughters'] AMS; daughter's A, S, B–C
358.20	State's] AMS; State S
358.23	and round] AMS; round and S
359.3	came] AMS; come A
359.6	But] A; *om.* S
359.7	slipped] A; slipped out S
359.10	circumstance] AMS; circumstances A, S, B–C

Word-Division

List A records compounds or possible compounds hyphenated at the end of the line in the copy-text (or in readings after copy-text if authoritative) and resolved as hyphenated or one word as listed below. If the word appears elsewhere in the copy-text or if Howells' manuscripts of this period fairly consistently followed one practice respecting the particular compound or possible compound, the resolution was made on that basis. Otherwise his periodical texts of this period were used as guides. List B is a guide to transcription of compounds or possible compounds hyphenated at the end of the line in the present text: compounds recorded here should be transcribed as given; words divided at the end of the line and not listed should be transcribed as one word.

	LIST A		
		38.19–20	wind-bowed
		45.2	catchpole
5.32	ground-floor	46.15	twenty-three
6.12	steam-pipes	52.32	finger-tips
7.3	mantelpiece	60.36	sleighbells
11.3	self-defence	71.32	elbow-room
11.19	commonplace	79.19	shoe-shop
11.35	railroad	89.22	headquarters
13.17	summer-folks	93.13	business-like
15.15	outgrow	93.25	friendly-looking
16.28–29	coachman's	96.6–7	home-life
18.26–27	house-coat	100.17	first-class
18.31	bed-room	100.24	wood-chopper
19.19	proud-looking	100.24	stable-boy
23.6	Good-night	101.34	counting-room
27.5	withholding	103.5	self-possession
28.13	waistcoat	107.7	note-book
33.8	anti-climax	110.7	stiff-necked

442

117.5	space-man's	289.36	blackguard
125.16	leg-burlesque	293.1	sphinx-like
139.5	stove-heated	297.11–12	piazza-steps
142.13	business-like	298.18	poverty-pride
173.5	everlasting	299.15	Good-by
174.29	overnight	299.31	farmhouse
178.3	countrymen	301.11	masterpiece
183.18	sunlight	303.2	house-keepers
183.27	far-off	306.19	everlasting
185.30	bean-coffee	307.14	soap-mine
186.6	make-believe	310.29	hand-writing
190.29	'omesick	311.11	first-rate
190.33	self-pity	311.22	leather-covered
194.6	Ha-ha	323.2	good-night
200.5	homesick	323.8	hand-bag
210.1	cousin-in-	326.26	coachman's
210.14	everyday	331.34	farmhouse
210.34	-a-days	335.7	van-like
213.36	wrong-doer	336.11	lawn-mower
232.19	twenty-five	348.24–25	travelling-companion
234.24	footfalls	349.4	undertaking
236.32	Good-bye	353.19	handcuffs
248.5	headstrong	355.2	shame-faced
250.3	warm-looking	358.1	stockholders
256.14	back-yard		
257.30	outstretched		LIST B
262.4	self-interest		
269.17	to-day	9.34	nickel-plated
270.7–8	wrong-doing	18.26	house-coat
274.7	postponement	32.36	half-patronizing
275.31	cold-bloodedly	38.19	wind-bowed
277.7	outlined	48.34	drawing-room
278.1	wrong-doer	71.34	dry-looking
278.27	drawbacks	85.16	self-abasement
286.4	-in-law	96.6	home-life
287.15	Good-night	103.1	self-possession
288.15	moneywise	119.14	*Chronicle-Abstract*
288.29	business-like	120.12	green-lined
289.26	brother-reporter	127.5	self-respect

172.11	Ha-ha	309.37	self-banished
192.3	'alf-hour	318.17	bark-sheathed
270.7	wrong-doing	337.3	drink-devil
297.11	piazza-steps	347.8	breast-pocket
305.4	English-speaking	348.7	self-interest
309.29	English-speaking	348.24	travelling-companion

THIS EDITION OF

THE QUALITY OF MERCY

has been set in Linotype Baskerville,

printed on Warren's Olde Style by Heritage Printers, Inc.

and bound by The Delmar Company.

The format is after a design by Bert Clarke.